AN IMMINENT THREAT

A ROB WALKER THRILLER BOOK IV

D1529101

JOHN ETTERLEE

As always, I'd like to thank my wife, Elizabeth for her continued support. I want to thank NYPD Officer José Tomas for his help, especially with scenes involving law enforcement and tactics. And, lastly, but certainly not least, I really appreciate all the readers who stuck with me. If not for you guys, I couldn't be doing this. From the bottom of my heart, thank you!

Terrorism has become the systematic weapon of a war that knows no borders or seldom has a face.

—Jacques Chirac

ONE

In a dimly lit and oddly shaped room with a piece of plywood blocking the only window, a group of Arab men of different ages perched in a row on a bench at a long wooden table, working in silence.

Many of the elders had black burn marks on their fingers or were missing a couple, something the young ones had yet to experience firsthand. On the table in front of them were dozens of sticks of dynamite alongside buckets of silver ball bearings, nails, and other small, sharp metal objects.

Along the street outside, the sounds of chickens clucking, goats bleating, and shop owners carrying on midday bartering at a local market were somewhat dampened by the tightly secured building. People at cafes smoked hookah on outdoor benches and bistro-style seating. Old men grouped together on plastic chairs outside in the shade, playing games of tawleh while sipping cups of sweet-tasting chai.

Inside, a sliver of daylight peeked through a tiny hole in the sand-colored wall, illuminating one side of a stack of wooden weapon and ammo crates in the corner. In the next room, a slew of large, sealed plastic bins full of radioactive powder sat tightly against one another.

Down a narrow corridor, a man wearing a white thobe—a traditional Arab dress—with a kufiyah and a full black beard with gray spots strolled slowly toward the end with one of his men. They spoke quietly in Arabic as they paused to embrace one another.

"Ibrahim," the man said. "Please, ensure everything is done right here, will you? We cannot afford any mishaps. I know you will take care of this for me. There is nobody I trust more with such a sensitive task."

The boss was Amir Hassan, a Lebanese-born al-Qaeda lieutenant. Ibrahim ran a hand through his brown beard, half his right index finger blackened and disfigured. He was a middle-aged man, slightly younger than Amir. But he still looked to him for guidance.

"Yes, Amir," he replied. "I will take care of everything, in sha' Allah. You have my word."

"Excellent," Amir said with a hand on Ibrahim's elbow.

Amir moved in close to his ear and lowered his voice.

"And if any of them give you trouble or don't obey," Amir continued, "you come get me, and I will handle it myself, okay?"

Ibrahim Abdallah was Amir's right-hand man, and he would've done anything for his mentor, even if it resulted in his death.

"Yes, yes, okay," Ibrahim replied with a grin, showing a gap where his front tooth used to be.

Amir let go of his arm. "Good," he said, gently shoving Ibrahim with one arm. "Go then, brother. Back to work. Don't waste more time talking to me."

While Ibrahim returned to the group, Amir pulled the wooden back door open, the light down the alleyway almost blinding him as it peeked over rooftops. With a squint, he stuck a silver key into the hole and locked the dead bolt.

Suddenly, Amir heard a vehicle approaching. He turned around, and a black Mercedes parked at the end of the alleyway. The driver hopped from the car and hurried to the back door. When he opened it, a tall figure climbed out. Amir saw the man's sandaled feet hit the ground under the car door. The driver closed the door and ran back around to the driver's side.

The man was an elder, in his seventies, with one glass eye, a light-gray beard, and the same style of clothing Amir wore. Using a hand-carved dark wooden cane, he ambled down the alley toward Amir. The old man slowly approached and set a hand on Amir's shoulder.

"As-Salamu Alaikum," he said. "How are you, Amir? Where are you going?"

Amir took the man's hand and kissed him softly on each cheek.

"Wa alaikum salaam," replied Amir. "Nowhere, sir. Just stepping out for some fresh air."

Surprised and shaky, he stepped back for a moment. The boss's presence always made Amir a little uneasy. "Boss, I did not expect to see you here. To what do I owe this visit?"

The old man, Aasim Abdul al-Bashir, was the leader of the Abdullah Azzam Brigades, otherwise known to western governments as al-Qaeda in-Lebanon. He was a Saudi national and someone everyone in that part of the world feared. The Abdullah Azzam Brigades had cells in Lebanon and other countries like Egypt, Jordan, Syria, and the Palestinian territory of Gaza. They all got their orders from al-Bashir and obeyed without question.

"I am checking on your progress, Amir," al-Bashir replied. "I am ultimately responsible if we succeed or fail. I want to know that I chose the right man for the job."

"Boss, I have this in hand," said Amir. "I'm sure you have other things to do."

Al-Bashir grabbed Amir by the sleeve.

"This mission is too important, Amir," he replied. "It is not that you aren't trusted or that I think you are incompetent. But there are too many moving parts in this machine, you see? We may only get one chance to make this work."

Amir leaned back against the wall. "You've come a long way, boss," he said. "Could I interest you in a cup of tea first?"

"No, Amir," al-Bashir replied, pointing down the alley toward the door. "Perhaps after I am satisfied you are still on track. Now, let's get on with this, shall we? I have other things to tend to."

"Yes, sir," Amir replied, nervously fumbling for the key in his side pocket.

Inserting the key, he tried to hide his trembling. Twisting hard and yanking it open by the latch, Amir held the door open for the boss.

"After you, sir," he said.

They entered the rear of the building, and Ibrahim spotted them from down the hall. He looked away, shocked, not wanting to get al-Bashir's attention. He didn't wish to be on the boss's radar for anything.

Amir and al-Bashir continued walking toward Ibrahim, and he stepped back toward the wall to get out of the way. The two men rounded the corner without acknowledging Ibrahim and walked into the room with the large table. Al-Bashir took a glance over the many workers keeping busy. Amir followed him as he paced down the line behind their chairs.

"Hard at work, I see," said al-Bashir. "God is good indeed."

They progressed further, and an old man toward the end of the table caught Aasim's eye. As he zoned in to the man's hands, al-Bashir got a glimpse of a cell phone as the man shoved it back into his pocket. He moved toward him, clutching the man by the hair and jerking him from the seat. Holding him with one hand, al-Bashir propped his cane against the table with the other and reached into the man's pocket.

"What is this?" he asked, retrieving a phone from inside his shirt. "What in God's name is this?"

The gentleman muttered something unintelligible under his breath.

"What did you say?" al-Bashir asked. "Speak up!"

Amir stepped forward to take a look, shaking his head.

"It is my cell phone," the man replied.

"A cell phone?" al-Bashir added. "And what are the rules about communication and recording devices in this building?"

He looked to the ground, too afraid to lock eyes with al-Bashir. "I'm sorry," the man replied, obviously scared to death. "I use this to communicate with my sick brother."

Al-Bashir held the phone up for everyone to see. "What is your name?" he asked the man.

"Muhammad," he replied, visibly trembling. "Muhammad Hadi."

Al-Bashir smashed the phone against the hard floor, breaking it into pieces. He took the man by the throat and squeezed.

"Well, Muhammad," he said. "I do not care. These rules, set by me, are nonnegotiable. And now you have just proven to me that you cannot be trusted."

Al-Bashir pulled a chrome-plated .45 pistol from his clothing and pressed it to the man's chest.

"I am sorry, sir," the man pleaded with his hands out. "It will never happen again, I swear on Allah!"

Al-Bashir held the man's chin with his left hand and

brought the gun up. "Nonnegotiable," he continued. "Unfortunately, now I have to make an example of you."

The old man raised his hands and started to scream. Al-Bashir pointed the gun at his forehead and pressed the trigger once. A loud *pop* was followed by a gaping hole with blood oozing from it. He let go of the man's chin and watched him fall back onto the chair, breaking it as his body made a loud *thud* on the concrete floor.

Al-Bashir stepped back and waved the gun around the room. He stared at everyone with rage-filled eyes.

"Let this be a lesson to you all," he said. "You disobey me or don't follow rules, and this will also be your fate. Without hesitation."

Every worker gazed straight ahead, utterly silent. They were all too afraid to speak.

"Now, get back to work!" al-Bashir continued. He glanced back at Amir. "Get rid of the body, discreetly."

"Yes, boss," Amir replied, waving down Ibrahim and a couple others to help.

They hoisted the dead body and began carrying it toward a truck at the back of the building to dump out to sea. Al-Bashir put the gun away.

"Boss," said Amir. "I had no idea."

Amir swallowed a gulp of air while al-Bashir wandered toward him.

"Amir," al-Bashir replied. "I like you. I do. You have been with me a long time. But this is your responsibility. And I will only say this once. If this happens again, you will not die a martyr in jihad. I will send you to meet Allah myself."

Amir didn't say a word.

"One more thing," al-Bashir added. "You will go with them to America to make sure there are no problems."

TWO

Sandyport Beach
Nassau, Bahamas

Rob lay back against a lounge chair on the white sandy beach, umbrella blocking the sun above his head. His eye wandered toward women in bikinis who were strolling along the edge of the water as he sipped his strawberry mojito through a straw. Rob tasted a hint of white rum, the cold mixture flowing down and coating his throat. Picking out the toothpick with the yellow umbrella floating in the glass, he dropped it on the white table beside his chair.

The rippling waves sparkled as people tossed frisbees up and down the shoreline. On the water, enormous yachts sailed by slowly, their huge sails vibrating steadily in the strong ocean breeze. In the distance, a group of college-aged kids played volleyball on the beach by stone steps to the street above. The afternoon heat blazed down. Rob set the glass back down and squeezed a little sunblock onto his palm. He removed his camouflage baseball cap and rubbed the lotion all over his face and shoulders and on the back of his neck.

On a short weeklong leave from the unit, he'd only recently completed the six-month Delta Operator course. One of only a handful in his class to finish assessment and selection, it was the toughest thing Rob had ever gone through in his life, much harder than Special Forces selection. Special Forces Operational Detachment-Delta, also known as CAG, or combat applications group, was one of the most secretive units in the US military. Only the name was known. The internal makeup, training, and operations were strictly top secret.

Wrapped around his neck, Rob's beach towel dangled over his bare chest. His muscular arms displayed half-sleeve tattoos as he snatched the now empty glass from the table. Rob carefully wrapped his Sig Sauer M17 pistol in the white hand towel under which it was hidden and stuffed it into his tan backpack on the ground. He stood and snagged his white T-shirt, tugging it over his body. Rob retrieved the bag by the handle and made his way back to the tiki bar at the edge of the sand.

He placed the glass on the glossy counter and put the pack by his feet. Rob took a seat on the wooden bar stool.

"How about another, sir?" the male bartender asked as he lifted his head from beneath the counter and wiped it with a damp rag. "I make a damn good mojito, wouldn't you say, bey?"

The bartender was a local man, speaking in the Bahamian dialect.

"Sure," Rob replied. "Why the hell not?"

"Excellent, mister," the bartender continued. "Coming right up."

The barkeep started making the drink while Rob turned in his seat and glanced back at the endless waves breaking. In the corner of his eye, he noticed a woman approaching the bar. The lady wore a blue bikini top with light denim shorts and had light blonde hair midway down her back. A round, white straw hat kept the sun out of her face. She placed her purse on the bar and took a seat.

"Hey," she said to the bartender, waving her hand. "Apple martini, please."

"Sure thing, pretty lady," he replied. "Excellent choice."

She dug into her purse and put a little money down on the counter. Rob caught her attention, and she glanced over at him.

"Hello," she said confidently with a nod of her head.

Rob turned his head toward her without making eye contact.

"Hello to you too," he replied nonchalantly.

The bartender placed Rob's drink down on a napkin and pulled another glass for the lady. Rob snatched his drink, slapped a bill on the counter, and headed back across the sand to his chair. He plopped down, stretched his legs out, and took a sip. Rob set the drink down, folded his arms behind his head, and peered out across the water. With his head back, he closed his eyes. After a few minutes, he'd just about drifted off to sleep when he heard a voice behind him.

Rob opened one eye and noticed a silhouette hanging over him in the bright sun. He looked up and saw her standing there, her long, yellow hair fluttering in the wind.

"Hi, again," she said. "Look, I'm not trying to be too forward here, and I don't mean to bother you. But I'm bored, and you look like you could use some company."

Rob was always leery when it came to strangers. He didn't know the woman. For all he knew, she could've been a foreign agent. Her persistence only made him more suspicious. Some might have called it paranoia. Still, the woman was stunningly beautiful. If she was a foreign adversary, Rob would find out. So he invited her to join him.

"Have a seat if you'd like," he replied.

She smiled and lowered herself onto the edge of the lounge chair next to him.

"I don't bite, I promise," she said.

"The name's Rob," he replied.

"I'm Rachel," she said, putting her drink down on the table between the two chairs.

Rachel leaned back in the seat with her legs crossed and stared ahead at the sparkling ocean. She wiggled her white sandals off with her feet, and they dropped to the sand.

"Beautiful, isn't it?" she asked as she watched random people playing in the water.

"Yeah, it sure is," replied Rob. "No place I'd rather be right now."

Rachel grabbed her drink and set her cell phone on her leg. Suddenly, the phone buzzed. She snatched it and read an incoming message. Rachel sighed and typed a quick reply. She hit send and put the phone down on the side table.

"Jeez," she said. "I'm on vacation, and my office is still blowing up my phone. I don't know what they'd do without me."

Rob grinned as he looked over at her.

"Not to get too personal," he replied, "but what is it you do?"

"I'm a lawyer," Rachel said, flipping her wavy hair back.

Rob sat up straight in his chair. "A lawyer?" he asked.

"Yep," she said. "I started my own practice five years ago, right after law school. We mostly do family law, stuff like that. It's very time consuming. This is the first break I've had in almost three years."

"I can imagine," Rob replied. "That's really impressive."

"Thanks," replied Rachel.

There was an awkward pause as Rob sipped his cocktail. Rachel broke the silence suddenly with a question he had been anticipating. It was the most obvious thing people asked whenever they were trying to get to know a person. For him, it wasn't so black and white.

"So, what do you do?" she asked, noticing the American flag tattooed on his arm.

"I, uh," he replied, shooting her a half glance, "work for the government."

Rob obviously couldn't tell her what he really did.

"Nice," she said. "Are you in the military or something like that?"

"Something like that," replied Rob.

Rachel took her phone and began going through her photos.

"My dad and his dad were both in the Army," she said. "My father retired as a JAG colonel a few years ago, and my grandfather was a pilot in the Korean War."

"That why you became a lawyer?" Rob asked. "To follow in your dad's footsteps?"

"You could say that," Rachel replied with a grin. "My dad is my hero. Living up to him was the most obvious choice for me."

She turned the phone so Rob could see. It was a photo of her father in his Army dress uniform, standing beside Rachel and a few of his junior officers.

"This is my dad, Colonel Nathan Wilson, at the JAG School in Virginia. He taught there for a couple years."

"Nice," Rob replied, glancing at the picture.

At that point, he knew she couldn't have been a foreign agent.

"He retired a few months after this was taken," Rachel added.

She turned the phone off and stuck it in a pocket of her purse.

"So, what do you do in the military?" she asked. "I hope I'm not being too forward here."

Rob just shrugged it off. "No," he replied. "It's fine. I'm in combat arms."

"Infantry, Ranger?"

Rob was purposely being vague. "Yup," he said.

Rachel uncrossed her legs and turned toward him in the seat. "You getting close to retirement?"

"Not as long as I still have gas in the tank," replied Rob. "I think I have at least a few more years in me."

Rob quickly changed the subject. He felt a little uneasy about the conversation, but he didn't want to make it apparent. Rob was also unsure if he could handle getting involved with a woman at this point in his life. Even he had a soft side, though, and he couldn't help but be attracted to her stunning beauty and bubbly personality.

"Listen, Rachel," he said. "Would you be interested in going dancing or something like that? There's a club down the street. Say, tomorrow night? I have a rental, so I can pick you up."

"Sure," she said, beaming back at him.

Rachel retrieved her phone again and handed it to Rob. "Here," she added. "Put your number in my phone, and I'll text you mine."

Rob typed his number and added it to her contacts. "Done," he said, giving the cell back to her.

Rachel googled the address of her hotel on Paradise Island, connected by bridge to the city of Nassau. She copied the link and sent it to him.

"There you go," she said. "Meet you out front at seven, tomorrow?"

THREE

Mecca, Saudi Arabia

Three CIA officers walked alongside a myriad of people down the scorching sidewalk toward the largest mosque in the world. Near Saudi Arabia's western border on the Red Sea coast, the humidity was high and oppressive. It was unlike much of the rest of the country, which was hot and extremely dry.

The men wore the traditional Saudi men's dress—white clothing with white and red checkered kufiyah on their heads. All were fluent in Arabic, and their disguises helped them mix with the local populace. The trio moved between two light-colored high-rise buildings, the horde getting larger the closer they got. One of these structures, a hotel with a tall clock tower, dominated the area high over the interior of the open-air mosque.

Known in Arabic as Masjid al-Haram, or the Great Mosque of Mecca, it was the holiest in the Islamic world. Every year, thousands of Muslims flocked to the city for their holy pilgrimage. Followers of Islam across the world aimed to visit the site, deemed the house of God, at least once in a lifetime, which was required by one of the five pillars of Islam. Formally called the Hajj, male Muslims who completed the trip were known as Hajjis, and females were known as Hajjas.

Security around Mecca was tight, as usual. In fact, non-Muslims weren't allowed within twenty-five kilometers of Masjid al-Haram. In addition, there was a force of roving patrols, and a sophisticated security surveillance system in and around the mosque and the city of Makkah.

The team slipped by a long line of Muslims on their way to conduct the Zohar prayer, the fourth prayer of the day as prescribed by the Qur'an. They neared a huge, beige-colored stone wall. Team leader Isaac Smith stood against it and peeked through one of the numerous doorway entrances. The other two men hung back, chatting among themselves so they didn't draw any unwanted attention from locals.

Smith peered at the masses inside, both men and young boys, searching for a face he'd studied extensively. It was like trying to spot a speck of glass in a pile of sand. The agency had received a tip from a Lebanese source who'd spent time with Aasim al-Bashir. A man previously thought to have been killed in Afghanistan years earlier, al-Bashir had been spotted and planned to visit the holy city and pray at the mosque. The team was tasked with his capture, but there was no way they could do it in such a crowded place.

Smith turned his head toward the wall.

"HQ," he said into the earpiece hidden by his head covering. "On location, beginning search."

The voice on the other end said only one word. "Copy."

They all knew if they were caught, they'd surely end up in a Saudi prison, or worse. The US would disavow them and say they acted on their own. The Saudi government and Prince Mohammed Bin Salman, or MBS, didn't play games when it came to securing the Islamic holy site. But the team had no choice. If they let al-Bashir slip away, they might never find him again.

Smith gave the signal, a simple head scratch, and proceeded inside with the other two men a short distance behind. They entered the mosque and split up as planned. Smith went right, while the other two headed to the left of the building. He walked a short distance and stopped, surrounded by praying Muslims.

Smith followed along, facing the wall in the middle. Muslims around the world prayed in the direction of Mecca. Inside Mecca, they faced the wall known as Ka'ba, the center of the holy site, with men and women in different areas. Smith pretended to pray on his knees, bowing and then glimpsing around the huge space whenever his head came back up. He remained in place, going through the motions.

The team stayed in place for over an hour, carefully eyeing everyone who came in and scanning throughout the interior. Smith was getting ready to cross the room when he received radio contact from one of his men across the way.

"Razor-one-one," his teammate whispered. "I think I got him over here."

Smith glared across the expanse to his right, spotting his man kneeling on the ground. He gradually rose to his feet and headed in that direction. Making his way around the crowd, Smith stopped a couple of dozen feet away and hit the floor. He peered to his right, and the team member bowed toward the wall. Smith peeked in that direction and bowed, closing his eyes as his head neared the floor. When he came back up, he took another quick glance.

He scanned north and spotted four men standing together. One of them looked familiar.

"Confirmed," whispered Smith. "It's him. Stand by."

The team waited there until the old man made a move. Minutes later, the man came to his feet and began walking with three others toward the northern exit. All Smith could see was an old, grizzled face, but it certainly did appear to be the man from the photo.

"Let's move," he said.

Smith rose and wandered to that side of the building, the other two trailing him a couple dozen feet back. They followed a line of folks down a long stretch of walkway. Suddenly, the old man and his company veered left toward the parking area. Smith, moving between the crowd, picked up the pace and watched them climb into the back of a shiny, black Mercedes. The team headed for their own gray BMW on the opposite side of the lot.

They hopped in, and Smith turned the key in the ignition. He took his Glock from inside his clothing and set it on the center console.

"Boss," one of the men said, glancing through the side mirror. "He just pulled out, headed east."

"Roger that," Smith replied, putting the car in reverse and whipping out of the space facing the road.

He shifted the vehicle to drive and quickly turned right to follow the Mercedes. Smith sped up a little, maintaining a few car lengths back from the target's vehicle.

***

Across the Red Sea outside of Cairo, Egypt, CIA personnel and their station chief, Dan Bailey, monitored the mission via satellite link from a compound in the blistering Egyptian Desert. West of the Nile River, the station, a two-story structure, was surrounded by a high wall in the middle of arid sands. It was a dust bowl dotted with sand dunes and the ideal spot to be left alone. On the other side of the iron gate, however, a large fountain sat at the front of the structure, surrounded by palm trees and a circular, paved driveway.

Short, green grass contrasted against the surrounding landscape. The place had surveillance cameras all over, two-man patrols across the yard, electric wire surrounding the perimeter just above the stone wall, and biometric locks on every door and entrance, including the front and rear gates. It also had a pool in the back surrounded by a concrete patio. The building was previously owned by a wealthy South African man living in Egypt who fled during the Arab Spring, leaving the place abandoned. The United States government decided to purchase it and put it to good use.

Inside, Chief Bailey listened while sipping a cold cup of coffee he'd been nursing for going on two hours. His ears fixated on the little radio traffic they'd received so far. Now, however, three CIA Operations Officers were in pursuit of a wanted terrorist who they'd believed died in a drone strike in Tora Bora, eastern Afghanistan, in 2008.

"HQ," Bailey heard Smith say through the radio. "Still on his trail. Just made a left, heading northeast on King Faisal Road."

Chief Bailey snatched the radio up. "Roger, razor-one-one," he replied. "Maintain distance, and stay with them."

On a large monitor across the room, a satellite feed relayed the team's current position. It followed the BMW as it increased speed, two hundred meters behind the target's vehicle. Matching the speed of almost every other car around, they didn't want to get the attention of the occupants in the Mercedes until they were ready. They kept a steady eye on the vehicle from the right lane while al-Bashir's driver veered into the other lane and around two cars in the front of them. Smith didn't budge.

Suddenly, the car made another turn on Highway Forty, a long stretch of road between Makkah and Riyadh. The road passed through open desert made of flatlands mixed with rocky, hilly terrain. Bailey and the others viewed Smith making the turn and pulling back a little behind two other cars.

"We're northbound now toward Riyadh, Razor-Six," said Smith. "When we're alone, we'll take 'em."

"That's a good copy, razor-one-one," replied the station chief. "Keep your distance until then so they don't make you."

"Will do," Smith replied.

The long highway seemed to go on forever. They passed by tiny towns in the distance, dust blowing over the pavement in front of them. A dust devil began to form off the highway to their right, traveling south. The team looked ahead, noticing a familiar and unwanted sight a few kilometers away.

"Shit," said Smith. "It's a goddamned sandstorm. A big one. Damn it, the timing couldn't be worse."

The men watched the sand wall growing taller and thicker. The wind picked up, and it began to turn red.

"Razor-Six," Smith said over the radio. "There's a gnarly sandstorm right in our path. Please advise, over."

Smith glanced back at his men in the back.

"This thing is going to be bad, man," one of them said. "What're we going to do now?"

The few other cars on the road stopped to turn around. They all peeled out away from the area in the other direction.

"All we can do is keep going," replied Smith. "We'll keep on until we can't go anymore. If we can't see shit, neither can they."

"We see the storm, razor-one-one," the chief replied back. "Just follow protocol. You know what to do."

Chief Bailey and the others in the room observed the storm getting closer to the team's location. They couldn't turn around. There was no way around it. All they could do was go straight through it.

"Cover your faces and hold on," Smith said to his team. "We're going to push through this mess."

The fine powder-like dust from such a storm could easily penetrate cracks in a vehicle. Everyone in the BMW slipped their kufiyah over their faces, tying them tightly against their mouths. Smith checked that the windows were rolled up. Chief Bailey and his people watched the vehicle overhead and saw it move headfirst into the stirring sand. The car vanished into the red dust cloud dispersed over a wide-enough area to fill the screen.

"Shit," said Bailey. "I hope we don't lose that bastard."

Then everyone heard a loud crash over the speakers.

"Oh, no," Bailey added. "Razor-one-one, are you good? What's your status, over?"

Nobody answered.

"Razor-one-one," he continued. "Razor-one-one, do you read?"

The chief paused for a moment.

"Razor-one-one?"

Chief Bailey peered around the room with heavy breaths.

"What the hell just happened?" he asked anyone who was listening.

"I don't know, Chief," an analyst replied. "Maybe they ran off the road."

Everyone in the station's operations room went quiet when gunfire erupted through the speaker system. They listened and watched in horror but could do nothing. They heard gunshots, moaning, and men shouting in Arabic and English. In less than thirty seconds, the ruckus was over and everything hushed. Chief Bailey listened for any sign of movement.

"Razor-one-one," he said. "You still with us?"

Suddenly, there was a voice on the other end. Someone had snatched a headset from one of the dead Americans.

"Your men are dead," the man said into an officer's earpiece. "If you do not want many more to meet the same fate, stop following us."

The blowing sands passed over, and they could see the figure of a man glaring into the sky. It was like he knew they were watching.

"I will bring the wrath of Allah to your door," he added. "You kill my people? Many more Americans will die!"

The chief heard the headset smash against the ground and go dead before he could respond. But he knew who the caller was.

"Shit," he said. "That's al-Bashir."

The sand cloud dissipated, and Bailey spotted the BMW at the edge of the road with three bodies spread around it. The Mercedes was long gone, racing down the highway. Bailey's hands were tied. The CIA wasn't supposed to be in Saudi Arabia. And he certainly couldn't launch a Hellfire at them. They had no choice but to watch al-Bashir escape from their grasp.

Bailey had to figure out how to deal with three American bodies on Saudi soil. He'd simply shut the operation down, and the agency would deny all involvement, per usual.

"All right," he said to his people. "This mission is FUBAR. Everyone, follow protocol and get rid of everything, any trace of this op, now. There should be nothing left when you're done."

All personnel in the operations room quickly began deleting files, hard drives, and video feeds and shredding top-secret documents.

"I want this done in ten minutes!" Bailey shouted.

FOUR

The Warwick Hotel
Paradise Island, Bahamas

Rob's eyelids began to part, the sun streaming through the east-facing window and onto the side of his face, warming his head. The hotel air conditioner cooled his feet poking out from the end of the blanket. Rob blinked to get rid of the fog.

His eyes opened slowly. He reached up and rubbed the short, prickly hairs on his cheek. His vision still a blur, Rob gradually rolled over onto his side, pulling the white blanket down from his body. He swung his legs across the sheet, and his feet met the plush area rug on the hardwood floor as he touched them to the ground. Rob stood by the bed's side, yawned, and brought his arms back into a deep stretch. He then swayed his head to the side, popping his neck.

Reaching to the chair beside the bed, he snatched his green T-shirt from the top of his pack and pulled it over his head. Rob unlocked the small combination lock and unzipped the front pouch of the backpack, retrieving his gun from the center of a folded towel. He looked around to make sure Rachel wouldn't suddenly surprise him.

Clipping his holster inside his waistband on the right, he shoved the gun in firmly until it locked. Rob tugged his shirt down low. He ran a hand through his short hair, then went and pulled the blinds to look through the glass balcony door.

Glancing back, Rachel's side was empty, and he wondered where she'd gone. Rob slid the glass door open and stepped onto the balcony of the sixth-floor room. From there, he could see the orange sun gleaming over the distant beach. Seagulls consistently flocked across the small island. Palm leaves fluttered as waves broke over sand and rocks. Rob took a seat on a white wicker chair and stared out at the endless water.

It was nine in the morning, a late hour for Rob to be getting up. But they'd had a good time dancing the night before, not getting in until almost three in the morning. It was the first time in a while Rob had gotten the chance to just relax and have a little fun. He surely wasn't expecting to meet a woman along the way. Yet here he was, sitting in her hotel room and wondering why he was there. He was attracted to her good looks and her personality, but what then? How could it possibly work with Rob's line of work? He questioned it all in his mind. He wasn't the type for one-night stands.

Suddenly, he heard the door of the room where he'd woken up open. A soft voice carried across the room as she noticed the empty bed.

"Rob?" she asked. "You still here?"

Rachel took a look around. She thought he'd ditched her.

"Of course," she added, shaking her head as she sat at the foot of the bed.

Then she glanced behind and noticed Rob's duffel still sitting on the floor by the table.

"Out here," Rob replied through the cracked door.

Rachel smirked as she grabbed the plastic bags. She made

her way to the balcony, opening the door the rest of the way and wandering out to meet him.

"Hey there," Rob said with a grin. "You thought I bailed, didn't you?"

Rachel took a seat and set the bags and two coffees down on the wicker table between them.

"No," she said, looking amused. "Why would you say that?"

"Yeah, you did," Rob replied with a chuckle. "The look on your face says it all."

Rachel faced him.

"Sorry," Rob added. "I didn't mean to laugh."

"Okay," she said. "So maybe I did for a second. It wouldn't be the first time, if I'm being honest."

"Yeah, well," replied Rob, "I'm not that kind of guy. I have a little more respect than that."

Rachel wasn't used to meeting guys who wanted more than a night.

"I see," she said. "How refreshing."

Rob stood and wandered to the balcony railing, leaning against it and glancing at the pristinely manicured grounds below.

"We had fun last night, huh?" Rachel asked.

"Yep," Rob replied, peering back at her. "We sure did. I haven't had that much fun in a long time."

He rubbed the side of his head. "However," he added, "I think I might've had a little too much to drink."

"Oh, I know," replied Rachel.

Rob turned around and returned to his seat, sitting on the edge facing her. He leaned into the bags. "What's in here?"

Rachel began taking things out. "Well, let's see," she replied. "I got cinnamon bagels, cream cheese, and a couple large coffees from this cute little place right outside the hotel."

She set a couple of bagels and cream cheese packets down on a napkin beside Rob. He reached into the bag and snagged a plastic knife from inside.

"Thanks," he said. "It sure smells good."

Rob pulled the bagel apart and spread a little cream cheese onto both pieces. He took a bite and glared out across the island. "Damn," he added. "This place is paradise, isn't it?"

"Yeah, it is," Rachel replied as she bit into hers. "I need to find the time to come here more often."

Rob took a sip of coffee and glanced at her. "I bet you stay pretty busy, don't you?" he asked.

"Yeah, it's chaotic at times," she replied. "Especially since the practice has been growing so fast. Honestly, I knew it would take a lot of my time. I didn't expect it to take off as fast as it did. But a lot of clients I had at the last office I worked followed me over. So, yeah, it's pretty time consuming."

Rachel took another bite of her bagel and put the half-eaten piece on the napkin on the table. "What about yours?" she asked. "I'm sure the Army keeps you occupied."

She had another question lingering, which she hesitated to ask. "I'm curious," said Rachel. "Do you go to Iraq or Afghanistan much?"

Suddenly, a myriad of memories flooded Rob's mind, the kinds of memories that were tough to process at once. He'd lost many friends to combat, and he didn't like to talk about it a lot. Rob looked out at the sea in the distance. Instead of answering her vocally, he acknowledged with a quick bow of his head.

If you only knew, he thought, forcing a smile.

***

Across the Atlantic in the London borough of Enfield, two Muslim teenage brothers prayed in a mosque on the north side of the city. The Adhan, or call to prayer by the muezzin, was done five times daily. It sounded in the background as Muslim men and boys gathered around the red, carpeted floor.

The mosque was one of several around the London area, but it was the only one within a short walking distance from the boys' flat. White caps on their heads and kneeling on prayer rugs, Ahmed and Faisal Ali bowed together, reciting verses from the Qur'an softly in their native language of Urdu.

The modest mosque was half full, with Muslims of different nationalities lined up in rows and praying together. Mumbled prayers filled the room as they echoed softly. The two boys had been recruited by a jihadi organization a year prior. However, the mosque was not involved, and neither the attending Muslims nor the mosque leaders knew about the brothers' extremist views or involvement in terrorism. In fact, the Imam, Daanish Aly, had strongly condemned extremists on many occasions.

Fifteen minutes had passed, and the prayer was almost complete. The pair bowed repeatedly, heads and hands to the floor and faced in the direction of the holy city.

"Allahu Akbar," the brothers said, making their final bows.

They each returned to their knees, popped up onto their bare feet, and adjusted their clothing. In a hurry to get back, the two ambled across the room toward the main double-door entrance. They neared the door and recovered their slip-on shoes from the rack, slipping them on. Both boys snatched separate bags from the shelf and turned toward the exit.

Ahmed, the older of the two, held the door open for his brother and they slipped out under a dreary, overcast sky. Dark clouds in the distance suggested a possible rain coming soon. The pair stepped out onto the sidewalk and began hoofing it half a kilometer toward their bland third-floor flat. The low-rent accommodations were paid for by the organization that recruited them.

A short walk and a few minutes later, they reached the rusty black gate and low brick wall that separated the flat grounds from the street. The gate creaked as Faisal jostled it open with his foot. The brothers made their way to the exterior metal staircase that led to the upper floor.

"Come, my brother," said Ahmed. "They are waiting for us."

Ahmed and Faisal were both from a tiny village in Pakistan. They'd immigrated to the UK years earlier with their families, but they'd grown agitated with the West, believing they were treated like second-class citizens. They were young, discontent, and the ideal targets to be recruited by a jihadi terror group.

They continued on from the top step, and Faisal entered his key into the lock and turned. They stepped inside and wandered down the hall to the small living area. Two of the windows to the flat faced the street and were always covered by dark curtains, allowing little sunlight to make its way inside. Occasionally, out of paranoia, the occupants would take a peek outside through the closed blinds.

Ahmed advanced past the small kitchen and peeked into one of the two bedrooms. Seeing the younger boys keeping busy, he headed inside.

"How is the progress in here?" he asked as one of the other two young boys placed a medium-sized black backpack on a wooden table.

His name was Umar, and he was even younger than Ahmed and Faisal. Wearing latex gloves, Umar finished wrapping the explosives with tape and sealed the canisters containing the radioactive material tightly between them. He stuck a finger under his gloves and removed them from his hands inside-out. Umar placed the gloves inside a Ziplock bag and sealed it, tossing it into a garbage can.

Faisal had heard them talking from the hall. He entered the room and noticed two other identical packs sitting upright against the wall in the corner.

"And those?" he asked.

"Yes," the fourth boy, Adeel, replied from across the room. "They are complete. Our mission is ready to proceed, in sha' Allah. All we wait for now is confirmation."

"I already received confirmation," Ahmed said, inspecting the inside of each bag.

He wanted to make sure there were as many explosives as they could fit and that the radioactive dust was filled and sealed in the container.

"We are to proceed as planned," Ahmed added. "The boss wished me to relay to you how proud of all of you he is. There is no higher calling than to rid this earth of infidels and nonbelievers."

Being the oldest boy in the group, he was the one to be contacted by their leader. The teens were zealots for the cause, having been influenced by the more extremist sects of Islam.

Ahmed and Faisal left the others in the room and strolled back to the living area next to the small kitchen. Ahmed grabbed them both glasses from the cupboard and filled them with water from the sink. He handed one to Faisal, and they both wandered toward the sofa.

They sat beside each other, and Ahmed snagged the television remote from the old coffee table. He turned it on and took a drink from his glass. Ahmed removed the prayer cap from his head, folded it, and placed it on the table. He started flipping through the channels, and something caught his attention. It was a documentary about Western involvement in wars across the Middle East. They aired an old interview of Bin Laden after the September 11th attacks in the US.

"There is America, hit by God in one of its softest spots. Its greatest buildings were destroyed, thank God for that."

Ahmed and Faisal both stared at the screen, mesmerized by the tall, lanky figure who'd caused America and the West so much suffering. The man had long been dead, but to them, his purpose in life would be never-ending until all Westerners were banished from Muslim lands.

"We will continue your jihad, in sha' Allah," said Ahmed. "In the name of Allah and all his martyrs, our true path will forever reign."

"Yes," Faisal replied. "Allahu Akbar!"

FIVE

The Chief of Staff of the US Army, General Mark Wilkins, marched down the long corridor of the Pentagon in his dress uniform toward his office in the back of the enormous structure. Through the halls, junior officers, high-ranking enlisted, and Department of Defense civilian personnel went about their day. They were important cogs in a giant and complex machine.

Briefcase under his arm and cap in his hand, the general's shiny, black Oxford shoes tapped the tile floor as he walked with a purpose. He turned the corner just in time to see his secretary rush into the office ahead of him. Her back to Wilkins, she obviously hadn't noticed him yet. On TV screens in other offices along the way, the general could hear chatter of some sort of a disaster unfolding overseas. He didn't yet have the slightest clue of what they were talking about.

He made a right into his office space and spotted his secretary going through some files on her desk. She took the tall pile of folders, stacked them on top, and shoved them into a metal filing cabinet. With bundled-up paper towels swiped from the supply closet, she wiped down a bit of coffee she'd spilled earlier. The secretary tossed the paper towels into the garbage can and turned up the volume on the television. She stared blankly at the screen on the wall.

"Michelle?" the general said, stepping through the open door and approaching her desk. "How's everything? Any messages for me this morning?"

She answered while staring at the television screen.

"No, General," she replied with a puzzled expression. Michelle got up from her seat. "Sir," she said. "You haven't heard?"

General Wilkins stopped mid-stride and pivoted toward her. "Heard what?" he asked. "What the hell are you going on about?"

She didn't respond in words. She just pointed and turned up the volume.

"What?" the general added. "What is it?"

General Wilkins shifted his gaze to the television. His jaw suddenly dropped. It was a derailed London subway train with a clear blast zone covering a wide area. Everything around the train had been blackened and blown to bits by some kind of explosion.

"Oh my God," said Wilkins. "What the hell is this?"

The general took a seat on a brown leather office chair and listened to the broadcast.

Today will go down as a dark day in British history.

At approximately eight o'clock local during the morning rush, a massive explosion ripped through the London metro just as many were on their early-morning commutes. There's an unknown number of dead, as well as hundreds of people wounded.

With the time difference, General Wilkins knew the attack had occurred hours earlier.

A large cloud of dust is dispersing throughout the immediate area, and it is not yet known what it is. Government experts are saying it may contain radioactive particles that could drift to other parts of the city.

They are in the process of sampling and testing. Emergency personnel in HAZMAT suits are beginning the daunting task of combing through the wreckage and debris, searching for survivors.

Several blocks around the London Underground are blocked off indefinitely.

As of right now, the chance of them finding anyone alive inside that train is looking grim. Rubbish, twisted black metal, and pieces of wall from the underground platform are piled up everywhere. All we can do is hope and pray that people are reunited with their families.

Currently, it is not clear who is responsible for this atrocity, nor is it known if there are more targets planned. We will update the public as soon as we know more.

Thank you. This is Jennifer Coolidge for BBC News.

General Wilkins stayed in the seat for a time, staring at the screen. "Jesus," he said, glancing back at Michelle. "That was no accident."

The general hopped up and headed straight for his office. He entered, leaving the door open. Wilkins snatched the remote from a table and turned on the news just in case. He wandered around his mahogany desk and took a seat on his high-back leather office chair.

For General Wilkins, it was just another day at the office as he got comfortable in his seat. Yet he had a feeling things were about to warm up. He pulled the keyboard toward him and flicked his computer mouse to display the screen. The general inputted his passcode and logged in. He began delving through random emails for the next few minutes.

Suddenly, his secretary yelled at him from the next room. "General," she said. "I'm forwarding you a weird email I just got. It's addressed to you. Maybe you can make sense of it, because I have no idea what it means. It's already been scanned, no viruses."

"All right, Michelle," General Wilkins replied. "Send it over, then."

The general waited a minute, then refreshed the window on his computer. He noticed an email addressed to his office with no subject. Wilkins clicked to open it. The email was short and bold and caught the general by surprise. It contained just three words.

YOU ARE NEXT.

"What in God's name is this supposed to mean?" the general asked himself.

General Wilkins glared coldly at the vague and unclear text. On a hunch, he picked up his secure office phone to call one of his CIA contacts at Langley. Before he could dial, however, Michelle shouted again from the front of the office.

"General?" she asked. "Did you get the email?"

"Yeah, Michelle," he replied, holding the phone between

his shoulder and chin. "I got it. Calm the hell down, would you?"

The secretary continued talking, but it was white noise to the general. He set the phone down, stood, and walked to his office door.

"Don't let anyone in here," he said, cutting her off midsentence.

"Uh, yes, sir," Michelle replied.

The general shut the door and locked it. He returned to his seat and snagged the phone again. He held it to his ear and dialed the number. Ring after ring, he waited for almost two minutes.

Then, suddenly, he picked up.

"Yes?" the voice on the other end answered. "To whom am I speaking?"

"David," the general replied. "How are you, my friend? It's General Wilkins."

There was a brief pause.

"General?" David said. "Something must be pretty important if you're calling me on this line. What can I do for you?"

David Spann was an old friend of General Wilkins and the deputy director of the CIA for operations. Based in Langley, he oversaw the collection of human intelligence, or HUMINT, with clandestine officers posted in countries around the world.

"I'm forwarding an email to you, David," Wilkins replied, hitting send with his mouse. "You should get it right about now."

"Hold on," Spann said.

The general waited almost half a minute for him to come back.

"All right," added Spann. "Email received."

General Wilkins could hear the concern in Spann's voice.

"You are next," said Spann. "Hmmm."

"My reaction too," replied the general. "Any clue what it means? Should I be concerned?"

Spann cleared his throat. "I might have an idea, yeah," he replied. "I understand this is a secure connection, General, but I'd much rather have this conversation in person, if you don't mind. A few decades with the Agency have made me paranoid like that. Never know who's listening."

"That's a fair point," said Wilkins.

"Good," Spann added. "I thought you'd see it my way. Meet me at the Iwo Jima Memorial, say, thirty minutes?"

"Fine, all right," General Wilkins replied. "See you there."

The general hung the phone up and spun around in his seat. He pulled a drawer out from his desk and took out a brown, wooden box. Wilkins opened it up and removed a cigar. He slid the cigar into his uniform coat pocket and closed the box, putting it back in the drawer. Snatching his keys from his pocket, the general hopped up and headed out. He yanked the door shut and secured it.

"Michelle, I'm going out for a bit," he said to his secretary. "Hold all calls and take any messages. I'll be gone for a while."

Before she could answer him, General Wilkins was already through the door and down the hallway. He made his way around the long corridor, through the main entrance, and out into the parking lot. The general marched halfway across the pavement to his parked black Chevy Tahoe. He clicked the keyless entry, opened up, and climbed in. Cranking it up, the general hit reverse, then swung out of his assigned parking space.

For the next several minutes, General Wilkins drove his vehicle north on Highway One. He'd gone under the Washington Boulevard Bridge and passed Arlington National Cemetery on his left. He passed over a hill, and the Iwo Jima statue suddenly appeared. Wilkins took a left onto the road between Arlington and the memorial.

As he came around a bend, he pulled the SUV into a small parking area and swerved into a spot close to the road. Taking a look around, the general put the Tahoe into park, opened the door, and hopped out. He placed his cover on his head and adjusted it. General Wilkins wandered onto a short sidewalk that led to a paved footpath.

Even though leaves were still scattered across parts of grass, the trees were beginning to turn green again, a sign that spring was fast approaching. General Wilkins advanced right, down the walkway and around a curve. The statue emerged up ahead, and the general spotted his friend alone on a park bench.

He traversed a set of concrete steps and reached Spann, who was sipping from a tall Starbucks cup. Wilkins took a seat beside him, crossing his arms and sitting back against the backrest. He recovered his cigar and cutter, snipping the tip off. He put it in his mouth, sparking it up with a silver lighter.

"So," General Wilkins said, taking a drag. "What're we really doing out here, David? I'm a pretty busy guy, you know? Give it to me straight."

Spann bent over, his elbows on his knees. He glanced around to make sure nobody was within earshot.

"All right, General," replied Spann. "Listen, I'm sure you heard about the bomb in London's metro station this morning, right?"

"Yeah, of course," replied the general. "I saw it on BBC. Why?"

Spann glared at General Wilkins. "Give me your cell phone," he added.

The general didn't argue. He just reached into his pocket for the phone and handed it over. "Here," he replied.

Spann checked to ensure the phone was off. "Okay," he continued. "What I'm about to tell you is top secret, still developing. It doesn't leave this bench, got it?"

General Wilkins bowed in agreement. "Of course," he replied, blowing smoke into the air.

"Good." said Spann. "Now, do you recall a terrorist leader named al-Bashir, Aasim al-Bashir? He was supposedly killed by a drone in Kabul in 2008."

"Of course I do," the general replied. "I was JSOC commander back then, deployed to Bagram."

General Wilkins had had a number of combatant command roles. Most notably, he was the commander of the US Army's most classified unit, Delta, in the late '90s and early 2000s before receiving his first star. He went on to command units in Iraq and Afghanistan.

"I know you were, General," said Spann. "As it turns out, al-Bashir isn't dead after all."

General Wilkins looked bewildered as his cigar dangled from his lips. Hearing that man's name sent a shiver down his spine. The hairs on the back of his neck seemed to twitch.

"Wait, what?" the general asked in a brash manner. "What the fuck are you telling me, David? How the hell could he have gotten out of there alive? For God's sake, we leveled the whole damned village."

Spann patted the general on the leg. "I don't know," he replied. "But believe me, he's very much alive. In fact, one of our Intel teams tracked him and some of his associates from Lebanon to Saudi. They trailed that bastard deep into the desert, but they never made it out. It was all on satellite feed. There's no denying shit."

General Wilkins sat up straight on the bench. He glanced curiously at his old friend.

"You asked me about the bombing in London," the general said.

"Yeah."

"So," Wilkins added, "why that? You think they're connected?"

"Listen, General," said Spann. "The email you received this morning. You aren't the only one to get it. That same message was sent to various other government officials. They apparently used a proxy server and a VPN, so we're having a tough time tracking its origins. We're pretty certain it came from the same man, though, or at least his people."

The general rose to his feet and stood over David Spann. "How sure?" he asked.

"Well, a few good officers died for it. The bombing meets the Abdullah Azzam Brigades' MO. The British Parliament has officers from multiple agencies working the scene. Our contacts in London are saying it was a dirty bomb and suspect radiation contamination. They're still conducting testing. I can't get into every detail of what we know so far, but trust that we are leaning on the side of pretty damn positive."

General Wilkins took a deep breath and peered up at the sky. Spann gave him his phone back, and Wilkins dropped it into his pocket.

"I don't believe this shit," he said. "Just keep me informed, would you? Washington brass is going to have a fit about this."

As the general turned to leave, Spann hopped up and stopped him.

"I'm sure I don't have to tell you this, General," he said, "but not a word to anyone. We never even spoke. The right people will know. Leaking this would cause a nationwide panic we don't need right now."

"Don't insult my intelligence, David," said the general. "I'm not a fool."

"Of course not," replied Spann.

He let go of Wilkin's arm and lowered himself down on the bench.

"Also, we're talking to British intelligence as we speak. We'll get to the bottom of it, don't worry."

"Right," the general replied as he stepped away. "Enough said, David. Just do your part, okay? And keep me updated on what the hell is going on. I don't want this to come back and haunt us."

SIX

Rob and Rachel roamed together along the street and through the island's main shopping center. A mix of luxury and locally owned shops, historical architecture, colorful buildings, and magnificent monuments dotted both sides of the street from end to end. The busiest part of the island, downtown Nassau offered many options for shopping and food.

It was the smell carried along by the ocean breeze, the year-round tropical climate, and the hospitality of the people that had drawn tourists to the islands for years. It would continue to do so for many more to come. Rob and Rachel were no different. The atmosphere seemed to work a magic that could sweep one's cares away with the warm ocean current.

Dressed in clothing that fit the island theme, the pair followed the flow of pedestrian traffic down the path and across a four-way intersection. Rob gripped a cold bottle of Kalik, the most popular locally brewed beer. They stepped off Bay Street, and Rob looked down at his blue shirt laden with palm trees, which had been bought at a local shop. He couldn't help but let out a cackle.

"Look at us," he laughed. "If this doesn't scream 'I'm a tourist,' I don't know what does."

Rachel wore a knee-length denim skirt and a shirt with an imprint of a palm tree sunset.

"Yeah, you're right about that," Rachel replied. "But you know what they say—when in Rome."

A few blocks ahead, a swarm of tourists began to flood the area from a cruise ship that had docked in Nassau Harbor. It was the heart of the Caribbean island's tourist economy. Rob and Rachel did their best to ignore the crowd. They were only there to grab a bite for lunch and take in the sights.

"What about this place up here?" Rachel asked, pointing to a yellow building with white pillars in front.

It was a quaint little bar and grill and didn't look to be too busy from the outside.

"After you," Rob replied, following her across the pedestrian crosswalk to the restaurant entrance.

Rob tossed his empty beer bottle into a garbage bin outside. They went inside, the smell of coconut rum and grilled steak lingering in the air. The place was hardly busy, with only a few patrons scattered here and there. A large flat-screen TV on the wall behind the bar aired American football. Rob and Rachel stood by the hostess station and waited to be seated. A short girl, early twenties with jet-black hair, appeared with two menus and greeted them.

"Hello there," she said in a Bahamian accent. "Just two?"

"Yes," Rob said, and they followed her a short distance down the aisle to a table by the window.

"Here you are," she added, placing the menus in front of them. "Your server will be over shortly."

"Thank you," Rachel replied with a smile.

The hostess left, and Rob took a look around the place and out to the street through the window.

"God, I love this place," he said as he browsed the menu, "people and all. It gets busy here at times, but it's nothing like where I'm from."

"That reminds me of a question I never asked," replied Rachel. "I assumed by your accent you're from New York. Am I right?"

"Yup," Rob said. "Brooklyn, to be exact. Though I don't care for it much anymore."

"Why's that?" Rachel asked as she watched pedestrians ramble outside.

"Too many people," he replied. "Also, crime has gotten way out of hand. I don't think I'll ever move back there again."

Rachel touched Rob's hand.

"I understand," she said. "So, where's home now ?"

Rob shrugged with a bitter grin. "Wherever I happen to be, I guess," he said.

"I can imagine," Rachel replied. "I bet you've seen the world."

"You could say that," Rob said as the waitress approached the table.

"Hello," she said. "I am Abigail, and I'll be your server. Are we ready to order?"

"Oh, hey," Rob replied, setting his menu flat and closing it. "Yes, I'll have the crab and rice and a cold glass of your most popular beer."

Abigail swiped his menu from the table. "And you, miss?"

"Um," Rachel replied. "I'll have what he's having, please."

"Excellent," the waitress said, taking Rachel's menu. "Thank you, bey. Coming shortly."

Abigail left for the kitchen, and Rob slid across the booth to the window. His back against the wall, he reached under the table where his pistol holster usually was. He'd left the gun locked away in a safe in his hotel room. Though he felt a little naked, it was better than the embarrassment of going to a Bahamian jail.

Rob peered across the restaurant and noticed the black-haired female bartender behind the counter, pouring his beer. In his peripheral vision, he saw a TV mounted on a pillar in the middle of the room. Rob's eyes shifted toward the screen while it played silently with English captions at the bottom. It was an image of destruction, smoke, and fire—the same image General Wilkins had seen earlier from his office.

Rob stood and slowly made his way toward the television. His eyes didn't deviate from the screen.

"Rob?" Rachel asked as he continued toward it. "What is it, what's wrong?"

He'd seen enough in his life to recognize a terrorist attack when he saw one. Rob glanced down at the captions beneath the chaotic scene.

"Shit," Rob mumbled.

Watching Rob standing there, Rachel could tell something wasn't right. With a grim look, Rob wandered back to the table and took his seat. He kept quiet, staring through the window, a light drizzle hitting the pavement.

"Rob?" asked Rachel. "Talk to me. What is it?"

The waitress returned with a tray and chilled glasses and set them down on napkins on the table.

"Here you are," she said.

"Thank you," replied Rachel.

"You're welcome, miss," said Abigail. "Your food will be out in just a minute. Can I get anything else for you two?"

"No, thank you," Rachel replied.

Abigail smiled and left the table. Rob, though, was in somewhat of a trance. Bouncing his leg from nervous energy, he had a feeling down in the pit of his stomach. Rachel glanced at him, her hands gripping one another on the table. She reached out for him, touching her hand to his. His tough exterior didn't budge.

"Come on, Rob," she said. "Talk to me. We've had a great time the last few days. Just tell me what's going on."

He couldn't do that. However, he could omit certain facts.

"I'm just pissed," he said. "I'm angry about what's happening in the world right now. That's all. I've lost a lot of friends over the years."

The waitress approached and set plates onto the table, and Rob's satellite phone began to vibrate in the cargo pocket of his khaki shorts. Rob reached into his pocket to retrieve the phone.

"Be right back," he said to Rachel.

Rob stepped outside onto the walkway, the phone to his ear.

"This is Walker," he said.

"Walker?" the caller said in a scratchy voice. "You having fun in the sun down there, son? Maybe half a bottle deep in Bacardi?"

Calling from Fort Liberty, formerly Fort Bragg, the man was current Delta commander, Colonel Mike Billings.

"Colonel?" Rob replied. "It must be something if you're calling me. What can I do for you, sir?"

"All right, I'll get to the point, then," the colonel said. "I'm sure you heard about the bombing in London, correct?"

"That's correct, sir," Rob replied. "Just saw on the news."

"Well," Billings added, "I'm afraid your leave is cut short. I can't speak more about this over the phone. You'll be briefed with the team when you get back here, understand?"

Rob knew it was a possibility he'd be called in, but now he was faced with the unexpected. He'd met a woman—one he enjoyed spending time with. He had to handle the situation with care.

"Okay, Colonel," said Rob. "Roger that."

"All right," Colonel Billings continued. "Be at the north side of Lynden Pindling Airport at fourteen hundred. There'll be a small jet there to pick you up. Look for the tail number NC11DF. The remainder of the team will meet us back at HQ."

The unit didn't normally use military aircraft for travel unless in a combat zone. Even then, there were no identifying markers. Delta opted to utilize civilian aircraft for most travel to keep from drawing any unwanted attention.

"Got it, Colonel," replied Rob. "I'll be there."

Rob ended the call and slipped the phone back into his pocket. He made his way back inside and to their table. Rachel looked curious.

"Rob," she said as he began to scarf his food down. "I'm far from an expert, but since when does an infantry soldier get a call from his colonel like that?"

Although Rachel had never served herself, having family members who had meant she knew a little. Rob looked into her eyes.

"Listen," he said. "I can't get into that right now. Can you give me a lift to the airport in a bit? I have a plane to catch."

"What?" Rachel asked. "You're leaving already?"

"Yeah," replied Rob. "It wasn't how I planned it. Something's come up."

Rob could tell Rachel was disappointed. She didn't even bother asking where he was going. She wasn't sure if she wanted to know.

"I promise I'll make it up to you," Rob added. "So, will you drop me off?"

"Yeah, sure," she replied. "Of course I'll give you a ride."

During the next few minutes, they finished their meal. Rob left enough cash on the table to pay for both with an added tip. He put his wallet back into his back pocket, and they headed for the door.

The ride to the airport would only take about half an hour or so. They exited the restaurant and started making their way to the other end of Bay Street, where Rachel had parked her rented blue Jeep Wrangler.

They both climbed in and buckled up. Rachel put the Jeep in reverse and backed up. She then hit the gas and hopped the curb out onto the road. Swinging left, they traveled southeast on Bay Street a short distance. Rob had to make a pit stop at his hotel down the street to grab his things. A quick pack of his backpack, and he was done. Downstairs, Rob quickly checked out of the hotel and tossed the key card onto the counter. He snatched his pack and left through the sliding doors.

Rob hurried to the Jeep and tossed his bag in the back. The engine still running, Rachel turned out of the lot and southwest onto Soldier Street. They headed toward the main road that would take them all the way to the airport.

A twenty-five-minute drive later, Rachel veered right onto the access road that led to the north of the airport. A few hundred meters away, Rob spotted the white twin-engine plane idling on the far end of the airfield. A man wearing khaki pants, a dark polo shirt, and black shades waited for him by the stairs. Rachel continued on for a couple hundred meters.

"Here," Rob said. "Stop here."

"Here?" Rachel asked as she tapped the brakes.

"Yeah," replied Rob. "It's better if you don't get too close."

Rob snagged his pack from the back floorboard and put it on his lap. He removed his Sig Sauer pistol from one of the pockets and racked the slide. Rachel didn't know he had a gun.

She was floored as he switched it to safe, slid it into the holster, and hooked it onto his belt. Rob pulled his shirt down to conceal it.

Rachel looked like she was on the verge of saying something, but Rob stopped her before she could.

"Listen," he said. "There is no time for explanation. And even if I wanted to, there are things I just can't tell you or anyone."

"Okay," Rachel replied. "Is that it? Is that all you have to say?"

Rob put his hand on her leg. "Look, Rachel," he added. "I've got to go now, okay?"

She looked like she had a million questions. Rachel had no idea what Rob was into, but it didn't seem good. Rob opened the passenger door. Rachel quickly popped the top of the center console and snatched a napkin from the inside. She took a pen and jotted down her phone number.

"Here," she said. "Call me when you can, okay? I don't know what the hell is going on. Maybe you can tell me when you get back."

Rob took the napkin, folded it, and stuck it in his wallet. He smiled, slamming the door and waving goodbye. Rob put his arms through the shoulder straps on his backpack and took off jogging toward the waiting plane.

SEVEN

The plain black helicopter soared low over the tall North Carolina pine trees. The rotor blades chopped forcibly in rhythm, whipping the surrounding air. Tree limbs swayed rapidly in the downdraft as the chopper passed over treetops and crossed a small pond down below.

The sun had faded, and the landing lights came into view ahead through the cockpit. The bird crossed over the two-lane road and perimeter fence on its way to the helipad.

In the backwoods of the west side of the base, the complex was hidden from the road by the thick wood line and the surrounding privacy-screened wire fence. Concertina wire topped the fence around the compound. Manned entry gates with jersey barriers and a hi-tech surveillance system with night-vision cameras maintained a high level of security.

Other gates around the large complex, built to keep people out, remained barred when not in use. Two men guarded each main entrance with M4 carbines and sidearms in black leg holsters over jeans and khakis.

The chopper began its descent over the grass, the pavement

getting closer. As it touched down on the deck, a man in jeans, a green button-up shirt, and a baseball cap waited across the blacktop. Feeling the helicopter rotors reduce power, Rob clutched his pack, shoved the door open, and leaped out. Holding his tan cap to keep it from flying off, he made his way across. The chopper pilot and copilot shut the aircraft down and climbed from the cockpit.

"Hey, brother," Rob's team leader, Sergeant Major Brian Meeks, said as Rob stepped onto the walkway. "How you doing, man?"

"I'm good," Rob replied as they slapped hands. "Good as can be."

"Yeah?" Brian asked. "How was leave? You look like you got a little sun."

"It was good," replied Rob. "Just working on my tan. Nothing like rum, bright sunshine, and women to make a man feel right at home, you know?"

"You can say that again," said Brian. "I've been down there a few times. It's a party paradise."

"Come on, bro, we'd better get inside. The colonel's in with the guys, and they're waiting for us."

"He been waiting long?" asked Rob.

"Yeah," Brian replied. "For your sorry ass to get back from Shangri-la. You're lucky he likes you."

"Yeah, I guess," Rob said.

As they left the helipad, Rob lowered the multi-cam backpack from his shoulder and carried it by the top handle. The two men advanced toward the headquarters building on the opposite end of the parking lot.

"So, have you heard about the shit that happened in the UK?" Brian asked as they got closer to the large structure.

"I heard something on TV," replied Rob. "The bombing in

London? I had a feeling it had something to do with this."

"Oh," Brian said. "It does all right."

They made it to the entrance past a circular driveway, and Brian entered a six-digit passcode into the keypad. The windowless metal door clicked, he yanked it open, and they slipped into the long hallway. The two advanced toward the last door on the right. They entered and saw their commander up front and three other operators sitting around a conference-style table. Two of them had hair to their shoulders and medium-sized beards. The other sported a brown mustache and a goatee.

"Well," said Colonel Billings. "Good of you to join us, gentlemen. Please, have a seat so we can begin."

Their immediate superior, the colonel was the commander of Alpha Troop, Golf Squadron.

"Yes, sir," Rob replied.

Nobody in the room wore uniforms, even the colonel. Lieutenant Colonel Billings was a hard charging combat veteran with tons of combat experience. He'd begun his career after West Point as a Ranger lieutenant, a platoon leader who'd served on many deployments to Iraq, Afghanistan, Bosnia, and other places. The colonel had tried out for and was accepted into Delta while he was a captain.

Rob and Brian took their seats, and the colonel switched the lights off and flicked the mouse to refresh the laptop as it displayed on the white pull-down screen on the wall.

"I hope you enjoyed your little vacation, Walker," Billings said to Rob, "because it's about time to punch in that time card, son."

Rob hated being called son, but in this situation, he decided to just grin and bear it.

"I know you're new to the team, Walker," the colonel continued, "but believe me, you wouldn't be in this room right now if I didn't think you were ready. So, do with that what you will."

"Roger that, Colonel," replied Rob.

Billings clicked the laptop mouse, and an image appeared on the screen.

"Men," he continued, tapping the screen with a pointer. "This is Aasim Abdul al-Bashir, mujahideen, bomb maker, al-Qaeda leader, and overall bad guy. Born in Riyadh, he's now the leader of the Abdullah Azzam Brigades in Lebanon, which is basically al-Qaeda's branch in the country. Al-Qaeda provides all their funding and training."

There was a brief silence.

"Colonel," Sergeant First Class Jamal Erickson said from a few seats down from Rob. Jamal was an African American team operator.

"I was a Ranger until 2009," he added. "I remember hearing that name back then. Wasn't he killed?"

Colonel Billings grinned as he sat on the edge of the table.

"Yeah, well," he said, "intelligence isn't always perfect, is it? Even if it does come from a large agency like the CIA. Or maybe I should say, especially. The Agency doesn't have the best track record, I know. But shit, this bastard fooled us all."

Billings got up and walked toward the screen.

"We were informed by the Agency that al-Bashir recently popped up in Beirut," the colonel added. "They had a team track him to the mosque in Makkah, Saudi Arabia. They trailed him, got caught in a sandstorm, and were never heard from again. One week later, a dirty bomb detonated in London's subway system during morning rush hour, killing dozens and releasing high levels of radiation into the air. Almost immediately after, a threatening message was sent to dozens of federal government officials, including Army chief of staff, General Wilkins. Naturally, it's got them a little on edge."

Colonel Billings changed slides, and a screenshot of the message popped up onscreen.

"Colonel," Rob said. "Could you refresh our memories? What is known about this man? And who found him in Lebanon?"

"He's a savage and ruthless," the colonel replied. "He hates everything the West stands for. That's why Bin Laden gave him his post prior to his death. He's an explosives expert, per their standards, anyway. A CIA asset in Lebanon watched his movements from his apartment window for a month."

Sergeant First Class Josh Reynolds chimed in. "Colonel," he said. "How do we know the source is credible?"

Josh was a former Army Ranger platoon sergeant from third battalion. He'd arrived at the team at the same time as Rob.

"We don't," the colonel replied. "But that's not our job, and for now, it's all we have. This directive is coming straight from the president himself. We have reason to believe that London was only the beginning, and his eyes are now on the US. That's where our intel ends. We think we have the who and what, with no idea about the when, where, and how. That's where you all come in."

"Meaning we don't know his next targets or his current whereabouts?" asked Rob.

"That's correct," replied Billings. "Although the CIA is working on it vigorously, the man's elusive. He seems to appear and vanish just as quickly. Also, the group's most likely using hawala to move money. Intel officials haven't been able to trace any of their finances. Going after their funding is key to shutting them down."

Hawala was a form of underground banking. Widely used in the Middle East since ancient times, it involved the transfer of money without any currency actually moving. Islamic extremist organizations almost solely used this network because it was virtually untraceable.

"So, what's the mission, sir?" Rob asked.

Colonel Billings stepped toward the laptop and changed the slide again. "We'll have a team here on standby in case anything pops off."

The colonel pointed to another photo onscreen. "Meanwhile," he added, "you five will meet up with this man in London to see what you can find out."

Colonel Billings touched his finger to the screen.

"He's an SIS officer heading the investigation into the bombing. This is crucial to try and determine where they might be headed next. We're sure they have big plans, but we just don't know much more. Our intelligence agencies are scrambling to get more information. So, that's what we've got so far. Any questions?"

Nobody in the room spoke up.

"All right then," the colonel continued. "Wheels up at zero two. See you then, gentlemen."

EIGHT

A group of men watched from inside a large, open aircraft hangar as the wheels of the C-130 touched the pavement with a puff of white smoke. The midday light easily outlined the top of the massive aircraft as it coasted down the runway. The plane slowed swiftly over the next several hundred feet. It came to a crawl, and the pilot made an immediate left turn onto the taxiway.

The plane rolled steadily toward the hangar. The rear cargo door swung down loudly and buzzed until it hit the ground. The gang of three Brits waited inside the structure next to two black armored Range Rovers and a private PA-31 Navajo prop plane.

"Hiya, mates," one of them said while Rob and the others, packs on their backs, made their way inside. "You must be Brian."

"Yup," Brian replied. "I'm Sergeant Major Brian Meeks, team leader. This is Master Sergeant Rob Walker, assistant team lead, and these guys are Sergeants First Class Jamal Erickson and Josh Reynolds, and Staff Sergeant Colin Mills. You're all with the Security Service, correct?"

MI5 was also known as the Security Service.

"That's right," he said with a handshake. "I'm Richard. These two chappies are Oliver and Benjamin, two of our junior officers. I haven't had the pleasure of working with you Delta blokes before, but there's a first time for everything, I reckon."

"Isn't there," Rob agreed. "What is your position in the organization?"

"I'm the lead investigator on this case," Richard replied. "It's my job to run this investigation and coordinate with any external organizations, such as you, for example."

Rob clutched Richard on the arm. "Listen," he said. "We're here to help find out who and what was responsible, and prevent these ruthless bastards from killing others. What have you found so far?"

Richard grabbed a handful of notes from the hood of the Rover and slid them into a folder.

"Come," he replied, wandering around to the back of the vehicle. "It's better if I show you. It's just a short drive from here."

He opened the rear door of the lead vehicle and Oliver climbed into the driver's seat.

"Benjamin," Richard shouted. "Take the rear."

Benjamin hurried around and hopped into the other Rover.

"Josh and I will take the front," Brian said to the team. "The rest of you get in the other car with Rob."

Rob climbed in next to Benjamin on the passenger side of the black Range Rover, putting his pack on the floor between his feet. Everyone else hopped into the backseat. The lead vehicle scurried out of the hangar while Rob's vehicle followed closely toward a chain-link gate exit not far away. The gate guard closed and locked the gate as they passed. The two vehicles dashed out into the left lane of a two-lane road for what would be a roughly twenty-minute drive to Piccadilly Circus.

"So, Rob, is it?" Benjamin asked as they took a right turn toward the heart of London.

"That's right," replied Rob. "Rob Walker."

The convoy began to pick up speed as they veered off the on ramp and onto a four-lane highway.

"Prepare to stop a few miles on," Benjamin added. "The whole area is barricaded for blocks. We have to put on suits because of the radiation contamination. Scotland Yard has personnel guarding the scene for us as their HAZMAT team continues the cleanup. It's going to take some time to get it usable again."

"Yeah," Rob replied. "I figured as much."

The vehicle sped down the roadway for another couple of miles, then took a right off the freeway. They neared the intersection down below, and they could see the HAZMAT tent up ahead on the right side of the street. The convoy turned left and slowed, coming to a standstill just before the white concrete jersey barriers.

"Here," Richard said over Benjamin's radio. "We're on foot from here."

Benjamin's vehicle pulled beside Richard's, and he, Rob, and the others stepped out. Rob reached in and grabbed his backpack, slipping his arms through the straps. Shutting their doors, an eerie silence surrounded them. That part of the city was unusually quiet, with not a single civilian anywhere in sight. There was no traffic, no public transport, not a sound that didn't come from personnel working the scene. Even the media was notably absent. Richard led them to a tent on the other side of the barriers.

He shoved the plastic door open. Inside was part of a HAZMAT team, some still in full suit.

"Hey," their supervisor said as he approached from the back. "You the investigative team?"

"Yup," replied Brian. "That's us."

"Yes," Richard interjected, glancing down at the man's name tag. "Officer Law, we're with the Security Service. We have an American team with us also. They are authorized by the British government to be here."

"Very well, then," Officer Law replied, reaching for a clipboard on the table. "Welcome to our command tent. Just need you to sign in here, please."

Richard took the clipboard and signed his last name. He passed it back to Rob and the rest of the team. Erickson was the last to sign the document and passed it back up.

"Here you are," said Richard.

The officer retrieved the clipboard and returned it to the table. "All right," he said. "Follow me."

Officer Law escorted the men to the other side of the tent where there was a separate room with HAZMAT suits hanging from the wall above plastic benches.

"Okay, gentlemen," Law said. "I just need you to put on a suit here before you can proceed."

"I haven't worn one of these in a while," Rob said, snagging a suit and taking a seat.

He dropped his pack by the bench, kicking it under. Rob pulled the pants up to his waist as the officer left them.

"I fucking hate these things," he added, removing the contents of his pockets.

"Me too," replied Brian.

For the next few minutes, each of them donned a suit and a HAZMAT helmet, pulled on a pair of rubber boots, and made sure everything was sealed correctly. Each man checked the one beside him. Lastly, they hooked the radios into their helmets.

"Testing, testing," Richard said, turning the volume knob. "You all reading me?"

"Roger that." Rob gave him a thumbs-up. "Good to go."

"Great," replied Richard. "Let's get on with it. We've got a lot to look at."

"We're right behind you," Brian said as they left the tent in a single line.

The team had a little hike ahead. The blast zone was half a kilometer away, but in full HAZMAT suit, it felt much longer. They continued down a footpath toward the Piccadilly Circus Station. As they got closer, powdery dust swept across the street in front of them. Debris and shrapnel were everywhere. Shop windows and doors were blown out, and glass littered the sidewalk. Light posts were blown to the side, almost coming out of the ground.

The men turned past a corner building, and they spotted a sign reading "London Underground" that was twisted, black, and tossed like litter. Emergency crews were on all sides, cleaning up and conducting radiation testing. A hole in the roadway in the middle of the intersection showed the direction the blast had originated. The bodies below had long been recovered by EMS. They'd been instructed not to access the blast site further, though, until they were given the all clear by authorities.

"Up there," said Richard. "Ahead is the entrance to the underground."

Rob directed his gaze to where Richard was pointing. He spotted a handrail coated in a powdery substance, with rubble burying the stairs beneath it. They made it to the entrance, and Rob and Richard pulled brick and other fragments away from the steps. Rob tossed a pile of junk out of the way with his gloved hands. They proceeded down slowly.

"Shit," Brian said. "This place was torn apart. Looks like the apocalypse down here."

"Got that right," replied Rob.

The inside of the underground structure was mostly caved

in, including the train tunnel on both sides. Chunks of asphalt had fallen through the massive hole and onto the top of the derailed train. Pieces of the platform were blown in all directions. It was a dreadful sight as they made their way around a blown-out wall and down to the bottom.

"God," said Richard. "What a bloody mess. Imagine being down here when it happened."

Richard continued toward the first train car. "Well, shall we?"

While Richard and his men started in what was the first car, Brian, Rob, and the rest of the Delta guys inspected the rest.

"Nobody could've survived this," Rob said. "And if they did, they'd wish they hadn't."

The train car leaned left toward them, held up by twisted metal wreckage underneath. They hopped down off the platform to take a look. The train was ripped in pieces, and the doors were no longer attached.

"Keep your eyes open for anything that might be connected to the bomb," Brian said.

"Roger, boss," replied Rob.

Rob pulled himself up by his hands and entered the car. Turning onto the aisle, he tilted his body to the side to keep his balance. Half the car was missing, blown down the tracks toward the tunnel. Everything inside was black, charred beyond recognition. The leather seats were burned away, revealing the metal frames. The scent of banana, caused by the nitroglycerin found in dynamite, lingered in the air.

"Hey," Rob said to Brian. "You smell that?"

"Yup, sure do," Brian replied. "That's dynamite all right."

Rob advanced ahead of Brian while the others checked the next car.

"Put all this stuff together," he added. "The powder,

explosives, nails and shit, the perfect recipe for a dirty bomb."

The detonation had totally obliterated the train, while outside were shards of pointy metal objects stuck in walls, on the floor, and all over. Spots of blood crossed the platform where people had been hit.

"They must've used a ton of dynamite," replied Brian.

"Yeah, no shit," said Rob.

Rob had almost made it to the end of the car, where it split in two. He kicked through the debris on the floor with his feet. Suddenly, he spotted something shiny. He bent over to pick it up, brushing the black remnants away with his hand. It was a piece of wire that looked to be ripped from the detonator in the explosion.

"Look," Rob said, turning to Brian. "Looks like part of the detonating device."

"Yeah," replied Brian. "Hang on to that. They'll want to see it."

For a time, the team continued searching through and around the wrecked train, but they found nothing else of importance. Rob and the others met Richard and his men outside on the concrete platform.

"Here," Rob said, handing Richard the piece of wire. "Part of the detonator. It was set off remotely. Most likely, the bomber or bombers watched their handiwork from a safe, elevated position."

Richard shoved the wire into a small Ziplock baggie and held onto it. "Okay," he said. "Well, guess we better head back, then."

Rob waved his hand forward. "Following you," he replied.

They all made their way back to incident command. It was getting dark, and the power was out for blocks around. The team hoofed it the half kilometer back to the police tent. They entered it and prepared to go through a decontamination shower to ensure no radioactive dust remained on them or the suits. One by one, they were sprayed down with water in a makeshift shower beside the tent.

They entered through the back tent flap and into the changing room. As they started to remove the HAZMAT suits to hang them up, Richard received an urgent call on his radio.

"Whiskey-four," the caller said frantically. "Come in, whiskey-four."

Richard removed the last piece of the suit and gripped the handheld radio. He squeezed the button. "Yes, this is whiskey-four, over."

He waited for a response while the others eagerly listened in.

"Whiskey-four," the caller added. "It's bravo-three-zero. This is urgent. We've received intel on a suspected terrorist safe house and require your assistance. Please acknowledge, over."

The caller didn't have to say who they were referring to. He already knew.

"Acknowledged, bravo-three-zero. I repeat, acknowledged. Send me the coordinates now. Whiskey-four, out."

Richard clipped the radio to the inside of his front pocket. "Bloody hell," he said. "We have to move, guys. Come on, I'll explain on the way."

Rob and the team followed Richard as he darted for their parked Range Rovers outside.

NINE

Downtown London

The convoy scrambled down the street and across the capital city toward a residential area in the North London borough of Enfield. Evening had turned to dusk, and the city street lamps dotted the sidewalks and neighborhoods. Moving briskly at a high rate of speed, they made an abrupt right, skidding over asphalt, and raced down a highway toward the northeast part of the city.

They came to an intersection, and Rob's vehicle, with Oliver manning the wheel, followed the lead car north onto Great Cambridge Road.

"Hey," Rob said to Oliver. "You going to tell us what's going on or what?"

"Yeah, sorry, mate," Oliver replied as he followed Richard, swerving around traffic. "SIS received intel on a suspected terrorist hideout. An SAS team is preparing to go in and asked us for assistance."

"A safe house?" Jamal asked from the backseat. "That can't be a coincidence."

"Nope," replied Rob. "I don't believe in coincidences."

The vehicles advanced down the roadway and took a sharp

curve right toward a decrepit-looking four-story brick building half a mile down. They crossed over into the right lane and approached a pair of armored Land Cruisers parked at the edge of the road a block from the building. Richard pulled up behind, and Oliver followed.

Rob's men snatched their stuff and followed Oliver out of the vehicle, slamming the doors shut. Those in the lead vehicle did the same. Oliver marched to the rear and popped the back hatch. Inside was a locked, hefty, black hard case. He touched the biometric lock with his hand and it popped open, displaying a pile of rifles and handguns at their disposal. The other half of the team had their own arsenal up front.

"Holy shit," Rob said as he took one of the weapons by the pistol grip. "Nice selection. This FN is mine." He was referring to the FN SCAR, a common weapon used in special operations in the UK and other countries.

Behind the case were stacks of metal ammo cans with full magazines and another case full of handguns. Rob picked three magazines for his rifle. The weapons case also included the C8 Carbine, similar to the American M4, and a few G36Cs.

Rob reached into the second case and snatched a Sig P226 nine-millimeter handgun. Stretching to the ground, he recovered his holster from the outside pouch of his bag. He wrapped it around his leg and attached the strap to his belt. Rob slid the gun inside.

Oliver reached to the side and pulled out a stack of black body armor.

"Come on and take what you want," he said, the rest of the team picking weapons and ammo from cases. "We need to move."

The men each took a vest and put it on, attaching Velcro straps. Oliver slammed the hatch, and they hustled to meet the SAS team. They approached a group of men in all black with C8s and FNs.

"Hey," one of them said. "I know who you blokes are. I'm Captain Williams, SAS team leader, Twenty-First SAS Regiment. But we can do introductions later. Have you been briefed?"

"Somewhat," replied Brian. "I'm Sergeant Major Meeks, team leader. This is my assistant team leader and the team behind him. You guys got intel on a terrorist safe house, correct?"

"That's affirmative," the captain replied. He pointed out a dark pathway toward the small apartment building. "Right over there. We need to move before these fuckers figure out we're coming."

"Yeah," said Rob. "We have questions that need to be answered."

Captain Williams gripped Rob by the hand. "Well," he said, "I trust you Delta chaps. Hopefully we can find those answers for you."

The captain waved down the sidewalk toward a low brick wall. Everyone chambered their weapons slowly and quietly. "All right," he added. "Two teams, us and Delta. We go in and clear this place and see what we find, got it? The rest of you remain in vehicles to watch the street. Keep your firearms hidden unless you have to use 'em. Don't want to draw any unwanted attention to us."

"You take point," Brian said to Rob.

Rob and the rest of the Delta team formed a line beside the captain and his men.

"It's your party, Captain," said Rob. "On your call."

They waited in the shadow of the wall for him to give the word. The streetlight glared over their heads while Captain Williams glanced up at a third-floor window covered by a curtain. He noticed a silhouette moving in the dim light.

"All right," he said. "On me, guys."

The teams moved side by side down the walkway toward

the exterior staircase. They neared the bottom step, and a random tenant suddenly emerged from the rear of the building. She jumped, startled by the presence of men with guns. The frightened old lady threw her hands up. Before she could scream, Captain Williams put a finger to his mouth to calm her.

"Shhh," he said. "We aren't here for you, miss. Just keep moving, you never saw us." The captain motioned for her to pass. "Go, go," he added, watching the woman slide by fearfully toward the street.

The men waited for her to move out of sight. Observing the woman flee in a small, yellow Volkswagen, the captain gave the signal, and they hit the stairs. Step by step, the teams gently inched their way to the fourth floor of the building. From the top step, they hugged the wall and rounded the corner to the apartment entry facing the street. Each team took opposite sides of the door.

"Do the honors, mate?" Williams asked Rob, standing by the doorway.

Rob grinned, gripping his rifle in one hand by the pistol grip. He stepped back and drove his right boot heel into the door, breaking the lock and sending the door flying back with incredible force, slamming it back against the wall. It dangled from a single hinge. They entered fast, each team moving around opposite sides of the room. Gunfire erupted and they mowed down three young Muslim men with Kalashnikovs before they could fire. Their bodies plummeted to the hallway floor with a splatter of blood coating the walls.

"Clear," Rob said, both teams stacking against two walls at the beginning of the corridor.

Captain Williams signaled, and each file pressed against both walls. They advanced, moving to a bedroom door on the right. Two men covered both ends of the hallway as the others lined up on each side of the closed door. Rob prepared to breach.

All of a sudden, a burst of AK fire peppered holes through the middle of the wooden door.

"Shit!" Williams said. "Get back!"

"Allahu Akbar!" one of the men screamed from inside the room.

Rob reached out with his hand and slowly twisted the knob. He nudged the door open. A longer volley of rifle fire went off and pounded the wall opposite the door.

"Get away from here!" the voice yelled once more.

"Just the master sergeant and I," the captain said. "Everyone else, wait here."

Captain Williams removed a flash bang from the side of his vest, tossed it through the doorway, and turned his head. There was a small explosion followed by a bright flash. Rob and the captain moved around the corner and through the doorway, weapons up. The two boys inside were disoriented, flailing their arms and rubbing their eyes.

"Get the hell down," Rob said, poking one of them with his rifle barrel. "Just give me a reason."

The one on the right brought his AK up and blindly aimed. Rob immediately popped him twice in the chest with his FN, and he fell face forward to the floor in a puddle of spurting blood. The captain disarmed the other before he could get ahold of himself and kicked him in the gut. He doubled over onto the tile floor, and Williams held him down forcibly with a boot to his back.

Rob rushed over, snatching up his AK. Captain Williams reached into his back pocket and recovered a set of plastic cuffs.

"Here," he said, tossing them to Rob. "Secure this fucker."

Rob put the cuffs behind the man's back and secured them tightly. He pulled him up by the arm.

"You infidel!" the man shouted, spitting on Williams. "You killed my brother!"

Rob drove a fist into his stomach, and the captain wiped his face with his sleeve.

"Yeah?" Rob asked. "You're damn lucky we didn't kill you too. You're only alive for one reason!" Rob jostled him toward the door. "Now, walk!" he added.

Rob handed the man off to Brian, and he and Williams began searching the room. On the table by the sofa, Rob found a closed laptop and secured it. They started rummaging through drawers and cabinets, looking for the slightest piece of intel. Captain Williams made a radio call.

"Sierra-one," he said into his mic. "It's bravo-three-zero. Site is secure. Repeat, site is secure, package in hand. It's yours to process, over."

The radio squawked. "Good copy, bravo-three-zero. We're on the way."

Laptop under his arm, Rob and the rest of the teams escorted their captive outside and to their vehicles down the path. They made it to Captain Williams's Rover, and he reached inside and retrieved a black sack. He slipped the sack over the man's head and opened the back door. Rob shoved him inside. Two of Williams's men slipped into the back with the package in the middle.

"If you lot want a jab at him," the captain said, swinging a leg into the vehicle, "then follow us."

Rob, Brian, and the rest of the Delta team headed back to the waiting SIS officers.

"Follow them," Rob said, climbing into the back.

"Will do, mate," replied Oliver.

The four-vehicle convoy sped away to an unknown destination, and the cleanup team moved in.

TEN

Secret Detention Facility
Northampton, England

The gang of vehicles turned off the country road just outside of town and onto a gravel drive that connected to a large, prisonlike complex in the English countryside.

Under cloudy darkness, they stopped briefly at the security checkpoint, headlights lighting up the entryway ahead. Captain Williams showed his face, and the guard hit the button to open the sliding gate.

"Thanks, mate," Williams said, rolling up the tinted window while they pressed on.

From the roadway near the small village of Quinton, the compound, which was built with thick concrete walls, looked like a massive, impenetrable bunker. Inside a tall electric fence with razor wire, the convoy backed down a ramp into an underground parking garage. As the last Rover passed the electric metal bay door, it quickly lowered to the concrete ground with a thump.

The convoy stopped in a line of spaces in front of the entrance to the interior of the building. They stepped out of the vehicles, and two of the captain's men, Staff Sergeant Beck and Sergeant Russell, escorted the package toward the entry, hood still over his head. Richard and his men departed the area in two cars while the others headed for the door.

The hardened structure was built as a bunker during World War II and repurposed with add-ons decades later. It saw significant use during the Global War on Terror. The SAS regiment, as well as intelligence officials, used it to interrogate terrorists and hold some in pretrial confinement. Guards with body armor and an array of weaponry roamed the grounds.

The thick, steel entryways weren't susceptible to most explosives. Around the fence line, metal guard towers and men with high-powered rifles watched the perimeter. A sophisticated security system with numerous high-definition day and night cameras surrounded the site.

"Where you taking me?" the man asked in broken English. "Infidel swine!"

Holding his neck with one hand, Beck punched him in his back with the other. The man dropped to his knees, and Rob grabbed him under the arms to lift him back up.

"You might want to behave, kid," Rob said, letting go of his grip, "or this is going to be much harder than it has to be."

Captain Williams unlocked the large metal door, and the men wandered inside. The door slammed, and Beck and another of Williams's men, Sergeant Myers, led the captive to a room at the other end. The captain opened up, and Beck forced the prisoner inside, shoving him down onto the cold, hard floor. The space was a huge square room with no windows except for a small, square piece of plexiglass in the door. There was a sloped floor and a drain in the center of the room.

Rob observed as the SAS captain marched inside and loomed over the man. He jerked the black sack from his head and tossed it across the room. Williams smiled down at him. He took a knee on the concrete.

"Now," he said. "Mister Ali, Ahmed Ali. We're going to ask you some questions, and you're going to answer them, right?"

Ali stared ahead while tensing his jaw muscles. He didn't utter a word.

"Yup," Williams added. "We know who you are. Somebody from the mosque sold your ass out. It turns out not all Muslims share your extremist views. What do you think about that?"

The captain snapped his fingers in front of Ahmed's face, seeing him blink.

"Oh," he continued. "You're going to talk, or you will suffer much unneeded pain."

"My brother is now a martyr!" Ahmed shouted. "Allah awards those who dispel nonbelievers!" He suddenly shot upward. Captain Williams gripped him by the arm and kneed him in the groin. Ahmed fell straight to the floor, bowing down in pain.

"Bad move, you arsehole. Let me tell you something. Your brother was nothing more than a filthy terrorist, like you. So spare me your righteous hogwash, little lad."

The captain forced Ahmed into a metal chair bolted to the floor. He took a chain from the corner and wrapped it around Ahmed's body, securing it tightly around his waist and arms.

"Okay, then," said the captain. "That's better. Perhaps now we can have a little conversation, huh? What do you think, Ahmed?"

Williams dropped down onto the seat, crossing his legs and arms. He smirked at Ahmed.

"Go to hell," Ahmed replied, spitting in the captain's direction.

Captain Williams rubbed his brown beard as he bent forward slowly in the chair. "Nope," he said. "You got it all wrong, matey. I'm not the one in hell here. You think al-Bashir gives a fuck about you? You and your brother both were just toys in his little game. You're expendable."

Ahmed tensed up, rattled at the mention of al-Bashir's name. He stared at the floor.

"Oh, that's right," the captain added. "We know all about him."

What Ahmed and his brother didn't know was that an informant had infiltrated the mosque. He was an Arab from Jordan—a peaceful man that had grown tired of brainwashed Muslims using the Qur'an for violent means. He'd spied on a small group of young Muslim boys while they were discussing their orders. The British government had agreed to protect him and his family in exchange for outing them. They would never reveal his true identity.

"Why do you think he recruits young lads like you?" asked Captain Williams. "Both of you were living on the street, no family, no prospects, no future. Just the two of you. He doesn't care whether you live or die. You're just pawns. Now that you've outlived your usefulness, what do you think is going to happen if we let you go? We'll just make him believe you talked. If you're lucky, you'd last a few hours, but my guess is no."

Ahmed tried to lunge at the captain, but the chain dug into his skin while holding him back.

"Nice try, you little wanker," said Williams.

Rob, observing the exchange from the doorway, stepped inside and shut it. The clank of the metal echoed off the bare cinder-block walls. He approached the captain while the other guys waited outside.

"Hey," Rob said, leaning against the back of the captain's chair. "Let me get a minute with him."

Captain Williams glanced back at Rob and cracked a smile. "Thought you'd never ask," he replied, springing from the chair. "He's all yours, mate."

The captain moved toward Rob's ear. "Feel free to rough him up a bit," he whispered.

Rob slipped his hands into a pair of tan Mechanix gloves as the captain headed for the door. While he and Brian conversed just outside, Rob stood to the side, an arm against the chair's backrest.

"Where's the next attack going to be?" he asked, moving around and bending almost nose-to-nose with Ahmed. "LA, New York, where?"

Ahmed closed his eyes, a cold, emotionless look on his face. Gripping the chain in his left hand, Rob balled his right fist. He swung, snapping Ahmed's head back hard. A drop of blood dripped down his cheek as sweat beaded off his forehead.

"We didn't kill your brother," said Rob. "Al-Bashir killed him the moment he recruited you. But Faisal is in a better place, right, seventy-two virgins in the afterlife and all that? There are only two ways this ends. Either you tell us where the next attack will be, or you rot in a filthy prison cell. They don't like terrorists in there. You'd have to watch your back for the rest of your miserable life."

Rob knew that was only partly true, however. Ahmed was headed to prison regardless, but they weren't going to tell him that.

"Well?" Rob added. "What's it going to be?"

He squeezed a fist once more and drove it into Ahmed's gut; Ahmed cried in pain, his body shuddering. Ali's head fell, and a bit of puke came up and landed on the floor by his feet.

"Damn, Ahmed," said Rob. "That's just nasty."

A little hung from Ahmed's lip as he tried to spit it up. Instead, the soreness in his throat sent him into a coughing fit.

"I ... will not ... tell... you anything, American," Ahmed said between coughs, spit flying from his mouth. "To be a martyr is highest honor. The West will leave our Muslim lands, or we will kill many more of you!"

"Really?" Rob asked. "You stupid, brainwashed punk. Well, you may just get your wish."

Suddenly, Rob heard the captain's phone ring behind him. He glanced back as Williams picked it up. Rob couldn't make out what he was saying, but he saw the concern on the captain's face. A few seconds went by, and he ended the call. Rob saw as Williams and Sergeant Major Meeks spoke briefly outside. The captain waved a finger, signaling for Rob to join them.

"Don't go anywhere," Rob joked with Ahmed. "Oh, that's right, you can't because you're tied up."

Rob left him dangling there and strolled through the doorway. He elbowed the door shut.

"Yeah?" Rob asked. "What's up? What is it?"

"I'll let the captain here tell you," replied Brian.

"Tell me what?" Rob asked.

Captain Williams put his cell back into his pocket. "That was one of our SIS officers on the phone. They're still on scene at the brothers' flat."

"And?" asked Rob.

"They are finishing up securing the site," the captain replied, "but it's not good news."

Rob glanced at Brian, then back at the SAS leader. "Meaning what?"

"Meaning," replied Williams. "Their plans are much more ambitious than we realized. SIS found a boatload of intel. We'll have to look it all over once it arrives. They got computers, hard drives, and handwritten letters. It looks like the main target was always the United States. The London bombing was just a trial run for the real thing."

"Jesus," said Brian.

Rob thought back to the messages the colonel had mentioned before. They were obviously a warning. With this new information, their true meaning was now beginning to materialize. They needed to contact Colonel Billings. If they couldn't locate al-Bashir, or figure out where the next target was going to be, many more people would die.

Brian tipped his head, indicating for Rob to follow him.

"We'll be back," said Brian.

"Hold on," replied the captain. "Let me open the door for you."

Captain Williams walked down the hall to a control room. He hit a button on the wall to let them out. Brian and Rob made their way up the side of the ramp and through the open door to the outside. Brian dialed a number and put the phone on speaker while it rang.

"This is Colonel Billings," the colonel said.

"Boss," Brian said. "We have the package in custody."

They could hear the colonel's concern and his heavy breathing. At almost the same time, Captain Williams received a call and stepped out of the room to take it.

"Tell me something good," Billings replied to Brian. "What's going on there?"

"We have one in custody, the other KIA on scene, Colonel. The Brits are finishing up searching the apartment now. Apparently, they found a treasure trove of intel. We'll have to sort that out once we get our hands on it. The boy isn't saying much, yet."

Rob watched Brian listening to the colonel speak.

"Yes, Colonel," Brian replied. "Will do, right away."

Brian ended the call and glanced back at Rob. "Looks like they got him," he said. "The Agency has a drone over his place in Lebanon."

"We can't touch him there," Rob replied. "It would be an act of war to shoot a missile into Lebanon."

All of a sudden, Captain Williams reemerged from the next room, his cell phone in hand.

"That's true," he said, "but we just got some solid intel that he's due in Syria in a few hours."

"What?" Rob asked.

"SIS recovered some documents, one of which showed correspondence between the boys and al-Bashir's second-in-command."

The captain showed the map location on his tablet.

"Right here," he added. "He's due for a meeting there. It's not far over the border."

ELEVEN

Tripoli, Lebanon

Aasim Abdul Al-Bashir roamed casually over the slightly uneven stone floor and down the cold stone-walled corridor. He trudged along in his brown sandals while gripping a wooden cane in his right palm. The dragging of his feet made a sandpapery sound with each step as he entered the large living area of the old house.

Al-Bashir owned the house in Beddaoui, a suburban village near the Port of Tripoli. A wealthy Saudi with ties to Saudi oil, he owned houses and compounds across both Lebanon and Saudi Arabia. Al-Bashir's father was a wealthy oil tycoon, and he'd inherited his fortune upon his death almost twenty years earlier.

Attending school in his home country, a young Aasim had befriended future al-Qaeda leader, Osama Bin Laden. The terrorist mastermind was a major influence on him as a teen. They both practiced Wahhabism, a puritanical form of Sunni Islam. During the Soviet war in Afghanistan, he rose up the ranks quickly. However, after Bin Laden's death, al-Bashir formed his own branch of al-Qaeda in Lebanon.

A few of al-Bashir's men rested on the floor along the wall, sipping tea while watching a football match on TV.

"Are they downstairs?" he asked one of them.

Seeing the boss standing before them, they rose promptly.

"Sit down," al-Bashir said, waving his hands down. "Sit. Are they still downstairs or not?"

"Yes, boss," one of them replied as he sat back down. "Salman is with him."

"Good," he replied as he continued toward the basement stairs.

As al-Bashir opened up the door, the cool subterranean air escaped through the doorway and swept over his face. With each stride, his sandals scraped across the steps on his way down the wood stairs. Al-Bashir stepped onto the bottom floor, his guard on a folding chair, watching the American captive hang from the ceiling pipe as he'd done for hours. The guard noticed al-Bashir and instantly jumped up.

"As-Salamu Alaikum, Salman," al-Bashir said to his guard.

"Wa alaikum salaam, boss," the guard replied, a little nervous to be in his presence.

Al-Bashir gestured for Salman to move out of the way. The young Muslim man snatched his rifle and rambled to the other side of the room. He stood still, caressing the barrel against the front of his body.

Al-Bashir strolled toward the American and stood before him. The American captive was bruised and battered, with purple welts around his eyes and cuts on his cheeks. Blood that had dripped from his nose had since dried and caked around his swollen lips.

"Hello," al-Bashir said to him.

He touched the tip of the American's chin. Al-Bashir pulled a shiny Damascus bone-handle knife from under his clothes.

"Do you know who I am?" al-Bashir asked, rubbing the side of the man's face with the blade.

The American's head shook weakly. "Should I?" he asked, his face quivering.

Al-Bashir grinned and brought the knife back. He smacked the American hard across the cheek with the tip of the handle.

"Of course you know who I am." He laughed, his breath reeking of cigarette smoke. "Why else would you be following me?"

The American's head dropped. Fresh blood dribbled from his lip. "I don't know what you're talking about."

"No?" asked al-Bashir. "Your friends are dead. Now, I'm trying to figure out what I should do with you. Nobody is coming to rescue you."

He snapped his fingers to get the guard's attention. "Come here, Salman," he said.

Salman hurried to his boss's side, his rifle across his belly.

"I appreciate the opinions of my men," al-Bashir added. "Tell me, Salman, what do you think I should do with this man?"

Salman stared at the American with hate-filled eyes. "Well, boss," he replied, "I think you should use him for insurance, leverage against the Americans. When you have no more use for him, kill him slowly."

Al-Bashir got excited, patting his man on the back. "You see?" he asked the American. "That is initiative. This is a born leader right here. He might one day be a lieutenant in the organization."

The American intel officer stared back at Salman. "Don't let him brainwash you, kid," he said with sweat pouring from his head. "He's nothing more than a murderous maniac, preying on young minds like yours."

"Shut up, American!" Salman shouted. "You know nothing about me!"

Without asking for his boss's permission, Salman smacked

the American in the mouth, and a bit of blood flew from his already cut lip.

"That is it, Salman!" al-Bashir said. "That's how you do it!"

He leaned in and whispered something in Salman's ear. Salman immediately headed for the staircase while al-Bashir stared the American down. A couple of minutes later, the guard returned with two more of his men, both clutching Kalashnikov rifles. They all surrounded the intelligence officer.

"What is this?" asked the American. "What the hell is going on here?"

Al-Bashir bowed his head, and they unhooked him from the ceiling chain. The American plummeted straight down and they caught him before he hit the ground. The two men propped him up, holding his hands behind his back while they tied his wrists with rope.

"Okay," al-Bashir said to the American. "Now, we go for a ride."

He headed for the door. His men following behind him, they thrust the American forward by their rifle barrels. One man on each side of him, they dragged and jostled the American up the basement stairs to the main level. Al-Bashir slammed the door and locked the large padlock. Four more of his men joined them, making their way to the street behind the house.

The door flew open, and three vehicles sat outside—two black Mercedes with a cargo truck in the middle. The men heaved the American up and shoved him into the canvas-covered flatbed. Two guards jumped in behind him, with another climbing into the cab of the truck. Three additional men joined them. A guard still in the building bolted the rear door from the inside as al-Bashir and the rest of his men climbed into cars. He got comfortable in the backseat of the lead car with Amir and Ibrahim by his side.

"What we waiting for?" he asked the driver, hitting the back of the seat. "Let's go!"

***

Eighteen thousand feet above Tripoli, the MQ-1 Predator drone with high-definition camera had picked up al-Bashir earlier while he and his men exited the house. From inside the GSC, or ground control station, the flight team monitored the house and the surrounding area. The drone operator, Greg Moore, had zoomed in to get a better look when he saw the group exiting the house and forcing a hostage into the truck.

From the CIA annex near Cairo, Egypt, they'd been sitting on one of al-Bashir's houses for a few hours by that point. The same source that had given intel officers intelligence that led to them tracking him to Saudi Arabia also gave up detailed information on multiple properties that al-Bashir owned. This information further confirmed the intel received from Britain's SIS officers.

The informant's name was Umar Aziz. He was a shop owner from Beirut with former ties to al-Qaeda. He'd grown weary, however, of the barbarism and hateful message the group depicted. Umar no longer wished to be affiliated with such groups and just wanted to live in peace.

He'd helped the Americans with the hope they'd sponsor his immigration to the United States. Umar was afraid al-Bashir and his men would find him and retaliate. His only hope was to get his family out of Lebanon.

The convoy raced toward the Lebanese–Syrian border in the southeast of the country. The drone pilot continued viewing the scene on the ground.

"Weapons off," Dan said to the drone pilot. "We can't engage within Lebanese borders."

Dan moved toward the screen to get a closer look at the vehicles.

"Where's the American?" he asked.

"He's in the middle," the pilot replied.

The chief took a seat at the module beside Greg's. He followed the enemy movement onscreen.

"What do you want me to do, Chief?" asked Greg.

Suddenly, the vehicles turned left onto a two-lane south of the port city.

"Follow them," replied Bailey. "What else? Let's see where they take him. If we can't take him out now, at least we might be able to report the whereabouts of an American hostage. Notify me of any significant changes."

"You got it, Chief," said Greg.

While Greg observed the convoy picking up speed, moving down the four-lane highway, Chief Bailey got up and stepped outside to make a phone call. He recovered his secure cell phone from his pocket, dialing the number as he sparked up a cigarette and leaned against the metal container wall. It started to ring.

"This is Mason," a voice on the other line answered.

Charles Mason was Bailey's department head in Langley. With a career spanning over three decades, he was from the old school of Agency spooks.

"Hey, boss," Bailey said with his cigarette in the corner of his mouth. "We have a problem, a big fucking problem."

The chief could hear Mason sigh over the line.

"Don't tell me problems," replied Mason. "Tell me solutions. What the hell is it, Bailey?"

"Boss," the chief added. "I have an update on al-Bashir. We have him in our sights, but he isn't alone. He has an American with him."

"What?" Mason asked.

"Yes, sir," the chief added. "We thought he'd killed them all, but apparently not. They're transporting him southeast toward Syria, it looks like. We're tracking their movements as we speak. Maybe start thinking about a rescue op? We might have to get that bastard on the ground."

Chief Bailey heard Mason fiddle with a stack of papers.

"Al-Bashir's not stupid," replied Mason. "He knows we're watching, and he's using the man as cover. Sending a ground team is going to be tricky, though. We have diplomatic relations, so it can't be done secretly. We'd need to get the Lebanese prime minister involved. He will almost certainly want to send a local team to assist and to make sure we don't break any peace agreements. They hate these terrorists just like we do, but the red tape can't be avoided if we don't want to piss them off."

"Understood," said the chief. "But this is time-sensitive. They won't hold him forever. Eventually, they'll have no more use for him."

"I know, Dan," Mason replied. "I know. I'll contact the appropriate people. Meanwhile, keep watching him. Let me know of any changes, however slight, okay?"

"All right, boss," Bailey said. "You got it."

Bailey hung up and pocketed his cell. He yanked the door of the GCS open and headed inside. He filled his coffee mug full of black coffee and returned to his drone pilot. Bailey took a seat, placing his cup on the table beside him.

The drone pilot had followed the target vehicles much farther up the highway when the convoy suddenly swung right. They traveled through jagged hills and grassy terrain, houses lining elevated streets off the main road. Green fields of grass mixed with trees and litter bordered the roadside all the way down.

"Where are you going, you bastard?" Greg mumbled.

They sped down a steep decline, and the vehicles veered onto an unpaved road toward a large house situated at the bottom of a hill. Dust clouds were left in their wake as the convoy raced down the path and stopped on a circular drive with a fountain in the middle.

"All right, Chief," Greg added. "They've stopped."

The house itself was fairly large, white with two floors and a terrace overlooking the backyard. There was an olive garden in the back and rose bushes around the perimeter. The chief and his pilot observed the occupants of the cars getting out. One of them opened the door for the boss and then headed toward the back of the cargo truck. He let the tailgate down. It was obvious he was shouting at the American as he grabbed him by the arm and dragged him feet first. The hostage fell from the bed, striking the back of his head on the bumper.

"Damn it," said the chief.

"Looks like Smith," Greg said, referring to the hostage.

"Yeah," replied the chief. "That's him. God knows how he survived to end up there."

Onscreen, they brought Officer Smith to his feet and poked him forward as both his legs wobbled. One of the guards took his AK and jabbed him in the back with it. Smith fell to the dirt again, two of al-Bashir's men forcing him up by the arms.

"Shit," said Greg. "He looks in a bad way."

The guards forced Smith toward the back, where they disappeared into the compound. The rest of the men, including al-Bashir, vanished inside and out of the view of the drone.

"That's it, boss," said Greg. "We have his location, at least."

"Okay," replied the chief. "I'll send the coordinates up the chain. We'll have a rescue op pending approval."

TWELVE

The bright moonlight sparkled over the calm sea. The team was perched in rows of webbed seating facing the center of the cargo plane. They thought they were on the way back home and had settled in for a flight time of several hours back to the States.

Drizzle began to form on the cockpit windshield as the C-130 exited UK airspace. Rob and the others had mixed feelings about the outcome of their operation in Britain. They surely hadn't left with the answers they were seeking. The team had learned, though, that al-Bashir recruited young radicals, and they planned to attack the United States. But that was the extent of their information-gathering.

They needed a fresh bit of intel, and fast. The team trusted the SIS would find something more of value they could use. They were unaware that al-Bashir was currently being tracked by the CIA in Lebanon. Their mission was about to take a drastic turn.

Rob and three of his teammates played cards to kill the time while the aircraft soared twenty thousand feet above the water. Brian sat alone on the opposite row of seats, reading a book and dozing off every few minutes. The team's weapons, armor, and most of their gear were spread out on the floor. There was little turbulence on the flight home, and they'd made it a few hundred nautical miles over the Atlantic.

Rob tossed his stack of cards down onto an MRE box.

"You out?" Josh asked.

"Yeah," Rob replied as he stretched out his legs and pushed himself up from the seat. "I'm done, man. I need to move around a bit. My leg's falling asleep."

Rob couldn't stop thinking about Ahmed. He was such a religious zealot, he was never going to talk. It might have been displaced loyalty, but Rob couldn't help but sort of admire his dedication. It was no surprise that a nobody like Ahmed felt some sense of purpose being recruited by such powerful men. Young extremists like him had no greater aspiration than to become martyrs for their cause, though most didn't fully understand what that meant.

"Hey," Rob said as he approached Brian. "You all right, boss man? What you doing over here being so antisocial?"

Brian nodded slowly. "Yeah, man," he replied. "I'm good. And I'm not being antisocial—just thinking about bad guys. I don't know what they're up to. The CIA better get its shit together before they do some major damage. This can't be another fucking nine-eleven. If the most powerful and sophisticated country in the world can't stop a bunch of medieval assholes with detonators…."

Rob stopped him there. "We will, man," he said. "All right? Even if we have to go in alone and unsupported, we'll stop them. We have to. I don't even want to think about the alternative."

Brian took a deep breath and sat up in the seat while Rob pinched a bit of Copenhagen from a can and put it into the side of his mouth. "And if we can't?" he asked. "What if the intel comes in late like it often does? What then?"

Rob knelt down beside Brian. "I don't even want to think

like that," he replied. "We can't think like that, boss. It's our job to stop them, and we will."

Rob sat down on the seat next to Brian. He took his cap off, dropping it onto the next seat over. He bent forward, his chin in his hand, and the plane's crew chief appeared and signaled for them to don their radio headsets. Both Rob and Brian snapped up and snatched the headsets hooked up inside the plane that were closest to them.

"Golf-Three-Six," a voice transmitted through the plane's onboard radio. "Golf-Three-Six, this is Alpha-Six-Actual, do you copy, over?"

Brian squeezed the button as everyone else took headsets to listen in.

"Good copy, Alpha-Six-Actual," he replied. "We read you, over."

The man on the other end was Colonel Billings.

"Roger that, Golf-Three-Six," he said. "There's been an update on the situation. You are being diverted to Lima Echo from your current position."

Lima Echo, or LE, was the NATO country code for Lebanon.

"You'll have a stopover in QA," the colonel added.

QA was the code for Qatar.

"There," he continued, "you'll board a private civilian aircraft en route. Once you land, you'll link up with a team from the local commando regiment at the airport, as well as one of our own intelligence officers. Your team will be briefed on the operation at that time. Understood, Golf-Three-Six?"

Understandably, Delta command didn't want to use US military aircraft in Lebanon. Effectively, they wanted to go in, conduct their mission, then vanish without anyone ever knowing they were there. It was part of what made Delta so secretive.

"Understood, Alpha-Six-Actual," Brian replied.

They held on, feeling the plane starting a hard left turn.

"All right, son," Billings said. "I'll be in touch. Have a good flight and try to catch up on some sleep on the way, huh? I know you boys have been up for a while. Alpha-Six-Actual, out."

The pilot and copilot had listened in on the call.

"We're setting a course now," the pilot said. "ETA, about four and a half hours."

"Roger that," replied Brian.

"You see what I was saying?" Rob asked as he spit a stream of tobacco into an empty water bottle. "Now's the time, man."

"Yeah, yeah," Brian replied. "Good call, as usual."

"Whooo!" Jamal yelled as he bounced from his seat. "Time to get to work, fellas."

Rob hopped up and made his way to one of the small portholes in the aircraft, staring out into the abyss. Soon, they'd be on the ground in another country. He returned to his seat, snatching up his weapons and gear.

"Make sure your stuff is in top shape, gentlemen," he said. "We won't have time once we land."

Rob pulled his assault pack from under the chair. He checked his night vision and the scope for his long rifle. Reaching into a small pocket, Rob snagged his tan and black checkered shemagh and wrapped it around his neck. He leaned back into the seat and closed his eyes. For the next several minutes, Rob slowly drifted off to sleep.

Hours later, Rob gazed through the window of the small twin-engine aircraft, its wheels meeting the runway of the Raffia Hariri International Airport in Beirut, Lebanon. Everyone stayed seated as the plane slowed from landing speed to a gentle crawl. Ready to finally stretch his legs a bit, Rob got up from his seat and recovered his pack from the bin above. Holding it up, he put his arms through the straps and buckled it across his chest. Rob reached to the floor to retrieve his weapons case from under the seat. He dragged it out and pulled it upright by the handle.

His teammates secured their gear and equipment as they got ready to disembark the aircraft. The plane took a right turn and moved down the taxiway. Rob peered through the window again to see a group of men waiting beside two black Land Cruisers at the far end of the airport. "Welcome to Lebanon, gentlemen," said Brian. "Where half the country hates you, and you can't tell friend from foe."

It was true, like it was in most Middle Eastern countries. The US and Lebanese governments were historically close. The US had even provided aid to Lebanon on multiple occasions. Yet, just under half of the Lebanese people had a favorable view of Americans. Approximately 34 percent of Lebanese were Christian. It was the Lebanese Muslims who were generally wary of Americans, especially ones who carried guns.

"That looks like our contact up ahead," Brian said, glancing through the window.

The plane squealed to a stop, and the copilot appeared from the cockpit and opened up the aircraft door. They shuffled to the opening.

"Thanks for the lift," Rob said to the copilot.

"My pleasure, sir," he replied.

As Rob headed down the steps with the team, the strong humidity of the Mediterranean coast smacked him in the face, as if it would suck the air right out of his lungs.

"Got to love that Middle Eastern air," Rob joked, his boot touching the blacktop.

They stepped away from the plane and a group of four Lebanese men drew near from their running vehicles. All had body armor with handguns on their hips. Though they didn't wear uniforms, it wasn't like they were trying to hide. In fact, most people knew who they were by their look and didn't bother messing with them. They were the most elite unit Lebanon had to offer.

"As-Salamu Alaikum," Brian said as they approached.

"Wa alaikum salaam," their commander replied with a hand over his heart. "Sergeant Major Meeks? Brian Meeks, is this correct?"

"Yeah, that's me," Brian replied as Rob stood next to him. "You speak great English."

"Yes," he replied. "It is required. We have to be proficient as part of our training."

"Great," said Brian. "This is my assistant team leader, Master Sergeant Rob Walker, Sergeant First Class Jamal Erickson, Sergeant First Class Josh Reynolds, and Staff Sergeant Colin Mills."

"Hey there," said Colin with a finger up.

"Hello, gentlemen," said the Lebanese commander. "Welcome to Lebanon. I am Captain Sameed Rachid, commander of the Commando Regiment. These are my men, Saib, Haasim, and Abdel, all NCOs under my leadership. Saib is sergeant first class and one of my trusted team leaders."

"Hello there," Saib said.

The captain guided them to the waiting Land Cruisers. "Men," he said. "If you would please follow us, we have a briefing set up for you at our headquarters in Roumieh. It's not far from here. You can load your equipment in the back of the vehicles."

Two of Captain Rachid's men popped the hatches of both Cruisers. Rob took the lead vehicle with Jamal, and they both began stacking their stuff in the back. Brian, Josh, and Colin tossed their gear into the rear of the second vehicle, and they all climbed in.

"I call shotgun," Rob said, hopping in next to Saib.

Saib appeared confused. "What does this mean, shotgun?" he asked.

Rob and Jamal both let out a short laugh.

"Oh," replied Rob. "It just means I call front seat."

"You call front seat?" asked Saib.

"Yeah," Rob replied. "You know what, never mind. It's just an American expression."

"If you say so," said Saib.

The captain stepped up onto the seat behind Rob, and they took off toward the airport exit. They departed the airfield through the gate, and Saib aimed the vehicle just to the east of the capital city. For the remainder of the drive, Rob gaped at the picturesque Lebanese countryside as it flew by. With its rugged rocky cliffs, winding roads, and luscious mountainous terrain, it was truly a beautiful sight to see. But that beauty hid something dark—the most evil anything or anyone could possibly be. And it operated right under the government's and the average Lebanese citizen's noses.

Twenty-five minutes and a little over twenty miles later, the two vehicles approached the main gate of a Lebanese military base. The guard put an arm out to tell them to stop. Saib rolled down his window.

"Identification, please," the gate guard said in Arabic.

They recognized a few faces in the car, but to keep unsavory types away, namely the terrorist kind, they were instructed to stop everyone. The captain produced his ID card and gave it to Saib. He handed the occupants' IDs to the guard. Behind, two more guards checked the rear vehicle. They inspected the occupants' IDs, and guards with vehicle inspection mirrors checked the undercarriage of both Cruisers for bombs and such.

"These other men are guests of the Lebanese government," Captain Rachid said from the backseat. "They are to be treated with respect."

The guard peeked inside the vehicle, looking everyone over. He handed back the ID cards.

"Very well, Captain," he said. "You may proceed."

"Thank you," Rachid replied as Saib hit the gas.

For a little over half a kilometer, they pressed on until arriving at a large building complex on the left. The Lebanese flag whipping rapidly in the wind, they pulled into a parking lot out front. They parked across the walk from the double glass doors and shut the vehicles down.

"This is our headquarters," Captain Rachid said as he opened the door and stepped out. "We have everything set up for you just inside. Get your things and we will begin."

Rob and the others roamed to the rear and began unloading their gear from inside. Rob secured his pack to his back and snatched his weapons case. Carrying it by the handle, he accompanied the captain and his men inside while the others followed.

They entered the building, and immediately noticeable were the rows of Lebanese military leadership photos down both sides of the wall. Captain Rachid guided the men halfway down and through an open door on the right. Inside, a high-ranking Lebanese officer waited. The commandos immediately stood at attention and Captain Rashid saluted.

"Relax," he said. "Come in, men, please. Sit. I won't make this a formal meeting."

The Americans followed the captain and his men, sitting around the table.

"My name is Colonel Imad Alawi, regiment commander.

We welcome you to our country. I know you want to get started, so here we are. Would any of you like some tea before we begin?"

"No, Colonel," Brian replied. "We're good."

"As you wish," said Alawi. "We shall begin, then."

The colonel produced an image of al-Bashir from a folder. "I believe this is the man you want," Alawi added. "This photograph was taken by us a few months ago outside one of his compounds. He moves between properties he owns all over Lebanon. Your government's source says he'll be at this one tonight."

Alawi gave the image to Brian, who passed it over to Rob and the others around the room.

"If you were that close," Rob said, glancing up at the colonel, "why didn't you take him then? Could've saved us all a lot of trouble, if you ask me."

Colonel Alawi took the photo back. "Because," he replied, "we were still gathering intelligence on this man. It takes time to perform these types of operations on Lebanese soil. Because your government has shared some information about his plans with us, you are now here. Unfortunately, we do not have the same resources the US has at its disposal. Our budget is spread thin. However, we are, after all, partnered with your country to combat terrorism, so…"

"I see," replied Rob.

"So you're here to babysit us?" Brian asked.

"No," the colonel replied. "We are here to accompany you. This is our country. We are responsible for what happens here. If one American dies here, your government may withdraw aid. This is a joint mission between our countries, nothing more. Is there anything you need from us before we begin?"

Rob looked Alawi directly in the eye. "Listen, Colonel," he said. "With respect, we aren't politicians. We're operators. We couldn't give a shit less about politics. What some pencil pusher in Washington thinks doesn't faze us. With that said, just let us go, support us if you can, or stay the hell out of our way."

THIRTEEN

Masnaa, Lebanon

In armored chevy suburbans, the team, with their Lebanese counterparts, zoomed down the highway to the southeast, just outside Masnaa. Rocky outcrops jutted out from the hill along the side of the road as the vehicles whizzed by.

The medium-sized town was situated just a few kilometers shy of the Syrian border, where weapons and munitions were smuggled in and out of Lebanon by terror groups on both sides. The further eastward and closer to Syria, the more sparse and desert the landscape became. Distant desert mountain peaks emerged as they came around a sharp curve of the three-lane roadway.

A safe distance from the compound, Saib turned onto a side road. He led the convoy off the pavement and onto an unstable gravel path beside a field with rows of cedar trees. He hit the brakes of the armored vehicle and slid a few feet across the rocks at the edge, sprinkling dust over the road.

"This is where we get out," said Captain Rashid.

As they exited, the sun was vanishing beneath the mountains, perfect for a stealthy approach. Rob headed to the back and opened the hatch. He popped the weapons case open to retrieve his long gun, his M4 carbine, and his vest. Securing the vest over his civilian shirt, he reached into his pack and snagged a pair of fingerless camouflage gloves. Rob slipped them on. Slinging the sniper rifle onto his back, he held the M4 down by his side. Everyone else took their respective gear and softly closed both hatches.

"Do you and your men have a plan to save that man?" Captain Rashid asked.

The captain outranked them all, but he would listen.

"Yeah, we do, Captain," replied Brian. "For this op, we split into two teams. You and your men are Alpha Team. We're Bravo. You guys cover the exits, Walker and Mills will be on overwatch, and the rest of us clear the buildings. If the intel is good, we'll find him here."

Captain Rachid cocked his AK47. He racked his Canik pistol and holstered it on his leg. "You don't need us with you?"

Brian removed the lens cover from the red dot optic on his M4. He lined the magnifier up with it and locked it in place. "No offense to you or your men, Captain," he replied. "I'm sure you know what you're doing. But there was no time for rehearsals, and we have never conducted an op with you. We've got this. Just cover both ends and make sure nobody gets in or out."

Brian recovered a map from inside his shirt. He made his way to the front of the vehicle and spread it out on the hood. He shone down a green-tinted flashlight.

"Captain," Brian added, pointing to spots on the map, "I need you and your men to cover here and here to make sure there are no surprises. Walker and Mills will be on this hill, covering us. The rest of us will head inside to clear the place and grab the hostage. If we get into any trouble, we will radio you for reinforcements. If all goes well, though, we should be in and out."

The captain signaled his men to join him. Everyone donned radio headsets.

"Whatever you require," replied Rashid, "but remember, this is our country. No breaking rules of engagement. We'll contact you when we are in position."

"Understood," Brian replied as Rashid and his men slipped between the trees.

Rob loaded a full magazine into his Remington 700 sniper rifle. He screwed the suppressor to the tip.

"Walker," Brian continued. "You two head to the overwatch position. The rest of us will take the other way around."

"Wilco, boss," replied Rob. "Let's go, Mills. You're with me."

With his sniper rifle on his back and his carbine at the low ready, Rob and his spotter headed northeast to the base of a dirt hill three hundred meters away. Crouched low, they snaked their way past the patch of trees and across open, flat ground. They got close enough to see most of the inside of the complex, and noted security lights all the way around the inside of the wall and at the front of the building. They hit their knees and crawled the rest of the way to the top of the rocky hill overlooking the yard.

Rob plucked his rifle from his back and unfolded the stock. He set it up on the bipod and placed his M4 carbine to his left.

"Golf-two-five," he said into his radio. "We're in position, over."

"Copy," the captain said. "Lima-Six is also in position."

With his M4 beside him, Colin retrieved his spotting scope from his pack. He quickly set it up on the tripod. Removing the lens cover, he peered through the glass to calculate the range to the target. With a keen eye, he studied the range and the indicators on the glass.

"Four hundred meters to the front door," he said. "Wind, five miles per hour coming from our two o'clock, half value."

Rob dialed his scope while he waited for the rest of the team to be ready. The radio keyed.

"Golf-Three-Six, in position," Brian said.

Rob situated the butt of his rifle firmly into the crevice of his right shoulder. With his left hand under the tan aluminum hand guard, he scanned through the high-powered Vortex scope. The compound was big but not mansion-sized. A tan-colored structure, it had a brick driveway from the main gate. A few black Mercedes were parked on the left, with an armored Suburban closer to the front entrance. They viewed the yard, where some guards were chatting up one another. Others roamed the grounds at random.

"Few guards out front," Rob said over the radio. "Six by my count."

"Hold on," Colin said, peeking through his spotting scope. "I just saw two more exit the front door."

Rob pivoted the scope right. He moved his dominant eye to the glass.

"Roger, I see 'em," he replied. "They're guarding something for sure."

Rob and his spotter continued surveying the compound. No other guards were visible. Rob yanked his gloves tighter on his hands and set the butt of the rifle down a moment.

"All right, Lima-Six, Golf-Two-Five," Brian said from his team's position by the wall. "Remember the plan. We move on Two-Five's call, not until."

"Copy," Captain Rachid replied.

"Yeah, roger that, Golf-Three-Six," said Rob.

Rob gripped his rifle's pistol grip. He snugged it against him and peeked through the glass. Two guards watching the front gate stood meters from one another. One blew cigarette smoke into the air as Rob settled his scope reticle in the center of his chest.

"Preparing to engage tangos out front," he said.

Rob squeezed the trigger immediately, watching red mist shoot out of the man's back when the suppressed shot punched through him. Like a statue, stiff, he fell backward into the sand. Rob immediately racked the rifle bolt and loaded another round into the chamber. He turned left instantly as the second guard noticed his dead friend on the ground. Before he could scream for help, Rob sent a round through his neck. The penetration of the bullet nearly decapitated him, and he toppled back, his neck and jaw a bloody mess.

"Tangos down," Rob said. "Clear to move."

Alpha and Bravo teams entered the compound. Brian and the rest of his team engaged fighters out front while Captain Rachid provided cover as they waited near the entrance. Taking cover behind the Suburban, Brian and the others sent fire into the enemy position by the house. Rob followed their movement in his scope. The enemy had ducked behind a low wall to the right. One of them popped his head up momentarily. Before he could duck back down, Rob put a bullet through his forehead, dropping him flat.

Bullets pinged off the walls and the house as the firefight intensified. Suddenly, the firing ceased. No sooner than it began, it was already over. With gun smoke filling the air like fog, Rob checked the perimeter. They were expecting more to exit the house, but no others came.

"Perimeter is clear," said Rob. "Repeat, perimeter is clear. Don't know about the interior. Something ain't right."

"Roger," Brian replied as they exited their covered position. "Nothing but bodies here. Wasn't much of a fight."

Jamal tightly gripped the sledgehammer at his side and prepared to breach.

"Moving on the building," Brian said. "Breacher, get ready."

Rob covered the entryway with his rifle.

"Now," Brian said. "Go, go."

Sniper and spotter watched as Jamal busted the lock off. But surprisingly, after the team entered, they heard no firing. They waited a few seconds, still nothing.

"Golf-Three-Six," Rob said. "What's going on in there, over?"

They heard a distinct gasp. There was a brief silence, then Brian spoke. "Golf-Three-Five," he replied. "You guys need to come see this for yourselves."

Rob glanced over at his spotter. "What the fuck?" he asked. "What is it?"

"Just get down here," Brian insisted.

"Copy that," replied Rob. "On the way."

The pair hopped from the ground and secured their equipment. Rob folded his rifle's stock and slung it. Both men headed down the hill, M4s in hand. They hoofed it a few hundred meters across flat land and through the front gate. They neared the broken door, and Rob elbowed it open, and they stepped inside. Immediately, they heard a loud voice. The two wandered through the nearly empty room to the next door. Rob peeked inside to see the rest of his team staring in shock.

"What the hell is this?" he asked as they entered the room.

In the center, an old box TV sat on a small table. On the screen, Aasim al-Bashir gave a stern warning to the Americans.

I applaud you for trying, infidels. I commend you for having the nerve when you knew you would fail. Nevertheless, you cannot catch me. You cannot stop the movement. And you cannot prevent what is to come. Brace yourself, Americans. For your homeland will suffer the consequences of meddling in Muslim affairs. We will show no mercy, as your government showed no mercy in killing our women and children with your drones!

Al-Bashir turned the camera on his captive, CIA officer Smith. Bloodied and battered, Smith sat bound to a chair, blood covering his white T-shirt. Barely able to talk, he hung his head and coughed, spitting up blood. The terrorist leader continued his monologue.

As of this recording, soldiers of Allah are converging on your country, preparing to bring His wrath down upon you. We will not stop until it is complete. Bow down, American imperialists, because soon, you will understand what it truly means for your brothers and sisters to burn while knowing you cannot do anything to stop it!

The recording stopped, and the screen went to static. Rob and the others were rattled, in disbelief.

"Shit," Brian said. "That asshole used his men as bait, sacrificing them just to get us in here."

"He sure as hell did," Colin added.

"Yeah," Rob replied. "We need to get this intel back to the colonel right now. I hope the CIA has got something for us. Otherwise, we're in the dark without a fucking flashlight. If we can't stop whatever they have planned, it's going to be a really bad day."

The team exited the building. Rob stepped away to inform Captain Rashid as Brian headed to the vehicle to contact Colonel Billings.

FOURTEEN

Sergeant Juan Torres and his partner, Sergeant Gabriel Santiago, had just exited the station, headed to their parked patrol car near the front entrance to the building.

Downing a little black coffee in a Styrofoam cup, Torres dumped the rest of the liquid in the dirt and tossed the cup into the garbage can by the walkway. He stepped toward the back of the car and popped the trunk. The officer took his black vest out and tossed one to his partner. They both put them on and fastened them. Officer Torres slammed the trunk and wandered toward the driver's side. Santiago went to the other side. They climbed in and buckled their seatbelts.

The police station, located in one of the most gang-ridden cities in Mexico, was located inside a walled compound with razor wire and a solid metal gate entrance. It was protected for good reason. The Los Lobos Cartel ran Juárez, like they did many other cities and towns throughout Mexico. They had a hand in everything. Drugs, guns, and piles of cash made their way through the city on a regular basis.

Unfortunately, many police officers and politicians across

the country were on the cartel's payroll. Others who feared them simply looked the other way. But a few, like Torres and his partner, couldn't be bought at any price. They risked their lives and those of their families for peace of mind, but to them, it was the price to pay for being on the right side of the law.

Officer Torres pulled the car up to the gate while another officer outside rolled it open. They drove through and waved back to him, and the officer shut and locked the gate behind them. Torres took a right onto the roadway headed away from the center of town.

"Where to, partner?" Santiago asked. "Or are we just going to drive around aimlessly?"

"We're just going for a ride, amigo," replied Torres. "Patrolling the usual spots, checking the sights. Just another day in Juárez, mi amigo."

It was the middle of the day in Mexico, but the sky had become nearly dark as night. The overcast clouds went from a fluffy white to pitch-black in a matter of an hour or so. Suddenly, a clap of thunder pounded from high above. Jarring vibrations rumbled, shaking the ground under them. As they stopped the police car at a four-way intersection, lightning streaked brightly across the sky in a web pattern.

"Looks like it's going to be a stormy one today, huh?" Santiago asked, the window trembling.

"It sure does," Torres replied, flicking the wipers on when droplets started collecting on the windshield.

In just a couple minutes, the drizzle had turned into a full downpour, and the rain began to douse the car faster than the wipers could clear it. The pair could barely see the red light suspended from the cable above the street.

"Shit," said Torres. "I can't see a damn thing."

"Just go slow," his partner replied. "I don't feel like crashing today, hombre."

"Funny," Torres said as the light turned green, and he pressed gently on the accelerator.

The streets were starting to flood over. Driving through puddles, the tires splashed water off the right side of the road and into the dirt. Officer Torres pressed on slowly, aiming for the outskirts of the city. The car moved on, and buildings and homes became less and less frequent. Stopping the vehicle at a stop sign, the officer swung right and headed for the city limit sign along Highway Two.

The desert outside the town was bare and bleak but for the occasional house and service station. The duo liked to patrol there because there'd been an uptick in cartel activity out in the sands. The higher-ups never did anything about it, but Torres and Santiago occasionally had run-ins with cartel associates, mostly drug mules paid to smuggle merchandise into the States. The partners weren't known to back down. It was a wonder they were still alive.

Although the rain had begun to lighten up a bit, it still fell at a steady pace as Officer Torres swerved onto a muddy back road toward the tiny border town of San Isidro. Slowing the patrol car, he came to a complete stop by a worn-out and rust-covered stop sign. He prepared to continue the drive, but the shape of a person appeared through the rain-covered windshield. Officer Torres and his partner rocked forward in their seats as he slammed on the brakes. They saw the unknown person fall forward, gripping the bumper and sliding to the street.

"What the hell?" Santiago asked.

As the figure fell out of sight to the soggy ground, Torres switched on the blue lights. He flung the door open with his knee and swung his leg out, drawing his nine-millimeter pistol from his duty belt as he exited the vehicle.

"Wait here," he said to his partner.

The officer crept his way forward, gripping his gun while moving toward the front of the car. Peeking around the front bumper, Torres saw a man on his knees, his head down with blood trickling from his face. The blood pooled on the pavement and the rain flow carried it away in a stream. The officer bent his knees and lowered himself to the ground to get a good look at the man's face. He stuck his arm above the hood and waved for his partner.

Officer Torres heard the door slam. Santiago made his way to him.

"What is wrong with him?" Santiago asked, bending down and pulling the man's head up by the chin.

He didn't seem to be able to talk. Every sound he made was a feeble groan.

"What happened to you, hombre?" Torres asked. "Who did this to you?"

The two officers stood over the man, and he suddenly started to vomit blood. Santiago jumped back to keep from getting it on him. Torres headed back to the car window to grab the radio. He reached in for the mic as he stuck his head through.

"Victor base," he said. "This is Victor one-one. We have a sick man here at Highway Two and Clemente Toquinto in San Isidro. We don't know what he's gotten into. Please send EMS."

"Ten-four, one-one. Dispatching EMS to the scene now."

Torres wiped rain from his forehead.

"Thanks, Isabella," he replied, putting the radio mic back inside the car.

"Hey, partner," Santiago called out from the front of the police car. "He's convulsing. We have to get him loaded up in the next few minutes, or he might not make it!"

Torres rushed to the front of the car.

"What happened to you, mister?" he asked, gripping his soiled shirt.

But the poor man was obviously in no shape to talk. His bugged-out eyes just stared into nothing.

***

At ISA Headquarters in Fort Belvoir, Virginia, intel Sergeant James Weber stood with his back against the break room counter, sipping from a cold bottle of Gatorade while munching on a piece of toast. Having stepped away for a bit to clear his head, he pondered alone to himself. Everyone in that office was eager to get to work, and they were getting antsy.

Part of JSOC, or joint special operations command, ISA stood for intelligence support activity. It was the premier intelligence collection agency for all tier-one units of the US military. An intermediate to the CIA, the ISA worked much more closely with units like Delta and SEAL Team Six. They'd been known by various names over the years, such as Task Force Orange, Field Operations Group, and Gray Fox. This was mostly to misdirect any probes into their activities or identities.

The ISA were one of the special operations groups most shrouded in mystery. Because they had their own dedicated team, these special mission units didn't need to rely solely on the CIA for intelligence gathering. But the ISA didn't only gather intel. More often than not, they fought side by side with the operators they supported. Many who knew them called them soldier spies.

The agency had been working around the clock, attempting to collect and analyze intelligence gathered in Lebanon and the United Kingdom; however, the information they had was thin. The rescue operation in Lebanon was a bust, as the only thing the Delta team had walked away with, aside from the video, was the confirmation Smith was most likely still breathing, for now.

Weber finished up the last little bit of drink and, fading

back like he was in a football game, tossed the bottle into the receptacle by the door. Suddenly, his friend Jack Conrad barged into the room. He marched straight for the refrigerator and pulled it open it, snatching a small bottle of orange juice. He removed the cap, tipping it back and bumping the refrigerator door closed.

"My eyes are starting to water," he said to Weber as he took a chair. "I hate staring at a screen. I'm not a damn analyst. I want to be back in the field."

Both men, dressed in street clothing, were staff sergeants in the unit.

"You come up with anything?" Weber asked.

"No," Conrad replied, putting his hands up. "That's the thing. Nothing in the intel we've collected points to any US targets—not from the Brits, the Lebanese, or our own intel community. We can't find a damn thing. If anybody besides the terrorists has any information, they sure as hell aren't sharing."

Weber popped the rest of his toast into his mouth and wandered toward Janet, one of the ISA analysts. He took a seat next to her.

"Just calm down, would you?" he said to Conrad. "I know it's frustrating. I'm with you. But we're the Unites States of freaking America, the most advanced country in the world."

"Exactly," replied Conrad. "Yet we can't figure out where they're coming from, or if they're already here. What if we're too late? I mean, these bastards murdered our own and have one man locked up in some shitty hole somewhere. Our technology, our drones, and we can't track a few of these slimy bastards?"

Since the warnings made against government figures at the Pentagon and in Washington, lawmakers and military leaders had been pressuring the Agency to validate the threat. Al-Bashir and his branch of al-Qaeda didn't leave paper or electronic trails.

Without human intel, the intelligence community had nothing.

Words typed in a message sent through a proxy server was hardly anything to go by. It was untraceable, no IP address included. The computers the team had located in Lebanon were being analyzed, but they had been wiped clean. Nothing of use was found. If al-Bashir and his associates were conducting any business online, they were surely utilizing the dark web to avoid surveillance.

"Damn it," Conrad said, marching to the door and propping it open. "We need to get in there. We can't do shit from here."

Their supervisor, Sergeant First Class Mike Epps, stopped him mid-stride. "You might just get your wish," he said to Conrad, clutching a stack of papers.

"What?" asked Conrad. "What do you mean, top?" He followed Mike back into the room.

"Have a seat, and I'll explain," he said, setting the documents on the table.

Mike grinned as they all settled around the table.

"I just got a call from JSOC," he added. "Apparently, Mexican authorities in Juárez contacted us about a man they found on the street. They say he was talking gibberish, but he got a few words out they understood."

Conrad and Weber both seemed bewildered, not sure of the connection.

"Boss," Weber said. "What does some guy in Mexico have to do with anything?"

Mike pulled one of the papers out with his finger and slid it across the table.

"Because," he replied as they looked over the photographs on the page, "he has radiation sickness. Evidently, he spouted something about bombs to the hospital staff before passing out. That's as far as they've gotten. He hasn't spoken since. But

Mexico isn't exactly a prime target for terrorists, is it? So that just leaves one other option."

Conrad held the document up. "Shit," he said. "That's horrid. Do we know who this man is?"

"They're working on it," Mike replied. "My opinion? He's probably some low-level hoodlum working for the cartel. He gets sick and dies, nobody cares, you know? How this is connected to terrorists, and most likely al-Bashir, isn't known, but with our porous southern border, you can probably imagine the rest."

Conrad stood for a moment, putting the document back on top of the stack of papers. "So, what you are saying, boss," he said, "is we're headed to Mexico?"

Mike took the stack and held it under his arm. "That's right," he replied. "I know you guys have been anxious to get going. Here's your chance. Three of you will assist a Delta team on the ground. There will also be a Mexican police presence on site. They won't know your true identities, only that you are military investigators."

"They want to babysit us?" asked Weber.

"Well," Mike added, "let's just say they want to make sure things don't go haywire. It is their country, after all. And with the cartel involved, it's understandable. So get with the rest of the team, have some chow, and square away your gear. You leave tonight at twenty-one hundred."

FIFTEEN

Hospital Ángeles
Juárez, Mexico

Heart monitors echoed down the hospital corridor, each one beeping out of sync with the other as patients lay in hospital beds. Doctors and nurses carrying clipboards dipped in and out of rooms, making the rounds and tending to critically injured patients.

Two Mexican National Guard officers, formerly the Federal Police, stood guard over one of the rooms with guns on their hips. Inside, a man lay on the bed, oxygen mask on his face and a rash covering most of his body. An IV line administering medications was taped to his arm.

Mexican authorities, already with low manpower, wouldn't normally provide officers for such a task, but the Americans had requested it, at least until they arrived. The Mexicans knew they were guarding someone of value. Otherwise, they wouldn't be there. But that was the extent of their knowledge.

As the guards stood on each side of the door, the patient suddenly woke. Shooting up in bed with cold sweats running down his face, he whipped his head around, tossing the mask across the room and onto the floor. The man yanked the IV needle from his arm and screamed in Spanish while rocking vigorously and vibrating the metal bed.

"They had…gas masks and plastic suits," he said. "I don't know what…they were saying, but…they were Arab men. Lots of stuff, gear…explosives!"

It seemed like he was having some kind of psychotic episode, undoubtedly a symptom of acute radiation sickness. The guards rushed into the room. One of them picked up the mask and pinned the man to the mattress as he struggled against them, forcing his head off the pillow.

"No…no…you will…not…take me!" the patient shouted. "No, Navarro, I won't talk!"

"Doctor!" one of the guards yelled while they gripped the man's arms to keep him from falling from the bed. "We need a doctor!"

The patient shouted drivel, and a doctor and nurse rushed through the door to his bedside. The policemen held him down, and the nurse injected a sedative into his right arm. Moments later, the yelling began to dwindle. They released the man's arms and he fell back onto the bed. His body went limp.

"You may return to your posts, gentlemen," the doctor said to the guards. "He'll be out for some time."

"Okay, doc," one of them replied as they stepped out and stood by the door.

The doctor placed the oxygen mask back onto the patient's face and inserted the IV back into his arm. He taped it to his skin. "There we are," he said to the nurse. "Monitor him, and let me know immediately of any changes in his status."

"I will, Doctor," she replied as they both left the room.

One of the guards pulled the door closed. A cell phone began to ring. The guard recovered it from his shirt pocket and noticed a familiar number.

"Yes, Inspector García?" he answered. "This is Officer Sánchez. How can I help you, sir?"

"Sánchez?" replied the inspector. "Listen carefully. I need you to go outside and meet the American team. Escort them to the patient's room and give them unlimited access. But watch them closely. We don't want this thing to get out of hand. We especially don't want to spark a war. If they are working with a bunch of terrorists, this could go haywire quickly. Okay?"

"Yes, Inspector," replied Sánchez. "I understand."

"Good," García said. "Get it done."

The line went dead. Sánchez pocketed the phone and headed for the double doors at the end of the hallway. He hit a button on the wall, and the doors automatically swung open. The officer made his way through the waiting area to a glass door that led out to the parking lot. He exited the building and headed down the walkway. A group of Americans met him by the curb.

"Sánchez?" Brian asked him. "You Officer Sánchez? We were told to meet here."

Rob and the rest of the crew, including a small team from the ISA, stood behind Brian, guns concealed on them.

"Yes," he replied. "I am Officer Sánchez. I was told to escort you to the patient. Right this way, please."

"Behind you, Officer," said Brian.

They all followed as Sánchez led them to the intensive care unit.

"Has he talked to anyone?" asked Rob.

"The patient?" Sánchez asked. "If you want to call it that. He shouted something about bombs and terrorists, but nothing is verified yet. I suspect that's why you are here."

"You suspect right," said Brian.

They entered through the hospital wing door. The doctor noticed and stood in their way.

"Who are all these men?" he asked. "What are you all doing here? This is a hospital, for God's sake. We don't need a crowd in here."

"That's need-to-know information, doc," Rob replied. "And you don't need to know. So please stand aside, unless you want us to contact your government."

Rob flashed his military ID card, covering his name.

"Our president was authorized by yours," Rob added. "This goes way above any of us, you see?"

The doctor backed away. "No, no," he said. "Fine. Please, proceed. But do try to keep it quiet."

The team continued on.

"Thanks, Doctor," Rob said as they passed by him. "We appreciate your cooperation."

Sánchez escorted the men further down the hall.

"This his room, here?" Brian asked as they approached the other guard by the door.

"Yes," Sánchez replied, returning to his post. "You may enter, but please keep it down. I don't want to hear shit from this doctor again."

"We'll try," said Rob.

Sánchez stopped him. "One other thing," he said. "During his babbling, he mentioned the name Navarro. Perhaps that may be of use to you."

"All right," replied Brian. "We appreciate that."

He and Rob stepped into the room and closed the door while the rest of the men waited outside. They neared the bed, and they saw the patient's rash-covered body.

"Jesus," Rob said. "This guy is seriously fucked up."

Brian waved to Staff Sergeant Jack Conrad, ISA team leader, who was standing right outside the door. Two other ISA agents, Staff Sergeant James Weber and Sergeant Gary Fox, had accompanied him on the trip.

Conrad slipped through the doorway and shut it. He approached the patient. "Damn, that's awful," he said.

Retrieving his camera, Conrad began snapping photos of the man's body to send back to HQ. Out of nowhere, the patient began to twitch. It appeared he was going to have another episode. Instead, he sat up in bed. With glassy eyes, he glared at the men, spitting a little saliva onto the sheet.

"Who are you people?" he asked, spit dribbling from his chin as he looked around. "Where's my wife?"

Rob took the blanket on the bed and wrapped it around him, folding it in front.

"You're in a hospital, sir," Rob replied. "Do you remember anything, or how you got here? Anything at all? What is your name? We can start there."

Conrad knocked on the door window to get Sánchez's attention. He cracked it open.

"Has he had any other contact?" asked Conrad. "He said something about a wife."

"No, no one," replied Sánchez.

Conrad nodded, securing the door. As he returned, the patient mumbled Incoherently.

"What, mister?" Rob asked. "What did you just say?"

The man made a writing motion with his hand.

"What? You need a pen?"

Rob snatched a pen and a magazine from the table by the window and handed them to him. With the magazine on the bed between his legs, the man turned it over and started scribbling something, hardly able to keep his hands from trembling. He jotted a few words and pushed the magazine to the foot of the bed. Rob held it up to read it.

Terroristas, bombas, América.

He showed the writing to Brian and Conrad.

"If I didn't know any better, gentlemen," Rob said, "I would say they are planning to smuggle bombs across our southern border."

Before any of them could react, they heard chatter coming from just outside the door. Officer Sánchez opened up and interrupted them. He handed Rob an ID card.

"This was recovered on the ground by a hiker in Las Palomas, in the Chihuahua Desert," Sánchez said. "This place is in the middle of nowhere, but it's just a few kilometers from the US border. Maybe this is where he came from."

"Okay, thanks," replied Rob. "We'll look into it."

Rob gave Brian the ID, and he ambled toward the man.

"Mister López, Diego López," he said, glancing at the ID. "Does the name Navarro mean anything to you, sir?"

López raised his eyebrows and pushed Brian away.

"No…no!" he yelled. "Navarro…no…he…very bad man!"

"Huh," Rob said to the others in the room. "I guess we need to find out who this Navarro character is. He seems to have something to do with whatever's happened to this poor guy."

The doctor overheard the commotion and hurried into the room.

"That is quite enough," he said. "This is a hospital, and my patient needs his rest. Please, will you leave him be now?"

They slowly wandered toward the door.

"All right, doc," replied Brian. "Sure, whatever you say. We're finished for now anyway."

They left the room, and the doctor proceeded to check on his other patients.

Conrad stopped the team in the corridor. "I'll do some digging," he said. "See if we can connect this name to anything."

"Roger that," Rob replied as they all headed for the exit. "I have a feeling we need to step on it. Whatever they have planned, it's already in motion."

SIXTEEN

Las Palomas, Mexico

The desert air was dry and boiling hot, even as the sun prepared to go to bed that evening. The region didn't provide much in the way of cover, but for the random sage brush and cacti spread across the barren land.

The population of the nearby town was low, in the double digits. It also wasn't an area of Mexico frequented by law enforcement types. Criminals ran the town, and they didn't care much for outsiders, unless those outsiders had money to burn. Most killings out there were never solved. They just became buzzard food and rotted out in the desert somewhere, never to be seen again.

The Delta and ISA teams ran two old Jeep CJs, loaners from the Mexican Police, down the remote and dusty road in the heart of the Chihuahua Desert. They'd run out of pavement almost fifteen kilometers back and bounced over potholes and uneven ground while they drove northwest to the tiny border town.

"Hey," Rob said to Staff Sergeant Conrad in the backseat. "You get the weapons we asked for?"

They all had handguns on their person, but gangs there were heavily armed, even more so than the police. Pistols wouldn't do much against high-powered rifles. While operating in Mexico, the team was sure to cross the cartel at some point. They needed better firepower.

"Sure did, buddy," Conrad replied, tapping on a large weapon box behind him. "They're right here."

"Good," replied Rob.

Conrad bent forward between the seats. "By the way, I got some intel on Navarro."

"All right, good," Brian replied. "What you got?"

"Well," Conrad added. "His name is David Navarro—cartel lieutenant, extortionist, money launderer, trafficker in everything from weapons to people, and all-around bad guy. He's a career criminal."

"Of course he is," replied Rob. "The exact person you'd need to smuggle anything across the border."

"That's correct," replied Conrad.

They drove for a few more kilometers, around bends and over bumpy hills through a valley between two canyons. Suddenly, Rob hit the brakes of the lead vehicle, jolting forward as the Jeep slid across the sand. They came to an abrupt stop by a berm and another road that seemed to lead to nowhere.

"Wait here a minute, guys," Rob said to the others, shifting the vehicle into park. "Going to check something."

He, Brian, and the ISA team leader jumped out and made their way to the middle of the turnoff. Rob checked the coordinates on the GPS on his wrist.

"Yep," he said. "This is it. This is where they found Diego's ID, right here at the crossroads."

"You sure?" asked Brian.

"Yeah, I'm positive," replied Rob. "It's right here. What the hell was he doing way out here?"

"Yeah," Brian said. "More importantly, where did he come from?"

They would've brought the man with them, but there was no way the doctors would allow Diego to leave the hospital in his condition. Hardly able to communicate, he was probably better off.

"Weird," Conrad said, standing in the middle of the road.

He studied the ground for footprints. All he found were tire tracks that seemed to cross over each other.

"This much traffic," Conrad added. "Way out here? There has to be something significant down there somewhere."

Rob gazed down the road. Dusk was settling over the hilltops ahead. "I say we see what this land is hiding so well out here," he said.

"I agree," Brian replied, walking up beside him. "Let's find out what that old man was running from."

They headed back to their idling vehicles and put them into gear. Rob hit the pedal and swung the Jeep right and then an immediate hard left. Tossing sand and pebbles, the vehicle bounced as the all-terrain tires skipped over a small embankment. They advanced down the road, looking for buildings or some sign of activity.

They pressed on, and most everything looked the same as far as they could see. Suddenly, coming up on the right, they spotted a single warehouse-type building surrounded by a fence with a flatbed truck parked out front. The only exterior light was a single yellow bulb lighting the front walk above a walk-in door. Rob pulled over on the opposite side of the road, out into the weeds. Jamal, driving the second vehicle, pulled behind Rob at a forty-five-degree angle. They shut the engines off.

"Okay, then," Brian said. "You got a plan? Or are we just winging it?"

"You're the boss," replied Rob, gripping the door latch. He hopped from the Jeep. "And, yes, I have a plan of sorts."

Rob leaned in and took a water bottle from the center console. He unscrewed the cap and took a long gulp. Rob tossed the bottle back into the Jeep. All of a sudden, headlights beamed toward them from down the road.

"Shit," Rob said, climbing back into the vehicle.

Without lights, he pressed the gas and moved the Jeep away from the road and farther into the desert. Jamal followed close behind. They came to a halt and quickly shut the vehicles down and hopped out. Kneeling close to the ground, they watched three vehicles close in and turn into the gated entrance.

Rob reached into the back for a pair of night-vision binoculars. He put the lens to his eyes and zoomed in on the building.

"What do you see?" asked Brian.

Hitting the ground, they crawled up over a small hill. Rob followed movement while one of the men got out of a Land Rover to unlock the chained entry gate.

"Three vehicles," Rob replied. "All Land Rovers, possibly a dozen or so men. Maybe cartel. This guy's got an AK slung. He's getting back in the vehicle."

The Land Rovers entered the warehouse lot as one man stayed behind to secure the gate. He locked the chain and continued toward the building, slipping inside. A large door lifted, and all three vehicles pulled in. The garage-style door lowered after them.

"They're inside," Rob added. "I don't see anyone left outside."

Josh slithered his way up beside Rob, spitting a little Copenhagen to the side. "What are we going to do, boss?" he asked. "We going in?"

Rob folded up the binoculars. "What do you think?" he asked Brian.

"Well," replied Brian. "If this is where Diego came from, we need to get a look inside."

"That's what I was thinking," Rob said, signaling everyone.

They returned to the Jeep and popped the weapon box open. Inside were M4s, AKs, suppressors, other gear, and a few shotguns, all for the choosing.

"Conrad," Rob said, putting a full magazine into an M4. "You guys stay here. A small team can infiltrate much quicker. Plus, when we exit, it's going to be quick."

Rob pulled a vest over his body and inserted three more magazines into the attached pouches. He fastened the Velcro and screwed a suppressor to his barrel. "When you guys are ready, we'll get popping," he said.

"Let's do it," Brian replied, racking the charging handle on his rifle. "On you."

"All right," Rob said as the four men formed a line behind him.

They began moving and advanced over flat, sandy ground toward the edge of the roadway. Looking both ways, they followed Rob, who led them to the fence and around the left side. The others crouched, securing their perimeter, and Rob also hit his knees.

"Give me the cutters," he said. "Come on, hurry up."

Colin passed the wire cutters over Rob's head. He snagged them and began cutting a small slit in the fence just big enough to crawl through. Rob laid his weapon flat, dragged it by the barrel, and snaked his way through the opening on his back.

"Come on." He waved to the others, rising to one knee.

One by one, the men made their way through the fence. They formed up in a wedge. The back of the building was completely black, but the front light was bright enough to reach the sides of the structure.

Rob took a look around. "Let's go," he whispered.

The team moved onward in unison, eyes trained on their weapon optics and scanning for any threats. They slowly made their way to the rear of the building and pressed their bodies against the metal wall. Suddenly, they heard men from inside conversing in Spanish. Rob peeked around the corner.

"We're moving," said Rob.

They turned and followed the wall to the front. Next to them was a door facing the yard. Rob leaned out again. "We're clear," he said.

He reached out and slowly turned the doorknob. "All right," Rob added.

Barely cracking it open, he and Brian slipped inside into the shadows. They huddled in the darkness of the doorway, the only light beaming from above the large main room. Looking out from the entryway, they spotted five men in all black standing around one of the vehicles. One of them yelled, his voice carrying through the building as he barked orders at the others.

"That must be el Jefe," Rob whispered. Then he noticed the undeniable outline of an AK47. "I see weapons," he added, taking a gander around. "A few AKs and submachine guns."

The cartel men hadn't noticed them lurking in the shadows. The rest of the team slipped in behind Rob and gently closed the door.

"Okay," Rob continued. "Each of you take one, but leave the tall one alive. On my mark."

Rob aimed his M4's red dot and flicked the safety off. He squeezed the trigger, sending a three-round burst into one of them. The full metal jacket bullets ripped all the way through his torso and splashed blood across the concrete floor. The other team members dropped the rest except one man, who dove behind a large work bench, screaming in Spanish.

"Los mataré, hijos de perra. Jódanse tú y tu puta madre!"

Gripping a gold-plated 1911 pistol, he fired back at them from behind the bench. Rob heard the metallic clink against concrete as he dropped a magazine to reload.

"Cover me!" he said.

They sent a hail of bullets to suppress the enemy, and Rob darted for a stack of wooden boxes halfway across the room. When the firing stopped, Rob peeked out and spotted a leg sticking out. He aimed and squeezed off a round. A bullet to the man's shin was followed by a blood-curdling scream.

Rob immediately rushed toward him and booted his gun across the floor. "All clear," he said.

Rob pressed his right boot to the cartel boss's wounded leg and watched him flinch and tighten his face as he held back a scream. "Navarro?"

The team all gathered around him.

"David Navarro?" Rob added. "Nice to meet you. You've been a very bad boy, haven't you, David?"

"Fuck you, puto!" David yelled, spit flying from his mouth. "Who the fuck are you, cabrones?"

Rob drew his pistol and pointed it at Navarro's head. "Don't fucking move," he said.

Brian bent down and retrieved Navarro's gun. Colin and Josh stepped away to take a look around. The place was nearly empty. But they spotted a long, metal table against the back wall. Almost-empty cans of nails and ball bearings sat on top, and a bundle of wires were piled up in the corner.

"Think we got something here," said Josh.

As Rob watched Navarro, Brian wandered toward the table and took a look inside the cans. "Yep," he said. "They've been here, all right."

Brian took his camera out and snapped a few photos of the

evidence. He glanced to the ground and squatted, searching under and around the table. Brian noticed a small pile of dust, almost like ashes, inside a medium-sized barrel. The container was almost empty.

"Don't go near this shit," he said. "I'd bet money this is what Diego got into."

Brian took a piece of scrap metal from the floor and a baggie from his cargo pocket. He scooped up some of the substance, added it to the bag, and zipped it. He dropped the piece of metal to the floor.

"Secure that bastard," Brian added.

Rob and Colin rolled Navarro onto his back. He tried to grab Colin's leg, but Colin punched Navarro hard in the back of the head.

"Stay still, asshole," said Colin.

Noticing a bulge in his back pocket, Rob put a hand in and recovered the man's cell phone. They forced Navarro's arms behind his back. Rob retrieved a pair of flex cuffs from his pocket. He placed the cuffs over Navarro's hands and around his wrists, pulling them tight. Snatching him up by his arms, they forced the cartel lieutenant toward the exit.

"Package secure," Rob said over his headset radio. "Meet us out front."

The pair of vehicles, driven by Conrad and Fox, busted through the metal entry gate. They pulled up alongside the team. Rob and Brian forced Navarro into the back. Jamal and Colin climbed in on each side of him.

Jamal, with his tall, muscular presence, stared Navarro down. "Don't you fuck around and try anything stupid," he said, "or I'll toss your ass out of this Jeep and watch your head splatter on the road for the fun of it. Just give me a reason."

Rob cut a U-turn and tore out into the roadway, tires spinning as he slammed on the pedal.

SEVENTEEN

Babícora Police Station
Juárez, Mexico

T he bare cell was filthy and stale, the only fresh air flowing in through a tiny, barred window in the corner close to the ceiling.

Navarro squirmed while two officers bound his hands and feet to a long, metal bench bolted in place. They secured the large padlock and left the room. The cell door slammed, a loud clank reverberating through the corridor.

Normally, they would've interrogated him in some faraway place away from witnesses. But since the Mexican authorities welcomed them, Rob decided to do them a solid and deliver Navarro to their door, with stipulations. The police in Juárez wouldn't cooperate unless they did.

Rob was a skilled interrogator, among other things. Being a seasoned sniper gave him the will and patience to go as long as he had to. It also was a role he excelled at.

Sitting at a table in front of the station, far away from the cartel lieutenant, Rob and Brian combed through the contents of the man's phone. Rob thumbed through his contact list, and he came across an American name, Roger. When he opened the text window, though, something was off.

The message was in English but didn't seem to be written by a native English speaker. It was suspicious, kind of like getting a scam email from a foreign company pretending to be American. Rob took a swig from a water bottle on the table and screwed the cap back on.

"Look at this," he said, turning the screen so Brian could see it. "You notice anything wrong with this picture?"

Jamal glanced over Rob's shoulder. "Yeah," Jamal said. "He's no fucking American."

"I agree," Brian replied. "There's something to this, and it's really all we have to go on."

They heard the creak of the door as Conrad and his two men entered the office.

"Hey," he said, taking a seat by them. Conrad glanced around the room to ensure no Mexican policemen were around. "All right," he added. "I just got off the phone with my boss in Virginia. It seems they found a secret bank account in the Cayman Islands. Our cyber guys did their thing and found this piece of shit's prints all over it."

"Is that right?" asked Rob.

"Yep," Jack continued. "There was a recent deposit of five million into that account. They are working on tracing the origins of the money transfer as we speak, but it looks to me like the jihadis paid off the cartel to move through their territory and, probably, for help smuggling bad stuff across the border."

Rob rose from the table. "Well," he said. "We certainly aren't going to sit around and wait for that information."

Brian got up from his seat and followed Rob through the hall toward the back of the building.

"Guardia!" Rob yelled for any guard close by.

One of the Mexican officers took a metal ring full of keys from his belt loop and unlocked the cell door for them. He left the key in the lock and stepped back. Brian lingered by the door as Rob strolled toward the middle of the room. He flashed Navarro a grin.

"Señor Navarro," he said. "David Navarro. Five million US dollars is a lot of money for anyone, isn't it? Who gave it to you? Who paid you off?"

Navarro sat straight up with his back against the wall. He stared ahead, flexing his jaw muscles. His black tattoo sleeves showed down both arms he folded in his lap. A little splatter of blood colored the bottom of his white T-shirt.

"Don't know what you're talking about, cabrón."

Rob pulled up a chair and sat a few feet from Navarro. "You know," he replied, "we could've easily killed you, like we did your friends. But, no, we wanted you alive." Rob tipped his hat back and wiped the sweat from his brow.

"What?" Navarro asked. "Am I supposed to be grateful to you pieces of shit? Fuck you, gringo. When the boss finds out where I am, he'll send a squad after you bitches."

Rob stood a moment and slammed the chair legs onto the floor. "Nobody knows where you are, dumbass," replied Rob. "We killed your guards. Nobody else was around to witness it. You're on your own now, cowboy."

Rob glared Navarro down, then glanced at the guard outside. "Enough fucking around," he said.

He pointed to the baton the officer carried on his duty belt. The policeman removed the stick and handed it over to Brian. He wandered into the room, and Rob signaled the guard to leave. He grabbed the baton from Brian and tapped it against his free hand.

"See this stick?" Rob asked Navarro. "Steel-reinforced wood, very powerful. It can easily break bone with minimal effort. So I'm going to ask you again, hombre. Who paid you? What are their plans?"

Navarro continued staring forward, not uttering a word.

"Fine then," Rob added. "Your choice."

He raised the baton to eye level and swung it hard against Navarro's kneecap. The sudden, stinging pain penetrated deep and radiated down Navarro's leg while a piercing scream traveled through the building. Navarro's body shook violently as he gripped the knee with his bound hands.

"Hijo de puta!" Navarro screamed. "Fucking gringo, I will kill your bitch ass!"

Rob glanced back at Brian, still standing by the door. "You hear that?" Rob asked with a chuckle. "He says he's going to kill me." Rob twirled the stick, flashing a smile. "That's funny," he added.

Rob swung again, this time striking the cartel lieutenant square on the shin. The leg bone made a fierce cracking sound, and Navarro howled at the top of his lungs. Rob watched the man, whose shirt was drenched in sweat. Blood trickled down the bottom half of David's right leg. He heaved in air with his eyes closed.

"That hurts, doesn't it?" Rob asked, sitting back down and scooting closer.

Navarro breathed hard as his bodied reacted to the sharp sting in his leg.

"David," Rob said. Navarro's body trembled. "Look at me, David."

Navarro's eyes barely cracked, his face in anguish while he looked back at Rob with watery eyes.

"I don't care about the money," Rob added. "I don't care if they let you go after we leave. All I care about is there is somebody on their way to my country with bad intentions. If you tell me where they're going, we can stop it, and your pain will end."

Rob gripped Navarro by the jaw. "You make a living hurting people," continued Rob. "Now, you're partnering with terrorists. For God's sake, do something good with your pathetic life for once."

Navarro cringed from the pain coursing through him. "Come closer," he whispered to Rob. "I need to tell your gringo ass something."

Rob moved in a tad closer. Navarro sneered at him. "It's already done, cabrón," he said. "You can't do nothing to stop it. All you can do is just sit back and watch."

Rob heard footsteps coming toward them from out in the corridor. Jack, his men by him, approached Brian, clutching a locked hard case. He whispered something in his ear. Brian waved for Rob to join them.

"Come here, Walker," said Brian. "You need to hear this." He shut the metal door.

"What's up?" Rob asked.

The men got close so they could hear each other.

"Listen," replied Jack. "HQ obtained satellite images of the depot you guys raided. When we found out the area we'd be searching, I had them monitor hundreds of square miles around. We didn't realize how significant this place was until later."

Jack turned to head back through the hallway. "Come here," he said.

They followed while Jack marched past the office area and shoved open the main entrance. He wandered toward the Jeep. Jack yanked the door and climbed into the seat. He put the case on his lap and activated the biometric lock with a touch of his hand, then opened it up, revealing a laptop inside.

Jack logged into his secure email and downloaded an attachment. He opened it and turned the computer so they could see it.

"All right," Rob said. "What we looking at?"

Jack pointed to the image. "This is the warehouse where you captured Navarro."

Brian looked closer. "Yep," he said. "I recognize the place. What about it?"

Jack scrolled to another photo. "This is the warehouse six hours before." Jack zoomed in on the image. A tall figure wearing a kufiyah head covering stood at the front, seemingly directing the six individuals assembled around him.

Rob studied the image. "That looks like Amir Hassan, al-Qaeda lieutenant," he said.

"Yeah," Jack replied. "And what are the odds of an Arab man being here by chance?"

"I would say zero," Colin replied from behind the group.

Rob gave Brian an unsettling look. He swiped his phone and snapped a picture of the satellite image. He marched straight for Navarro's cell. "Guardia," he said.

The guard quickly unlocked the cell door. Rob stormed inside and approached Navarro. With his phone, he zoomed in on the man onscreen. He flipped the phone around and put it in Navarro's face. "Who is that?" he asked.

Navarro kept his mouth shut. With an open hand, Rob swung at his cheek. Navarro's head flew back. Blood formed on his lip.

Rob showed him the image again. "Who is this?" he asked.

Navarro squinted up at Rob, a mix of pain and hatred in his eyes. "Puto," Navarro replied, spitting on Rob's boots.

Rob rushed Navarro, gripping his windpipe and squeezing. He shouted so loud, he almost lost his voice. "It's Amir Hassan, ain't it? The man who paid you? Tell me where he is, where he's going, and I might not kill you!"

A couple officers heard Rob shouting and hurried to the

room. They pulled him back by the arms to keep him from killing Navarro. Rob elbowed them both away.

"I'm fine," he said. "Get the hell off me."

The cartel lieutenant hadn't paid much attention to the image. He broke out laughing in Rob's face.

"Maybe I do know him," he said. "Maybe I don't. Long as I get paid, I don't give a fuck who he is. But I do know this. They have big plans. I guess you will just have to wait and see, huh, pendejo?"

Rob tightened a fist and sent a haymaker into Navarro's head, whipping his skull back into the wall. Not knowing what to do, the Mexican policemen just stood there.

"We got your ass, though, didn't we?" Rob replied. "Have a nice life in prison, you sick prick."

Rob headed through the doorway and slammed it. He made his way back to his men to get the hell out of there. Navarro wasn't going to say more. Cartel types weren't the talking kind. They would report his location to the FBI, but the team had no hand in it. They weren't law enforcement. Their jobs were to act on intel to take down immediate threats.

The old Jeeps sped out of the lot, heading across town to the US–Mexico border.

EIGHTEEN

Near The Border
Mexico

Rob and the team were almost to the Juárez border checkpoint and the Bridge of the Americas, trying to figure their next move. Earlier, the ISA agents had caught a flight to nearby Fort Huachuca, Arizona, to meet with other intel agents. They needed to come up with more actionable intel, which they hadn't found down in Mexico.

Behind the wheel, Rob drove the Jeep down a two-lane road on the northwest side of the city with Jamal and Josh. Brian and Colin followed close behind in the other vehicle.

Juárez was a city prone to violence. Cartel activity there was common. Murders had risen more than a hundred percent in the previous year. More recently, shots had even been fired across the border into El Paso. The urban blight was a direct result of a city controlled and terrorized by armed thugs and gang-on-gang conflict.

They could see the checkpoint a little over half a kilometer straight ahead. Rob slowed gradually and came to a screeching halt in a long line of cars headed north. The incoming breeze had provided some relief from the blazing heat while the vehicles were in motion. But with no tops on the old Jeeps, and no working AC, they had little protection from the baking desert sun while they idled. The line inched forward painfully slow, sweat soaking through their clothes.

"I don't know what's hotter, man," Rob said, tipping a bottle of water. "Iraq or freaking Mexico."

"They're both balls hot if you ask me," Josh replied as he leaned forward from the back seat.

Rob passed the bottle back to him. "You can say that again," replied Rob

Suddenly, they heard a squelch through the radio speakers. It was their team leader in the other vehicle. Having received a call on his SAT phone, he'd put it up to the radio mic so everyone could hear it.

"Golf-Three-Six," the caller said. "This is Alpha-Six-Actual."

"Alpha-Six-Actual," Brian replied. "It's Golf-Three-Six, yeah, we read you."

A few seconds later, they heard noise in the background as the commander continued.

"Golf-Three-Six, there's been a change of plans."

Brian glanced over at Colin.

"Roger, Alpha-Six-Actual. Go ahead."

"Golf-Three-Six, we've received intel there's been an attack at the border checkpoint in Puerto Palomas. Four Border Patrol agents reported killed and others wounded, shot by a submachine gun. The driver, of Middle Eastern origin they think, fled into the New Mexico desert with unknown cargo. They weren't able to inspect the vehicle, but he obviously wanted to protect it. There's a strong possibility of a connection."

Rob shook his head as he listened.

"What would you have us do, Golf-Three-Six?" asked Brian.

"I need you to head to the coordinates I'm about to send you. From there, you'll board a bird into the States to look for the truck. I'll contact you if anything changes. Golf-Three-Six, out."

With no room to back out, the cars at the border crossing were packed tight, almost bumper to bumper.

"Damn it," said Brian. He pressed the mic on his radio. "Walker, go give us some space, would you? We're jammed in here."

Rob got out of the old Jeep and made his way to the vehicle immediately behind Brian's.

"Hey, sir," Rob said. "Can you back up a little, please? We need to get out. It's kind of urgent."

Rob got a closer look, and he noticed the man was an old vet, gray hair and wearing a Vietnam Veteran hat.

"Sure, young man," he said with a nod as he backed his old Ford pickup a few feet.

Rob waved to him, dashing for the Jeep while traffic started to pick up again. He quickly climbed in. Rob put the stick into reverse and did a three-point turn, with Brian cutting a U-turn behind him. They sped in the other direction and made an abrupt right turn, heading west toward open desert.

Two hours of driving through a barren wasteland led them to a single turn north toward the pickup spot. The Jeeps came barreling over a small hill, and Rob tapped the brake near a dirt road to a distant mountain. He veered right and checked the coordinates on his GPS. The landing zone had been chosen for its isolated location.

"LZ, straight ahead," he said.

They continued for another few thousand feet until they arrived at a large clearing in the desert landscape. Rob swerved off the road and parked side by side with Brian, the helicopter arriving overhead. The bird drifted to the side and hovered over the landing area. Operated by a couple pilots from Delta's Echo Squadron, the aircraft was a Blackhawk, black with no identifying markings of any kind. It descended, and the team hopped from the vehicles and snatched up their gear and equipment. Heads low and holding on to their caps, they made their way to the bird. A crewman slid the door open.

They tossed packs and gear onto the floor between two rows of seating and climbed up. Strapping in, they put their headsets on.

"We're good to go," Rob said to the pilot. "Let's get out of here."

The aircraft rose again and made a quick turn north toward the border. It zoomed over the desert landscape at a high rate of speed. Flying at an altitude of only five hundred feet, they spotted the border checkpoint ahead. Numerous local police and Border Patrol vehicles surrounded the scene with lights flashing. Guards on the Mexican side blocked traffic in cooperation with American law enforcement.

The pilot brought the aircraft over a flat, rocky area between two roads and went in for a landing. The men left everything but the handguns they had on them and hopped down onto the hard ground. They hustled across the street toward the Border Patrol office. The agent in charge met the team outside by the building.

"Hey," he said in a Texas drawl as they approached. "I'm Agent Rodríguez, Luis Rodríguez."

Rodríguez was a Mexican American. Born in Mexico City, he'd been raised in Laredo, Texas, since he was four. He sported the brown Border Patrol uniform with matching Western-style cowboy hat.

"Y'all the Army team?"

Brian reached a hand out. "That's us," he replied. "Care to walk us through what happened?"

"Right this way, gentlemen," replied Rodríguez. The agent escorted them toward the pavement. "Don't know why y'all are here and not the FBI," Rodríguez added, "but that came from above my pay grade."

"Oh, I'm sure the FBI will be here soon," said Rob. "We just happened to beat 'em here."

Yellow crime scene tape circled the perimeter next to Border Patrol cruisers with lights whirling.

"This is where it all went down," Rodríguez said, tearing up a little. "We lost a few good agents right here, and a couple civilians. A team of agents and state police are searching for the suspect right now. The driver managed to evade through the desert. There are no roads where he was going. Bastard must have a death wish."

Rob knew Rodríguez wouldn't like where the conversation was about to go. "Agent Rodríguez," he said, "I need you to tell them all to stand down."

The agent seemed perplexed. "Come again?" he replied.

Brian intervened. "Do it," he said. "Don't put this shit out over the radio, either. The last thing we need is a damn panic."

Rodríguez was visibly frustrated. His face tensed. "You know I can't do that," he insisted. "Come on, they are doing their damn jobs. Who are y'all to show up here and tell us how to operate?"

Brian recovered his phone from his pocket and pulled up a number. He held it out for Rodríguez to see.

"We're losing time here, and we don't have time to explain. You want to call the Pentagon and tell them why you won't cooperate?"

"Cooperate?" the agent asked. "You want the suspect to get away?"

"Yes, he is getting away while you argue," replied Rob. "You have no idea what you're dealing with. If you don't want more to die, you'll comply. Otherwise, we'll dial the number and let you explain to Washington brass why you refuse."

Agent Rodríguez eyed them curiously. "Who the hell are y'all, really?" he asked.

"That's not important," Rob replied. "Now, tell 'em to stand down, please. We won't ask again."

Rob moved in closer to Rodríguez. "Trust me," he added. "I know what you're thinking. He will get his due for what he did here."

The agent reluctantly grabbed his radio. He took a long breath. "This is Rodríguez," he said into the microphone while staring at Rob. "Stand down the ten-thirty-one. I repeat, all personnel, stand down the ten-thirty-one. All units return to your posts immediately."

"Ten-nine?" an agent replied over the radio. "You sure about that?"

"Yes," Rodríguez replied. "Just do it!"

"All right," the voice replied. "Ten-four."

Agent Rodríguez clipped the radio back to his shirt. "There," he said to Rob and the team. "You happy now? Anything else I can do for you?"

"Other than staying out of our way?" Brian asked. "Nope. But thanks for the cooperation."

The team hurried back to the aircraft, rotor blades still whirring up dust across the road. The suspect had a huge head start. With luck, they could make up some time and pinpoint his location before he did any more damage.

NINETEEN

In the air

They monitored the police frequency through the radio inside the helicopter while the bird sailed over the desert roadway a few miles south of the New Mexico village of Sunshine. Police chatter filled the airwaves, some giving directions they'd gotten from random passersby who'd claimed to have caught a glimpse of the suspect vehicle. The directions were spotty at best, though.

"Damn it," Rob said into his earpiece microphone. "Looks like it's already reached local police."

To keep a low profile, they favored them when operating domestically.

"Either that," Brian replied, "or we really pissed someone off down there."

With that thousand-yard stare of his, Rob gazed out into the expansive desert. "Could be some two-bit sheriff's deputy looking for his moment of glory," he added. "And to think, not long ago I was sitting on a beach, sipping rum through a straw."

"Yeah?" Jamal asked, patting Rob on the back. "We can all have some rum when we get back. It's on me."

"I'll drink to that," Colin said with a grin.

The terrain below was mostly flat all around but for the distant canyon, miles from the village. Traffic was scarce, so it should've made spotting a fleeing vehicle not too difficult, especially with cacti and the occasional sage brush being the only cover. The pilot gunned it across the sky.

They passed over the tiny village in a blur, heading toward a set of peaks that towered over both sides of the paved road. The bird climbed higher, clearing the tops of the plateaus and swaying right to the other side. When the village was almost out of sight, a radio call came through.

"Golf-Three-Six," the voice said. "This is India-One-Sierra. Golf-Three-Six, it's India-One-Sierra, do you copy, over?"

It was Agent Conrad with the ISA.

"Yes, India-One-Sierra. Golf-Three-Six reads you Lima-Charlie, over."

"Roger, Golf-Three-Six," Jack added. "We've been monitoring movement with our handy eye in the sky. We think we spotted the target vehicle, a black Nissan pickup with a white camper shell on the back. It pulled into a parking garage in Silver City."

Brian averted his gaze toward Rob.

"You think it's rigged to blow?" he asked Conrad.

There was a few seconds' delay.

"We don't know," replied Conrad. "It's a strong possibility. Just move in, proceed with caution, you know the drill. If anything changes, we'll let you know. I'll guide you to the target once you're close."

"Roger that," replied Brian.

Rob glanced up at his friend and team leader.

"What the hell are we about to walk into?" he asked, certain he didn't want to know the answer. "He could very well be prepared to level that garage and anything in it."

In a combat zone, they would've simply destroyed the truck with a Hellfire missile. Domestically, that was out of the question in a populated area.

"You're right," Brian replied. "That's why we're going to set you up on the long gun. You and Colin will be watching from afar. Whoever he is, we don't want him to know we're there until we can neutralize him. Pray to God we get there in time."

Rob had his Remington sniper rifle folded and stowed in his drag bag, along with his M4. He recovered it from the floor and began setting it up. The pilot had been monitoring the radio and prepared for insertion.

"We're going to drop you guys off on the outskirts of the city, near the hills," he shouted back.

The bird passed over a few desert mounds, and the small city emerged as the land became flat again. A strand of rolling hills bordered the west side of town where arid desert turned into a patch of thick greenery. Swooping low, the pilot aimed for the base of those hills. They descended over treetops and came in for a landing at the base of the tallest bluff.

Every man on the team grabbed his respective gear and hopped down from the helicopter. With packs on, they moved out away from the bird and waved to the pilot as he took off again. Since they weren't in a combat zone, each took only the necessary gear, mostly handguns hidden under clothing. Rob and his spotter were the only ones with long rifles. They got set to climb the hillside and find a good hide site.

"You two go," Brian said to the pair. "The rest of us will head into town within sight of the parking garage. We'll blend until we get ready to move."

"Got it, boss," replied Rob.

The rest of the team departed, and Rob and Colin began climbing the steep incline. Moving at a steady pace, the soles of their hiking boots dug into the soft sand and gravel. It was an ideal spot, away from traffic and people. The nearest road was close to half a mile away.

Reaching the overlook, they began to set up. Rob had his rifle, complete with suppressor and Vortex scope, sitting on its bipod, while Colin situated the spotting scope. Caressing the pistol grip in his right hand, Rob snugged the butt of the high-powered 300 Winchester Magnum rifle firmly into the crevice of his shoulder.

"What you got?" he asked.

Colin turned the spotting scope to the right. "They're moving down the road, separating to the right and left."

Rob peered through his scope, pivoting to the right and zooming the lens. "Got 'em," he replied. He moved the glass up a tad. "There's the garage beyond those houses down there. First floor is partly hidden by bushes, but the second and third are clear."

Colin got line of site to the parking garage. The particular spotting scope he used had a built-in range finder. "Five hundred and twenty-five meters to the vehicle entrance," he said.

Rob did some quick calculations in his head and adjusted the elevation knob on his scope.

"Wind, two miles per hour from our twelve o' clock, no value."

There was no need to adjust the windage knob.

"Got it," replied Rob.

Colin surveyed the interior of the garage that he could see. Beginning at the ground floor, he scanned left to right on one floor, right to left on the other. The parking structure was mostly full of cars belonging to employees of nearby banks, shops, and the town's only hospital. It was packed, and it was getting dangerously close to rush hour.

"I see people coming from the hospital," said Colin.

He scanned up to the third floor and crossed the floor through the lens. There, its tail end facing them, was a black Nissan Titan pickup.

"Target, black Nissan with camper shell three floors up and six spaces to the right," Colin added.

Rob shifted the glass up and to the right. He read the wordage on the tailgate. "Roger, got 'em," he replied.

With a full magazine, Rob pulled the rifle bolt back and rode it forward, inserting a round into the chamber. "Golf-Three-Six," he said into his earpiece. "Eyes on target vehicle, but no view of the target yet. Standing by, over."

They could hear breathing through the radio.

"Copy, Golf-Three-Five. We'll be on location in five mikes."

Rob and his spotter observed the men all splitting up and heading toward different buildings just down the street from the parking garage. Brian had taken a seat at a coffee shop's outdoor seating area and snatched a newspaper from one of the benches. Rob watched the scene through the glass, then momentarily glanced down at his watch.

1630.

"Damn it," he said, knowing in the next several minutes, people would be leaving workplaces and heading to their cars to go home.

Rob viewed the team in position, and Colin caught a glimpse of something. "Wait a minute," he said, zooming in on his spotting scope. "I see movement."

It was a young-looking man, wearing a black hoodie and jeans. From what Colin could tell, it appeared he had a dark complexion. He also seemed nervous, wandering down the aisle. Rob trained the scope on him.

"I got him," he replied.

The boy looked back. Rob was just able to see his face before the boy climbed into the vehicle.

"Golf-Three-Six," Rob said into his mic. "We have eyes on a young male fitting the description. He just entered the black truck. Please advise, over."

"Roger, Golf-Three-Five," replied Brian. "Is the target confirmed?"

"Just saw his face," Rob replied. "Confirmed."

"Copy," Brian said. "You have a shot on him?"

"Hold one," replied Rob.

They needed to take him out, but the last thing they wanted, aside from the vehicle exploding, was to get into a shootout in broad daylight. Rob's suppressed rifle would minimize that, if he could get a clear shot. He peered through the truck's back glass. Rob noticed the outline of the target's head disappearing below the seat.

"Negative," Rob replied. "No shot. He just dipped down in the seat. I lost visual, over."

"Damn it," Brian replied. "Copy that, Golf-Three-Five."

Rob could hear Brian's frustration through the speaker.

"You think he knows we're here?" Colin asked Rob.

Rob shook his head. "I don't see how he could," he replied.

"If he's planning to blow himself up," Colin asked, "why would he give a shit if we saw him?"

"Good point," replied Rob. "But he looks like a young kid, probably scared shitless."

Rob set the butt of his rifle down for a moment. He reached into his breast pocket and removed a can of Copenhagen. He packed it in his right hand and opened it up. Rob picked a little and stuck it into the corner of his lip, slipping the can back into his dark green T-shirt. He spit to the side and recovered his rifle butt from the ground. Rob glanced through the glass again.

"Golf-Three-Six, he's not moving," he said. "And we're getting close to having a crowd to contend with."

"Roger," Brian replied. "Watch our backs, Three-Five. We're moving closer."

"Will do," said Rob.

He and Colin observed the team exiting their locations and moving out separately. They headed out down sidewalks on both sides of the road toward the entryway to the parking structure. The team casually entered the building and made their way up the ramp and toward the upper floors.

"Hold," Rob said as they reached the second story. "He's one floor up and almost directly above you, right around the corner on the far side of the lot."

Rob took another glimpse at the pickup. He still couldn't see the driver.

"All right," he added. "As you turn that corner, the target vehicle is on the opposite side to the right, six spaces down. Recommend moving behind that row of cars to avoid detection, and stay low."

The team knew they had to catch the driver by surprise so he wouldn't have time to detonate whatever explosives he was carrying. They followed Rob's advice as they crept closer to the vehicle, and took a knee on the concrete behind two cars.

"How we looking, Golf-Three-Five?" Brian asked, drawing his Sig Sauer pistol and holding it close to his body. "We clear of civilians?"

Rob took a quick glance around. "Affirmative," he replied. "The floor is clear, for now."

"Good," Brian replied as he peeked around the tail end of the car toward the truck. He got ready to move. "You guys hold here," Brian said to Jamal and Josh. "Three men are easier to spot."

Brian stayed low and turned the corner. "Moving in, Golf-Three-Five," he said.

"Roger, I see you," replied Rob.

But before Brian could make it far, he received another call.

"Golf-Three-Six," the voice said. "It's Alpha-Six-Actual. I was just notified that the Border Patrol contacted local authorities. You may have company soon. When they arrive, show them your credentials and give 'em the number. We'll handle it."

Rob and his spotter watched the exchange from their hide on the hill and listened in. Suddenly, Rob caught a flash in his peripheral vision. He moved the scope down a bit and noticed a series of police cars racing toward the parking structure.

"Three-Six," Rob said over the radio. "Be advised, you've got four police cars headed your way. About half a mile out and closing fast, over."

"What?" Brian asked. "Idiots, I told them to stay out of it."

"I guess he couldn't handle a higher authority," replied Rob.

"Come on," Brian said. "Time for a meet and greet."

They heard footsteps pounding the concrete and getting closer while they made their way around the corner and down the ramp. They'd almost made it to the first floor, and a group of six officers hustled toward them with their guns drawn.

"Whoa, whoa, whoa!" Jamal said. "Hey, what're you doing, damn it? Jesus, put those guns down, would you?"

"Who are you?" asked Officer Mills, the officer in charge. "We got a report of a bomb in this building. Where's the vehicle?"

"Yeah, it's a suicide bomber," Brian replied. "I wouldn't advise going up there. We're here under orders from the Pentagon. We have this under control, Officers."

The officer pinched the radio mic clipped to his shirt.

"Two-six-five to dispatch," he said into the radio. "Show us ten-eighty-four at that ten-thirty-three. Assessing the situation, will report back soon."

Brian displayed a card to Mills, with mostly false information but with a phone number directly to the colonel. "Just call this number," he added. "They'll explain."

Glancing at the card, the officer gave them a funny look.

"Just who are you guys?" he asked. "Federal agents? FBI, CIA?"

"Something like that, Officer Mills," Brian said, glancing at the officer's name tag. "We're investigators, and there's a very dangerous person up there getting ready to do some awful shit. But there's a much bigger picture at play here, bigger than you can imagine. If you don't want another nine-eleven in your town, then let us go."

"Look," Officer Mills replied. "I served four years as a Marine after nine-eleven. A lot of us did. So I understand. If this checks out, you'll have no interference from us. Right now, until the device is verified, we're all just going to back away. Sound fair?"

"Yes," replied Brian. "We have a shooter prepared to take the target out when he gets a clear shot."

Seeing the group from his position, Rob radioed in.

"Three-Six, we've got another group of officers entering from the other side. They're headed right for the target."

Suddenly, people started flooding into the parking garage from the elevator.

"Shit," said Brian, waving people out. "Get out of here, now! Bomb in the building! Everybody out!"

The top of the target's head popped up, barely visible over the seat. Rob took aim quickly, but not before the team heard a scream down below.

"Allahu Akbar!"

Just as Rob squeezed the trigger, a giant eruption rocked the ground as the bomb detonated, sending several cars and gray smoke skyward. They watched Brian, the team, and the officers with them diving over the concrete wall and onto the pavement outside. Punching a gaping hole into the floor above the blast, the surface gave way, dumping twisted metal and chunks of blackened concrete and bricks below.

"Fuck!" Rob said, pounding the rocks around him. "God damn it!"

The explosion had obliterated the pickup and buried everything around it, including the officers upstairs, in a thick pile of debris. The target vehicle was burned to a crisp. Shrapnel, including pieces of nearby cars, had shot across the lot and landed all over the grass and drive outside.

People outside screamed and shouted as they ran away. Others near the building had been tossed to the ground like rag dolls. Drivers passing by slammed on brakes, causing collisions in the middle of the adjacent roadway. The explosion had created an enormous dust cloud that was rising high and growing.

"Shit," Rob said, watching the carnage. "God damn it, what the hell were they thinking?"

"I don't know," Colin replied, searching for movement through the glass.

Rob's forehead hit the dirt. He rocked his head up and down against the ground.

"It's my fault," he said. "It's all my damn fault. If I'd been quicker on the trigger..."

Colin stopped him. "No," he replied. "Don't do that to yourself. You didn't have enough time, maybe a second or two, at a target you could barely see. It wasn't your fault."

Below, covered in ash and a pile of debris, Brian crawled

away and painfully pushed up onto his knees. His legs wouldn't stop shaking. He attempted to stand up straight, causing him to fall back down. He caught the ground with his hands. Brian touched his ear and noticed his missing earpiece. He began searching the ground for it. He was surprised to find it intact, albeit much dirtier, under a pile of junk.

"Alpha-Six-Actual," he said into the radio, spitting up dust. "It's Three-Six. We've had a vehicle-borne IED detonation at this location. Number of casualties unknown, possibly dozens."

Brian began coughing and wheezing forcibly. The rest of the guys, under a blanket of ash, struggled to get up. Josh had a ringing in his ear that pierced right through his head.

"Shit," Brian added, wobbling from the blast site. "I can't believe we just walked away from that."

"You mean barely?" Jamal asked, stumbling over his own feet.

"There are at least four police officers KIA," Brian continued over the net. "Send EOD and someone to deal with local law enforcement and media, over."

EOD stood for explosive ordnance disposal. The team had no time to deal with that. They still needed to maintain their cover, so they'd be gone by the time news reporters showed up at the scene.

"Damn, Three-Six," said Rob. "Holy shit, you guys made it out."

"Yeah, we made it out, all right," Brian replied, hacking from smoke inhalation. "I think everybody's still got all their limbs."

He wrapped his tan kufiyah around his face.

"Hold tight, Three-Six," Rob continued. "We're coming to you."

Rob and Colin began securing their gear to assist the rest of the team and the officers with them. There was no need to contact police, fire, or EMS. They could hear more coming from down the street. The police chief was about to get a serious earful from Washington brass.

TWENTY

Most of the team was being tended to by doctors while Rob and his spotter waited, antsy, in the hospital's emergency room lobby. They were given oxygen and examined for concussions due to their proximity to the explosion.

Rob heard Brian from down the hall, pleading with the doctor to let him check out. But orders were orders. The colonel wanted them checked out as a precaution. Everyone else thought they were wasting time they could be in the field, chasing bad guys.

The closest post to the site of the explosion, Holloman Air Force Base, was a hop, skip, and jump east of White Sands Missile Range. It was out in the desert, a few dozen miles north of El Paso, Texas.

Flipping through a *Stars and Stripes* newspaper he'd found lying on a table, Rob glanced periodically at the TV on the white wall straight ahead. He finished reading a short article, folded the paper, and placed it neatly on the side table by the sofa. Rob's eyes bounced from the television to the newspaper and back, and an image of the bombed-out building appeared onscreen. He couldn't hear the reporter's voice but could read the captions shown down below.

A giant blast was set off in a parking garage today in downtown Silver City. Many that were a distance away, or driving on the highway, felt a powerful tremor as the building went up in flames. The cause of the explosion and the number of dead haven't immediately been determined, while emergency crews work through the rubble.

The police chief, Jason Campbell, hasn't said whether this was a gas explosion or an incident of foul play. As usual, we'll keep you informed of details when we learn them.

I'm Bob Castle for KDAT, channel seven action news.

Rob glanced back at Colin with a shake of his head. "Such bullshit," he said. "Be right back."

He pivoted around and made his way to Brian, who was sitting up on the bed with a hand over his head. Rob slid the curtain aside and squatted by Brian on the mattress.

"How you feeling, brother?" he asked.

Brian looked up with squinting eyes. "How do I feel?" He chuckled, yanking the oxygen tube from his nostrils. "I feel like we're wasting time in this place. There's nothing wrong with me. Fuck, I hate hospitals, man."

"You're just lucky you guys weren't closer," Rob added. "The floor above would've come down on top of you."

"Yeah, no shit, huh?" replied Brian. "We didn't get the worst of it, did we? Damn, what the hell were they doing up there?"

"I have no idea," Rob replied. "I don't think we'll ever know for sure."

Rob turned to leave. "Just chill out for a bit," he said. "I'm going to go check on the other guys. Be back in a bit."

Rob fist-bumped Brian. He drew the curtain open and caught a familiar voice talking to one of the nurses. Rob peeked around the corner and spotted their commander marching toward them from down the corridor.

"The colonel's here," he said to Brian.

Colonel Billings waved to Colin as he walked past and went straight for Brian's bed.

"Colonel," Rob said as Billings moved the curtain aside.

The colonel stepped around Rob and took a seat close to Brian, folding his arms in his lap. "How we doing, Sergeant Major?" he asked.

"Well, Colonel," replied Brian, "I'd be just great if I could get the hell out of here."

"Soon," said the colonel. "Soon enough, all right?"

Colonel Billings leaned forward in the chair. "The good news," he said without delay. The colonel was one for getting to the point. "The blast contained no radiation," he added. "The bad news, it killed twenty civilians in addition to the four police officers."

"Ah, shit," replied Rob.

"ISA thinks it was just a dry run," Colonel Billings continued. "A diversion to get the others through holes in our southern border, which is probably why he shot those border agents. Homeland Security isn't doing much. Hell, they're completely understaffed and can't even handle the influx of migrants we already have. It's a shit show, is what it is. But the terrorists knew the response would be swift. It always is when law enforcement officers are killed. We focus on an area, meanwhile, the assholes operate somewhere else under the radar. We know there are other bombs, we just have no idea where they are. It's a safe bet they plan on killing many more people, though. We'd better find something soon."

Brian didn't say much, but regret was written all over his face.

"So, you guys all set to go?" Billings asked.

"Hell yeah, Colonel," Brian replied. "Just show me where to sign."

"Good," the colonel said, retrieving his phone from his shirt pocket. "Because there's something else." He held up a photo for both men to see. "This," he added, "is a SIM card the intel team retrieved from the site. We pushed the police back and made sure they had room. The police chief didn't like it much, but we're the United States government. He'll get over it."

"This is from the site?" Rob asked, snatching the phone and zooming in on the image.

"Well," the colonel replied, "it was found under the seat of his burned-out pickup. It's amazing this little piece of metal survived at all. The rest of the phone is nowhere to be found. The police don't know about it, and they won't. We don't need any loose cannons causing a stir."

Rob handed the phone back to the colonel. "We need to get this looked at ASAP," he said.

"They're on it now," the colonel said. "The ISA is analyzing it as we speak."

Sooner than expected, Agent Conrad and his colleague, Agent Weber, appeared behind them.

"Already did," replied Conrad.

The colonel was startled, hopping to the side. "Damn," he said. "Don't sneak up on people like that. I almost knife-handed your ass."

"Sorry, Colonel," replied Conrad, unable to keep from grinning. "Our team just finished up the analysis."

There was a moment of silence while the agent gazed them over.

"Well?" Rob asked. "What is it?"

"It's not good," Conrad said. "Is there somewhere we can talk in private?"

"Yeah," Rob replied. "Come on, follow me."

The two ISA agents and the colonel followed Rob down the hall toward an area outside with picnic tables and benches. They passed through the exit and made their way across to one of the tables. Rob and Colonel Billings took a seat, the others settling opposite them.

"All right," Conrad said. "We had to decode the card's encryption. We were lucky to get anything at all because of the fire damage. But we recovered some texts in Arabic between the holder of the phone and someone we believe to be al-Bashir himself. They probably figured the phone would be unrecoverable in the explosion anyway."

"How do you know it was al-Bashir?" Rob asked. "I'm sure they didn't use names."

"Because he was giving orders," Conrad replied without skipping a beat. "He's their leader. Every order they follow comes from him. It's the same old story. They believe they got seventy-two virgins waiting for them to become martyrs."

"Believe me," Rob replied. "We know the type all too well, all of us."

"Is that all?" Colonel Billings asked. "That doesn't tell us where he is."

"We wish it was, sir," Weber replied, taking a seat across from Rob. "We think he's still in Lebanon. He's smart. He wouldn't risk showing up here. Al-Bashir's got people for that.

He's well prepared to sacrifice young Muslim boys, giving them orders from halfway across the world. And…"

Rob waited for Weber to continue.

"And what?" he asked.

Conrad rested his hands on his lap, sitting sideways on the bench.

"The evidence we've gathered so far points to Mardi Gras," he replied. "The text highlighted crowded American holiday events as prime targets. Mardi Gras just happens to be coming up soon. It's huge in New Orleans, as we all know. People from around the country and the world attend that event. We would be remiss to overlook it."

"Yeah," Rob replied. "I've been there a couple times. That place is a madhouse. All those people… Damn."

He glanced down at the date on his Garmin watch.

"Shit," Rob added. "Mardi Gras starts in two days and lasts for two weeks. That's a large window in a crowded city. How the hell are we supposed to know when and where he'll be?"

"We don't," said Conrad. "We'll have to find him, somehow. I don't even want to think about what'll happen if we don't."

Rob raised his brow. "And here I thought this was going to be hard," he sarcastically replied.

But inside, Rob was nervous, unsure if anything would go right this time.

Colonel Billings chimed in. "So, New Orleans it is," he said. "You two are going with them. We need an intel team on the ground. I'll clear it with your boss."

"Roger that, Colonel," Conrad replied.

He gave Rob a questioning look as he and Weber left the area.

"As much as I don't want to do this," Colonel Billings said, "we're going to have to coordinate with the FBI. A terrorist threat of this magnitude and not informing them? I'll never hear the end of it."

The colonel placed a hand on Rob's shoulder. "All right, son?" he asked.

"Yeah, Colonel," replied Rob. "I got it. I'll pass it on to the rest of the guys."

"Good," Billings said.

The colonel stepped away, and Rob made his way back inside to speak to Brian. They had some preparations to make.

TWENTY-ONE

FBI Field Office
New Orleans, Louisiana
Two Days Later

The Delta team and two ISA agents waited inside the cold meeting room, twiddling their thumbs and chatting with one another to pass the time. Colonel Billings sat close to the front of the room, checking his watch every few minutes while glancing through a local newspaper and sipping a cup full of black coffee.

At just past six in the morning, they needed to get an early start before the day's events ramped up. In the corner of the table, Rob had just finished field stripping and cleaning his Sig Sauer nine-millimeter pistol. Putting it back together, he inserted a full magazine into the magazine well and tapped it once on the bottom with his palm. He put the small cleaning kit back into the outside pocket of his pack resting on the floor by his feet.

Rob holstered the gun and pulled his shirt down over it, and they heard the double doors crack open. The doors echoed down the corridor as they slammed shut, and pairs of footsteps stomped the tile floor as they got closer. Colonel Billings came to his feet when the group of men were turning the corner.

"Colonel?" one of the five men asked as they entered the room. "Colonel Billings?"

"Yes," Billings replied. "I'm Colonel Billings, Alpha Troop commanding officer."

The colonel began pointing out the men. "These five are under my command. The two down there are our intel team from the ISA."

"Hello, gentlemen," the man said, glancing at them while gripping Billing's hand firmly. "I'm Special Agent Rick Campbell, HRT commander. Sorry to keep you guys waiting. We had to catch an early flight from Quantico."

HRT stood for hostage rescue team. They were the premier counterterrorism unit of the FBI and the US federal government. The team's mission profiles included high-risk raids, hostage rescue, assault, and more. With a selection process almost mirroring that of US Army Delta, it was no surprise they trained and worked with special-mission units like Delta and SEAL Team Six from time to time.

"Well," the colonel replied. "We're all here now. Let's get on with this, shall we? We don't have any time to waste."

"It's your show, Colonel," Campbell said, pulling out a chair.

The other four members of the FBI team took seats by their commander on one end of the table.

"All right," said Billings. "Down to business then." The colonel moved toward the projector in the back of the room. "This outfit will collectively be known as Task Force Black for the duration of this operation," he said. "Campbell, your call sign is Hotel-One."

Billings pointed to each HRT member under Campbell. "The rest of your team are Hotel-One-Alpha, Bravo, Charlie, and Delta. Got it?"

"Understood, Colonel," replied Campbell.

"All right, then," the colonel said, turning the projector on.

Al-Bashir's face was displayed on the white screen at the front. It was a photo taken by US intelligence officers in Lebanon. The photo, captured from a slightly elevated position, clearly showed Al-Bashir with a scruffy beard, a scar down his cheek, and wearing a head covering as he walked with his men.

"This man," Billings said, "is Aasim Abdul al-Bashir, leader of the Abdullah Azzam Brigades, otherwise known as al-Qaeda in Lebanon. His organization was responsible for the London bombing and has now infiltrated our border here."

The briefing, given by the colonel, was more for the FBI team, to get them up to speed on what was going on.

"Now," the colonel added, "intel we've obtained, with the help of the ISA guys sitting beside you, points to an attack happening in New Orleans during Mardi Gras. The where and when has not been determined, so we have to use our best educated guess."

"Which is?" Agent Campbell asked.

"Downtown," Rob said.

The colonel returned to the projector and changed the slide. It showed an image of mid-city New Orleans from a high vantage point. "Correct," he continued. "The Krewe of Endymion parade. It's an easy target and the biggest by far. If I were a terrorist looking to do mass harm, that would definitely be on my radar. Blending with that diverse crowd of lunatics wouldn't be too difficult."

Campbell nodded, folding his arms and glancing at his men. "So," he replied. "What did you have in mind for us?"

Colonel Billings sauntered toward the table and perched on top of it. "I'm glad you asked," he said. "We need three of you on the ground with our team, mixing with the people and ready to move on a moment's notice. The other two will be in the vehicle with the signal jammer. We'll have our sniper team covering everyone from above. Now, since we had no time to rehearse together, are you guys comfortable with this?"

Campbell grinned, looking over his team. Without a word spoken, the answer was written on their faces.

"We're good to go, Colonel," replied Campbell. "Just say the word."

Brian rose and waved Campbell toward the door. "You guys are with us," he said. "Let's get to it."

The colonel shut the projector down as all teams headed outside to catch a ride to their destination, blocks away.

Hours later, along the Street, pedestrians packed the city streets from one side to the other as far as one could see. Street performers danced and juggled, and people gathered along the sidewalks. The Mardi Gras celebration was almost in full swing.

Drunk college-aged boys with multicolored beads dangling from their necks ran through the street. They tossed them to women, who readily flashed their breasts in return. Bright lights radiated from outside bars and clubs, lighting up areas full of party-goers across the French Quarter. People on balconies drunkenly shouted down at folks on the walkways beneath them.

Five floors up and half a mile down, Rob glanced down the roadway through his high-powered rifle scope. He could hear the parade approaching from behind, police moving rowdy people out of the way of the coming floats. Set back a few feet from the window, Rob and Colin scanned the crowd. The mass of people was so thick, the road was barely visible under their feet.

They'd been waiting there since long before the festivities began. Vantage points were carefully chosen, and personnel on the ground were dressed to blend with the mob. There were many along the street when the team arrived, but hours later, the place was swarming with people.

Rob squeezed the talk button connected to his earpiece. "One-Sierra," he said. "We got the parade coming up behind us. You guys got anything on that end, over?" Rob waited for a response.

"Negative, Three-Five," Conrad replied. "Nothing yet but a bunch of drunk fools. Still searching."

ISA Agents Conrad and Weber were posted on opposite ends of the Street. The rest of the Delta team and HRT were positioned in random spots on the ground between them.

"What about you, Two-Sierra?" Rob asked Weber.

He could hear the music from a nearby bar while Weber keyed his mic.

"No," Weber replied. "Nothing here yet. The parade is halfway around the corner, though."

"Roger that," said Rob. "Three-Six," Rob continued. "Anything on the ground?"

"Nope," Brian replied, trying not to be obvious as he stood against the wall outside a restaurant. "Nothing unusual down here yet except a bunch of idiots."

"Yeah, copy that," Rob said.

Mardi Gras was well known to the New Orleans police for getting out of hand at times. Officers walked the beat in pairs along the edge, making their presence felt to everyone. Colin, peeking through his spotting scope, saw one officer cuffing an intoxicated, shirtless man with his partner by the doorway of an old hotel.

"Looks like they're out in force today," he said.

They heard the music getting closer to their location.

"Keep watch on this end," Rob replied. "Be right back."

With his own rifle next to him, Colin kept his eyes glued to the spotting scope. Rob picked up his weapon and moved to the window with a view of the other side of the street. Peeking through the glass, he saw the first large float behind rows of dancing girls in red, sparkly outfits almost a quarter mile down the roadway. Closer to Colin's side, a police squad car, a white Ford Escape, turned right off a side street away from the parade. The car's horn blared, causing people to disperse from the street and onto the walkways. Policemen on the ground herded them out of the way while the cruiser passed by.

Rob and Colin heard the marching band bumping. The dancers moved to the beat of the drums. Glaring through the window, Colin watched up and down pathways on both sides of the road. Suddenly, something got Colin's attention. A dark-skinned young man stood by a hotel. He leaned over and set a gym bag down on the ground by a city garbage can.

"Come here," Colin said to Rob. "Take a look at this."

Rob hurried over to the window and glared through Colin's scope. After a few seconds, the kid took off down the sidewalk through the horde of people before melting into the crowd.

"Shit," Rob said. "Golf-Three-Six, we got a gym bag down here on the corner by the bar with the blinking lights. It's close to the road in front of the door by that big trash can. A kid just dropped it and ran, white hoodie with torn jeans and a black, backward cap. You see the bag or the kid from your position, over?"

Rob knew they couldn't physically check the bag yet. If it was set to detonate remotely, there would surely be someone watching it.

"I see the bag, Three-Five," replied Brian. "No visual on the kid. All black elements, be on the lookout for him—dark complexion with white hoodie, backward cap, and jeans."

"I'll contact the police chief," said Campbell. "I have his direct number."

"Copy that," replied Rob.

Rob and Colin eyed the gym bag closely while others searched the ground for the kid. Random passersby meandered past it, oblivious to what was just feet away.

"Two-Six," Rob added. "We need to get those people out of there."

A couple minutes later, a New Orleans police car came out of the same side street and blocked the parade, lights flashing. He got out and held his hand up to stop them. The participants all halted in place, still playing music and dancing in the street.

A black Chevy Tahoe with tinted windows parked on the side street by the building Rob and Colin were in. People out on the street, losing signal, started checking their phones.

"Looks like it's working, Three-Five," said Brian. "If they planned to detonate remotely, it sure won't work now."

FBI personnel inside the Tahoe were using a signal jammer to jam cell phone signals.

"Yeah," Rob replied, peeking through the glass down below. "It's working, all right. Good job, Hotel-One."

"Just another day at the office," said Campbell.

A group of police appeared and began pushing the mob of patrons back far away from the site. A few cops took temporary barriers from their trunks and placed them across the pavement facing both ends. People below were angry and shouting, not sure of what was happening. It was probably better they didn't. Police officers spoke to the masses over loudspeakers in attempts to control a situation that could easily get out of control.

"Three-Six," Rob said through the radio. "You're clear to move, over."

Any remote signal nearby would be jammed, but if there

was a bomb in the bag, it could still be detonated manually. Brian hoofed it down the walkway toward the bag's location.

"Be careful, Three-Six," Rob said.

"Shit," Brian nervously joked. "If I'm going to go, it might as well be with a bang."

Brian stopped in his tracks at the side of the road, the bag right at his feet. He kneeled down over it. "I got it. It's right in front of me."

The crowd behind the barriers and the parade were crazed and hard to control. They had no idea what was going on and weren't happy their holiday was being interrupted. Many cursed and threw beer bottles into the street.

"This is exactly what they expected," Rob said under his breath.

Colin moved away from the lens and glanced over at him. "What was that?" he asked.

"Well, think about it," replied Rob. "They had to have anticipated the cops would clear the area. What do you see?"

Colin glanced ahead again. "I see a load of people packed on the other side of the barrier," he said.

"That's right," Rob said.

They watched Brian unzip the white gym bag. He had a flustered look on his face.

"Shit," he said. "It's empty. There's nothing here."

Suddenly, Rob and Colin heard a police radio transmission over the scanner.

All units, this is two-five. We have a report of the 10-79 suspect fleeing westbound on Ursulines Ave. toward the interstate in what looks like a black Mercedes, possibly stolen.

The radio squelched. A few seconds passed, and the officer continued.

We're moving to intercept. Requesting backup from any available units.

As the cops went after the car, Brian noticed a sticky note stuck to the bottom of the bag. Rob watched him pull it out. The note contained a single word.

Boom.

"Three-Six," Rob said. "What is that? You find something?"

"Yeah," replied Brian. "It's a note. Clever, damn it. They knew we'd be here. We were fucking played."

Rob took his rifle and placed it inside a large guitar case. He and his spotter packed up.

"Come on," Rob said. "Hurry, we got to move."

They both snagged their stuff and sprinted down the stairs and out toward the road.

"Three-Six," Rob said into his earpiece. "We're mobile."

He and Colin jogged down the path toward an intersecting street.

"Everyone hold," Rob added. "We're going after him. Tell them to pull the cops back. I have a feeling this was a ploy, a diversion to get us away from the real location of the bomb."

They continued on for a quarter of a mile. Rob spotted a man getting into an old black Ford Mustang. He rushed in and grabbed the car door before he could shut it.

"Sorry, sir," Rob said. "We need your car. It's an emergency."

"No!" the man yelled. "I'm not giving you my wheels. This is a classic. Get your own damn car."

Rob held the door so he couldn't close it. "We need this car," he added. "Please, sir."

"No!" the man shouted again. "Get out of here before I call the cops."

Rob tugged at his shirt, showing his Sig pistol in its holster.

The man saw it and climbed out of the vehicle. He backed away with his hands up. "All right, man, take it," he said. "Shit, I don't want any trouble."

Rob snatched the keys from the man's hand. "Thank you very much," he said.

He and Colin jumped in, tossing both guitar cases onto the backseat. He fired up the Mustang and peeled out as the man yelled for help. The muscle car's engine roared, tearing down the road toward Ursulines Ave. Rob yanked the wheel left, blaring the horn and fishtailing onto the one-way street. People along the road jumped out of the way of the speeding vehicle.

Veering around parked cars at sixty-five miles an hour, Rob bolted straight for the I-10 freeway. He swung right and skidded across pavement. Straightening the car, he shot up the highway on-ramp and out onto the four-lane roadway. Up ahead, they saw police lights whir with sirens blaring.

He put the pedal to the metal, and as he got closer, the police cars slowed, their lights suddenly switched off. The men knew the colonel had called it in. They had no authority over the police, but not many police chiefs wished to piss off shadowy government officials, especially ones in direct contact with the office of the president.

"There it is," he said, passing the police cars. "There's the Mercedes. Hold on."

Rob swerved left across three lanes of traffic. All of a sudden, he had a thought. "What is the range of one of those signal jammers?" he asked Colin.

"What?" Colin said, glancing at Rob while holding on to the door handle.

"The jammers the FBI used," Rob added. "What's the range?"

"I'm not certain," Colin replied. "Maybe a mile or so."

"Shit," Rob replied.

He zoomed toward the fleeing Mercedes and transmitted over the radio. "Three-Six," he said. "I think the bomb is set somewhere outside of the range of those jammers! Is there another crowded area nearby?"

"Stand by," replied Brian.

They were almost bumper to bumper with the target vehicle.

"Three-Five," Brian added. "I was just told there's a huge party happening at the city park, lots of people."

Rob prepared to ram the Mercedes off the road.

"Then get there! We're going to snatch up this kid."

"Roger," Brian said, he and the rest of the men darting for their vehicles.

"Hold on, partner!" Rob said to Colin. "Hold the fuck on!"

Rob swung the car wide left. He pressed harder on the accelerator and jerked the wheel to the right. The front end of the Mustang struck the left rear corner panel of the Mercedes, sending it sideways and spinning out toward the guardrail. Flipping sideways off the end of the bridge, the vehicle plunged twenty feet into a grassy area and landed on its side. Rob hit the brakes and skidded to a stop at the edge of the road.

"Come on," he said.

They darted down the gentle slope toward the wrecked vehicle. They neared the car and spotted a black kid, late teens, attempting to climb through the shattered window. Rob reached up, grabbing him by the arm and dragging him out to the ground. Colin pinned him with a boot to the back.

"You little shit," Rob said, taking zip cuffs from his back pocket and wrapping them around the kid's wrist. "You're coming with us, punk."

Rob and Colin forced the kid uphill toward the car. Rob

drew his pistol as he popped the trunk. The boy tugged on his baggy jeans and pulled down his New Orleans Saints jersey.

"Get in," he said to the kid, "or I'll send you straight to hell, boy."

"Okay, okay," the kid replied with his arms out. "I'm going, damn."

Colin shoved him in the chest, knocking him back into the trunk. Rob grabbed his feet and swung him around. He slammed the trunk. They rushed to get inside, and a huge blast erupted off in the distance. They could see the smoke cloud rise over the city.

"Shit," Rob said. He keyed his mic. "Three-Six, we just saw an explosion. You guys okay, over?"

There was no answer.

"Three-Six, you copy?"

They weren't sure why their team leader wasn't answering his radio. But Rob gunned it across the city.

TWENTY-TWO

City Park, New Orleans

The park loomed from blocks away as pandemonium broke out in the city streets. An enormous cloud of black smoke lingered high above, spreading slowly.

Many rushed to help injured people stumbling across the road in shredded and disheveled clothing. Across the grass, the dead were laid out over a wide area along the ground where they'd fallen. Numerous sirens sounded, police and emergency crews racing to the scene. What was a wide patch of grass had turned into a crater at the site of the detonation. Those closer to the blast never had a chance. Even people farther away had suffered from shrapnel wounds and smoke inhalation.

The team made sure to stay well away from the immediate area of the explosion. Rob stopped the car blocks from the site. Brian and the FBI team in the van behind him pulled up along the curb. Rob and Colin hopped out, and they heard the kid pounding on the inside of the trunk.

"Get me out of this fucking trunk, you bitches," he said. "I can't breathe in here!"

Ignoring his pleas, Rob and Colin met the gang at the back of the vehicle.

"I swear when I get out of here, I'm gonna fuck you up, yo!" the kid added.

People in the streets up ahead coughed violently, like they'd hack up a lung. The dark cloud over the city drifted away from them.

"Alpha-Six-Actual," Brian said into the radio. "It's Three-Six. FBI is on-scene with us. It's devastation down here. Send EOD and a CBRN team for possible radiation contamination, over."

CBRN stood for chemical, biological, radiation, and nuclear. Since radiation couldn't be seen, smelled, or tasted, testing was necessary. They knew that radioactive dust from a dirty bomb would pose a more serious threat and more immediate illness to those close to the blast, but when carried in the wind, the radiation could be dangerous if inhaled farther away.

"We'll evacuate five blocks around the site," Brian added. "We've got the kid, over."

"Copy that, Three-Six," replied the colonel. "I'll make contact now. Keep me updated. Alpha-Six-Actual, out."

Police and EMS lights and sirens came from every direction and closed in fast.

"Damn," Agent Campbell said. "We have to stop these guys before they get too close. They have no idea what they're walking into."

"Roger that," replied Brian.

"Come on, guys," Campbell said to his team as they headed for the back of the van.

He popped the door open and reached inside, snatching masks and tossing them to his men. They put them on and left to delay police and EMS personnel before they made it to the scene.

"Hey," Rob said to Brian, standing by the back of the car. "Why didn't you answer your radio?"

"Because," he replied, "the jammer was fucking with our signal. Where's the kid? You catch up to him?"

"Sure did," Colin said, pointing toward the trunk. "He's in there."

Brian kicked the rear tire of the Mustang. "Fuck!" he yelled. "How could we not see this coming? The bastards played us like a fiddle!"

"Yeah," said Rob. "They're definitely cunning, I'll give them that."

Brian snatched the car keys from Rob's hand. "Let's see what this asshole has to say," he said.

He stuck them into the keyhole and popped the trunk. It opened, and the young boy, his hands cuffed, sprung up in an attempt to get out. Rob squeezed a fist and punched him in the face, knocking him back inside and onto his back. He slammed the trunk closed again.

"As you can see," Rob said, "he's a feisty little shit."

"Yeah," Brian replied. "What I don't get is why would a black kid be involved in this?"

Agent Conrad interjected. "He was probably paid," he said. "It makes sense to use poor, inner-city kids like this who won't say no to easy money."

Rob leaned his back against the back of the car. "Not so easy this time, though, huh?" he replied.

He glanced back and saw Agent Campbell and his team waving down emergency crews. Rob noticed a flag down the street whipping to the northeast. Since the wind was blowing away from them pretty hard, the team should've been in the clear where radioactive dust was concerned.

"What are we going to do with him?" Weber asked, tipping his head toward the back of the Mustang.

"I have an idea," Brian replied. "Follow me. I know the city."

Rob and Colin ducked into the car again to follow Brian to wherever he planned to take them. Rob cranked the engine, hitting the gas and whipping the car back around in the opposite direction as Brian pulled around in front of them. They headed back down the street to the southwest. Rob wondered where they were going as they passed underneath the highway bridge.

Coming almost to the end of the road, Brian took a sudden right. Rob trailed him, driving a block over, then taking another right turn to the north. Brian slowed the Suburban and swerved into a row of spaces along the left side of the street. He put the SUV into park. Rob killed the Mustang's engine, and they climbed from the car, slamming doors behind them.

"This is the NOPD's second district station," Brian said. "I called the colonel and had him relay to them that we were bringing a suspect in to interrogate, and we'd need a room. They think we're federal agents."

"Well, all right then," replied Rob.

Rob opened the trunk again, and he and Colin dragged the kid from the back by his arms. His feet hit the pavement, and Rob placed a hand on the cuffs and another on his shoulder and shoved him forward. He stopped a moment.

"Cuff his legs," Rob said.

Colin reached for another pair of zip cuffs and stooped down. He wrapped them snugly around the kid's ankles and tightened them.

"There," Rob added. "Now you can't try to run."

"Man, come on!" the kid shouted. "Why you bitches fucking with me? Stupid ass crackers! I ain't got shit to do with shit."

Jamal butted in. "Do I look like a cracker to you, boy?"

Rob gripped the kid's arms tightly. "Brian, Colin, I, and the ISA guys will go in," he said to the team. "The rest of you wait here."

Rob glared at the young boy. "Move," he said, prodding him forward with a poke.

They escorted the kid down the walk and toward the steps and the glass door front entrance. Colin opened up for them, and they stepped inside. Brian quickly flashed an ID at the officer on desk duty.

"Federal agents with one in custody," Brian said. "Our boss called earlier."

The policeman got up from his seat and put the sandwich he was eating on a napkin. He pointed to the left.

"Yes, sir," he said in a strong Cajun accent. "Straight down the hall, last door on the right."

The station was almost empty, with most police in the city busy due to recent events. They were in for a disappointment, though, as the feds had taken control.

"You got a set of metal cuffs we can use?" Brian asked.

"Yeah, sure," the officer said, reaching for a table in the office. He tossed the cuffs and a key to Brian.

"Thanks," Brian replied, catching them midair.

The team headed down the hallway.

"You guys hear about that bomb downtown?" asked the officer.

"Who hasn't?" Rob replied, leading the kid down the corridor. "Crazy times we live in."

The officer evidently had no clue that the detainee had anything to do with the bombing. He met them by the door with a large ring of keys and unlocked it.

"Thank you, Officer," Rob said. "Please leave us. We require a little privacy."

Rob waved for the officer to join him outside in the hall. He glanced down at his nametape. "Where are your security cameras, Officer Boudreaux?"

"Here," he replied, stepping toward the office and showing Rob to the surveillance system in a small back room.

"I'm going to need you to disable the camera in that room," said Rob.

"I can't," the officer replied. "My boss would have my ass."

"The US government would have everyone's," Rob said, smacking him lightly on the cheek. "We aren't law enforcement. We work in a different part of the government. If your boss has a problem, direct him to us."

"You…uh…CIA or something?" the officer asked anxiously.

"Or something," Rob replied with a grin.

Rob got his point across. Officer Boudreaux wasn't going to pry any further. He was certain he didn't want to know. Instead, he pushed a few buttons on the console. The monitor connected to the camera in the interview room cut out.

"Thanks, Officer." Rob added, "Nobody comes back here, got it? I don't care if it's the chief."

"Sure," replied the officer. "Whatever you say, sir."

"Good boy," said Rob.

He marched down the corridor and back into the room, and Brian and Colin watched the entrance outside. He yanked the keys from the solid metal door and slammed it after him. The kid was perched on a metal bench, his cuffed hand now secured to a metal bar bolted to the wall. Rob stared him down.

"What the fuck?" the kid asked, Rob standing a few feet away. "What you want from me, white boy? Why you bitches manhandling me like that? I didn't do nothin' to nobody!"

Rob knelt down in front of him. "What's your name, kid?" he asked.

The kid bucked at him, tugging against the chain. "I ain't hiding shit. Name's Maurice, but they call me Money. Why, what's yours, asshole?"

"My name's not important," Rob said. "Listen, Maurice. I need to know how you came across that bag you left on the sidewalk. You're not in trouble—yet. If you're honest with me, you can walk right out of here."

"Don't know what you talking about," Maurice replied.

Rob squatted next to the kid on the bench. He bent forward and looked Maurice in the eye. "Look, Maurice," he said. "Just calm the hell down, all right? A bomb just went off in this city that hurt a lot of people. That bag has something to do with it. I need to know where it came from."

Maurice's jaw dropped, his gold front tooth glinting under the overhead light.

"Yo, man," he replied. "Nobody said shit about no bomb! They run drugs and gats out here, but ain't nobody fucking with no bombs and shit. We ain't about that, homie. Even the rag-heads stay away from that shit 'cause of the stereotype."

"All right, Maurice," replied Rob. "I need you to think hard, okay? Who gave you the bag? Was he Middle Eastern? What did he look like?"

"Dog, come on," Maurice said. "They all look the fucking same. Brown, beard, towel wrap or some shit. Oh, and he was smoking some nasty-ass clove cigarettes. Hate that fucking smell. Dude paid me like a hundred bills to leave the bag there. I figured it was a dead drop. That shit's common around here. Anyway, I needed the dough, so I took it."

"You didn't think it odd coming from a Middle Eastern–looking individual?" asked Rob.

"Bruh," replied Maurice. "All types be slinging that shit 'round here, you know?"

Rob got up and stood in the middle of the room, his back to the kid. "You didn't look inside the bag?" he asked.

"Nah," Maurice replied. "You can get your ass shot for shit like that 'round here, you know?"

"All right," Rob said, turning around to face him. "These cigarettes, what did they smell like?"

"Cherry or some shit," replied Maurice.

There was a quick knock on the door. Rob left Maurice sitting there. He gripped the doorknob and yanked it open. Wandering through, Agent Conrad pulled up an image on a tablet.

"You need to see this," he said. "We were able to get a recording from a security camera a few blocks from where the bag was found."

Conrad showed Rob the screen. He hit play and let it run for a few seconds, then paused it. He zoomed in to an alley between two buildings.

"See that?" Conrad asked. "See the handoff?"

"Yeah," Rob replied as Conrad zoomed in even closer.

They could clearly see a bag being exchanged.

"See the face? You recognize him?"

His head covered, only the man's face was visible. Rob studied it closely. The screen was frozen, a puff of hazy cigarette smoke rising.

"That's Amir Hassan," he said. "Al-Qaeda lieutenant and second-in-command under al-Bashir. He disappeared years ago after his boss was suspected of being killed in Afghanistan."

Brian moved in between them to take a look.

"Yeah, I heard about him when I was with the Rangers. It wasn't my unit who thought they'd killed his boss, but we all knew about him. He was ruthless as fuck."

Rob left them, entering the room again and closing the door behind him.

"All right, Maurice," he said. "One final question. Did he say anything to you? Anything that sounded strange?"

"Nah, man," Maurice replied. "Dude just flashed his cash

and told me where to put it. That's all the fuck he said, I swear."

"Shit," said Rob.

He took the key and unlocked the cuffs around Maurice's wrist. Rob strolled to the door and opened it. Maurice stood from the metal bench and rubbed his wrist. He walked toward Rob.

"This is why you stuffed my ass in the fucking trunk?" Maurice asked. "Can I go now, then?"

"Yeah, kid," Rob replied, pointing him toward the exit. "Go on. Get out of here."

Maurice gave them all a hard stare as he headed for the door.

"Go!" Rob said to him. "Get the hell out of here before I change my mind."

Rob returned to the team as Maurice left the building.

"This is a dead end," Brian said. "Damn it."

Rob smacked him on the shoulder.

"No, it's not," Rob replied. "At least we now know who's behind it. Let's find this bastard and make him pay."

TWENTY-THREE

The president's motorcade traveled rapidly down Highway 395 toward the off-ramp that led directly to the vast Pentagon parking area. The fleet of armored Chevy Suburbans and other vehicles, all full of Secret Service agents, and the president's limo swung right onto the off-ramp. They circled around the bend toward the lot and the executive entrance located at the far side.

Republican president Kevin Tyler was hyper-focused during most of the drive from DC, not paying attention to his national security adviser, Neal Rampart, sitting across from him. During the ride, the president had been rummaging through the many documents inside his leather briefcase. The motorcade came to a halt by the covered entrance, and the president shoved the papers back into the case.

Just into the second year of his first term, this president, unlike most, came from humble beginnings. His father worked offshore while his mother was a stay-at-home mom. Growing up in Denton, Texas, he'd played football all his life, including at Texas A&M. The president joined the military straight out of college and went to officer candidate school. He was later commissioned as an ensign in the US Navy.

One of the Secret Service Agents held the door of the limo open, and President Tyler and his adviser climbed out and headed inside under one of the covered executive entrances.

"What do we know so far?" the president asked, marching through the corridor with agents surrounding them.

President Tyler paused a moment, waving the Secret Service agents off. "Adams," he said to the senior agent. "You all wait outside. I'm good from here."

"Yes, Mister President," he replied as he did an about-face.

The remaining agents followed Adams back to the exit as President Tyler picked up his step again.

"So?" the president continued.

"Three attacks, sir," his adviser replied, walking in cadence. "The one at the border, multiple agents dead; the bombing in Silver City, New Mexico; and the most recent being a packed Mardi Gras celebration in New Orleans."

"Silver City? What the hell is significant about that place? Hell, there's nothing there. My God, all those innocent people. We have to get to the bottom of this, and fast. We need to send a message that no one will come to America and push us around."

Rampart continued following his boss, speed-walking toward the meeting room a little farther down.

"Sir," Rampart replied. "Intel agents believe New Mexico was some kind of diversion for New Orleans, a way to get us looking the other way while they sneaked into the country."

The president stopped abruptly just before the room entrance. "How the hell would that work?" he asked. "How could they just slip right past our border guards undetected like that?"

"Mister President," Rampart replied. "We are being told they had help from the cartel. They know the border well and, of course, all the weak points. It would be very difficult to traverse the desert without them."

"Jesus," Tyler replied. "Let's make sure we send a team down there to see what they need. They know the border better than anyone. I plan to visit myself soon, and I want you with me, Neal."

"Absolutely, Mister President," replied Rampart. "I'll get on it immediately."

Rampart gripped the door latch, and his boss set a hand on his arm.

"One more thing before we head in," the president added. "What's the current status of the Delta team?"

"They're on the ground in New Orleans as we speak, Mister President," said Rampart. "The FBI's HRT team is there also, coordinating with local police and assessing the damage."

Rampart held the door for his boss. President Tyler continued on through the doorway with his adviser in tow. Rampart shut the door, and they wandered through another short hallway. Before entering, they both dumped their cell phones onto a pile of others in a bin by the door and headed into the conference room.

Waiting inside were General Wilkins; Colonel Billings; the CIA Directorate of Intelligence, Henry Kitchens; Defense Secretary Bob Gates; and Executive Director Rob Holm, head of FBI Intelligence. The five of them rose from their seats as the president entered. Rampart followed his boss and remained by a chair while President Tyler continued around to the head of the table.

"Please," the president said, setting his briefcase on the floor by his feet. "Have a seat, gentlemen. We can skip the formalities, all right? Let's just get to the point of why we're here, hmmm?"

President Tyler took a glass from the table and filled it with water from a pitcher. He was known to get straight to the point. He had nerves of steel, but this was the second major attack on American soil. He wanted answers.

"Three attacks," the president said, gulping a bit of water. He swallowed it down.

"Two bombings in less than a week," Tyler added. "Border Patrol Agents murdered at a border checkpoint. Can someone intelligently explain to me what the fuck is going on here?" Tyler leaned forward on the table, waiting for a response.

"Mister President," Kitchens replied. "I'm sure you received the intelligence briefings. We lost good officers following these men. We don't know what happened. The next thing we hear is about an attack in London."

President Tyler set his glass on the table and calmly glared at the CIA Directorate.

"Yet," he said, "somehow the Agency wasn't able to track these terrorists to our borders. Now we have bombs going off in our cities. I think I would call this a colossal intelligence failure, wouldn't you, Henry?"

"Mister President…" Kitchens replied before President Tyler cut him off.

"Save it, okay?" Tyler said in a raised voice. "Y'all completely dropped the ball on this one. You're losing the trust of your own government, especially our special operations community. The same thing happened before the attacks on the Twin Towers. You guys sat on intelligence on Bin Laden that could've very well proven to be the difference."

Kitchens gazed at the president, his hands folded together on the table. "Yes, sir," he replied.

President Tyler swiped his briefcase and put it on the table.

He directed his attention to the others in the room. "Now," he said, opening the case. "Give it to me straight. I want the full workup. What do we know so far, and what are our options?"

"Mister President," General Wilkins said. "If I may."

"Well, of course, General," replied Tyler. "Sure, I'm all ears."

"Yes, Mister President," Wilkins said. "This is basically al-Qaeda 2.0."

The general got up and popped his case open, retrieving a stack of images. He handed them off to be passed around the room.

"That first image is Aasim al-Bashir, al-Qaeda leader in Lebanon," Wilkins said as they each glanced at the photo. "He was reported deceased by the seventy-fifth Rangers back in 2005—"

The CIA Directorate cut him off. "This man was recently found and tracked via drone by a team from our agency stationed in Egypt."

General Wilkins appeared annoyed. "Yes," he said. "And you know, Mister President, they were killed before they were able to capture him. It's a shame, too. It might've prevented this whole damn thing."

The CIA Directorate appeared ghost white.

"He's right, you know," said the president. "I'm sorry about what happened to your officers, Henry. But it could've been prevented if not for faulty intelligence the first go around."

Kitchens stayed silent.

"Please, General," President Tyler said. "Continue on."

"Yes, Mister President." The general added, "The second photo is al-Bashir's right-hand man, Amir Hassan. Delta and the ISA believe they caught a video of him on the street before the attack in New Orleans. The Delta team have been following his trail since the London bombing."

"I know," the president said with a quick nod. "Who do you think approved the operation? What's the situation on the ground in New Orleans?"

Director Holm of FBI intelligence interjected. "Mister President," he said, "I received an update from my agents at the scene before arriving here. They are saying the bomb contained radiation particles that have spread north of the blast zone. The majority of the destruction was contained within a two-block perimeter around the park."

"How many dead?" Tyler asked.

"Best guess so far," Holm replied, "a hundred fifty, with a good chance of others developing some kind of radiation sickness in the near future."

President Tyler rested his hand on his chin and bowed his head. "My God," he said. He got up from his seat and walked around the chair, pacing in short steps back and forth.

"I thought we'd learned our lesson since nine-eleven," he added, hitting the wood table with two open palms. He leaned back against the table with folded arms. "But apparently not," the president continued. "Now we have a bunch of religious extremists running loose in this country, planning God knows what. When I was a pilot in the Navy, we'd just bomb the hell out of the enemy like we did during the Gulf War. Never did I ever think the fight would land on our doorstep. This is a new age we're living in, and it stinks to high heaven!"

The room went eerily silent. But while they waited to see if the president would continue, they started to hear footsteps pounding on the floor outside and getting closer. Suddenly, Secretary of State Ken Powell barged into the room.

"Mister President," he said loudly. "Mister President, you've got to see this!"

Powell made his way to the flat-screen TV on the wall halfway across the room.

"See what, Ken?" the president asked. "What in the hell are you talking about?"

Powell grabbed the remote from the table and turned the TV on. The secretary of state fumbled with the buttons until he got to a news channel. He turned the volume up as they played a recording that had been sent to the news agency.

The man in the video had a black balaclava over his head, revealing just his nose and eyes. The voice was distorted, but there was no denying who it was from as those in the room listened in horror.

This message is for your United States president and for all Western leaders who believe the American imperialist nation and others must police the world and interfere in Muslim affairs. For too long, we have watched as you have killed our men and women and made orphans out of our children.

Your bombs and your drones have decimated cities and villages, and your soldiers have killed without mercy. Now is the time for you to pay for your crimes. And you will. We, the Abdullah Azzam Brigades, will bring you infidels to your knees until you beg us for mercy. But you will get no mercy.

The man paused a moment. He moved closer to the camera, his penetrating eyes staring into it.

Mister President, swine leader of imperialist America, enemy of Allah, we will come for you. There is nowhere you can hide. But first, you will watch us rain fire down on your people. Then, when enough have suffered as we have, we will come for you. We will not show mercy.

The recording cut out as the lady news reporter continued the broadcast. All noise faded into the background, President Tyler staring into space, his jaw hanging open.

"Mister President?" the national security adviser said, turning the television off.

But the president didn't answer.

Rampart snapped his fingers in front of him. "Mister President?" he added.

"Yes," Tyler replied, snapping out of his stupor. The president flashed a half-baked grin. "Sorry about that," he added.

"Mister President," Rampart continued. "This is a very serious threat. We should take it as such. I recommend we move you to a secure location immediately. How do you want to handle it, sir?"

President Tyler reclined back in the chair with his hands interlocked behind his head.

"First," he replied, "I want to know how they obtained this recording before us. How did we not get our hands on this?"

"Mister President," the CIA Directorate said, "most likely, the news agency was sent the recording directly. In that case, intel officers would've never intercepted it. If we get an unedited copy of it, maybe we can analyze the background to determine the probable location it was recorded."

The president elbowed his national security adviser in the arm. "Get my family and the VP to the bunker now," he said. "And get an unaltered copy of that damn video, all right?"

"Yes, Mister President," Rampart replied. "What about you, sir?"

"What about me?" Tyler asked. "I'm a fighter, Neal. I'll be okay, just do what I ask."

"Yes, Mister President," Rampart replied. "I'll get to it right now."

"Then go," said Tyler. "Contact me when it's done."

Rampart stood and pushed his chair in. "Mister President," he replied, tipping his head and taking off toward the exit.

The president turned to Wilkins. "General," he said. "What's the status of the Delta team currently?"

"Mister President," General Wilkins replied. "Colonel Billings is in a better position to answer that."

President Tyler diverted his gaze to Billings. "Colonel?"

Billings placed both arms on the table. "Mister President," he replied, "my boys, working closely with the ISA and the FBI team, are following the trail of breadcrumbs. They know what they're doing. It's only a matter of time before they find something."

President Tyler paused to collect his thoughts. "Understood, Colonel," he said. "Let's hope that happens before these bastards end up on the White House lawn, hmm? We need actionable intelligence yesterday. Everyone, get to work! And get me a landline, now. I want to speak to the Delta command team directly."

TWENTY-FOUR

Al-Zabadani, Syria

CIA officer Isaac Smith sagged with his arms stretched high above his head and chained by his wrists to an exposed metal pipe on the ceiling. His shoeless feet were chained by the ankles to a metal contraption fixed to the cement floor.

It was a square room of a small building made of mud-baked bricks that were uneven in many spots. There were no windows. The only tiny bit of light came from a small hole in the wall close to the ceiling behind him. It barely lit up the dust-covered floor in front of Smith's feet.

He was grimy, and dried blood collected around his nose, mouth, and on his bare chest. His pants were torn and bloody, and his belt and everything he had on him had been removed. Smith had been stuck in that position for so long, his entire body was virtually paralyzed, so aloof he could no longer feel the metal pressing against his skin.

Smith's head was drooping. Barely conscious, he didn't have the strength to lift it. He saw double through his cracked, bloodshot eyes. The man's face was spattered with a mixture of dried sweat, blood, and sand from being pinned to the desert ground. He could hear the squeaking of rats every couple minutes as they scampered across the hard, uneven floor. He was too numb to feel it, but some nipped at the open sores on his toes.

Smith could vaguely hear voices coming from outside, but it was just a bunch of jumbled noise to him, like someone or something was covering his ears. Suddenly, the door lock budged. A bright beam of daylight swept across the room and blinded him further. Smith closed his eyes, a faint moan emitting from his mouth.

"What shall I do with you, American?" one of his captors asked, marching into the room with an AK slung over his shoulder.

The man, like them all, was a member of the Abdullah Azzam Brigades. He'd been entrusted by al-Bashir to watch over the captive while they carried out their mission. Reporting to Amir Hassan, he also happened to be his much younger brother. The man's name was Basim Hassan. Desiring to prove himself to his boss, he was even more cold-blooded than his sibling.

Another man clutching an AK stood guard by the door as Basim approached the hostage. Basim lightly smacked the side of Smith's bruised face and moved close to his ear. "I will break you," he whispered, his breath smelling of raspberry hookah smoke.

He strolled to the corner of the room, snatching a folding chair, and returned, placing it a few feet from Smith. Basim took a seat. He removed the AK-47 from his shoulder and set it across his lap.

"You are strong," he said to Smith. "Very strong American. But you will break eventually. They all break, you see?"

Basim cracked a smile. "You are alone," he added. "Your men are dead. No one is coming to save you. What do you think about that?"

Smith slowly glanced upward through his fuzzy eyes and

spit onto the ground in front of his captor. "Fuck you," he replied.

Basim leaped from the chair and jabbed Smith in the face with his wooden rifle butt. A trickle of blood flowed down from the bridge of Smith's nose and onto his lips. He spit up some of the blood onto the dusty floor, much of it now coating his front teeth.

"It's too bad your country will have to see you like this," said Basim. "It is a shame for you, I imagine."

Basim removed a small, handheld radio clipped to the inside of his pants pockets and brought it to his mouth. "Begin the preparations," he said into the mic in Arabic.

He clipped the radio back onto his trousers. A few seconds later, a few of his men stepped into the room, two carrying large lights and another toting a camera attached to a tripod. They set the lights on each side of Smith, facing him from a few feet away. The cameraman placed the camera with its stand behind Basim and facing the captive. Running cords under the door, they plugged in the lights. They turned them on, and a flood of white light in the dim room blinded Smith. His head pointed toward the floor, and he closed his eyes.

"Soon," Basim said to Smith, "you will be displayed for your masters to see what a pathetic excuse for a man you have become. Then we will truly know whether they care if you live or die. I am betting not."

Suddenly, a tall silhouette of a bearded man appeared in the doorway, blocking the outside light. The beam in Smith's face obscured everything but the outline of his robed body. The man ambled forward, his sandals popping with every step. Basim snapped upward as the man reached the chair.

"As-Salamu Alaikum," Basim said with a kiss on each grizzled cheek.

"Wa alaikum salaam," he replied with an embrace.

The man moved forward and kicked the chair out of the way, sliding it across the floor. He moved closer to the American, and his identity became clear.

"Do you know who I am?" the man asked.

Smith glared upward in disgust. "Yes," he replied, stuttering with his swollen mouth. "You're al-Bashir, butcher of... Lebanon and overall... evil bastard."

Al-Bashir gave him an evil grin. "That is right," he replied. "So you have heard of me? Excellent. You know who I am. But who are you—CIA, Navy SEAL, commando, what?"

"I'm the tooth fairy," Smith quickly replied.

Al-Bashir smacked Smith hard across the cheek, his red hand print visible through the American's beard.

"I will find out who you are," he said. "I think it is safe to assume that you know what I will do if I do not get what I want, correct?"

"And what is that?" Smith asked, struggling against the chain.

Al-Bashir hunched forward close to the American's face. "I am glad you asked," he said. "I want you to denounce your government on camera. I want you to express censure of your country's involvement with Middle Eastern affairs. And I want you to express to the whole world that America and the West are nothing more than imperialists who kill our people and destroy our cities. They can push us around no longer!"

Al-Bashir gripped the American by the jaw. "You do not think that I knew you were following me?" he asked. "I have scouts everywhere. They spotted you before you ever made it to the mosque. What were you thinking entering Makkah, infidel? You did not think you would get caught? Allah will strike you down for your blasphemy!"

The CIA officer stared through al-Bashir. "Like I told your man back there," he replied, "fuck you."

Al-Bashir squeezed a fist and struck Smith square in the mouth. Spit flew across the room, and blood began to drool from his cut lip.

"You think you are amusing?" he asked, his face inches from the American's. Al-Bashir spun around and signaled his men. "Get ready," he said in Arabic. "No more of this nonsense."

Al-Bashir pointed for his men to release the captive man from his chains. They unlocked them, and the CIA officer plunged to the floor in a weakened state. Hoisting him up and forcing his battered body into a metal chair, they wrapped the chain tightly around him. One of them put the lock into place, securing him to the chair.

The boss and four of his guards snatched black hoods from a table by the door and slipped them over their heads. Through small slits cut in the fabric, their eyes were the only thing visible. The four of them stood behind the American with AKs and a submachine gun in hand. Another adjusted the light and then manned the mounted camera.

Al-Bashir planted himself in the middle while one of his men hovered over the back of the American, clutching a large bowie-style knife.

***

Across the globe in Louisiana, the last of the bombing victims had long been loaded up and transported to nearby hospitals and morgues. Local authorities were well into the process of notifying the families of the deceased, those who could be immediately identified. Dental records, and in fewer circumstances, fingerprints, of those who couldn't be identified had been put through the system.

New Orleans police officers and other law enforcement personnel from surrounding cities and parishes blocked every street close to the site of the bombing. Barricades were set up, and blue lights could be seen for blocks around. The mayor of New Orleans had called a state of emergency, and feds from various agencies were also flooding the scene.

That part of New Orleans looked like a ghost town, cleared of civilians for many blocks surrounding the site. The FBI's hazardous materials response unit was operating in full HAZMAT suits. They processed and investigated the blast area to determine what type of materials and explosives had been used.

Leaving the FBI team behind, Delta and the ISA prepared to catch a helicopter flight from Louis Armstrong Airport in New Orleans back to Fort Liberty, North Carolina. Everyone waited on the tarmac, bags at their feet. Leaving his stuff in place, Rob stepped away to make a phone call. He retrieved his personal cell from his pocket. Thumbing through his contact list, Rob pressed the number under her name and waited. Five rings later, the phone picked up.

"Hello?" she said.

Rob took a breath. "Hey, Rachel? Uh, hey, it's me, Rob."

He could hear her typing away on her computer on the other end.

"Rob?" Rachel asked. "Hey, how are you? I was wondering if you'd ever call."

"Oh, yeah, sorry about that," Rob replied. "Been busy with work, you know? I had a few minutes now, and I was just wondering what you were up to."

Rachel heard the sound of a plane's engine screaming in the background. Rob put his hand over his ear to better hear her.

"I'm just doing a little bit of work," she said. "What're you doing? You at an airport?"

"Yeah," replied Rob.

"Going somewhere?"

Rob paused briefly. "I can't really talk about that over the phone," he said. "You understand?"

"Okay," she replied. "Well, when can I see you again? I'm back in DC. I'm getting ready to head back home from the office in a bit. Maybe you can tell me in person."

As they spoke, Rachel flipped through the channels on her TV until she came across a news channel. Rob could vaguely make it out as they reported on the bombing.

"Oh my God," she added. "You hear about what happened in New Orleans?"

Though she didn't want to say, Rachel suspected Rob was involved somehow.

"Yup, sure did," said Rob. "It's awful. Can't imagine what those people are going through."

The buzzing of helicopter rotor blades grew louder by the second.

"What's that noise?" Rachel asked.

Rob could barely hear her over the deafening sound.

"Hey," he said over the noise getting closer. "Look, I've got to go. But, uh, I'll call back when I can, okay? I promise."

Rachel answered back, but Rob couldn't understand her.

"See you!" he continued, ending the call.

Rob turned the phone off, stuffed it into his pants, and hurried back to grab his stuff. Clipping his cap to a belt loop, he took his long gun case and his assault pack by the carry handle. The crew opened the doors as the team quickly lined up to board the bird. They all tossed their gear in and climbed up. They took their seats, and Rob buckled his seat harness and settled in. The aircraft took off with the doors still open and crossed the airfield, heading east.

A while later, and now above the state of Mississippi, the black, unmarked bird soared through the sky at a high rate of speed and an altitude of one thousand feet.

With headsets on and staying mostly quiet, most of the team opted to rest their eyes during the calm flight. But Rob couldn't sleep. He sat on one end of the bench, and his dreary eyes stared through the window at the ground far below. Beneath each seat was a black case full of weapons and ammo. Closer to the cockpit, behind Rob, Agent Conrad's attention was directed toward his work tablet. He appeared taken aback, like he'd seen a ghost. He tapped Rob on the back of his shoulder.

"Hey," he said. "A friend of mine from the unit just sent me this. You guys need to see it."

Conrad passed the tablet over Rob's shoulder. He took it and held it near his lap. In the video, he saw the American chained to a chair and surrounded by masked Islamic terrorists. One of them was significantly taller than the others. His height certainly got Rob's attention.

"I'd bet ten to one that's al-Bashir right there," he said. "We were probably less than an hour from capturing his ass, too."

Conrad gave Rob a set of headphones. "Here," he said. "Use these."

Rob backed the video up a few seconds and paused it. "Thanks," Rob replied, snatching the headphones and plugging them into the side of the tablet.

He inserted them into his ears under the headset. Rob hit play and watched. At just under a minute long, he let the video play out in its entirety.

"That son of a bitch," he added. "He's taunting us."

Brian, resting back with his eyes shut, suddenly opened them. Without moving his head, he glanced right and caught a glimpse of Rob. Rob noticed Brian waking and elbowed him in the side.

"Hey, boss," he said, handing over the tablet and earphones. "You need to take a look."

Brian let out a yawn and swiped the tablet from Rob. He played the video quietly, his face expressionless. Jamal began to wake up, and curious as to what Brian was watching, he looked in.

"What the hell?" Jamal asked. "That's Smith, the Agency spook we were looking for, ain't it?"

With one earphone in, Brian finished the video. "Yeah, it is," he replied, setting the tablet on his lap. He reached behind and gave the tablet back to Conrad. "Make sure command gets ahold of this," he said.

"A threat on the president's life like that?" Conrad replied, slipping the tablet back into his backpack. "Shit, I'm pretty sure they've already seen it. I'm surprised he hasn't made contact yet."

"That asshole thinks he's outsmarted us," said Rob. "He thinks he can hold America hostage to his jihadi ideals. Not going to happen."

Conrad prepared to send the video to Special Forces Command over their secured network. Brian was about to contact their commander via radio to inform him of the video message. However, the colonel beat him to it.

"Golf-Three-Six," Colonel Billings said over the net. "This is Alpha-Six-Actual. I say again, this is Alpha-Six-Actual. How copy?"

"Roger, Six-Actual," Brian replied into his mic. "We read you, over."

The whole team listened in.

"Good, Three-Six," said the colonel. "Listen, I'm setting your new destination as India, Alpha, Tango, Alpha."

India, Alpha, Tango, Alpha, or IATA, was the airport code for Eglin Air Force Base in the Florida panhandle. It wasn't far from Alabama.

"When you arrive," Billings added, "you'll meet me and another team inside a hangar on the far side of the airfield."

"Six-Actual," Brian said. "I'm guessing you've seen the message?"

They weren't going to get into specifics over the radio.

"That's affirmative, Three-Six. We'll discuss it when you land. Just get here ASAP. Alpha-Six-Actual, out."

TWENTY-FIVE

Eglin Air Force Base
Florida

The blackhawk helicopter coasted in for a landing on a helipad to the left side of a large, open aircraft hangar. The last hint of daylight had sunk beneath the horizon a couple of hours before. Colonel Billings waited outside by the open door, wearing his class A uniform and puffing on a cigar, his green beret in hand. The man sure loved his cigars.

With its white lights blinking, the colonel followed the bird's movement across the airstrip while it taxied toward them. He waved to the men. At the same time, the aircraft slowed and got closer to the ground. Rob's head jolted as the back wheel touched ground and rolled a bit across the pavement. They came to a stop, and everyone unbuckled. Three of them snatched their things and jumped out, making their way over to the building. Jamal and Colin unloaded the black weapon and ammo cases from the aircraft.

Rob, Brian, and Josh pounded pavement straight for the colonel, the other two toting the cases and setting them just inside the entrance by the wall. Conrad and Weber lingered outside.

"What's going on, Colonel?" Rob asked. "What the hell we doing in the Sunshine State, sir?"

Billings glanced at them both with a frustrated smirk and gritted his teeth. "Follow me," he said.

"Okay," replied Brian.

They all followed the colonel inside the bay, where a few men were hanging out by a folding table at the other end. The rest of the building was empty but for a Chevy Tahoe and a black, twin-engine plane. The team continued to the table and dropped their bags to the floor in a stack. Four unknown men, also in civilian clothes, stood by on the other side.

"What's this?" Rob asked.

"Hey there, Colonel," one of the strangers said.

Colonel Billings approached the table. "Hi, boys," he replied. He faced Rob and Brian. "These guys are from SOG," the colonel added. "They have some information to share with us."

SOG, or special operations group, was a clandestine unit from the Special Activities Center of the CIA. They were a small team consisting of less than a hundred operators and recruited mainly from special-mission units of the US military.

"Share, you say?" Brian asked bitterly. "The Agency ain't known for sharing, Colonel. Everybody knows that."

The CIA didn't have the best reputation among the special operations and special forces community. And the team was reluctant to work with them. But they didn't have a choice.

"Yeah, well," Billings continued, "that's what they're here for. This came straight from the president's mouth, so you all might as well get used to it."

One man among them addressed the team.

"Hi, guys," he said. "Name's Chris, but they call me Chief."

Chris "Chief" Trotter was the senior CIA officer of the

team. He was formerly of SEAL Team Six, DEVGRU, and understood Brian's concern.

"Look," he added. "I don't know who from the Agency you've worked with in the past, but you haven't been with my team. I run a tight ship. Every damn one of us are former special ops or special forces. We know very well what it's like to be you, believe me. So give us a chance, huh?"

Rob stepped out in front. "Okay then, Chief," he replied. "Can we get down to what we're doing here?"

Colonel Billings glanced across the table at Conrad and Weber. "You two can catch the next flight back to Virginia," he said. "We won't need you on this particular op. Go check in. I have you on a flight leaving in an hour."

The pair was obviously frustrated. In their eyes, the CIA wasn't to be trusted. But orders were orders. They had to comply.

"Yes, sir," Conrad replied. "If you need us in the future, just ask."

"Will do," replied the colonel.

Conrad and his man snatched up their gear and headed outside through the open door.

"As for the rest of you," the colonel added. "You get another shot."

"Come again, Colonel," said Brian.

Chris answered instead. "The Agency has tracked our captive officer to a town in Syria, not far from the Lebanese border. That man spent a lot of time studying al-Bashir's men and collecting intel on their activity and movements before he was captured. His whole team had a wealth of knowledge after being on the ground for weeks at a time. They even had a safe house down the street from his compound, where they observed them around the clock. But as you know, he's the only one still alive. If they kill him, all that information dies with him."

Rob kept his cool, but one thing stood out to him.

"Doesn't the Agency usually cut the cord if you're caught?" he asked. "That's been my understanding."

One of Chris's men stepped forward. "Under certain circumstances," he replied. "In this case, we need to get him out. This is a SAR mission, off the books."

SAR stood for search and rescue.

"He never had a chance to report in," the man added, "and we need to know what he knows. That's how we stop these terrorist fucks. If we find him, maybe we'll find al-Bashir, too, provided he doesn't find out we're coming."

"And you are?" Brian asked.

"Name's Tony," he replied. "My nickname is Flash."

Tony "Flash" Isdell was a former Recon Marine and second in charge. The other two behind him, both former Rangers, remained relatively quiet.

"Well," Rob replied, "perhaps we don't have a choice here, but you guys better share every piece of intel you have with us, got it? If we're risking our men to go in and get him out, it's the least you could do."

"Understood," said Tony.

"Also," Rob said to the colonel, "we need to go after their financing. Being a terrorist mastermind comes at a cost. If we stop the flow of money, we could cripple their operations. This mission is twofold. We stop the attacks, but we also hit 'em where it hurts."

Chris answered instead. "You're right," he replied. "All we need is intel on their couriers to point us in the right direction."

Suddenly, they heard vehicles approaching. Rob backed up and gazed out across the airfield toward the runway. At the end of the tarmac sat a blue and white plane, a VC-25. It was the president's transport, Air Force One. A four-vehicle convoy of dark Suburbans pulled up in front of the hangar, blocking the view. Men in suits with guns on their hips climbed out of each vehicle. One made his way to the rear of one of the vehicles and opened the door.

President Tyler stepped out and readjusted his suit coat and tie. He made his way around the SUV toward the hangar, agents surrounding him on all sides.

"Well, this just got more interesting," Rob said.

The president entered the building, and his Secret Service agents waited near the doorway.

"Commander-in-Chief on deck, attention!" said Brian.

"Relax, you guys," President Tyler said, walking briskly across the hard floor.

It wasn't unheard of for a US president to address the team personally. He was the one who approved their missions.

"Colonel Billings," he added as he came near. "How are you and your men doing?"

The colonel gripped his hand firmly. But he was concerned for the president's well-being.

"Mister President," he said. "Shouldn't you be locked down somewhere, sir? This is a valid threat."

The president shrugged him off. "I'm a fighter pilot, Mike," he replied. "I don't scare easily. Besides, I'll be operating mostly from the air. I just wanted to stop by and talk to your boys."

"Well, Mister President," Billings said, "we all appreciate that. I think I speak for everyone when I say they are ready to kick some ass, especially after the recent attacks. They just need the green light."

Everyone gave the president their undivided attention, gathering around the table.

"Well, they have it," he replied. "Understand something. This isn't just a man you are rescuing. If we are right, it could be an intelligence gold mine. The building they've got him in is a fortified building in the Syrian desert, where guards work around the clock. It appears much more important than a holding facility of some kind. The SOG guys here have all the details."

The president certainly had their attention now.

"We believe," the president added, "this particular building is their Syrian headquarters."

President Tyler glanced at Colonel Billings. "I'm sorry," he said. "You already go over this? I didn't mean to take over your briefing."

"No, Mister President," the colonel replied with a hand out. "I was gettin' there. It's quite all right, sir."

"Okay," President Tyler said. "Now, I don't want you guys to feel like you're abandoning your responsibilities here by going back. We will have another team rotate in and take over where you left off. The sad reality is that we have very little intel to go on. Anyone we know who might've known something is dead. So we need to go to the source. This team has more experience in that part of the Arab world. It's unfortunate but necessary. Questions?"

Rob spoke up. "Mister President," he said. "If we see al-Bashir?"

"If you do run across him," President Tyler replied, "it's kill or capture. If he's shooting at you, dust his ass. But if you can get your hands on him, do so. Those are your options."

Rob nodded once. "Copy that, Mister President," he replied.

"All right," President Tyler continued. "I've got to run, gentlemen." He whistled to signal his Secret Service guards. "Colonel, I'll leave you to it. Remember, nobody fucks with America and gets away with it."

"Yes, Mister President," Billings replied as the president took off toward his men.

Chris took a tablet from a nearby table and laid it out in front of them. He brought up the map and zoomed in on a black *X.*

"All right, guys," he said. "This is a two-day-old image of the target in Al-Zabadani, Syria, courtesy of our analysts at Langley. It's just under fifteen kilometers from the Lebanese border. We'll be in a C-130 over the Mediterranean from RAF Akrotiri, Cyprus. From there, we'll cross over Lebanon and, once in Syria, we'll conduct a HALO jump a few kilometers from the compound."

HALO stood for high altitude, low opening. This type of jump not only allowed jumpers to stay undetected by jumping high and opening parachutes low to the ground, but it also allowed planes to fly above the range of surface-to-air missiles.

Colonel Billings jumped in. "You'll hike in to the compound from there," he said. "Delta, you are the assault team. The rest of you guys back them up and collect any intel you find. If you find al-Bashir, snatch him."

"Roger that, Colonel," replied Brian.

"In case you do get him," Billings continued, "you will be diverted to an Agency black site. If not, well, you know the rest. Chris?"

Chris reached for the tablet. He zoomed in on the building. "This compound is well guarded," he said. "There are quite a few stationary guard posts, roving patrols, vehicles, and some light armor."

He pointed to different spots on the property. "These positions need to be taken care of before we rush in," Chris added. "My team will be positioned here, on the back side of the compound. We'll need to scale the wall to get in. You Delta guys will enter from the front, and we'll move on you. We'll need a sniper team to cover us and to take out the guards. Once in, we blitzkrieg their asses and locate Smith. This op is completely off the books. Any questions?"

Rob glanced at the satellite image. "What's our exfil?" he asked.

"A pair of our pilots flying Blackhawks at low altitude, in and out. Anything else?"

Nobody spoke up.

"Okay, ladies," said the colonel. "We have cots set up in back so you can get some rack time. Be ready to leave by zero nine tomorrow morning."

TWENTY-SIX

Over The Mediterranean Sea

The C-17 cargo plane sailed through the clouds as Rob waited with his team in a single row of seating. The aircraft hit a little turbulence during the last leg when it climbed up to jump altitude. The plane flattened, reaching a height of twenty-eight-thousand feet.

SOG personnel sat together on the other side, facing the Delta team. Oxygen masks and parachute packs on, they all waited quietly for the plane to reach the drop zone. Rob hunkered down at the end, reading a book while listening to radio chatter through his electronic headset.

The aircraft had just passed over Beirut, heading toward the Syrian border. It didn't take long to reach Lebanese airspace from RAF Akrotiri on the island of Cyprus. They'd conducted buddy checks prior to takeoff, but they'd do one more just to be safe. Rob rose to inspect Brian's parachute rig while Jamal checked his.

The men reached down and inspected each other's rucks, held on by straps at waist level. Each jump without fail, they'd scrutinize one another's gear numerous times before ever leaving the aircraft.

"You're good to go!" Jamal said into his mic.

Rob tipped his head. "You too!" he yelled to Brian, smacking him on the back.

The rest of the team finished up, and Rob took his seat back with his ruck suspended over his knees. He adjusted his black helmet with night-vision goggles mounted. Rob tightened his black tactical vest and checked his wrist to ensure his altimeter was firmly attached. Peering back through the porthole and into the clear sky, he glanced downward at the bright, glistening moonlight on rippling waves.

All personnel waited in complete quiet for a while, preparing mentally for what was to come. Then a call from the pilot over the headset speakers broke the silence.

"Five minutes," the pilot said.

Brian held five fingers up high. "Roger that," he said, bouncing to his feet.

Rob took a Ziplock baggie and placed his book inside it. Sealing it tight, he reached down and stuffed the book into an outside pocket of his ruck. He snapped the button down and yanked the strap tightly over his pack.

Everyone formed a line facing the rear of the aircraft. The jump master pressed a button, and the ramp thrust open and lowered itself with a ringing hum. Brian and Rob were the last of their team in line, followed by the SOG team. As the raging wind howled outside, Brian looked back at his buddy one last time before they jumped.

"Can't get enough of this!" he shouted, he and Rob bumping fists.

"You know it, man!" Rob replied.

Brian faced the front, and the light by the door turned yellow.

"One minute!" shouted the jump master.

They'd crossed into Syria a few minutes earlier. The area they were jumping into was out in the middle of the desert, far from any town or villages. As he waited the final few seconds, Rob just hoped they didn't overshoot the landing zone coordinates. A night jump dressed in all black should help conceal them well enough.

Rob stared at the light as it went from yellow to green. The jump master shouted to them in quick succession. "Go, go, go!" he yelled.

At two-second intervals between jumpers, they took off and jumped feet first into the black void. Rob sailed down and began rocketing headfirst through the sky at terminal velocity. Catching the powerful wind with his body, he soared downward, his arms and legs slightly bent and straight out. Seeing lights below dotting the landscape here and there, he glanced at his altimeter.

Eighteen thousand feet.

Gliding through the air, Rob pressed his arms together and ducked his head. Falling a few thousand feet in seconds, he spread his limbs and caught the gust again. He checked his wrist a second time.

Ten thousand feet.

Beneath him, Rob could just make out the white speck of the first parachute opening, then the second. This time his eyes were glued to the altimeter as it counted down.

Six thousand, five thousand, four thousand…

At the three-thousand mark, Rob yanked his rip cord. The chute deployed and carried him upward as the air collided with the canopy. It eased up and began carrying him back down slowly toward the desert below. Not able to accurately see the surface beneath his feet, Rob had to rely on his altimeter. On his other wrist, a GPS marked the landing zone. He steered himself in that direction.

The ground came up fast, and Rob got set to land. His feet touched the desert floor, and he buckled and rolled to the right. Catching himself with his hands, he popped up as the parachute fell around him. Rob removed the rig from his back, balled up the parachute, and stuffed it into the pack. He released his ruck to the ground, taking a knee as he opened the top flap to retrieve one of two rifles. In two pieces, he inserted the takedown pin on the weapon and pressed it into place.

Gripping the M4, Rob spotted Brian almost fifty feet away and took off toward him. He made it to his team leader's side as he radioed in.

"This is Golf-Three-Six," Brian said. "We're Oscar, Tango, Mike. I repeat Oscar, Tango, Mike, how copy?"

Oscar, Tango, Mike was the military acronym for on-the-move.

"Copy that, Three-Six," the voice said. "We're tracking you."

The others made their way to them through the dark night. They dropped their parachute packs and masks to the dirt, piling palm tree leaves on top to conceal them. The men knelt in the dirt while Brian pulled up the target building on his handheld GPS.

"All right, guys," he said. "We have just over a four-kilometer hike to go. Rob, you and Colin are on overwatch outside the walls. Intel on the area says there should be some abandoned buildings here to choose from."

Brian pointed his tiny, red-lensed flashlight at the map. "It's about four hundred meters to the west," he added. "Should give you a clear view of both sides."

Rob studied the satellite image. "Roger that, boss," he said.

"This moonlight should give us just enough light to navigate," Brian continued.

They had their NVGs (night-vision goggles) fixed to their helmets in case.

"Sierra, you guys know your mission."

Sierra was the code chosen for the SOG team.

"We'll get your man back. Just do your thing, back us up if needed. Roger?"

"Yep," Chris replied, M4 at his side. "Copy that, man."

Brian checked his watch.

2315.

He stood up and took point. Rob and the rest moved up behind him.

"All right," said Brian. "No time to waste. Let's move out."

A meter between them, the group began hoofing it across the rocky, desert plain covered with the occasional patch of greenery. They were headed toward a row of high hills that towered over one side of the enemy compound.

Syrian daytime temperatures could easily reach over one hundred degrees Fahrenheit. At night, it could hover around seventy. With high humidity, though, it seemed even hotter. Sweat dripping from his head, Rob wiped his forehead with the brown shemagh around his neck. The group continued moving at close to jogging speed, making good time toward their destination.

Minutes went by as they marched through the darkness. The land was mostly flat with a hill here and there. As they got closer to their objective, however, palm trees and desert brush became more frequent.

They circled a hill and climbed up loose sand and gravel, and came to a two-lane road they had to cross. While the group looked both ways, headlights suddenly appeared from the east, moving fast.

"Vehicle inbound," Rob said.

Everyone hit the ground and buried their heads in the dirt. The white, four-door sedan came around the bend, a beam of light glaring over the men, the car passing by within meters. They waited for it to move out of sight.

Rob peeked over the mound. "All right," he said. "I think we're clear."

The men got up and dusted the dirt off their black clothing. Brian gave the gesture to move, and one by one, they traversed across the blacktop toward a group of palm trees on the other side. Brian checked the GPS again to get their bearings. Rob glanced over his shoulder. Just over a kilometer to go.

Brian signaled them to continue, and they followed him low among a row of palms. In the distance to the north, they spotted an area lit up among a row of houses. A couple Syrian men were perched outside on plastic chairs, holding what appeared to be AKs. Brian retrieved his binoculars from a pouch on his black vest and peered through.

Men with rifles were nothing new in that part of the world, but these men appeared to be guarding something. From that distance in the dark, there was no way the Syrians could've seen them. One of them got up, flicking his cigarette to the ground as he began pacing across the yard.

"Think they're with the target's network?" Rob asked.

"Could be," Brian replied. "Or he could be out for a stroll. Who the hell knows? You know it's hard to tell in this fucking place. Let's just stay out of sight. We'll stir the hornets' nest when we have to."

"Copy that, boss," replied Rob.

They pressed on, silent as cats on the hunt, making their way closer to the target coordinates. The further they went, the greener it became as they closed in on the city. They could see residential lights from a vantage point on a small hill. They took cover next to a row of bushes.

"All right," Brian said, taking a knee. "There's the compound. Sierra, you guys wait in this wooded area for the go-ahead. When I give the signal, head inside and help us clear the place. Then sweep for intel while we look for your boy."

"Copy," replied Chris.

"Rob," Brian added. "You and Colin get into position here on this hill." Brian pointed to an area on the map. "The rest of us will get into position in this field just outside the compound and wait for Rob's go-ahead. Rob, you two are our eyes. We move on you, agreed?"

"Thought you'd never ask," Rob replied.

TWENTY-SEVEN

Al-Zabadani, Syria

Rob glared through the night vision mounted to his M2010 enhanced sniper rifle while it rested on top of his assault pack, suppressor attached. As he and his spotter lay on the grassy, rocky hillside, Rob trained the scope over the wall of the enemy compound.

By his side, Colin had his sniper rifle set next to him as backup. His spotting scope lens pressed to his eyes, he did a quick calculation in his head.

"Four hundred fifty meters to the gate entrance," Colin said. "Wind from one o'clock, ten miles per hour."

Colin regarded the tall grass and palm leaves swaying gently in the breeze. "A quarter value," he added.

A shot from that distance was like child's play to Rob. "Got it," he replied, dialing his windage knob.

Rob had a small night-vision optic attached in front of his Leupold Mark V scope, effectively converting it to night vision. He steadied the rifle and spotted the team trudging low through the waist-high grass.

"This is Three-Six," Brian said over the radio as they stopped. "We're in position."

"Roger," replied Rob. "I see you."

Rob inched the glass across a dirt drive toward a cluster of palms in a field. He saw the SOG team hug the sand-colored wall and hunker down.

"Sierra-Six, we're in position, over," said Chris.

"Copy that," Rob affirmed.

In addition to marksmanship, snipers were also trained experts in observation and reconnaissance, surveillance, and target acquisition. That was exactly what they were going to do. With his gloved hand on the pistol grip, Rob followed the dirt road from a mile out, all the way to the compound gate. Around the perimeter, he noticed the absence of guard towers, likely so they wouldn't draw unwanted attention.

To the right, Rob spotted pieces of farm equipment not far from the team and zoomed in to get a better look.

"Three-Six," he said to Brian. "There are a tractor and plow about a hundred meters north of you. Might be better cover than being in the open in case any lights come your way."

"Yeah, roger that," replied Brian. "We'll check it out."

Rob observed the three men crawl toward the tractor and press themselves against the large tire. Suddenly, Rob caught movement to the left. He pivoted the scope toward the drive and saw a lone figure walking down the path, clutching an AK47. A beam of light appeared as the man waved a flashlight toward the ground in front of him.

"All elements, hold tight and stay quiet," Rob said. "I've got a rover over here between you."

The radio was silent as Rob followed the man. All of a sudden, he stepped off the path and out into the grass.

"Three-Six," Rob added. "He's moving in your direction from the road, two hundred meters out. Going to drop him before he gets too close."

Brian didn't want to alert the enemy guard, so he didn't respond. Rob moved the glass upward to double-check that nobody was around to witness. No one else was in the vicinity. Rob lowered his rifle quickly and followed the man through the grass, reticle directed at his upper torso as he moved. Rob took a deep breath through his nose and let it out through his mouth.

"Four hundred meters and closing," Colin said, peering through his spotting scope. "Wind, no change."

At that distance, dialing his scope wouldn't be necessary. Rob led the target slightly to the right, aiming for the side of his rib cage. He breathed in, let out some air, and held it. The tip of his finger felt the cold metal trigger as he squeezed. Red mist sprayed out from the enemy's side, and the force of the suppressed shot sent him hurtling to the side. His body landed motionless on the ground.

"Three-Six," Rob said. "Tango down."

"Good copy," Brian replied.

Rob and Colin watched Brian and Jamal creep toward the middle of the field. They saw Brian bend down, seize the AK, and toss the flashlight. He and Jamal both gripped the dead body by the feet and dragged it further away from the road. Stopping on the edge of flat ground, they released him. Jamal used his boot to roll the body down an embankment toward a drainage ditch. They hurried back to their position.

"We're good to go," Brian said.

"Roger that, Three-Six," replied Rob. "Stand by."

By now, Rob and his spotter had already moved on, examining the compound and its surroundings. Four buildings made up the complex, three of the same small size and one much larger structure in the middle. A single overhead bulb lit up the yard in front.

"Sierra-One," Rob said into the mic. "Any idea which building the package is in, over?"

He waited for a response.

"Negative, Three-Five," Chris replied. "We tracked him here and haven't seen a sign of him since."

"Copy that," Rob said.

He and Colin scanned the complex. There were no vehicles, guards, or signs of any activity behind its walls.

"Strange," Rob said, removing his eye from the scope. "The place looks deserted."

They scanned outside the walls and down the hill on both sides and saw nothing. But when Rob backed away again to relieve his eye, headlights appeared from down the way. Rob took his binoculars from his vest. He scanned south.

"We've got a vehicle here," he said. "Looks like a black Mercedes G-Class, and it's headed right for the gate."

Brian radioed back when the luxury car stopped in front of the entrance. "Got 'em," he whispered. "Let's see what they're up to."

"Copy," replied Rob.

He set the binoculars down, and through his rifle scope, he viewed the vehicle's lights blink twice. The gate opened, and the car proceeded inside. It stopped just shy of the largest structure. Three men hopped from the vehicle, and one opened the door for a fourth in the backseat. Rob zoomed in on him as he climbed out with the help of his host. In a white jubbah, a white taqiyah cap, and the usual beard, he seemed to command their respect.

"Three-Five," Brian said. "What're you seeing?"

Rob quickly reached into a large outside pocket of his pack and recovered his MX50 tactical tablet. He pressed the screen and turned it to the side.

"They've stopped," Rob replied. "I've got my eye on the probable leader of the group. Let's wait it out."

The front door of the building came open. A man with a brown beard, dressed in a robe and Muslim prayer cap, approached the car. He exchanged greetings with the other and kissed each of his cheeks. The men stood by the car, talking for a time. After a few minutes had passed, the man with the prayer cap escorted the other toward the door, walking just in front of him.

Rob zoomed in and held the tablet in place. The man turned to look at his guards and made a hand gesture toward them. As he spun around, Rob snapped a headshot.

"Bingo," he said.

Rob tapped a few times on the screen and pressed send. "Sierra-One," he said. "Just sent you a mugshot, over."

As he awaited a reply, the two men entered the building while the guards remained outside watching the front.

"Roger, just got it," replied Chris. "Hold one."

While the SOG team leader inspected the high-resolution photo, Rob radioed his boss. "Three-Six," he said. "They've entered the building. Three guards posted outside, please advise, over."

The whole mission couldn't be planned, so they would make decisions on the fly.

"Use your best judgment, Three-Five," Brian replied. "We've got to get inside that building."

"Roger," Rob said, observing the guards dispersing in two directions.

Two men took a stroll toward the right of the yard, and one wandered to the left. The lone gunman walked around the left side of the building toward the rear. Rob looked back at the other two. The pair of men stopped by the smaller structure on the right, chatting up one another and leaning back against the wall. Both had AKS-74Us strapped over their robes.

Rob lightly kicked the side of Colin's leg with his boot.

"Need you on the gun on this one," he said. "Don't want to alert them to our presence just yet."

Colin gripped his rifle's bolt knob, pulled the bolt back, and drove it forward again. He flicked the scope's dust cover open and snugged the butt into his shoulder, finger crossing the trigger guard. Colin inched the scope right until he had a good view of the target.

"All right," Rob said. "You get the one closer on the right, I got the other guy. Okay, on three."

Both men cycled through their breathing. Settling his crosshairs on his target's chest, Rob counted down.

"Here we go," he added. "Three... two... one..."

Within a fraction of a second from one another, both men squeezed their triggers and sent two high-powered suppressed rounds toward the enemy guards. Rob's target was hit just above the sternum, knocking him straight back, blood splashing from his chest. The other caught a bullet a little more right of center, causing him to spin to the side and drop like concrete to the dirt.

"Good kill, good kill," continued Rob. "Three-Six, two guards down, one to go."

Rob moved the scope left, but before he could get a bead on the third target, a man exited through the front door.

"Shit," Rob said. "He's going to see the others, damn it."

Then he had an idea. Rob brought the scope higher and aimed for the pole light just inside the black metal gate.

"What's your status, Three-Five?" Brian asked.

Rob pinched the mic button. "Stand by," replied Rob. "We got more company."

Rob squeezed the trigger and let a round go. The bullet pierced the yellow bulb, leaving shards of glass falling to the ground below. Hearing the glass bust, the guard went to investigate. They watched the man, who appeared confused as he shone a tiny flashlight overhead. The man plucked a small handheld radio from his pocket and brought it toward his mouth.

"Don't think he suspects anything," Rob said. "Lights bust sometimes, right?"

Rob caressed his rifle trigger with the tip of his index finger. He breathed and watched the rise and fall of the reticle through the glass. At center mass of the enemy guard's body, Rob squeezed. The force of the large bullet knocked the enemy back, his knees buckling, and he dropped onto his back. A pool of blood stained the dirt from the exit wound in his back.

"He's down," said Rob. "Just one guard left that we can see."

But as Rob trained his scope on the other guard, he vanished behind the building.

"Damn," Rob cursed. "We just lost visual on him."

Both he and Colin checked the area, waiting for the enemy fighter to reemerge. Suddenly, Rob picked up the sound of rustling in the brush behind them. Glancing back slowly, he saw a man approach, standing over them and pointing his AK in their direction.

"Don't move," the man said in Arabic.

"Shit," Colin said, lying motionless while glancing left. He slowly keyed his mic. "Three-Six," he said. "We've been spotted, over."

The enemy crept forward and moved the barrel of the AK47 closer to Rob's head.

"Give me a SITREP," Brian replied. "Three-Four, SITREP, over."

The enemy fighter stepped forward and pressed the rifle barrel to Rob's head. In a quick, reflexive action, Rob popped up while grabbing the barrel and forcing it to the side. The rifle went off, echoing through the night air as the bullet kicked up dirt near the road.

Rob managed to wrestle the weapon away, kicking the man in the stomach and belting him in the face with the butt of the rifle. He fell to the ground, and Rob continued whopping him with it until he was no longer moving. Blood poured from his nose and his cracked skull. Rob tossed the AK into the bushes.

"Three-Five," Brian said. "Where'd that come from?"

Rob took a quick breath. "Three-Six," he replied. "One tango down here, but we're compromised. Somebody had to have heard that shot. Get ready for contact, over."

Rob lay back down and gripped his weapon again, watching the team through the scope. He noticed them repositioning for incoming enemy fire.

"Fuck," Brian said. "Copy that."

Enemy fighters began flooding out of the structure, making a dash for the Mercedes. They jumped inside before Rob had a chance to fire. The vehicle reversed quickly, spinning around and heading for the gate. Colin, his finger on the trigger, prepared to shoot. Rob reached out and grasped him by the shoulder.

"No," he said. "Don't bother. The vehicle is armored."

The Mercedes broke through the gate, knocking it off the hinge. It flipped over the vehicle's roof and slammed onto the ground behind it. The Delta and SOG teams began firing at the car from their position in the field just outside the wall. Their bullets just pinged off the armor. Rob followed the car in his scope as it sped away.

He aimed for the rear tire, leading it a few mils up and to the left. The vehicle had almost made it to a curve in the road when Rob fired. The rear tire popped, and the Mercedes began to fishtail. The driver tried to regain control, and the car slid to the side, hit the embankment, and flipped sideways, rolling down the steep decline.

"Three-Six," Rob said into his headset mic as they rushed to break down their equipment. "Enemy vehicle down, moving to intercept, over."

"Roger," replied Brian. "We're moving to clear the building. RV here when you're done."

"Will do," replied Rob.

The two men secured their weapons and packs and readied to move.

"Hurry," Rob said while clutching his M4 and shouldering his pack. "We need to get down there, now."

TWENTY-EIGHT

By The Road
0150 hours

Smoke emanated from the bottom of the ravine. Rob and his spotter scampered across the dirt roadway toward the wrecked vehicle. Most of the occupants of the Mercedes had been killed on impact when they plummeted thirty feet over the edge.

The vehicle, now resting on its roof, looked as if it would explode any moment. The hood had been ripped off, and sparks shot out inches from the leaking fuel line. Rob and Colin slid down the grassy hillside just south of the hilltop and landed on rocky ground at the bottom. As they pushed themselves up, a man, clearly in pain, crawled from the backseat. Bruised and bloody, he collapsed just outside of where the door used to be, his face to the ground.

"Come on, partner," Rob said to Colin.

They took off toward the injured man. They stopped and stood over him, and Rob nudged the side of his body with the inside of his boot. Noticing the shallow rise and fall of his back, they could tell he was still breathing.

"He's still alive," said Rob.

Rob stooped down and gripped the man by his bloody robe. He reached for his side and rolled him over, face up. Blood dripped from a gash just above his forehead and from his nostrils.

Rob took a peek into the overturned vehicle. "The package isn't here," he said.

He grabbed the injured man by the arm. "Let's get him up," Rob added. "We need to get away before this thing blows."

They both reached down and yanked the man to his feet. Holding him still, Rob recovered a pair of zip cuffs from his back pocket and fastened them around his wrists.

"Hold him up," said Rob.

Arms under his, the duo guided the man away from the steep bank.

"Three-Six," Rob said into the radio. "It's Three-Five. Three tangos down, one in custody. What's your status there, over?"

Rob waited for a response as they made their way up a path cut in the dirt.

"Preparing to breach," Brian whispered. "Leave Three-Four to watch the entrance and RV with us, over."

"Copy," Rob replied.

He and Colin made it to the road and dragged their captive past the busted entry gate. An explosion suddenly rocked the hillside hundreds of meters behind them.

"Damn it," Rob said. "That's going to draw attention."

Fire erupted high above the road in a billowing cloud of black smoke. The bitter stench of burning fuel filled the air.

"Better hurry, Three-Six," Rob added, "before somebody shows up to see what the hell's going on."

Rob left Colin to guard the captive and their exit and made his way to the team. He stacked behind the other men, night vision on while the SOG team waited along the wall on the other side of the door. Brian counted down with three fingers. He brought his right leg back and kicked the door in, slamming it against the wall, and they entered the building. The teams moved around the wall toward the corridor opposite the front door. It was dark and bare inside, not one piece of furniture anywhere.

"Clear," Brian said, peeking around the corner of the wall.

They waited for a minute, listening for any slight noise. Brian glanced around the wall again, and suddenly, a volley of machine-gun fire broke out from the shadows, pounding holes in the wall and the floor around them.

"Shit," Rob said, planting himself against the wall. "Take cover!"

They stacked in a single-file line, low against the wall. Rob plucked an M67 frag grenade from a pouch on his vest. He crawled on his knees to the front of the pack. Yanking the pin out with his teeth, he brought his arm back and tossed it underhanded toward the gunner's position.

"Frag out!" he yelled.

Rob dove back into position. The concussion from the blast rattled the house. Smoke and fire engulfed the interior as it took out the machine gun position and wiped out the surrounding walls. Everything went silent, and they waited for the smoke to mostly dissipate.

Colin made a radio transmission. "Three-Six," he said. "A truck full of men just found the crash. Looks like they're moving to investigate, over."

"Copy," replied Brian. "Maintain position and keep an eye on them. Let us know if they get close."

"I'm on it," Colin said.

Brian signaled the team to proceed, and they inched their

way down both sides of the corridor. Three rooms, one on the right and two to the left, were still intact. They moved down gradually, and heard a door slowly creak open. AK fire popped from the second door on the left. The men ducked into the room on the right, noticing it was clear, and huddled against the wall. AK bullets zoomed past them, plunking holes in the dusty walls.

Rob moved to the other side of the door as the firing continued. He spun around and caught a bullet in the left shoulder.

"Damn it!" he said, making it to the other side of the door. "I'm hit. Fuck, that stings!" Rob checked the spot with his hand.

"You okay?" Chris asked from behind.

The bullet only grazed him, leaving a bloody gash on his shoulder. Small droplets of blood coated his sleeve around the wound.

"Yeah, yeah, I'm good!" Rob replied. "Just a flesh wound. I'll live."

Rob waited for the shooter to reload. When he heard the magazine drop, he darted across the hall into the other room. The two rooms were connected by another door. Holding his hurt shoulder, Rob moved to the wall by the adjoining door. The enemy opened fire again, and Rob yanked his knife from the sheath on his leg.

The enemy fighter fired at the team, and Rob got ready. Kicking the door open, he pressed toward the man, grabbing his AK barrel as the enemy caught sight of him. Shoving him against the wall, Rob tore the weapon from his hand, and the man gripped his forearm. The rifle fell to the ground with a clink while Rob thrust the knife blade into the side of the enemy's neck.

The Arab man's strength suddenly drained from his body. Blood poured down from his carotid artery when Rob jerked the knife back out. He released his grip. Clutching his neck with both hands, the man dropped straight down to his knees as he bled out. Rob stepped back, and the enemy fighter fell forward and smashed his head on the tile floor. His body went limp. Rob wiped the bloody knife on the dead fighter's pants and sheathed it.

"He's done," he said. "All clear."

"Roger," replied Brian.

The teams hurried across and joined Rob in the other room. They moved to the other door. Standing in front, Brian cracked it and glanced out. Jamal noticed something peculiar.

"You feel that?" he asked.

"What?" Rob replied. "What is it?"

He moved a little closer.

"Wait," he added. "Yeah, I feel it now. Cold air."

Brian booted the door open hard. They advanced around the room to clear it, but it was empty. Rob glanced down, spotting a cigarette butt still smoking on the floor.

"What the hell?" Rob asked. "Something ain't right."

"I know the package is here somewhere," said Chris. "We followed them all the way here."

The flow of cool air became stronger as they'd entered the room. A large area rug covered the majority of the floor, with a long wooden table and chairs over it. They were puzzled at the emptiness of the place. They'd expected a larger enemy force.

"This is no coincidence," said Rob. "Al-Bashir is smart. Otherwise, he wouldn't still be alive. No, there's a reason nobody is here."

He and the others glanced around the room. But as Rob gazed to the floor, he had a thought.

"I wonder…" he said as he started moving chairs away from the table.

Rob gripped the end of the table with both hands. "Help me with this," he replied.

The men all took the heavy table in their hands and slid it across the room. Rob snatched the dark rug and drew it away. Tossing it aside, it unveiled a hidden door in the floor underneath.

"Well, look at that," said Rob.

Rob bent down and unsecured the metal latch. He yanked it open.

"Holy shit," he added. "There's a tunnel down here."

Inside was dark, and they couldn't see the bottom. A ladder on the side led straight down. Rob swiped a chem light from his vest and snapped it. He flung it into the hole, took his flashlight, and climbed down.

"Be careful," said Brian. "You don't know what's down there."

Rob descended toward the bottom. His boots touched the dirt below, and he brought his carbine rifle up. He couldn't see much inside, but he noticed a dim, green light coming from the other end. Rob edged his way on, a sudden cool washing over his face. He made it halfway down and recognized the outline of a chair.

Getting closer, Rob realized the area was covered with remnants of torture. Blood coated the walls of the cave. The chair had scratch marks and other signs of a struggle. And he noticed drag marks leading away from the site.

"Three-Six," Rob said over the radio. "I think I found where they were keeping him."

The low light came from a chem light on the ground to the right side of the dugout. Rob used his flashlight to have a look around. He glanced behind the chair and saw another cigarette butt on the ground, still burning. He felt the cooler air circulating from beyond. Rob followed the drag marks with his light, revealing a section of the tunnel that led further beyond.

"Three-Six," he continued. "Looks like an escape tunnel. Don't know where it goes, but it seems we just missed 'em. The guards above must've been meant to slow us down. It explains how they vanished. They can't be far away."

Rob stepped toward the light and saw several sets of footprints. Suddenly, Colin called them over the radio.

"Three-Six," he said. "These bastards have pulled the dead out and are now headed our way. Need assistance, now."

"Roger, Three-Four," replied Brian. "Solid copy. Sierra team is en route to you."

In the tunnel, Rob snaked his way forward. "Three-Six," he said. "It's all clear down here."

"Copy, Three-Five."

Rob could hear the rest of the Delta team make their way down the ladder behind him. As the last man touched down, they moved toward him.

"Careful," Rob said, following the tracks. "I have no idea what's up here."

They lurked through the underground space a couple hundred meters, and suddenly they hit an uphill climb. Glaring upward through the tunnel, they could see stars in a partly cloudy sky. They climbed up and out and began looking around. With his night vision, Rob could barely see a group of men carrying someone to a waiting truck in the distance.

"Shit, there. I think I see 'em."

Before they could take off, gunfire came from further back.

"Three-Four," Rob said. "We found an exit. Looks like the enemy is trying to get away. You guys good back there?"

Through the speakers, the team could hear the unmistakable ruckus of rifle fire.

"Give me a sec!" Colin shouted. "Kind of busy right now!"

What was supposed to be a covert operation had turned into anything but as they waited for the gunfire to fade. Now on the other side of the compound wall, Rob stopped a second to get a look behind them. The orange glow of rifle muzzles radiated from the front of the structure. Rob turned around as the truck ahead began to move. They dashed for it.

"Shit," he said. "We'll never catch up!"

They heard an explosion followed by more firing from behind. Suddenly, the shooting ceased. They ran across the stretch of land as fast as they could go, and the men caught a vehicle coming from behind.

"Get in!" Chris yelled from the passenger seat of the bullet-riddled, white Nissan truck. "Come on!"

They dove over the side and into the bed. Inside, the captive man Colin had been guarding was tied by his wrists. The vehicle sped up again as Rob got his balance. He glanced down at the man on his back, clothing torn and bloody.

"Well, that works, I guess," he said, gripping his rifle. On his knees, he saw bullet holes in the back glass. With the butt of his rifle, he punched through it.

"Hey!" Brian shouted to the driver. "After that truck!"

Colin slammed on the accelerator, and the pickup slid to the side over loose dirt. It jumped a rocky bump in the ground, tossing those in the back into the air like dolls. Slamming against the back of the cab and landing on his M4, Rob hung on by the side of the bed. He took a look out at taillights ahead in the pitch-darkness. Colin swerved out onto a two-lane road and gained traction, advancing on the enemy vehicle.

"Okay, guys," Rob said. "The package should be in that truck. We can't do anything stupid here, all right?"

Colin spotted one of the enemy fighters leaning through the window and aiming something at them.

"Shit, RPG!" he yelled, white smoke trailing through the air.

He swerved left abruptly, the RPG barely missing the truck and exploding on the road behind it. Those in the back held on tight, and Colin jerked the wheel back to the right. Enemy AK fire erupted from the backseat of the enemy vehicle, shattering the front glass.

"Keep it steady, man!" Rob shouted to Colin.

Brian kicked the busted windshield out, and Rob rested his rifle on the roof of the pickup. He held the red dot on the enemy driver.

"Hello, you son of a bitch," he said.

Rob squeezed the trigger once and released. The single bullet tore into the driver's neck and splattered blood over the front windshield like paint. The enemy fighter slumped in the seat, and the vehicle swerved to the left. The passenger tried to get control, grabbing the wheel and attempting to move the body out of the way.

The enemy vehicle strayed across both lanes. It scraped its left side down the metal guardrail and coasted until it struck a light pole head-on. The impact caved in the bumper and radiator and spilled green coolant all over the road.

Colin hit the brake and skidded across the blacktop. Everyone jumped out. As they hurried across the road, two enemy fighters attempted to climb out. One in the front seat stuck his AK barrel through the window. Rob popped him once with his M4, and Chris and Colin went for the other two. Two quick shots, and they were out, their blood coating the worn-out seats and the glass.

Brian checked the backseat between them while Rob and Chris ran up beside him. Arms and legs bound together, the man looked like he'd seen better days. He had a deep laceration on his head and welts from his chest down. It was obvious he'd been beaten.

Chris leaned in. "Hey, brother," he said. "Glad you're still alive. Let's get you the hell out of here, huh?"

Smith could hardly see or speak, peering up with swollen eyes. Rob took his cutters and removed the cuffs. He and Chris clutched his arms and legs and slid him out. They toted him to the vehicle. Sitting him upright in the backseat, they climbed in beside him. Colin took the wheel again, and the others hopped in where they could. From the bed of the truck, they heard Brian call for their ride out of there.

"Angel-One-One," he said. "This is Golf-Three-Six, requesting exfil, how copy?"

Seconds later, the pilot responded. "Good copy, Golf-Three-Six," he replied, rotors whirring in the background. "Be on location in ten mikes. Angel-One-One, out."

Rob pounded the back of the driver's seat.

"Step on it!" he said. "Head to the LZ before more of these assholes show up!"

TWENTY-NINE

RAF Akrotiri, Cyprus

Rob settled on the concrete barrier, checking the bandage over the wound on his shoulder and making sure the tape was tight. He inspected his kit, topping off rifle magazines with ammo they brought with them. With Rob, Brian had been on his SAT phone with the colonel for the past few minutes.

Not far away, CIA Officer Smith had been transported to the UK's Royal Air Force Base clinic. His condition was severe but stable.

After a few hours in the rack and a shower, Rob felt somewhat refreshed. His sleep was spotty at best, though. He took a Styrofoam cup full of his caffeine fix and guzzled it. Rob crumbled the empty cup and tossed it into the trash receptacle a few feet away.

"Sir," he overheard Brian say to the colonel over the phone. "Any news from Bravo team?"

Rob noticed the frustration on Brian's face.

"Oh, I see," Brian replied. "I understand."

He gave Rob a perplexing look.

"Yes, sir," Brian added. "Loud and clear. Yes, Colonel. All right, out here."

Brian hung up the phone and reclined against the large slab of concrete.

"So," Rob said. "What's up?"

"Well," Brian replied, smacking his lips and crossing his arms. "Bravo team has nothing."

Bravo team was the other Delta team that rotated in to take their place Stateside.

"Not a peep since we left," Brian added. "No attacks, no contact, nothing."

Rob sat there, kicking the barricade below him with the heels of his boots. He popped up onto his feet.

"Let's go interview this asshole," he said. "Come on, I'm getting antsy."

"All right," Brian replied, jumping up and grabbed his carbine. "Lead on."

Brian accompanied Rob to a building across the street. It was the base headquarters of the Royal Air Force Police, or RAFP. MI6 also had a presence there. They were especially interested in the interrogation of a foreign enemy of state the American team had brought to their doorstep. After all, London was the first city to be attacked. To the east was a hotbed of terrorist activity, just a short flight over the Mediterranean Sea.

The structure itself was well kept but old. They passed by a towering flagpole, the British flag waving as they made their way up the concrete steps. When they stepped through the glass door, they passed by the supervising agent, Kent Bradford.

"Hey there, gents," he said, meeting them by the entrance. "Your men are in with the prisoner right now."

"They aren't our men," Rob replied. "Those guys are with a different outfit."

Bradford grinned back. "Yes," he said. "CIA? I get it, chaps. Anyway, they are down there with your man. I left a guard by the door."

They slipped by Bradford as he headed for the door.

"Thank you," Brian said.

"Ah, don't mention it," replied Bradford.

He left through the door, and the men made their way toward the stairwell and down to the basement level. MI6 had the entire level to themselves. The team neared the door, and a lone guard stood by, Beretta pistol on his hip. He punched a six-digit code into a panel. The door flung open, and they stepped inside.

The basement was dark and gloomy. Their footsteps seemed to echo through the empty corridor as they made their way to the other side. Much like a regular police interrogation setup, it was connected by a two-way mirror and an observation room.

As they approached a door, Chris and two of his men looked on from the other room as Tony questioned the subject. Rob knocked twice. Chris stretched out to open the door.

"Hey, guys," he said. "Just in time for the show."

They all gathered around, and they could hear Tony speak to the detainee over the speaker system on the wall. A second guard was posted just outside the interrogation room door.

"What were you doing at that compound?" Tony asked him. "We know you're connected to al-Bashir and his network. It would serve you best to speak to us."

The man didn't answer. He just sat with his cuffed wrists in his lap and focused on the table.

"Has he talked yet?" Brian asked.

"Nope," Chris replied, taking a drink from a bottle of water. "But he will. We know more about him than we're letting on. We'll set the trap and let him walk right into it."

"Yeah?" asked Rob. "What do you know so far?"

Chris sat on the table, facing them with his back to the glass.

"Well," he replied, "his name is Muhammed Barakat. He's a Saudi national currently living in Syria—Damascus, to be exact. He's got a wife and two children, girls, ages six and ten. He's a courier and a hawala broker for al-Bashir's network and others."

"You know this how?" Brian asked.

"Smith," Chris replied. "He got tons of intel on them before he was captured. We'll debrief him once he wakes up, but his team got really close. They would've led us to exposing their plans until they were ambushed."

"Interesting," said Rob. "Let me get a crack at him."

Chris pressed the button on the intercom. "Sierra-Two," he said into the receiver. "A word."

Though he'd only just started, Tony got up from the table. He snatched up a stack of documents on the bench and tapped on the door. The guard opened up, and Tony made his way into the next room.

"Take a break, man," said Chris. "Rob here wants a shot at the bastard."

"All right," replied Tony. "If you say so, boss." He gave the documents over to Rob. "This is what we've got on him," Tony said.

Rob flipped through the stack of papers. It was full of intel that was sent back by Smith's agency team. They, and a series of local assets, had trailed the terrorist network across Lebanon, Syria, and Saudi Arabia.

"Yep," he replied. "I can definitely work with this."

Rob took the stack and passed through the doorway. The guard opened up for him, and he ambled toward the bench opposite the detainee. Taking a seat, Rob dropped the pile of documents onto the table.

"Well, Mister Barakat, Muhammed Barakat. You're in quite a pickle now, aren't you?"

The man didn't make eye contact with Rob, still looking toward the table. Rob thumbed through the pages. He recovered a single document from the stack.

"I know your type," he said to Barakat. "You don't care about your own life. Nah, you'd welcome being a martyr to protect the organization, wouldn't you, Muhammed? Especially your boss, Aasim al-Bashir."

Barakat showed no emotion, his eyes fixated on the shiny, metal table. Rob knew he would have to get dirty to get the info they needed. With the document in hand, Rob dropped it in front of Barakat. The man's eyes twitched.

"That's right," he said. "We know where your home is. We know who your family is, your wife and two daughters. We know where they are, right in the middle of a terrorist safe haven. It would be a shame if they got caught in the crossfire. And believe me, we have people watching."

While in custody, Barakat pretended not to understand English. But Rob could tell he understood what he was saying. He pulled out a satellite image of Barakat's house and slid it in front of him.

"Everything you love, everything you know, gone. Your only chance is to work with us. Then, maybe we can arrange something. If you don't, boom."

Rob retrieved images of the bombings in London and New Orleans. He hopped up from the chair and shoved them in Barakat's face.

"Look at this!" Rob screamed, gripping the man's jaw in his free hand. "Look at it! I'm not wasting any more time on you! We know you're his courier. We know you have a hand in the financing. You decide in the next five minutes, or this will be the fate of all you hold dear. And we will force you to watch it all. Your time starts now!"

Rob returned to the door, and the guard yanked it open.

"Damn, he's good," Chris said to the men as Rob joined them in the other room.

"What now?" Colin asked.

Rob stood there, arms folded and observing Barakat through the glass.

"Now," he replied, "we wait."

Barakat showed emotion for the first time. His demeanor suddenly switched. A single tear formed in his eye and trickled slowly down his cheek. He tilted his head and began slamming his forehead against the table. Barakat shook wildly in his seat, pounding his fist on the metal. Then all of a sudden, he stopped. He closed his eyes and started praying, sweat coating his white shirt.

As they watched, Barakat seemed to be mumbling to himself, which they couldn't understand. He stopped, sat straight up on the bench, and shut his eyes. A few seconds later, they opened wide, and he stared straight ahead. Barakat spoke to them for the first time.

"I'll do it," he said.

"Wow," Rob said. "He speaks."

Rob glanced at his watch. Time was up. He headed back toward the room, and the guard closed the door after him. Rob took a seat on the top of the table by Barakat, a hand on his knee.

"You'll do what, exactly?" Rob asked, moving closer.

Barakat barely moved, other than glancing toward the floor. He looked back up and locked eyes with Rob. "I'll tell you," he replied. "I will give you their finances, brokers, shell companies, everything. Just don't hurt my family. I do not care if I die, but they are everything to me."

"All right, then," Rob said, getting up and pacing around the small room. "Tell me about these shell companies. Where they are, how much gets laundered through them, the brokers, all that."

The cuffs were tight around Barakat's wrist, and his skin was almost raw.

"Most of them, the big ones, are in the States," he replied.

"Wait," Rob said, grabbing a chair and moving it around the table. He plopped down. "You're saying these people, your handlers, launder money in the United States? How much are we talking about?"

"Millions," replied Barakat. "Not just through companies, but also through mosques. One in particular. They even recruit from there."

"Which one would that be?"

"Look," Barakat said, his face flush and sweating bullets. "If they find out I talked to you, I'm dead, my family is dead. They will torture me much worse than you. Then they will cut my fucking head off in front of my family before they do the same to them. If I tell you more, I need protection for myself and my family! Otherwise, there is no point because I am dead anyway."

Rob peered back at the mirror while the others looked on.

"All right," he replied, his head snapping back. "We will get your family out and put you all up in a safe house where you'll be guarded."

Barakat calmed himself, leaning to the side and wiping his face on his short sleeve.

"Okay," he said. "Okay, I will cooperate. I will do whatever you want." He knew at that point he was safer with the Americans.

"Good," replied Rob. "I'm glad you see reason. Now, tell me about this mosque."

On the other side of the mirror, a surveillance system connected to cameras seen on a series of monitors along the far wall. Above Rob's head, a camera pointed down from the corner of the ceiling. Everything that happened in the room was video and audio recorded.

"It is in New York," Barakat said. "Many members come from there, especially the ones willing to fight jihad in the States. They live among Americans. One day, they receive a call."

Barakat paused.

"And?" Rob asked. "I didn't tell you to stop. I need details, names."

Barakat inhaled deeply. His mouth made a whistling sound as he let the air out.

"I cannot believe I am telling you this," he added. "Fine, okay. The Imam there is named Habib Atallah. His mosque is in Queens. He helps recruit young boys. Money flows through from private donations all over the Muslim world. It is then laundered through front companies. But you heard nothing from me, okay? I will die a slow death if they find out."

"Look," replied Rob, "I already told you."

Rob moved his head to within an inch of Barakat's face.

"But," he added, "if you mislead or otherwise fuck with us, just one time, I will make it known everywhere that you helped us. I'm willing to bet you wouldn't even make it back home."

Rob backed up and propped his arm against the table. "Where's the next attack going to be?" he asked.

Barakat buried his head in his cuffed hands. "I don't know about such things."

Rob rammed his hand into Barakat's chest and locked his elbow, almost knocking him off the bench. "What was that?"

Barakat moved his face away from his hands and rested his chin on them.

"I said I do not know about such things," he replied. "I only know about finance. The Imam has a personal relationship with the boss, though. He would know, even though I do not think you can make him talk."

"We'll worry about that," said Rob.

Rob left Barakat and marched toward the metal door. He turned to him one last time. "Remember what I said," he added. "You don't want to mess with us."

Rob slipped through the doorway, and the guard secured it. Agent Bradford turned the corner from the stairs as Rob made it to the door of the observation room.

"Hey there," Bradford said. "How goes it?"

"Can you guys transfer him to a cell?" Rob asked him. "I want to know where he is around the clock. We'll work on getting him transported to a safe house soon."

"Sure," the agent replied. "We can do that right away. No worries, mate."

"Thanks," Rob added. "We appreciate the assistance."

Agent Bradford gripped Rob's hand and gave him a pat on the shoulder.

"Like I said," the agent replied. "No worries. We were more or less ordered to from on high, so it's not as if we had a choice in the matter."

Rob returned to his team, and Agent Bradford and the guard prepared to move the detainee to a temporary holding cell.

THIRTY

Safe House
Queens, New York

The Queens neighborhood of Elmhurst had already woken from its slumber early that Friday morning. The area was always bustling, with many shops and markets lining the sidewalks for several blocks. Black exhaust fumes were spit out from vehicles continuing through the four-way intersection. An ambulance siren grew louder, drawing closer and cruising around traffic on an intersecting street.

Young children waited with their parents at the school bus stop, playing kids games as their bus turned the corner a block down. Men and women began filling the sidewalks, ambling in each direction. Many people passed by, unaware they were being watched. Rob and Brian were looking for someone specific—a man who was the religious leader of a well-known local mosque. Rob wasn't far from where he grew up in Brooklyn, and he wondered how his mother and sister were doing. There certainly wouldn't be any time for social calls this go-around, though.

This was a three-man operation, and the remainder of the team had flown back into Pope Airfield and Fort Liberty the night before. The duo had been at the safe house since long before the sun rose that morning. Colin waited in a blue van a few blocks away. Intelligence they'd received laid out the Imam's schedule.

Friday was an important day to Muslims because it was the most important prayer of the week. Known as the Jum'ah prayer in Arabic, it was a congregational prayer required of Muslim men, though women did attend. Information they had received suggested Atallah didn't drive a car. As the leader of the mosque, he was said to arrive in the morning every week to prepare for prayer in the early afternoon.

Rob pressed the binoculars to his face and rested his elbows on a small table. He peered over the fire escape through a crack in the second-floor window curtain at people coming and going down. It was the suggested route Atallah took to get to the mosque. If the intel was spot-on, he'd show up in their sight shortly.

"Anything yet?" Brian asked, sitting on the floor against the wall and examining Atallah's photo.

"Nope," Rob replied. "Not yet. Just random folks going about their business. Barakat better be right, or I'm going to be pissed."

"You and me both," said Brian. "But I think you scared the man shitless, to be honest."

"Here's hoping," replied Rob.

The safe house itself, with one keeper downstairs, was owned by the Agency. The CIA higher-ups agreed to let them use it.

Brian snatched his binoculars and moved to a different window.

"Hey," said Rob. "Let me see that photo again."

Brian slid the large image across the floor. Rob picked it up and leaned it against the glass on the windowsill. Every minute he looked on with bare eyes, the crowd outside seemed to grow larger.

"So what you thinking?" Rob asked. "We capture that asshole and make him talk, or we bug his office and see what we get?"

"If we could get in there unnoticed, we might gather more info that way," Brian replied. "But that's a big if. If we're spotted, this whole operation would be in jeopardy, and we would be worse off. The way I see it, we grab him when nobody's looking, no witnesses."

Rob inched the binoculars closer to the building down below. "Of course," he said.

He picked up a small handheld radio. "Three-Four," he said. "How're you doing over there, over?"

The radio squawked.

"Bored as shit," Colin replied. "Pumping myself full of caffeine."

"I hear you," said Rob. "And gettin' paid for it, too, courtesy of the US government."

"Yeah," replied Colin. "Living the dream, buddy, that's for sure."

Brian spotted someone moving just beneath his window and past the front walk gate.

"Heads up," he said to Rob. "Coming toward you, white prayer cap."

Rob rose and put his head to the window. He glanced down at a group passing by on the walkway. Between them, he spotted a man wearing a long, white thobe over dark pants and a white taqiyah cap on his head. The man stuck out among other New Yorkers around him.

"Got him," replied Rob.

Rob lowered himself to his knees and eyed the man, who was walking at a casual pace moving farther away, closely through the binoculars. Brian moved up beside Rob. While they observed, a young Arab-looking boy along the street suddenly called for him. The man stopped, his face visible as he turned to talk to the boy. Rob looked closely at the picture.

"It's him," he said. "See for yourself."

He handed the binoculars to Brian, who took a look.

"Affirmative," Brian replied with a quick nod. "That's the target all right."

Rob cocked the slide of his nine-millimeter pistol and put it back in the holster tucked under his pants. He pulled his shirt down over it.

"Three-Four," Rob said into the radio. "Target identified. Hold tight, we're mobile. Going radio silent, over."

"Copy, Three-Five," replied Colin. He knew that meant no contacting them until they radioed first.

Rob switched the knob on the small radio off and slid it into his pocket. "Let's go," he said.

He and Brian headed through the door and down the stairs to the first floor. With a chance of rain in the forecast, Rob snatched an umbrella from the coat rack by the door. They slipped through the doorway and down the concrete steps to the entry gate.

They continued down the sidewalk, and taxi cabs and random cars beeped from the adjacent street as the light went from red to green. Brian hung back to create some distance between them. Rob walked with the flow of pedestrian traffic, past a row of brick town homes toward apartments on the right.

Up ahead, he could just make out the bobbing of a white Muslim cap. He watched the man take a right at another intersection and walk past the residential area toward a slew of businesses and storefronts down the road. Rob followed, cutting through the apartment building's parking lot.

He glanced back and saw Brian on the footpath, taking the

long way around. Rob continued walking, ambling toward the parking lot exit. He turned the corner by a short brick wall and spotted the target on the opposite side of the street. Brian turned the corner at the end of the block just as Rob picked up the pace across the road. They made their way up the slight hill and passed by Colin in the blue van parked in the alleyway. The side of the van read "Joe's Catering" in large white lettering.

Suddenly, Atallah froze in his tracks in front of a gas station. He swung back and glared down the path in Rob's direction. Not wanting to make anything obvious by reacting, Rob continued walking at a casual pace. Seeing what was happening, Brian ducked between two buildings.

The man continued eyeballing Rob as he got closer.

"Sir," Rob nodded, passing by him.

Rob passed the stop sign and made his way across another street. He turned his head just in time to see Atallah continue down the same road Rob had just crossed. He stood on one side of the wall, peeking around the corner. The target made it further on, and Rob continued his pursuit. Through the gas station lot, Rob spotted Brian moving between buildings. He continued down the walk. The mosque emerged a couple blocks down on the left, and Rob walked close to the buildings to keep from being seen.

The mosque wasn't a mosque in the traditional sense. It had no dome and wasn't shaped like a mosque you'd see in Middle Eastern countries. The place looked more like a small school. It was a rectangle-shaped, beige-colored brick building with glass front doors and a loading dock in the rear. A large sign out front read "Al-Rashid Islamic Center" in both English and Arabic.

Rob looked ahead as Atallah cut left and moved out of sight. Rob stepped behind a building and waited for Brian to join him. He plucked the radio from his pocket and squeezed the button.

"Three-Four," he said. "He's inside."

Rob and Brian waited there along the roadway for Colin to show up. They saw the van make a left turn directly toward them. Colin pulled up by them and tapped the brakes. Rob peeked around a bush and saw Atallah turn his key to enter the structure.

"We're clear," he said.

Rob slid the van door to the side, and he and Brian climbed in. Colin continued toward the building and made a left into the driveway. He drove around the mosque and kept going to a back entry road. Colin did a U-turn and parked between the road and a smaller building before shutting the engine off.

"All right," said Brian. "Our source said Atallah would normally end up back here on Fridays, once they cleaned up. Apparently, they don't employ housekeepers or any other outsiders. So get comfortable. We've got at least a three-hour wait or more."

Colin's leg had fallen asleep while waiting up front. He adjusted his body in the driver's seat to keep it from going completely numb. In the back, Rob and Brian were on the floor, legs straight out and backs pressed to the side of the van. They could just see over the dash and through the front windshield. Most attendees had already made their way to their cars and left for the day.

"Almost four hours," Colin said, glancing at his wristwatch. "But who's counting, right?"

Rob let out a chuckle. "Best damn job in the world," he replied.

Rob peeked over the dashboard, and he spotted a man in a gray robe and prayer cap with a few large garbage bags draped over his shoulder. He watched the Muslim man slip on a pair of sandals by the door.

"What do we have here?" Rob asked.

The man walked with purpose down the metal steps and toward the dumpster. He stopped for a moment, then heaved the bags over the side. He returned to the doorway and removed the sandals again, leaving them by the door as he entered. As soon as the door shut, though, it popped open again. A tall man stepped out into another pair of sandals. Holding a couple of bags himself, he made his way down the short staircase.

"Hey," Brian said. "That's him. That's the bastard. Wait until he drops those bags, then we got his ass."

Colin cranked the van. The Muslim leader wandered to the dumpster and tossed the bags over his head. They were parked far enough away to not draw much attention. Colin glanced around to make sure nobody was within sight.

"Here we go," Colin said as they slipped balaclavas over their faces.

The man turned around, and Colin slammed on the accelerator while Rob and Brian got ready at the door. Colin hit the brakes abruptly, sliding forward on the asphalt. They opened the door quickly, and the Imam looked to see what was going on. By the time he saw them, Rob and Brian had already grabbed him by both arms and yanked him inside, slamming the door. Colin peeled out through the front drive.

"What are you doing?" Atallah asked. "This is a place of worship. I am an Imam!"

Colin aimed the van toward the safe house. Rob stuffed a handkerchief in Atallah's mouth and tied it around the back of his head. The Imam tried to scream, but all they could hear was gibberish. Rob secured his hands behind his back. With another piece of cloth, he blindfolded Atallah. Rob shoved him down.

"Now sit there and shut up," he ordered.

Bypassing the four-way intersection, Colin took a left down a long, narrow alleyway. He cruised up behind the building, the door within touching distance. They peeked to make sure nobody was looking, and Rob and Brian quickly slid the door open. Brian hopped out and pressed the button on the intercom.

"Golf-Three-Six and Golf-Three-Five, coming in," he said, glancing up at the hidden camera. "Plus one party guest."

The dead bolt unlocked. Brian opened up and they dragged Atallah inside.

***

In the basement of the Agency safe house, Habib Atallah squatted on the cold, tile floor. His hands were secured by a chain to an eyebolt attached to the wall behind him. His face was still covered. Having been in that position for hours by that point and exhausted, his body went limp every couple minutes. The jolt of the chain pulling against his skin was what snapped him out of it. Rub marks had begun to appear around his wrists.

The room was completely soundproofed. Atallah couldn't see or hear a thing outside. All of the Imam's Muslim attire had been stripped away, including his prayer cap. He was blindfolded and left in just his boxers on the hard floor, a sure insult to a devout Muslim leader.

On the other side of the bolted door, Rob and Brian secured their firearms in a locked container in the arms room. Stepping into the short hallway and holding a black coffee in one hand, Brian entered a passcode into the keypad. The electronic lock buzzed and the dead bolt turned.

"After you," he said.

Brian entered the basement after Rob and secured it. They wandered toward Atallah as the yellow overhead bulb radiated down over his head.

"Hey there," Brian said, snapping his fingers in front of the man's face.

Startled, Atallah flinched. His eyes popped open. The sweat on his face glistened under the basement light. His head hung; his sore neck tried to lift it. Rob stepped behind the Imam and removed one of the chains, leaving the other hand still attached.

"Do you know why you're here?" Rob asked. He glanced down and realized the rag was still in his mouth. "Oh, shit," he added. "I'm sorry, you can't answer."

Rob untied the handkerchief and jerked it from the Imam's mouth. He dropped it by his feet. "There," he continued. "Much better. Now we can have a conversation."

Still blindfolded, Atallah could only smell the cup of lukewarm coffee Brian stuck in his face. Brian grabbed the man's hand and touched it to the Styrofoam cup. Atallah snatched it tiredly from Brian's hand and gulped it down. A bit of liquid trickled down from his lips to his chin. Atallah wiped it with his hand.

"You must be thirsty," said Brian.

Atallah dropped the cup to the floor. Rob stood over him and placed a hand on his head.

"You have something to tell us, Habib? I think you do."

Atallah bucked and shoved Rob back with one arm. He grabbed the man's wrist and bent it, causing him let out a pained moan. Atallah's face began to turn red.

"Okay, okay," he said, Rob twisting his arm.

"You try that shit again," replied Rob, "and I'll break it, got it?"

"Yes, yes," Habib said, getting ahold of himself. "I promise."

Rob let go of his arm.

"Who are you people, huh?" Atallah asked, resting the arm on his lap. "You undress me and tie me up like a dog? I am an Imam, a religious scholar, a pillar of this community, and a youth leader. You have the wrong man!"

"Yeah?" Rob replied. "That's not what your people in Syria say. They sold your ass out to protect their own skin. How do you feel about that, Mister Youth Leader?"

Atallah looked puzzled. "I do not know who you are referring to," he said. "I do not have contacts in Syria or Lebanon. I am American."

Rob bent forward and shoved the man's head back against the wall. It made a clanking sound as his skull met hard brick.

"We didn't say anything about Lebanon, Mister Atallah," replied Rob. "You see? We know you're lying. Save yourself the pain and suffering and just tell us what we want to know. Where's the next attack going to be?"

Atallah didn't respond. He just shrugged him off.

"I can assure you," Rob said, "things will heat up fast if you don't answer."

The door cracked open. Rob glanced back as Chris waved for them. Rob secured Atallah's free hand back to the chain.

"Don't go anywhere." He smiled. "Be right back."

He and Brian headed for the door and secured it. They stepped into the next room with Chris.

"What is it?" asked Brian. "We're kind of in the middle of something here."

"I just got a call from the powers that be in Washington," Chris replied. "There's been another bombing at a Saint Patty's Day parade in Chicago. At least a hundred fifty dead so far."

Chris was the only guy from his team at the safe house. The rest were busy elsewhere.

"Come here," he added. "You've got to see this."

They all walked to the living area by the front entrance foyer. Chris took a seat on the leather sofa and snagged the remote from the coffee table while the two men stood behind him. He aimed at the flat-screen above the old brick fireplace and hit the power button.

A scene began to unfold onscreen. A thick cloud of dust and debris blanketed the area. People screamed as their loved ones suffered or they themselves were hurt. A topographic view from a news helicopter showed green parade floats torn apart. Their blackened remnants were strewn all over the street and surroundings.

People covered in white ash—some dead, some injured—were spread up and down the roadway and sidewalks. Police, EMS, and fire engine sirens sounded nearby. Numerous adjacent buildings had glass and other fragments blasted out from the percussion. The walls of offices and storefronts were crumbled and knocked down.

"Jesus," said Rob. "We need to make contact and warn them of what they're dealing with. That radiation could contaminate every last one of 'em. That alone would be far worse than an instant death."

"Yeah," Chris replied, snatching up the secure landline from the table. "The FBI has responded. We plan to notify them right now. Of course, we all know who's behind it. If we don't get to the bottom of this shit, many more will die. I guarantee it."

They watched a bit more of the chaos that was playing out in Chicago. Rob was losing his cool and suddenly thrust the heel of his boot into the back of the sofa. Chris jumped up, phone to his ear.

"I've seen enough," Rob said. "This dude better start talking, or I'm going to fuck him up."

He marched toward the basement while Brian trailed him. Rob punched in the door code and went straight for Atallah. He tightened a fist and sent a haymaker toward his face. The force of the blow whipped the Imam's head back hard.

"I am all out of patience, Habib!" Rob said. "There was just another bombing halfway across the country. You want to end this? Talk, or I'll make you wish you were dead!"

The man winced from the pain and readjusted himself on the floor.

"We know you are one of al-Bashir's couriers," Rob added. "We know you are highly involved in the finances. And we know you recruit and launder money through your mosque. If you admit that and help us, I can make sure your time is more pleasant. If not, things will get very uncomfortable for you. See, we can do things others can't. We can make you disappear, and your family will never know what happened to you. Nobody will."

Rob reached down and pulled the blindfold from the man's face. He stooped down to eye level with Habib and poked the bloody gash on his cheek.

"Do you want that, Mister Atallah?" he asked, moving in close. "Family is important, wouldn't you agree? It would be a shame for your young daughter to grow up without a father. What is she, six or seven? We know you sent them upstate a couple weeks ago. Why is that?"

Atallah seemed to stare into space. He bounced his head up and down.

"If you continue down this path," Rob continued, "that's exactly what will happen."

Rob stood up, looming over Atallah, seeing his expressionless face as he crossed his arms. What the Imam didn't know was that officers were finishing up a search of his place several blocks away. The Agency had a limited scope when it came to operating on American soil. But these were dire circumstances, and what they found was interesting.

Rob felt a vibration in his feet as the front door slammed. He knew someone had just entered the safe house. Rob left Atallah to ponder all he'd said and wandered to the door. As he stepped through, he met Tony and another member of the

Agency team named Greg. They carried two large tote cases to a table near the kitchen.

"What's this?" Rob asked. "You guys score or what?"

Tony reached over and unfastened the buckles on each case. He flipped the lids open. "You could say that," he replied. "Check this out."

Tony began pulling stuff out. "We got laptops," he added, "a dozen burner phones, a few external hard drives, and ten flash drives. It'll take some time to analyze, but there's got to be something to it."

They had plenty of evidence to sift through. They would bring Atallah to another location for the FBI to pick him up pending analysis of all the intelligence they'd gathered.

"All right," Brian said to Tony and Chris, stepping between them. "I know you don't work for me, and I'm not giving you orders, but get him ready to be transported, if you would. We need to make contact with our CO and see what he wants to do. If anything changes, please let us know."

"Not a problem," Chris replied.

Rob and Brian went to the next room to get Colin. They needed to regroup with the rest of the team and figure out their orders. Brian whipped out his phone to call the commander, and the three men headed out into the evening dusk toward their vehicle parked a block away.

THIRTY-ONE

President Tyler peered through the window as the plane passed above gray clouds, thirty thousand feet over northern Virginia. It was a calm, partly cloudy day. Most of the staff were into something and hyper-focused.

Four thousand square feet in size, the plane's interior boasted three separate floors. It had a giant suite for the president himself, a large conference room, an office, galley, dining room, a staff area, and tons of living space. President Tyler's Secret Service agents were mostly grouped together in the living area, playing cards to pass the time.

The plane had been circling for a few days and had refueled midair three times so far. The president had been awake for a few hours, receiving his daily brief and meeting with various members of his administration. Now, from the culmination of stress and heartache over what was happening to the country, President Tyler spaced out for a time. The sound of those around him in conversation was all muddled in his ears.

As Tyler gawked at plowed farmer fields and patches of woods down below, he detected a voice a little louder than the others. It was his national security adviser, and he was attempting to get the president's attention. President Tyler could vaguely make out the man's voice, like it was happening in a dream, but the voice grew louder.

"Mister President," Rampart said. "Mister President!"

President Tyler snapped his head back.

"Mister President! You all right, sir? You look a little flustered."

The president rubbed his fingers over his eyelids and bowed his head. He glanced at his adviser. "Yeah, Neal," he replied sluggishly. "I'm fine, don't worry. Just a momentary daze. Sorry about that. I have a lot on my mind."

Rampart took a seat across from his boss's desk. "Sir," he said. "I understand. Perhaps you should go lie down for a while. I know you haven't been resting much. Maybe it'll do you some good. Reset your body, you know?"

President Tyler rested his chin in his hand. "Yeah, well," he replied, "I don't see how I can rest, knowing what's happening down there while we're circling around up here. Besides, I don't want to be curled up in bed while my staff is busy working. Not a good example."

Rampart looked at his boss with worry. "Of course, Mister President," he said. "It was just a suggestion."

"It's fine, Neal," replied the president. "I appreciate the concern."

"Sure, Mister President," Rampart said.

President Tyler glanced across the plane at the TV in the corner. It showed footage of the recent bombing with captions below. The more he saw, the angrier he got. Pressing his fists together and popping his knuckles, Tyler diverted his eyes back to the man in front of him.

"So, where are we now?" he asked.

The national security adviser unsnapped and opened a leather-bound notebook and placed it on the mahogany desk between them.

"Well, sir," Rampart replied. "The vice president and his team, plus the joint chiefs, are currently in the underground bunker as you ordered. The FBI are on scene at ground zero in downtown Chicago."

The president rapped his knuckles on the hard wood. "Shit," he said. "If they'd been prevented from crossing the border in the first place, none of this would've happened. How did we not see this coming?"

"Mister President," replied Rampart, "I hate to say it, but with the lower manpower at checkpoints, they blended right in with other migrants. Unfortunately, not getting congressional approval to reinforce our border has come at a high cost, higher than any of us could've predicted. I mean, we already have the cartels smuggling people and drugs into the country. It's the perfect cover for any terrorist network."

"Yeah," President Tyler said. "Well, we tried to warn them, didn't we? Now, let's hope they've had a change of heart."

"Yes, sir," Rampart replied.

CIA director Nathan Powell came into the room and approached the desk.

"Mister President," he said. "I'm sorry to interrupt, sir, but there's an update."

"For God's sake, Nathan," Tyler replied. "Have a seat, would you? I don't feel like looking up at you."

"Yes, Mister President," he said, taking another chair next to Rampart.

"So," President Tyler added. "What is it?"

"I just got off the phone with the directorate of operations," Powell replied.

The directorate of operations, Mike Como, was the executive head of the CIA's SAC/SOG unit. These two paramilitary units were responsible for overt political action and covert operations, respectively.

"Okay," the president said. "What did he have to say?"

Powell set his elbows on the table and interlocked his hands. He met the president's gaze.

"Well, Mister President," he replied, "the Agency team, in collaboration with Delta, found some interesting intel when they raided the house of one Habib Atallah. The D boys captured him outside his mosque and brought him to the safe house, sir. They began interrogating while at his apartment was being searched. They're following the money, sir. They think they're getting closer to crippling al-Bashir's network."

"All right," replied Tyler. "What did they find there?"

"A treasure trove of intel, sir," Powell said. "And they uncovered communications between the terrorist leader and Atallah. This confirms his involvement. Also, his mosque was used to recruit at least twenty young boys that we know of. Last contact I had, sir, they thought they were close to locating the front companies Atallah used to launder money sent to al-Bashir's organization."

President Tyler held a finger up. "One minute," he said, snatching the secure phone from the end of the table.

He dialed a number and waited. Five rings later, a voice picked up. "Hello, Director Esparza?" the president said.

Angel Esparza was the Director of the FBI.

"I need you to send a team to shut down a mosque in Queens, New York. Al-Rashid Islamic Center. Search the office, but no shooting unless there's a direct threat. We don't want an even bigger international incident over this. I'll get the rest of the details over to you. Understood?"

The president paused a moment to hear the director's response.

"Yeah, yeah, okay," he replied. "Thanks, Angel. Send me an update. Yup, all right, bye."

The president hung up the phone, and his national security adviser raised his brow. President Tyler glanced through the interior of the plane, looking for his chief of staff, Jason Riley.

"Anyone seen Riley?" he asked loud enough for those around him to hear.

Two staff members pointed next door.

"Sir?" Riley replied from the communications room. He stepped into the president's office, approached the desk, and began to sit.

"No, don't sit," President Tyler said. "This won't take but a second."

"Mister President," the chief of staff replied. "What can I do for you, sir?"

"I need you to set up a video conference, Jason," Tyler said, "with the two clandestine teams on the ground—the Delta team from Golf Squadron and the Agency assets currently attached to them. Set it up soon, okay?"

Riley turned to head for the door. "Yes, Mister President," he replied. "I'll get on it right away, sir."

"Thanks, Jason," the president replied as Jason rushed to the conference room.

President Tyler glared at his national security adviser and the Agency director. "Now," he added, "let's see if we can get to the bottom of this."

Just as Riley made it to the doorway, President Tyler stopped him.

"Oh, and Jason," he said.

"Sir?" Riley asked, turning his head.

"Let's head back to Andrews, huh? I want to pick up my family and head back home to my ranch for a while."

His adviser quickly spun around and marched toward the president. "Mister President, I don't think that's a good idea, sir."

The president leaned forward with his elbows on the desk.

"Just leave my Secret Service team with us. We'll be fine, don't worry. Those guys know what they're doing."

***

Further south, outside of Fort Liberty, Rob had just woken up in his own bed after a six-hour rest. The team had flown back in late the night before. Having just stepped out of the shower and gotten dressed, he munched on a bagel while sipping on a mug full of hot coffee.

Rob finished up the last of his breakfast. He washed the mug out in the sink and set it upside down on the mat to dry. Taking a seat at his dining table, he bent down and put on his mid-top hiking boots. He pulled each of the laces tight and tied them in a bow. Rob tugged the bottom of his khaki pants legs over his shoes. He finished buttoning the top few buttons of his untucked, short-sleeve, button-up shirt.

The small TV on the counter in his kitchen, its volume low, showed coverage of the Chicago bombing. Rob glanced at it for a second, then snatched the remote to shut it off. He dropped the remote onto the table.

"Enough of that," he said to himself.

Rob grabbed his Garmin watch and fastened the leather band to his wrist. He removed his personal smart phone from the charger and put it on the table in front of him. Rob got ready to head for the door, and the phone beeped at him. Unlocking the screen, he noticed it was a text message from Brian. He opened it.

Video conference with POTUS, 0900.

Rob took the phone and pocketed it. He snagged his hat from the table, put it on, and made his way out the door. He secured the dead bolt and marched for his old Mustang parked in the driveway. He climbed in and fastened the seatbelt. After he started it up, Rob hit reverse and backed out onto the two-lane road. He slipped the stick into drive and went straight for the gate a few miles away. Droplets formed on the car's windshield, somewhat cooling down the muggy, North Carolina heat.

That side of the base was mostly wooded, with tons of pine trees and red dirt. It was the least used gate and only open for a few hours in the morning. From the northwest side of the base, it only took Rob a few minutes to get to work. Most of the guys lived somewhere nearby. The gate cropped up over a hill just a mile ahead. Approaching the gate guard, Rob slowed. The guard recognized him and waved him through.

"You're good, Master Sergeant," he said. "Have a good day."

Rob continued on, around a curve to the left and down a long stretch of road that passed by the firing ranges. The compound appeared in the middle of woodlands on the left. Rob swerved left toward the gate, and the guard, who knew him, waved him through. He swung the Mustang around and parked in front of the building by the pathway to the helipad. Brian waited outside, leaned up against the wall with a bottle of Gatorade while Rob shut the engine off.

Reaching for his bag in the back, Rob shoved the door open with his knee and slid out. Slamming the door, strap over his shoulder, he joined his team leader out front.

"What's the word, boss?" Rob asked as he walked briskly toward him.

"Not sure yet," replied Brian. "I just know the president wants to talk to us."

Without stopping, Rob headed inside with Brian. They marched for the team room, where everyone else waited. As they entered, they made their way across the room, and Rob tossed his pack to the floor by the table. They took their seats.

"Hello, gentlemen," Colonel Billings said. "Right on time. Stand by for the president."

A couple of minutes passed while they stared at a blank screen. Then, the live feed popped up when President Tyler joined them.

The entire team popped to attention.

"No, no," the president said. "None of that. Please, sit. This'll be informal. Is everyone with us?"

Everyone took their seats. The colonel checked the feed to make sure the Agency guys were on. The screen split, and Chris and Tony popped in. They had the same view of the president as everyone else.

"We're on, Mister President," said Chris.

President Tyler took a sip of his morning coffee.

"Very good," he said. "Good morning from the friendly skies, gentlemen. I've got to tell you, I sure do miss being on the ground right about now. I know that sounds odd coming from a pilot, but this is the longest I've ever been in the air at one time."

Everyone in the room snickered.

"Well, down to business," the president continued. "I need to hear it straight from you. Chris, what have you guys come up with?"

Chris cleared his throat. "Sir," he replied. "These guys, al-Bashir's men and co-conspirators, meticulously covered their tracks. We weren't able to find any direct evidence. We did, however, uncover patterns in their communication that seem to lean toward a few companies the group might be using to launder their money."

President Tyler adjusted his screen and moved a little closer. His curiosity had been piqued. "Please explain," he said.

"Well, Mister President," Chris added, "communication via email and phone. Our support team analyzed burner phones and computer hard drives, including Atallah's personal phone, which didn't show much. Most of the content was encrypted. We were able to decipher a lot of it, including phone call and email recipients. They're still analyzing the intel, but a pattern is developing."

A somber look washed over President Tyler's face.

"By now," he said, "I'm sure you guys know about the recent attack in Chicago. The FBI has been investigating. So far, nothing substantial has turned up. I feel this is only going to intensify if we don't put a stop to it. These people think they can come here and push us around. Hell, they threatened me directly. But it's not me I'm concerned about. It's the innocent people just out with family and friends, in the wrong place at the wrong time."

Then the president did something he hardly ever did: curse.

"They need to know they can't fuck with us."

Colonel Billings paced the floor behind his boys, his hands behind his back while the president spoke.

"Mister President," he said, "just give us the green light, and we'll go after those shell companies. Nobody in his inner circle has any idea Atallah was caught by us, or the intel we have on them. As far as they know, he just vanished. Let my boys go in and shut these bastards down, sir."

President Tyler bent his head, rubbing the side of his face.

"Very well, Colonel," he replied. "You are a go. You all will continue domestic operations and go after these guys. But make damn sure you are right. Also, for the purpose of inter-agency communications, I'm adding a team from the FBI's joint terrorism task force, because they will be the ones responsible for arrests made. Agreed?"

"Agreed," said Colonel Billings. "Thank you, Mister President."

The president bent toward the screen and rose from the table.

"No, Colonel," he replied. "Thank you, all of you. Godspeed, I'm out."

They saw President Tyler move his hand toward the device, and his screen went blank.

"You heard him, men," Colonel Billings said to all in attendance. "Get ready to rock."

THIRTY-TWO

Queens, New York

The blue van hustled down Thirty-Sixth Street in Queens on its way from LaGuardia Airport toward the Ed Koch Queensboro Bridge to Midtown Manhattan. In the driver's seat, Rob took a quick right onto Queens Boulevard. Beside him, Brian kept a watchful eye out for any potential issues with traffic.

Intelligence gathered at Atallah's residence pointed to three companies used to launder al-Bashir's money. Of course, the information would never suggest they were actually shell companies, but when analysts dug deeper, they found the companies were owned by a distant relative of the terrorist leader, who had no other ties to the organization. In fact, it was pure luck they came across his name buried in a mountain of emails.

In the back of the vehicle, the rest of the Delta team, plus two pairs from both the Agency and FBI, sat on both sides, facing one another. Up ahead, traffic began to back up as they hit the bridge over the East River. The van slowed, a few feet from the bumper of the car in front.

"Damn, this New York traffic," Rob said.

Brian look stumped. "What?" he asked. "You're from here, aren't you?"

"Well, yeah," replied Rob. "That doesn't mean you ever get used to it. Shit, it was one of the reasons I left. There are more people in this city than some states."

"That's crazy," Brian said. "I'm from Billings, Montana. I thought that town was large at a hundred and something thousand people."

"Yeah," Rob replied. "I think I'd rather have that at this point."

Brian leaned between the seats toward the back of the van. "Where are you guys from?" he asked.

The FBI agent closest to him was the first to respond. "I'm from upstate," he said. "Buffalo."

"Ah," Brian replied. "A fellow New Yorker, Rob."

Brian pointed to the other agent sitting by his partner. "And you?" he asked. "Where are you from?"

"A little town you've probably never heard of," the agent replied. "Alcoa, Tennessee."

"Nice," said Brian.

Traffic began to pick up, and Rob pressed on the accelerator. Their speed increased to a steady pace while crossing over the water. The van cruised across the bridge in the direction of Central Park. Slowing again and hitting the off ramp just past the bridge, Rob veered right toward the bottom and onto East Sixtieth Street in Manhattan. He progressed further up and swerved right onto Second Avenue.

"Okay," Rob said, passing between towering office buildings on each side. "The place is ten blocks up ahead on the right. Get ready to move."

The van coasted through a few green lights until they got stopped by one red light. They could see the store two blocks down on the right. A sign above the entrance read "Imperial Laundry Services." The light turned green and cars began passing them on the left, and Rob continued in the right lane and pulled the van in front of the shop.

"All right," he said, shifting into park. "Here we go."

Rob swung the door open and stepped out. Jamal remained inside to watch the entrance. Guns concealed under their clothing, the rest hopped from the van, and they all made their way unnoticed toward the business entrance. Josh broke away from them and headed for the exit in the alley behind the shop.

They approached up the steps, and business hours were shown on a sign on the glass door. Rob gripped the handle and yanked it open, and they entered the premises. Without any workers noticing, he reached back, locked the door, and turned the Open sign to Closed.

"Can I help you gentlemen?" a middle-aged Arab woman asked in fair English as she approached.

Rob smiled, putting his hands on the counter. "I sure do hope so," he replied. He glanced back at the men, then to her. "Where can we find Farzan Beydoun?"

Her face turned white.

"No," she replied. "No Farzan here, mister. Never heard the name. Maybe you have wrong address?"

"Nope," Rob said, making eye contact with Brian. "I'm pretty sure we're in the right place."

The woman went silent, afraid to speak. Rob gazed beyond the counter toward the back of the shop. A man appeared from behind a row of hanging clothes. He froze as he glared at Rob and the men. Suddenly, he took off, darting through the rear exit. He busted through the doorway and down the alley, and Josh grabbed him outside and shoved him to the ground. He dove on top of him and pinned him down as the others came rushing over.

"Well, well," Brian said. "What do we have here?"

"The innocent don't run," Rob added.

Rob gripped the man by the collar as Josh hopped up. He pulled him to his feet and held on to his collar.

"You got that right," Rob replied.

He stared into the man's eyes. "What are you hiding?" he asked.

Rob handed the man off to the senior FBI agent, Agent Tanner. The agent slapped cuffs on him.

"Who are you?" the man asked. "What do you want with me?"

Rob retrieved a handheld radio from his pocket.

"Golf-Three," he said to Jamal. "Move to the rear exit. We have a pickup."

"Roger," replied Jamal.

Jamal circled the block and swung into the alley, pulling the van in beside them. He hit the brake and put it into park. The two FBI agents opened the back door of the van and loaded the man inside. Tanner's partner climbed in beside him and shut it. The others followed Rob and Brian back into the shop.

"All right, attention everyone!" Rob shouted for the employees to hear. "This store is now closed until further notice!"

"What?" the front desk clerk asked. "What have we done? By whose authority are you making us close?"

"The federal fucking government, lady," Rob replied as Agent Tanner flashed her the badge around his neck. "Now step aside, or they'll arrest you too."

The lady moved to allow them behind the counter. The men began snatching anything they could that would contain records and communications. They took the computer from the desk and a file cabinet under the counter. Brian snatched an empty box from the floor and stuffed every piece of paper he found into it.

"Where's the office?" Rob asked the lady.

"This is a private business, sir," she replied. "You can't go in there!"

Rob ignored her plea. "Where is it?" he insisted. "Back here?"

He wandered down the center aisle toward the back. Glancing around, Rob spotted the top of a door above a rack of clothes. He brushed the clothes out of the way. Behind them, he found a solid locked door with a dead bolt.

"Found the office back here!" Rob yelled to the others. "Get the keys from her!"

Rob heard Brian shouting to the clerk.

"Give us the key, now!" Brian said.

"I don't have it, mister!" she replied.

Rob keyed his radio mic. "Foxtrot-One," he said.

Before he could finish the transmission, Tanner stepped back into the shop through the back door. He locked it behind him. Seeing Rob in the corner, he approached.

"You called?" Tanner asked.

"Yeah," replied Rob. "You find a set of keys on him?"

Agent Tanner recovered a key ring from his pocket. "Sure did," he said, handing them over to Rob.

"Excellent," said Rob.

He fumbled through the numerous keys, trying to fit each one in the lock. Finally, one of them worked. The lock turned, and Rob jerked the door open. They both stepped inside and saw stacks of papers on a desk and a combination safe on the floor in the far corner. Rob bent down in front of it.

"What do you bet this contains something of value?" he asked.

Rob got up as Brian entered the room. He headed back through the door and out to the van. Rob tapped on the door of the vehicle, and the agent inside opened up. He hopped inside, pulling the door closed, and sat on the bench across from the detainee.

"I have a few questions for you," said Rob. "Think hard before you answer, because once you leave here, things will get worse and a lot more uncomfortable for you. You can help yourself by being honest."

The man refused to make eye contact.

"Look at me," Rob added. "It would benefit you to cooperate. What is your name?"

He didn't budge.

Rob grabbed his face and forced it upward. "Look at me!" He let him go. "Give me your name," Rob added. "This is the point where you answer. Don't take the rap for these fools. We know you are related to al-Bashir. Why do you think we're here? Do you really want to go down for money laundering and supporting terrorist activities?"

The man appeared scared. His hands trembled.

"Make this easier on yourself," said Rob. "Give us your name."

He anxiously glanced up at Rob. "My name is… Farzan… Beydoun."

Rob let go of him. "Good, good, Farzan," he replied. "That's a start. You are a cousin of Aasim al-Bashir, correct?"

Farzan's whole face went blood red.

"Tell me the truth, Farzan," Rob said. "Don't let this man intimidate you any longer. He forced you, threatened you, said he would kill your family if you didn't comply. Something like that?"

Farzan's head sank.

"Look at me," Rob insisted.

Farzan's eyes slowly looked up. "Yes," he replied. "If he ever finds out what happened here, I am a dead man. He will torture my family while I watch, then kill me slowly."

Rob knew that was al-Bashir's MO. He despised disloyalty and would make an example of anyone he thought had betrayed him or his cause.

"Okay," said Rob. "We'll get to that later. I have one other question for now. What's the combination to the safe?"

Farzan turned in his seat, his cuffed hands behind him.

"No, please," he replied. "I swore on Allah I would never give it up. They made me!"

Rob moved toward the front and snagged a pen and small notebook from the van's dash.

"This can go bad really quickly, Farzan," he replied. "And you were doing so good. Now, I will ask just one more time. If you don't give it to me, we'll do this the hard way, and you won't get another chance at any sort of redemption. Sure, we could get a safe cracker, but that kind of thing takes time. You get what I'm saying?"

Farzan began cursing in Arabic. "If I tell you," he said, "you have to immediately get my family out of the apartment, or they won't make it through the day. You protect them. That's the only way I will help you."

Rob glanced over at the FBI agent, who nodded in agreement.

"Deal," Rob replied. He opened the notepad and prepared to write.

"Okay," Farzan said while Rob prepared to write. "The code is twenty-three, forty-eight, thirty-two."

Rob tossed the pen up front and closed the notebook. He patted the side of Farzan's face. "Now," he said, shoving the door open and jumping out. "That wasn't so hard."

Rob slammed the door and headed back inside and into the office.

"Got it?" Brian asked.

"I think so," replied Rob.

He crouched low and began turning the numbers on the dial. He reached the final number, and the safe made a clicking sound as it unlocked. Rob opened it up. Inside, he found stacks of one-hundred-dollar bills in shrink wrapping and a folder containing documents.

"Jesus," he said.

Brian found an empty canvas bag near the desk and tossed it to Rob. He and Tanner stuffed everything from inside the safe into the bag.

"Looks like everything," said Rob. "Agent Tanner, you want to contact the local field office and get the other team in here to shut down this joint? We've got a lot of it to go through."

"Yup," the agent replied, stepping away with his radio. "I'm on it."

Sure the manager was the main culprit, they didn't arrest any of the employees. They did, however, guard the doors so they couldn't leave. There were more questions that needed to be answered. They would wait there in place for the FBI team to arrive.

THIRTY-THREE

Suburban Hospital
Bethesda, Maryland

Rob and the team exited the elevator and marched for the entrance to the hospital's intensive care wing. Stopping for a moment, Brian bumped the electronic button on the wall with a fist. The double doors swung open, and they continued on toward the nurses' station halfway down the corridor.

They reached the counter, and one of the nurses sat with her head buried in a three-ring binder, not noticing them at first. Rob leaned in to get her attention, tapping his finger on the counter. She glanced up at him.

"I'm so sorry," she said. "Can I help you gentlemen?"

"Yes, ma'am," Rob replied. "We're looking for a patient here, last name Smith."

Josh glanced toward the waiting area and noticed Chris and Tony sitting there.

"Hey," Josh said, elbowing Rob in the side.

Chris spotted them as Rob turned to look. He waved them over.

"Thanks, miss," Rob said. "Never mind, we're good."

"You're welcome, sir," the nurse replied as they stepped away from the counter.

"Hey," Rob said, wandering into the waiting room.

The pair of men had been watching news of the Chicago bombing on the muted television on the wall. Chris motioned toward it with a tip of his head.

"Yeah, we know," said Brian. "Damn, this is bullshit."

Rob jumped in before Brian could say any more. He wanted to distract from it for the time being and focus on the reason they were there. Smith had just woken up for the first time since being back. Other than seeing how Smith was faring, they needed to finally have a talk with him.

"How's he doing?" Rob asked Chris.

"In and out," replied Chris. "Lots of pain meds. He's doing better now. He had a few broken ribs, a fractured tibia, concussion, fractured eye socket, and his back is broken in two places. Those terrorist fucks did a number on him, I'm telling you."

"Can he talk?" Jamal asked, taking a seat by Rob on the bench.

"I don't know," Chris replied. "Maybe. We haven't been in for a while. He might be awake by now. We've just been waiting on word from the doctor."

Rob rose back to his feet. "I think I'll give it a shot," he said. "See if he's coherent enough."

"Be my guest," Chris replied as Rob and Brian slowly walked toward the hospital room door.

Rob peeked into the dim room through the tiny window. He gripped the knob and turned. They stepped inside the dark room, and Rob closed the door quietly. They made their way to a love seat–sized bench and had a seat.

Smith looked rough, with a bandage over most of his head

and one eye. His face was beet red and swollen. The blanket pulled up to his neck concealed his bodily injuries. An IV line dangled from his right arm and over the edge of the bed. A heart monitor on the other side made a pattern of continuous beeping sounds. Multiple wires suspended from the machine were attached to his bare chest under the covers.

It appeared the patient was out, so Rob snagged a magazine from the side table and started flipping through the pages. Brian began to doze off periodically as he leaned his head back against the wall.

"I hope he remembers something," he said to Rob as his eyes closed.

Rob tossed the magazine back and took another one. A doctor stepped into the room.

"Evening, gentlemen," he said, turning the light brighter and approaching Smith's bedside. "You friends, or perhaps family?"

"Good friends, doc," Brian replied as the doctor checked the IV.

The Indian doctor took a syringe and administered meds into the IV line.

"Well," he replied, "I am Doctor Sunger. You should know this man is on a lot of pain medication. He may not be able to talk for some time."

The doctor lifted the blanket to peek at the injuries underneath.

"We know, doc," said Rob. "We just wanted to come check on him."

Doctor Sunger finished up and tossed the syringe into a biohazard bin by the wall.

"All right," he said, heading for the door. "I have no issues with you being here if you respect the posted visitation hours, okay? Have a good evening, gentlemen."

"Yeah," replied Rob. "Thanks, doc."

The doctor dimmed the light. He stepped through the doorway, leaving it cracked. For almost half an hour, the two men sat still in the room while everyone else waited outside. Chris had checked on them through the window a couple of times as they sat in the darkness. Rob's head turned to the right against the back of the seat, and he suddenly began hearing a shallow noise coming from the bed. He sat straight up.

Rob peeped across the bed, and he saw Smith's head begin to turn and twitch. His right eye blinked rapidly.

"Hey, boss," he said to Brian, nudging his arm.

Brian's eyes popped open. "What's up?" he asked. "What's going on?"

He glanced at Rob and then to Smith, who started turning in bed and moaning gibberish. Rob got out of his seat and made his way to the door. He opened up halfway and motioned for Chris across the room. The CIA team leader marched across the hospital floor toward Smith's room.

"What is it?" he asked Rob. "Is he awake?"

"Looks like he's coming out of it," Rob said when Chris entered.

Chris went straight for the hospital bed and gripped Smith by the hand, squeezing. Smith began panting heavily, sweat rolling down his cheek. Suddenly, he jolted upward and opened his eyes. The pain from his ribs made him cry out in agony.

"Ugh…shit…" he said in a panic. "Where…am I?"

Chris wrapped his arms around him and lowered him down to the mattress.

"Calm down, brother," he replied. "Don't worry. You're in a hospital in Bethesda. Come on, we're here, man. Just relax. You'll be all right."

Smith gasped. His head hit the pillow. His face went from bright red to ghost white.

"Shh," Chris added, trying to calm him. "You're good. It's okay. Just lie back and breathe slowly. Just breathe, man."

Chris held Smith's arms by his side.

"Breathe, just breathe."

Smith copied Chris, breathing hard through his nose and out his mouth. His breath started to slow, and his body calmed down.

"There you go," said Chris. "It's all right. Just calm down."

The rise and fall of Smith's chest slowly returned to normal.

"Ah, shit," Smith said. "I can't fucking see anything."

Chris took his hand. "Just relax," he replied. "Just chill."

Rob got up from his seat and approached Smith.

"Hey, man," he said, taking another chair from the corner and sliding it up alongside him. "Look, I'm sorry about your men. And I know you're hurt. We'll get them back for what they did to you and your team. But..."

Smith interrupted.

"Oh, man," he replied, his head tilting back, facing the ceiling. "You've no idea... those barbarians, what they did... to... me. I'm surprised I... made it out... alive. That room was so dark... and cold. It smelled like piss."

Rob rested his hand on Smith's arm. "Yeah," he said. "But you did make it out. You're alive. And there's a reason for that."

Smith's head fell to the side and away from them. "Maybe," he replied.

Rob scooted the chair closer and touched a hand to Smith's cheek. He moved Smith's head to face him.

"Listen," said Rob. "I need you to focus and try to remember right now, okay? Can you do that for me?"

Smith's head nodded weakly.

"Oh," he replied. "I remember everything, everything those barbarians did to me."

Rob looked to the door to make sure nobody was near. The doctor had no idea who any of them were. As far as he knew, they were just visiting a friend.

"Do you remember anything else?" he asked. "Anything they said about their plans or something like that? I know you've been out a while, but this is crucial."

Smith scanned up through his swollen eye, only just able to see Rob. He grabbed his hand and squeezed as hard as he could in his frazzled state.

"I do remember something," replied Smith. "I overhead him. I think it was the boss."

"Al-Bashir?" Rob asked.

Smith nodded. "Yes, him," he replied. "The ruthless prick who got off watching his men beat me."

"What happened to you guys out there?" asked Rob.

Smith turned his head away. He took in a gulp of air.

"We were following them, you know? Tracked them to Saudi. But we got caught in a real bad sandstorm and boom, somehow they killed my men and dragged me into the damn car. I woke up later in some damn place, hot as hell. Syria, I think."

"Were you drugged?" Rob asked.

"I think so," Smith replied. "I don't even remember how I got there."

Rob tapped on Smith's arm. "Look at me," he said.

Smith rolled the best he could and glanced at Rob out of the corner of his eye.

"What else do you remember?" asked Rob.

Rob waited for a response, and Brian got up from the bench and wandered closer.

"This is important," he said. "We need to know. It's a matter of national security."

Smith looked down at Brian, standing by his feet at the

other end of the bed. "They mentioned hijacking a missile launcher," he replied.

Rob and Brian glanced hard at each other, then at Chris.

"I never told them I spoke Arabic," Smith added, turning his head and coughing into his shoulder. "He asked me countless times. They didn't know I understood them. There was talk of a big deal with a Mexican cartel. They planned to buy some powerful weapons from them, but I don't know where or when. They have big plans. I can't remember anything more. I'm sorry. They beat the shit out of me after that, and I blacked out."

Smith slowly adjusted himself in the bed to better see them.

"I'm sorry I wasn't able to warn you guys about the border," he continued. "I knew how they planned to get into the States."

Brian grabbed Smith's foot. "No, no," he replied. "You have nothing to be sorry for, man. You just get better, all right? We got this."

Smith closed his eyes. A single tear formed under his right eye and trickled down his face and onto his white hospital gown. The men prepared to leave as Doctor Sunger stepped into the room.

"Okay, gentlemen," he said. "Visiting time is over. The patient needs his rest. You can come back tomorrow if you wish."

"Yeah, doc," replied Chris. "We're going right now, thanks." He patted Smith on the leg. "Just rest, man," he said. "We'll check up on you later."

Rob and Brian headed for the door. They heard Smith mumble something. Rob doubled back.

"What was that?" he asked.

Smith coughed twice into the blanket. "I said, thanks for getting me out of there."

"Don't mention it, brother," replied Rob. "Rest up and take it easy."

The three men slipped into the hallway and shut the door gently.

"Tough son of a bitch," Brian said as they stood just outside the door. "Tortured nearly to death and didn't give up a fucking word."

"Yeah," replied Rob. "Rare breed."

They made their way back to the others in the waiting area.

"Well?" Jamal asked, pushing himself up from his seat. "You guys were in there a while. What's the verdict?"

"He's doing okay," replied Brian. "Let's get out of here. We'll explain everything else on the way. We've got work to do."

THIRTY-FOUR

Cuchillo Parado
Chihuahua Desert, Mexico

An old brown GMC Sierra pickup truck veered off the road and stopped in front of a drive-through chain-link gate by a rickety shack with a rusty, brown tin roof. Two Los Lobos Cartel guards with AK pistols over their chests approached both sides of the vehicle. One checked the pickup's bed. The other approached Amir and glanced inside the cab. He poked his head in toward Amir's face and spoke in Spanish.

¿Aquí para recoger?

But Amir didn't understand Spanish. He just shook his head.

"Here for pickup?" the guard asked in fair English.

"Yes, yes," replied Amir. "I am on time, no?"

The guard signaled another at the gate, and he rolled it to the side.

"We don't give a fuck, pendejo," the second guard by the truck said, pointing inside. "Move!"

The truck rolled through and across the dusty desert ground to the front of the large, brown bay door entrance. Across the grounds were men with rifles and submachine guns guarding various buildings or joking with each other and killing time. Each one of them eyed Amir as he made his way through. Amir stopped the pickup, and two men, both with slung AKs, rolled the warehouse doors to the side and waved him in.

Vamos, vamos.

Another man stepped to the front and guided the truck in. He held a hand up, and Amir braked in the center of the open building. The cartel member whistled, signaling the al-Qaeda lieutenant to shut the truck's engine off. The other two closed the doors behind him. Amir slowed to a complete stop. The guard walked slowly toward the driver's side door. He wrapped his hand around his throat, shouting in Spanish.

"Apágalo!"

He didn't understand, but Amir nervously turned the key anyway.

"Afuera!" the guard added, motioning for him to step out of the vehicle.

Large canvas bag in hand, Amir stepped out. Another cartel guard approached and forced his arms up. He frisked Amir from head to toe. He finished searching him and smacked him flat-palmed on his chest.

"He's clean," he said to the others in Spanish.

Suddenly, a dozen cartel men appeared and circled Amir. He felt a shiver through his leg as they glared him down.

"Jefe!" one of them shouted. "Jefe!"

Amir had traded his Muslim attire for dark Western-style pants and a button shirt. A brown kufiyah dangled from his neck. Muslims in that part of the world were uncommon, and he didn't want to stick out among the locals.

Amir heard footsteps coming from the back and noticed a billow of cigar smoke filling the air. Behind the gaggle of men, he noticed a man wearing dark-colored slacks, a red and black plaid shirt, leather cowboy boots, and matching cowboy hat. The man reached up and took a drag from his cigar, illuminating him slightly. It revealed his clean-shaven face with a neat, thin mustache, a shiny gold bracelet, and a diamond ring. Two of his personal bodyguards ambled alongside him. Wearing nice slacks and shirts, they were dressed better than the others.

His name was Juan Castillo. He lowered the cigar and centered himself under the yellow light bulb overhead. Clearly in charge, he stopped between both groups, his personal protection behind him.

"Bueno, compadres, miren lo puntual que son los árabes, eh?" Juan asked. "Or, good for business, the gringos would say."

Juan was as cold-blooded as they came, and violent. If you were no good to him or the organization any longer, he'd just as soon kill you. His men didn't dare do anything to anger him. "Now we speak English," he said, his gold tooth glinting while he smiled. "You do speak English?"

"Yes," replied Amir. "I do. Very well."

"Good," said Juan. "So, Arab, that was a big order your people made, you know? You got the kind of cash to pay for something so sophisticated?"

Amir tossed the bag in his right hand at Juan's feet. "Like we said on the phone," he replied. "It is all there. You can count if you wish. I will wait."

Juan crouched down and unzipped the bag. He grinned, thumbing through stacks of crisp bills.

"No," Juan said. "That's okay. I believe you. Besides, I know where to find your boss if anything is missing."

Juan closed the bag and tossed it back to one of his men. "Encárgate de eso."

Juan retrieved a cell phone from his shirt pocket and dialed a number. It rang twice, and he uttered a single word.

"Listo."

Amir held his arms out and took a quick glance around.

"Okay," he said. "Where is the product we ordered?"

Juan flashed him a wide smile. "Don't worry, Arab," he replied. "It's on its way."

A squeaky rumble resonated from behind Juan. One of his cartel cronies emerged, pushing a flat cart across the floor. On the cart were several hard, black cases piled a few feet high. The man rolled the cart between the cartel lieutenant and his guest.

"Ah, here we are, my friend," Juan said. "Just as agreed. You may inspect if you'd like."

Amir gripped one of the boxes and flipped the latch. He opened up and inspected the contents. He continued down the top row until all of those boxes were checked. Not wanting to go through each one, he popped the lids closed and locked them.

"Very good," replied Amir. "I think my boss will be pleased."

Amir grabbed the cart handle and pushed it along the side of the pickup.

"Excelente," Juan said. "What are your plans with these, anyway?"

Amir flashed an evil smile. "You'll just have to see."

"All right, hombre," Juan added. "Let us help you, heh? You were my number-one customer this month." Juan laughed. "Call it our dedication to customer service."

Not willing to get his hands dirty, Juan yelled at his men, as manual labor was for the grunts. "¡A trabajar!"

They rushed over and helped Amir load the cases into the rear of the truck. One by one, they stacked them up two high until the bottom of the truck bed was covered. Amir strolled to the cab and retrieved a large tarp from behind the seat. He tossed it into the back and began tying it down to the corners with rope.

"Remember, mi amigo," he said. "My men will meet yours

at the coordinates I gave you. They will help you get the cargo over the border. But do not keep them waiting. It's hot as fuck out here."

Juan waved, walking away with his personal guards.

"Now, get the hell out of my building."

***

A gang of cartel henchmen remained up top, equipped with AKs and gun trucks with mounted machine guns to guard the tunnel entrance. On the opposite end of the tunnel was the tiny Texas border town of El Indio.

By the time Amir and the guard with him made it into the elaborate underground tunnel system with the cargo, it was pitch-black outside. Green glow sticks were the only light they had, one on each end and another in the hands of the cartel soldier leading him.

"This tunnel is very long," he said to the guard. "It must have taken a long time to dig."

"Not for us," the guard replied. "Keep moving! We don't have time for chatting."

They'd pushed the cart a couple hundred meters over soft soil by then. It wasn't especially heavy, but the wheels kept veering off the wood planks spread across the tunnel floor and into the soft soil. Amir tried to correct it, but the guard snatched his hand away.

"I'll do it," he said. "If I let you, we will be here all night!"

The guard jerked the cart handle and kept moving toward the green light. They made it to the end, and the soldier held the glow stick up toward a wooden ladder that pointed out. He pounded on the ladder with a fist. On top, a round cover scraped across rock as it was tossed to the side, revealing the stars in the moonless sky above.

A man outside began lowering a chain with a glow stick attached to it toward the bottom. At the end of the chain was a large metal hook. He lowered the chain until he reached eye level with those inside. The cartel soldier at the bottom tugged on the chain, and the man above held it in place.

He wrapped the hook around the handle of one of the cases. The man above felt the weight, and he began hoisting it up. For the next several minutes, they repeated the process until each box had been raised and loaded into the bed of a white van. They finished up, and the cartel soldier shoved Amir toward the ladder.

"¡Ve, date prisa!"

Amir began to climb. As he made it to the top of the twenty-foot ladder, his man, Omar, took his hand and helped him up. The second cartel guard climbed in after Amir and headed down. Omar slid the cover back over the hole and tossed dead brush over the top of it. He squeezed Amir's hand and yanked him to his feet.

"You okay, boss?" Omar asked in Arabic. "You seem a little distracted."

"Yes, I am fine," Amir replied, dusting off his clothes. "Those Mexicans, they are a strange group."

They went to the van. Amir swung his leg onto the passenger seat and yanked the door while Omar hastily organized and covered the boxes in the back.

"Hurry," Amir added, smacking the inside of the door. "Let's get away from here before the American Border Patrol shows up!"

"Yes, boss," Omar replied, shutting the rear doors and locking them from inside. He stepped over the boxes and climbed into the driver's seat. Omar turned the ignition but left the headlights off.

He gently pressed the accelerator and rolled the van across the sand a few hundred meters toward a two-lane back road. They met the blacktop, and Omar swung onto the road and turned the lights on. They drove straight into the night, away from the small, Texas border town and north toward the I-10 freeway.

THIRTY FIVE

Miracle Valley, Arizona

T wo border patrol F-150 pickups whisked down the isolated piece of road toward the town in close proximity to the Mexican border wall. The blistering Arizona heat was out in full force as radio traffic constantly transmitted through the speakers inside the cab. The semi-arid land gave way to distant mountain peaks on the horizon. The two trucks passed by a few small, decrepit houses and run-down trailers, and it was evident that poverty was prevalent in the tiny Arizona community.

Earlier, the nearest Border Patrol station reported receiving a call from the Cochise County Sheriff's Department about a concerned neighbor claiming to have seen a suspicious vehicle in town. The border patrol received meaningless calls often, but when they came from known cartel routes, they tended to take them seriously.

The vehicles took a right onto another country road and traveled toward a little farmhouse just over a mile down. In the rear vehicle, a rust-colored, short-haired German Shepherd, part of the agency's K-9 program, perked up with his tail wagging. Up ahead, a single patrol car waited at the edge of the property.

They saw the deputy speak to someone as he rested against a worn-out chain-link fence.

"Hey, bud," Agent Austin King said over the radio to his partner behind him. "Wait in the truck, all right? I'll go up there and see what's going on. Just keep the dog inside for now. I don't want to scare her or cause him to overheat."

The radio squawked. "Ten-four," his man replied.

King's partner was a Mexican American by the name of Alex García. He was the first generation of his family born in the States.

"Whatever you say, amigo," García added.

The trucks began to slow, King steering right and onto a patch of gravel off the side of the road. He halted the vehicle just shy of a rusted chain-link gate in front of a faded, old house with broken, gray shutters and an old, shabby front porch. The truck kicked up dust, sliding across loose rock. Gun on his hip, King put it in park, donned his white cowboy hat, and hopped out. A short, old lady with gray hair ambled down a walkway and toward the front entry using a brown, wooden cane.

"That her?" King asked the deputy as he hopped out of the pickup.

"Yeah," he replied. "She called it in earlier this morning. Could be something or not."

The agent made his way toward the yard.

"Missus Adams?" King asked. "Are you Missus Adams, ma'am?"

She stumbled through the gate, falling forward and nearly slamming into King's pickup. He and the deputy caught her halfway and helped her steady herself.

"Whoa," King said, gripping her around the arms. "You okay, ma'am?"

They helped keep her on her feet. With one hand, the woman leaned up against the door of the pickup.

"Yeah, sonny," she replied, gasping to catch her breath. "I'm just fine. At my age, I ain't so nimble no more, you see? Nothin' works like it used to."

"So, you are Missus Adams, right?"

"Yes, young man," she replied. "But you can call me Roxanne."

The deputy headed back to his car.

"Okay, Roxanne," said King. "What is it that you would like to report, ma'am?"

King followed as she limped around the truck and across the dusty roadway, her palm gripping her cane. Leaning to one side against the wooden stick, she pointed over the desert brush to a parallel road across the way.

"There," Roxanne said. "That's where he saw it."

"Who?" asked King.

She squinted from the sun's glare and shielded her eyes with her hand as she glanced up at the tall man.

"My husband," she replied. "He saw a van over yonder from our porch. It just didn't belong here. Not many people in this Podunk town. We all know one other, you know?"

"Okay," said King.

"Anyway," the lady added. "It sat right there for a really long time, half the day, without moving. Then these men just appeared out of nowhere."

Agent King swiped a small notepad and pen from his breast pocket and started jotting notes.

"All right, Roxanne," he said. "Anything else you can tell me about this suspicious van?"

"He said it looked like they were loading something, but it was real dark. He saw what looked like a green light, and these people moving around doing something. That's all I know, son. Like I said, it just didn't seem right."

Agent King waved for his partner. The dog barked as the two exited the vehicle. Using a leash, García led his canine partner across the road.

"Max, sit," he said as they approached.

The dog sat, wagging his tail and panting. García tightened the lead against him while King pointed across the field of red dirt and dead shrubbery.

"Missus Adams," he said to his partner, peering down at the old lady, "I'm sorry, Roxanne, claims her hubby noticed a suspicious van across the way. So, let's go see what ole Max can turn up, huh?"

King set a hand on Roxanne's shoulder. "Thank you, ma'am," he added. "We'll be right back. This shouldn't take too long."

García gave the leash a little slack, and they marched forward over dusty ground. They traversed the pavement just past the square patch of land to the other side. Inspecting the disturbed dirt and grass, it was clear someone had been there. The dog sniffed, concentrating on one spot with obvious human tracks and soil that was dug into.

"Looks like we got a hit," said García.

Whoever had been at that spot, the dog quickly picked up the scent. The canine caught a strong whiff of something.

"He's onto something," García added. He let the leash fall to the ground. "Go get it, boy," he said to Max.

The dog took off into the underbrush. He looped around tumbleweed and Joshua trees and up a rocky, unstable hill as he tracked the scent. The two agents followed Max as he ran ahead, momentarily moving out of their sight. It seemed like they followed him at least a mile, sweat trickling down their heads and soaking through their uniform shirts. Passing over a hill, they caught sight of him again a football field's length away. Max stopped in place, sitting with his nose up and barking into the air.

"He's found something," said García. "What you got there, mijo?"

The men picked up their pace, jogging the rest of the way. At first, they didn't see anything, but Max kept resting his paw in a single spot. Agent King brushed and kicked the dead vegetation away with his foot. He stooped on the ground and felt it with his hand.

"What is it?" García asked.

King moved his hands over an object covered with red dirt and sage. "Damn," he said, reaching down with both hands. "There's something here, all right."

Gripping the sides, he lugged a round piece of solid metal out of the way. "Shit," King added. "There's a hole here."

Shining his Maglite down into the hole, he noticed the ladder attached to the wall but couldn't see the bottom.

"Holy shit, partner," he continued. "I think we just found another cartel tunnel."

Max sniffed around and circled the hole. Agent King petted him on the top of the head and ran his hand down his back.

"Good job, boy," he added.

Agent García dropped to his knees and peeked inside. "We climbing down to check it out?" he asked.

"No," King replied, rising and sliding the light into the holder on his belt. "Not yet, my Mexican, American friend. We need to call this in first. We don't know what's down there."

García spoke in Spanish. "Odio a los carteles. I fucking hate those assholes," he added. "They're the main cause of my parents coming here, man. My uncle, my dad's brother, got involved running that shit for them until he messed up and snitched. They shot his ass and left him in a ditch in the Sonora Desert. Ruthless sons of bitches, hombre."

"I know, brother," King replied, patting his partner on the shoulder. "I have no love for them either. But now you get to fight back, don't you? Come on, man, let's head back so we can let Samson know."

King bent down and covered up the hole. He and his partner made their way back to their vehicles across the patch of bare ground. The midday heat rained down like the sun was falling toward them. Sweat had accumulated in their shirts and down the sides of their faces. They walked, and Agent King retrieved a clean rag from his pants pocket and wiped off his face. They approached the trucks, and García hit the keyless entry.

"Get up there, Max," he said, loading the dog into the back. "Good boy."

Max's panting had increased.

"You thirsty, boy?" García asked. "Yeah, I bet you are, huh?"

He grabbed a small cooler of water from the floor and unscrewed the top. He poured some into a bowl he'd left for Max on the seat. Max began lapping up the cool water, and the agent slammed the door. Marching around to the driver's side, he yanked the door open and reached in. He inserted the key, cranking the truck, and turned up the air conditioning for his canine partner.

Up front, Agent King had leaned into his pickup and snatched his radio mic from its receiver.

"HQ," he said. "Be advised, investigating that ten twenty-seven. Possible ten thirty-six. We're ten twenty-five at this time."

King was requesting supervisory assistance before they investigated further. He waited for a response.

"Ten four," a voice said through the speaker. "We'll ten thirty-eight at that location."

"That's a ten four," King replied.

He set the mic back inside the vehicle.

"Hey, King!" the sheriff's deputy hollered from his car not far away "You need me to wait, or what?"

"No, thanks," replied King. "You're good. We've got the cavalry coming. We appreciate the assistance, though, per usual!"

"Ten four, man!" said the deputy. "Call if you need anything."

The deputy climbed into his running car and shut the door. He swung a U-turn and took off down the roadway. All the Border Patrol agents could do for the time being was sit tight where they were and wait for backup to arrive.

THIRTY-SIX

Agents King and García waited in their respective vehicles with the air conditioning cranked up all the way. The late-afternoon sun had begun to dip behind the far-off peaks. King checked the time on his black Timex wristwatch.

"Come on," he mumbled to himself. "What the hell is taking this guy so long?"

The men had been sitting there, unable to act, for almost an hour. King's eye had been pressed to his binocular, trained on the surrounding area around the tunnel the majority of the time. He could see the heatwave stream over the desert floor as it baked down. Agent King had expected somebody to pop their head up out of the hole at any time, but no one ever did.

Tired of sitting still, King keyed up his radio mic.

"Five-five," he said. "What's your ten twenty? We've been ten seven for almost an hour, over."

He waited, bouncing his leg out of boredom. King wasn't a guy who liked to wait around.

"Almost there," Agent Samson replied. "Sorry, got caught up in something here. ETA, five minutes."

"Ten-four," King said, setting the mic back down.

In his truck's side mirror, he could see the boss's SUV kicking up dust behind it over flat ground a couple miles away. King watched Samson zoom down the roadway and take a right half a mile behind them. Samson came up fast down the last stretch of pavement.

The Chevy Tahoe pulled up behind García and shut down. García and his partner exited their vehicles and wandered toward the Tahoe as Samson made his way around and popped the hatch. Inside, he snatched up two M4s, one for him and the other for Agent Bryant, who was with him. He tossed Bryant the rifle, and the agent approached from the passenger side. With his rifle on safe, the Border Patrol supervisor slapped a magazine in and released the weapon bolt.

"All right," Samson said. "Show it to me."

"All right, boss," replied King. "Follow me."

With vests on and gripping their weapons, they hustled across the hardtop. The agents tread over red dirt and dead grass toward the tunnel. Firearms were ready as they approached the site.

"Stop," he said, pointing downward. "There it is, right there."

Agent King stretched a hand down and found the tunnel cover once again. With vegetation covering the lid, it was hardly noticeable to the naked eye. King slid the hunk of metal out of the way. Agent Samson circled around with his flashlight in hand and shone a beam down into the darkness.

"Okay," he said. "There's really no way around this. We have to climb down to make sure nobody is down there before we demolish it."

"Got it, boss," replied García.

"It's crazy, though," Samson added. "After we cave this one in, there'll be another one somewhere to take its place."

"Yeah," replied King. "It's a never-ending freaking battle, ain't it?"

Agent Samson put a foot on the top of the ladder to make sure it wasn't rotted and was stable enough to hold their weight. He shifted all his weight onto it. "All right," he said. "I'll go first, you boys follow. One at a time, gentlemen. We don't know how much weight this thing can handle."

Samson slung his M4. He grabbed the top rung of the wooden ladder as he bent over and stepped lower onto it. Gripping the top with both hands, he began his descent. It took him a minute to reach the bottom because he stepped warily, one boot at a time. When he hit flat ground, King could see the boss's light turn on while he flashed it further ahead.

"Looks clear," Agent Samson shouted up, "but we need to go further ahead to make sure. Start climbing down!"

Agent García was the next to enter the hole. He holstered his firearm and stepped cautiously onto the ladder, climbing down to meet his boss at the bottom. One by one, they each headed down until at last, Agent Bryant's boots hit the subterranean soil.

"Okay," Samson said, turning on his weapon light. "Let's hurry and get this over with so we can get back up top. Kind of damn musty down here."

"Right behind you, boss," King replied.

Agent Samson stepped off slowly, moving the beam of light side to side.

"It must've taken forever to dig this," said García.

Samson froze in place, his light flooding the tunnel.

"Shh," he said. "I'm trying to listen."

He couldn't hear or see a thing up ahead. They crept through at an agonizingly slow pace, listening for the slightest bit of noise. All was eerily quiet. Then, a sudden clanking sound further on caught their attention.

"Does that sound like a…"

Before King could finish, gunfire erupted from the other end. Agent Samson was immediately struck by a bullet to the thigh. He quickly fell to his knees, then his face, dropping his rifle and wailing in pain. "Fuck!" he shouted. "I'm hit. I've been hit!"

"Shit," King said. "Everybody, get down!"

The men hit the deck. They began crawling over the cool ground. King took Samson's rifle and wrapped the sling around his off-hand. Kissing the soil, he fired indiscriminately through the dark. The others discharged their weapons at the same time, not sure of where the enemy was or where they were aiming. The AKs ceased fire. Not sure what was happening, King lifted his head. But they were met with even more intense fire as machine-gun rounds pelted the tunnel around them.

"What the hell?" García asked, recognizing the sound from his time in the Marines. "That a fucking SAW?"

He was referring to the M249 SAW, or squad automatic weapon, mostly used by US Army and Marine Corps infantry squads.

"Sure sounds like it!" King yelled over the rapid noise.

The ear-splitting racket of automatic gunfire overwhelmed them as it bounced off the tunnel walls. Dust blinded them while incoming bullets cut through the surrounding dirt. They tried to return fire on their bellies, but they couldn't see what they were shooting at through the haze of dust and gun smoke.

"We're outgunned here!" King yelled to them. "We have to get out of this hole, now!"

The agent grabbed his boss's collar and tried to drag him toward the ladder.

"Hey, help me!" King added over the ruckus. "We need to get him out of here!"

García made an attempt to get closer and assist King in moving Agent Samson, but when his head popped up, he caught a bullet to the forehead. Blood splattered back onto King's face as he painfully attempted to get his boss out of the line of fire. García's face was a bloody mess when he hit his back. A few feet away, Bryant was in a frenzy, shooting his M4 wildly through the dark.

"Hey!" King shouted to him. "Let's get the fuck out of here!"

Agent Bryant released the trigger and moved on his knees toward the tunnel exit. But when he got ahold on Agent Samson's arm, a burst of machine gun rounds tore through Bryant's back. Blood spilled from his mouth and down his chin, and he fell to the earth, slamming his head into the ladder. King ducked low in an attempt to roll him over. When he saw the red liquid coating the back of his vest from top to bottom, he knew Bryant was gone. King let go of him.

Samson had been bleeding profusely as they'd moved him a dozen feet or so, leaving a trail of blood-soaked soil in his wake. Bullets hit and ricocheted around them, and King took Samson's chin and turned his head. He'd been in and out of consciousness. Agent King swiped a tourniquet from his belt and began wrapping it around the top of his boss's thigh. He tightened it hard and tied it off.

'Boss!" King said, trying to keep him awake by smacking him several times in the face. "Boss, look at me. Stay with me. You have to stay awake!"

Agent Samson, his eyes half shut and fuzzy, glanced up weakly.

"Boss, I'm going to grab you now, okay?" said King. "You hold on with your hands, okay? I'll try to lift you out."

As hails of bullets struck the tunnel wall around the ladder,

Agent King heaved Samson up just enough for him to grab it. Backward against the wall, he lifted his boss up with his back.

"Come on, you bastard!" he screamed, his face apple red as he struggled. "Get up there!"

Suddenly, King heard the distinct impact of torn flesh above him. Agent Samson lost the already weakened grip he had. He plunged from the ladder, over King and ten feet down onto his back. He didn't budge. Blood pooled outward from under Samson's body.

"Boss, boss!" yelled King.

He climbed down and kicked the side of the boss's leg to see if he'd react, but it was no use. The man was dead, a single exit wound at the center of his chest. Agent King pounded on the ground.

"You motherfuckers!" he screamed at the top of his lungs. "You cartel bastards will pay!"

He plucked the rifle from the ground and let go of a few shots. He was no match for the volley of fire coming his way, though. His only other option was to escape. King calmed a bit, trying to slow his rapid breathing.

"Okay," he said, letting out a little air. "Okay, I can do this."

King slung the M4 onto his back. He picked up the pistol he'd dropped on the floor of the tunnel and holstered it. Bullets continued toward him sporadically while the enemy waited to see if anyone was left. He took a deep breath and climbed onto the ladder.

"All right, here we go."

King climbed four rungs. Before he made it to the fifth, three rifle rounds shot toward him, striking the back of his right leg. He nearly buckled, but his death grip on the ladder kept him from falling.

"Shit, damn it. Fuck, that hurts." King punched the side of the tunnel wall. "God damn it!!"

He pounded his head on the ladder. "All right," he said. "Keep going. Got to keep moving."

In agony, he slowly made his way up a few more rungs. He continued upward, and another shot rang out and hit him in his left calf. King nearly lost his grip and plunged to the bottom.

"Damn you, bastards!" shouted King.

Not able to put all his weight on either leg, he tightened his hand grip. He began to make his way agonizingly toward the tunnel entrance. As he finally reached the top, he set his hands on the ground surface and pushed against his body weight, hoisting himself out the rest of the way. He reached for the cover and mustered all his strength to move it back into place.

On his hands and knees, Agent King began to crawl painstakingly back toward the roadway and his patrol vehicle. Seeing double from a mix of high temperatures and the loss of blood, his movements were cumbrously slow. He didn't know what time it was or how long it was taking him. Seeing anything was nearly impossible while the salty sweat accumulated and trickled into his eyes.

For nearly half an hour, he poked forward, leaving a trail behind in the sand. King caught the silhouette of his pickup ahead and knew he was getting close. He clambered on for twenty more feet, finally feeling pavement under his palms.

The agent could just make out the outline of a person across the road. King removed the rifle from his back, wrapping his fingers around the barrel. He tried to push himself up by the rifle butt. He almost made it, but as he tried to extend his legs, Agent King became dizzy, losing his balance and crashing down on the hot asphalt. Quivering on his side, he could barely make out a faint shout and someone coming toward him.

"You okay, sir?" a muffled voice asked. "Sir?"

The mysterious woman wrapped her arms around him to feel for an injury. Then she noticed his bloody legs.

"Sir, we need to get you to a hospital!" the lady said.

Then everything went dark.

THIRTY-SEVEN

Plains, Texas

Hundreds of miles away in the state of Texas, Deputy Sheriff Dale Thomas of the Yoakum County Sheriff's Department had just left from getting his coffee fill at a small, locally owned coffee shop.

Without fail, he'd stop by every evening before his night shift and opt for a large black with two sugars. That day was no different. He was used to the routine of free coffee they'd give out to all law enforcement officers in the area. Southwest of Lubbock, the area was a small, tight-knit community not known for violent crime. Anticipating a quiet night on the job, the deputy headed through the lot and back to his patrol car, a shiny black and white Dodge Challenger.

Thomas unlocked the door and climbed inside, setting the cup into the drink holder between the seats. With the sun still out for a time, and wearing silver aviator shades, he removed his white cowboy hat and placed it on the passenger seat. The deputy slipped a hand into the pocket of his brown uniform shirt and retrieved his phone, plugging it into the charger on the dash. Peering at himself in the mirror, he ran a hand over his short, brown hair. He stuck the keys into the ignition and fired it up, and one thousand horses under the car's hood galloped noisily, vibrating his feet on the floor.

Deputy Thomas rolled through the small parking area and stopped just short of the side road. Waiting for a car to pass, he swung out into a four-way intersection and pressed the brake when the light turned red. The Challenger's engine rumbled deeply, drowning out every other car on the road. In his usual attentive manner, the deputy glanced at vehicles on both sides of him. He checked his rearview mirror, adjusting it as a black GMC Sierra pickup pulled up behind him.

Radio chatter sounded through the speaker as he waited for the light to change. It turned green, and Deputy Thomas pulled out slowly with traffic. He flicked his right turn signal, glancing back to make sure the lane was clear. Facing forward, he veered into the far right lane to turn onto the highway half a mile ahead.

The night before, the department had received an APB, an all points bulletin, from the Bisbee, Arizona Border Patrol Office of the Tucson sector. They were looking for the white van first reported near the southern border in Arizona. The Arizona Sector Chief, Jason Mullins, figured it had something to do with his agents' recent ambush by cartel members.

Thomas swerved his patrol car onto the off ramp and around the sharp curve toward the highway. He maintained speed, zipping toward the freeway and merging into traffic. The midmorning traffic was light, having missed the morning rush by a couple of hours. The deputy remained in the right lane, maintaining speed with the flow of traffic.

The land in that part of West Texas was mostly flat and desert-like with the occasional cluster of trees. The farther east a person got from the town, the greener the state became. With no destination in mind, Deputy Thomas patrolled the county as he traveled down US Highway 82 toward Brownfield. It had been an uneventful morning for the sheriff's office. That part of Texas wasn't known for high crime. Except for a few domestic calls, mostly drunken disputes, nothing really happened within the county's borders.

Thomas clicked his right blinker and got ready to turn off onto another side street before heading back. He started to swing right when a certain vehicle caught his eye through his side mirror. On instinct, the deputy turned back onto the highway. His body shook as he ran over the rumble strip at the bend between the off ramp and the highway's right lane. He swerved left and jerked back quickly to straighten out. The van in question had rushed by and was now a few hundred feet away. Deputy Thomas increased speed and moved around traffic for a clear line of sight. He glanced at the license tag.

Thomas snatched his radio mic, steering right.

"Central," he said, clearing his throat. "It's two-two-five. Got eyes on a vehicle matching the description of the APB put out by the Arizona BP eastbound on Highway 82. Nothing suspicious at this time. Going to follow unless there's an active PC to stop."

"Ten-four," replied HQ personnel.

"Tag is two, seven, five…eight, four, Juliet," Thomas added. "Be advised, I'm about to cross the county line into Terry County, over."

"That's a ten-four," said HQ. "We'll inform that department now."

"Ten-four," replied the deputy, setting the mic down.

He continued along the roadway, following the white van and crossing over the county line toward Brownfield. A few car lengths behind, Thomas trailed them without incident for just over five miles. He glanced to his right and spotted a Terry County Sheriff's car, a blue Ford Mustang, pulling out behind them from a side road. The Terry County deputy hung back a bit.

As Thomas maintained his distance to the van, he received a call from central.

"Two-five-five," the voice said. "That ten-fourteen just came back as ten-sixteen out of Tucson."

Ten-sixteen meant the vehicle was reported stolen. Deputy Thomas held the mic to his lips and squeezed the button. "Ten-four, central," he replied. "I'm in pursuit."

The deputy flipped the siren and lights on and mashed hard on the accelerator. He zoomed in behind the van quickly. The Terry County deputy behind him followed suit. Thomas saw the driver of the van glaring at him through the van's side mirror. He didn't appear willing to come to a stop.

The van increased speed in an attempt to get away. Deputy Thomas stayed on its tail, and the other deputy swerved into the left lane. Trying to box the van in, he whisked by Thomas until his patrol car was even with the driver of the van. The Terry County deputy, Bradshaw, gave an order over his car's PA system.

"This is the Terry County Sheriff's Department," his voice bellowed over the external speakers. "Pull the vehicle to the side of the road, now!"

Behind, Deputy Thomas could just make out the driver's face through the van's mirror. He appeared to have a dark complexion, as someone from west Asia would. Thomas could just make out his beard, brown with spots of white.

Deputy Bradshaw came over the PA again. "Pull your vehicle to the side of the road," he ordered. "I won't ask you again!"

Deputy Thomas noticed as Bradshaw got ready to perform a pit maneuver. The traffic on that isolated roadway hadn't picked back up yet. Deputy Bradshaw swung slightly to the left. He swerved back right to strike the van's quarter panel, and the rear doors suddenly popped open. Only ten feet in front of Thomas's Challenger, he immediately spotted an M240 Bravo, or M240B machine gun barrel pointed directly at him.

"Shit!" the deputy yelled while 7.62 bullets tore through his windshield and hood.

Glass shattered across the dash. He promptly jerked the wheel to the left. Thomas knew those rounds would tear right through his body armor, not to mention cut through his vehicle like a knife to warm butter.

"Central!" he shouted, grabbing the radio mic. "Incoming automatic machine-gun fire in pursuit of ten-sixteen…"

Before he could finish, the van's passenger began firing an AK at Deputy Bradshaw through the passenger window. Bullets riddled his passenger door and smashed the passenger-side window. Bradshaw hit the brakes to let the van pass and slowed until he was even with Thomas's car.

The van gained distance, and they passed by the city limit sign for Brownfield, Texas. The vehicles zoomed past a high school football stadium with a game in session. A local news helicopter buzzed around the stadium, gathering aerial shots. The machine-gun fire persisted, striking the front of Thomas's vehicle. Oil spurted up through holes in the hood. Green antifreeze gushed all over the roadway, leaving a liquid trail as his patrol car began smoking and rolled to a sudden stop. Deputy Bradshaw pulled up to check on Thomas.

"Damn it, central," said Thomas. "I'm disabled. Repeat, vehicle disabled. Requesting tow and SWAT eastbound on eighty-two entering Brownfield, over."

"Ten-four," replied central. "I'll contact the commander now. Just sit tight."

The machine-gun fire ceased. Having witnessed the carnage on the highway, the news helicopter rolled live footage as it glided toward the moving van.

Thomas barely noticed one of the men in the van shouldering a large, green tube.

"Shit, central!" he shouted. "Contact KCBD news and tell 'em to get that helo away from here. They're being engaged!"

But it was too late. The gunner in the back of the van moved out of the blast zone, and the other man fired the tube. A streak of white smoke sailed through the air at an angle toward the medium-sized helicopter. An intense *boom* followed by a bright orange flash erupted just to the right of the tail rotor. The rotor spun wildly, and the chopper began to spin out of control. Deputy Thomas watched helplessly while the helo dropped like a twirling pile of concrete into the grass at the edge of the road. It exploded in a huge ball of fire.

Bouncing out of his car, Thomas dashed for the burning chopper. Bradshaw followed. The flames loomed over them, and the heat was unbearable. Sure there were no survivors, the deputy snatched the radio clipped to his uniform.

"Central," he said, backing away from the intense heat of the flames. "Got a downed news chopper here, crashed and on fire from some kind of shoulder-fired rocket. Send EMS, fire, and additional units to assist, over."

"Ten-four," central replied.

Thomas booked it back to his car and hopped in. Deputy Bradshaw tapped on the window, and he rolled it down.

"Hey!" said Bradshaw. "You okay, you good? Your car took a beating there."

"Yeah, I think so," replied Thomas. "Just fucking rattled, man. Hang back, though. That thing will turn your car into Swiss cheese. SWAT is on its way."

Bradshaw gave him a thumbs-up and headed back to his patrol car and climbed in.

"Central," he said. "Lost sight of the subject. Again, just lost visual. Need ten seventy-one. I repeat, in need of ten seventy-one."

"Ten-four, two-five-five," replied HQ.

The subjects in the van slammed the doors shut. Thomas observed while the vehicle pressed on and made a right turn, moving swiftly out of his field of view. The only thing they could do now was wait.

THIRTY-EIGHT

Vice Admiral Kenneth Lipstein, the JSOC commander, escorted the First Special Forces commander, Major General Anthony Gold, a short distance down the shiny hallway and into his office close to the end. In a hurry, he'd just seen the news coverage of the downed helicopter in Texas a few minutes before. Suspecting a terror attack, he rushed to get that information through the chain.

General Gold, a 1992 West Point graduate, had been commander for almost two years. Under his command were each Special Forces groups and all their support elements. On the other hand, Vice Admiral Lipstein graduated from the Naval Academy in Annapolis in the late eighties. He was responsible for special mission units (SMUs) like Delta (CAG) and SEAL Team Six (DEVGRU), and a few other "tip of the spear" units.

He and the general entered the office, and Gold immediately noticed the billowing smoke from the crash site on the commander's TV, taken from a second chopper sent to the scene. Many lights flashed bright while emergency crews surrounded the smoldering helicopter. Eastbound traffic was blocked as a mile-long line of cars in all lanes remained in place, unable to turn around. Their view of the scene changed as the news helicopter circled the wreckage.

It was approaching dark, and the spotlight from the bird lit up the highway under the late-evening dusk. The gigantic fire did a good job of illuminating the rest.

"What the hell?" the general asked. "What's happened, Admiral? What am I watching?"

"You haven't seen this?" asked Lipstein.

"No, Admiral, I haven't."

"Well," Lipstein replied, "by the look of things, I'd say it's a terror cell on the loose on our highways, General. Probably the very one your boys have been chasing."

The general hesitated for a second as he watched the screen. The captions below did a good job of generalizing the incident, but local crews and police had no idea of the real tragedy that was unfolding right under their noses.

"But why there?" the admiral added. "Southwest Texas? What's the significance? That place is in the middle of nowhere desert, not a lot of people. It doesn't make any sense. If these are al-Qaeda terrorists, what's the target?"

Before the admiral could answer, three of the phone lines in his office blew up and began ringing constantly. The buttons on the phone all lit up like a Christmas tree.

"Sarah!" he shouted to his secretary in the next room. "Sarah, can you handle that, please? Take messages if you have to. I'm sort of in the middle of this mess right now. If it's important, I'll call them back!"

He heard Sarah press the button for one of the lines.

"Yes, Admiral!" she replied before answering the call.

General Gold plunked down on the admiral's office chair, tossing his service cap on the polished, brown desk. He stared blankly at the TV screen, his hand on his face. The general stomped his Oxford dress shoe on the floor.

"Oh, shit," he said, shooting back up out of the seat. "Damn it!"

Admiral Lipstein had yet to catch onto what the general was uneasy about.

"What?" he asked. "Come on, General, what is it?"

General Gold slowly glanced over at the admiral. "The president, Admiral," he replied. "His ranch is in Denton. It seems whoever shot down that chopper is on a direct path. That can't be a coincidence."

"What?" asked Lipstein. "I thought the first family were in the bunker with the rest of the cabinet."

"Negative, sir," the general replied. "He was mobile. His family was underground. But he refused to stay any longer. They flew back to Denton a couple days ago with their security detail."

Admiral Lipstein situated himself on top of his desk. He lowered his head. "My God," he said. "Why am I just now learning about this?"

"I don't know, Admiral," replied Gold. "I found out from Colonel Billings. Perhaps somebody dropped the ball."

"I would say so," the admiral said, quickly snatching his secure landline from the desk.

"Damn it!" he added, dialing a number. "Why didn't we pick up on this sooner? A few Secret Service personnel with handguns and a rifle or two won't do with that kind of threat. We've got to respond right away!"

A voice on the other end of the line answered. "This is Colonel Billings," the voice said.

"Colonel," replied Admiral Lipstein. "We've got an ongoing, time-sensitive emergency situation. You alone?"

The admiral heard Colonel Billings fumble with the phone.

"Yes, Admiral," he replied. "I am, sir. What's the situation?"

"Turn on the news, Colonel," replied the admiral. "We have reason to believe POTUS is in danger. We have maniacs on the loose with shoulder-fired missiles, machine guns, and Lord knows what else. Every second, we are losing precious time. We have to mobilize, right now!"

The admiral could hear through the line as Billings turned on the television. The colonel let out an audible gasp.

"That's right, Colonel," Lipstein added. "The POTUS ranch isn't far away, and he and his family are presently there. No more time to talk, Colonel. Round up your men. We need to get them in the air, now."

"Yes, Admiral," the colonel replied.

"I'll scramble a bird," Lipstein continued, "and meet you at the airfield in twenty minutes, out."

Admiral Lipstein slammed the phone down. He stood from the desk and moved closer to General Gold.

"General," he said, "I will contact POTUS and the entire emergency contact list. I need you to get Fort Bliss Command on the horn and scramble a couple Apache Helicopters. We'll track the terrorists' movement, but if the team can't get to the president in time, we'll have no choice but to take them out with a Hellfire."

"My God, on American soil, sir?" the general asked.

"We may not have any other option," Admiral Lipstein replied. "Of course, I'd get approval from POTUS first. Now go!"

***

Many miles away at Pope Army Airfield, butted against Fort Liberty, a C-17 Globemaster had been topped off with fuel and sat at the head of the runway. With a few dirt bikes loaded on a pallet inside by the rear door ramp, and the plane's crew conducting their final checks, the aircraft was almost ready to depart. It was a bleak, overcast night

In the parking lot by the terminal, Rob pulled his Mustang into a space just in front of the glass door entrance they'd need to take. With Brian riding shotgun, they both hopped from the vehicle. Rob reached behind the black leather seat and snatched up two camouflage combat packs. Brian shouldered his backpack while Rob locked the doors, and they made their way inside the building.

Headed to the back, they ran into Colonel Billings. They had no time for a drawn-out briefing, just a quick word as the rest of the team gathered around.

"Fellows," Colonel Billings said, meeting them in the corridor. "Walk with me."

They accompanied the colonel outside to the tarmac.

"Listen, men," the colonel added as they marched toward the plane. "I don't have to tell you how critical this is. We've never seen a situation like this. There's an imminent threat against the president. If we can't get there in time, 227th Aviation Regiment Apaches have been authorized to take the vehicle out with missiles. You all know this introduces a new set of problems, collateral damage. We can't allow deaths of American citizens, so there's only one option here."

Rob and Brian stepped onto the plane's ramp with the others.

"Roger that, sir," said Brian. "Don't worry, we'll deal with the bastards."

"Now," Billings continued, standing in the middle of the metal ramp, "they lost the van in Brownfield, but the choppers are on their way from Fort Cavazos to track them."

Rob waved to the colonel on the way up.

"Get it done, men," said Billings.

The five-man team boarded the aircraft. Inside, a stack of parachute deployment packs sat neatly inside an open hard case. The men each snatched one of the packs. They found their seats at the side of the plane and dropped their gear to the floor. Like the others, Rob donned a black helmet and his radio headset.

By the row of seating sat a large weapons case full of handguns and rifles that had been loaded earlier. He bent forward, snagging his HK416 and Sig Sauer P320 pistol. The HK416, made by Heckler & Koch, was similar to the M4 but more compact for ease of movement.

The rest of the team hunkered down around him as the crew chief buzzed the ramp closed with the push of a button. Retrieving his rifle and pistol magazines from an ammo can, Rob began loading them with his speed loader. He took out a small gun-cleaning kit from his cargo pocket to lubricate his firearms.

The pilot radioed from the cockpit. "Gentlemen," he said. "Please relax, sit tight, and fasten your seat harness. We're about to push off. Enjoy the flight. Next stop, the great state of Texas."

The plane's turboprops began to scream as they throttled up. The pilot contacted the tower.

"Tower, this is Conic-Two-Five. Conic-Two-Five requesting takeoff on runway two, over."

Seconds later, the air controller answered. "Conic-Two-five, you are clear for takeoff on runway two. I say again, you are clear. Have a good flight."

The aircraft's engines were booming at full throttle. The wheels slowly began to roll and picked up speed quickly. The C17 booked it down the runway, coming to a steep incline as it lifted off high into the black sky.

Three hours later, the large cargo plane soared through the clouds, thousands of feet above Highway 380 through Dallas,

Texas. The men snapped to their feet and performed buddy checks, strapping their gear and weapons tightly to their bodies. As they fixed helmets and goggles in place, the pilot interrupted with a radio announcement.

"Five minutes to drop zone!"

Brian and Rob took the lead. Hooking cords to the static line, each soldier held on to them and shuffled to the door. Ahead of them, the palletized motorbikes were hooked in and ready to deploy. The jump master, Master Sergeant Anthony Rico, stood to the side by the ramp. Rob, with black gloves on his hands, adjusted and tightened his helmet strap. They waited there a couple of minutes for the announcement to be made. Rob reached for the ruck suspended between his knees and tightened the straps.

The pilot came over the radio a second time.

"One minute, clear for drop!"

Several seconds went by, and their ground transport was released. The pallet shot through the opening as the chute deployed.

The jump master, holding a hand up, brought it down, shouting, "Go, go, go!"

Master Sergeant Rico snatched the end of each cord as they jumped. One by one, the men plunged feet first through the opening. The static line extracted cords, and the chutes thrust open as the men drifted across the darkened sky.

Sailing toward the Texas ground, Rob peered down below at the few lights that dotted the landscape. Checking the small GPS on his wrist, he steered the parachute toward the intended coordinates.

At one thousand feet and falling, Rob sailed through the clouds over the top of a farmer's field and a small patch of trees. Heading away from civilization and to open country, he steered over a lake and toward dusty plains half a mile away. He spotted a downed parachute below being dragged across the dirt and knew it was Brian's. The ground came up fast. Rob's feet hit the deck, and he ducked and rolled forward, landing on his back. He bounced to his feet and gathered up his chute while others landed across the meadow.

Rob released his ruck to the dirt and retrieved his attached HK416 rifle. His Sig already holstered, he flipped the ruck onto his back. Rob reached up and buckled the cross strap.

Brian adjusted his radio headset and pinched the mic. "Alpha-Six-Actual," he said. "This is Golf-Three-Six on location, how copy?"

"Solid copy, Golf-Three-Six," the voice replied. "Clear to proceed. Six-Actual, out."

Brian gave the rallying sign. "Let's get a move on, ladies!" he said.

With weapons ready and packs secured, the team darted across the terrain toward the five waiting motorbikes.

THIRTY-NINE

Jacksboro, Texas

Five black dirt bikes, headlights bouncing, zipped through the Texas countryside, past abundant farmland and over a dirt road toward a two-lane road.

With weapons in specially outfitted holders, the Christini AWD-450 bike engines revved and hummed while swerving around pothole after pothole off the side of the pavement and into the grass. Lightning bugs floated along through the air over the field and road. Racing down the roadway at fifty-five miles per hour, Rob hit a button to brighten the time on his Garmin watch.

2215.

They kept an eye out for cops; the last thing they needed was to get stopped and risk the target van slipping from their grasp. Tapping the brakes to slow down, they didn't bother coming to a complete stop at the four-way. They drifted right, and Rob spun a tire in a patch of gravel at the edge of the road. He hit the gas harder and hopped a small ditch back into the lane.

"Golf-Three-Six," a transmission suddenly sounded through radio headsets. "Golf-Three-Six, this is Archangel-

Seven. I say again, this is Archangel-Seven, how copy?"

They could hear the scream of helicopter rotor blades whirring in the background.

"Roger, Archangel-Seven," Brian yelled over the wail of dirt bike engines. "Good copy, over."

"Copy that, Golf-Three-Six," replied the lead pilot. "We're on station approximately five klicks due east of your location and conducting a recon of the area. No sight of the target at this time, continuing search, over."

The pilots and copilots operating the pair of Apache helicopters were flying with night vision so the enemy in the fleeing van wouldn't see them. Likewise, the adapted motorbikes the team was using had the capability to operate in blackout mode. These dim lights were used in nighttime operations so they could see one another up close, but the enemy could not spot them from afar. Five sets of headlights zipping down the street would be a dead giveaway.

As the dirt bikes zipped across the plains, the ISA at Fort Belvoir had been monitoring police radio traffic in that area of Texas. They'd just picked up something significant.

"Golf-Three-Six," Colonel Billings said over the radio. "It's Alpha-Six-Actual. India-One-Sierra has an update. I'm patching him through."

"Roger," replied Brian.

A few seconds later, Agent Conrad came through. "Golf-Three-Six," he said. "We've picked up police radio traffic at grid 33.2149024, 98.15889582, break."

The team listened in for Conrad to continue as he monitored the situation in real time.

"A van matching the description of the target vehicle," Conrad added, "just rammed a state police checkpoint in Bridgeport and is engaging with AKs and machine guns, over."

The team suddenly saw a giant explosion miles away, followed by a deafening boom.

"Damn it!" Rob said, slamming a hand on the bike's handlebars. "Alpha-Six-Actual, this is Golf-Three-Five. They're firing missiles. Can you call the police off before they all get killed? We can't afford to have that threatening civilians on the roads. They don't know what they're messing with, over."

"In the process," the colonel replied. "They don't want to listen. We're contacting the president's office now. That should perk up their ears a bit."

"Roger that," said Rob. "Three-Six, pull over a second, would you?"

Brian didn't feel the need to question Rob, but he wondered why he would slow down in pursuit of an enemy target. He slowed down anyway and coasted off the side of the road and into the dirt. The others pulled up behind him.

"India-One-Sierra," Rob said into his headset microphone. "Can you repeat those coordinates again but slower, so I can punch them in, over?"

He tugged his coat sleeve to reveal the GPS attached to his wrist.

"Roger," Conrad replied. "It's 33.21, 49, 024, break."

Rob finished the last number of the first line as Conrad continued.

"98.15, 88, 95, 82," Conrad added. "How copy?"

Rob hit a button on the GPS. "Good copy," he replied. "Thanks for the assist."

"Three-Five," Brian added. "Since you have the grid, you take point. We'll follow you."

"Roger that, boss," Rob said, pulling the bike ahead of Brian.

His back tire spun ,and Rob punched it out of the dirt and back into the road. The rest of the team behind him, he pointed the bike toward the east side of Bridgeport, Texas, a short drive away. They entered the town, and Rob quickly glanced at his GPS and made a right turn onto a highway on-ramp. The set of coordinates led only a few miles down the freeway.

Suddenly, the Apache pilot radioed them.

"Golf-Three-Six," he said. "Archangel-Seven here. We just passed over the police wreckage. It's a slaughter down there. We've spotted the target vehicle heading eastbound toward Decatur, over."

"Archangel-Seven," Rob replied. "It's Golf-Three-Five. Be advised, do not engage. There are more vehicles on this highway and a greater chance of collateral damage. We'll move in to intercept. Unless we call for a last resort, do not fire, over."

"Roger, Golf-Three-Five," replied the pilot. "Understood."

They sprinted around a curve, and the remnants of the police checkpoint turned up half a mile up. It was a ghastly sight as the men pulled up near the wreckage. Bullet holes riddled the sides of vehicles, but it was the armored Lenco Bearcat SWAT transport in the middle that got their attention. Even though the vehicle was hardened, the missile had ripped through it like it was made of cardboard. Armored police SUVs had been tossed across the highway like rag dolls. Body parts and pieces of armor were scattered across the pavement, still smoldering from the inferno.

The team could see the blinking lights from the Apaches straight ahead. Cars on the highway suddenly stopped, frightened by the shocking scene playing out in front of them.

"Alpha-Six-Actual," Brian said as they rolled by the towering fire and smoke. "Contact local EMS, would you? We also need someone to handle this traffic, over."

They began to hear sirens off in the distance. They peered back and spotted swirling lights moving fast in their direction and a civilian helicopter approaching from the west.

"Disregard my last, Alpha-Six-Actual," Brian added. "EMS is en route. But get rid of this goddamned news chopper. They can't get any closer, or they'll risk being shot down!"

"Copy that, Golf-Three-Six," replied the colonel. "I'll make the call."

Rob spun tires, leaving blacks tread marks across the blacktop, and they took off again. Farther ahead, they suddenly detected a flame spark and a trail of white smoke shooting into the sky. The Apaches performed evasive maneuvers, making a hard right turn. The missile missed the tail of the lead helicopter by mere inches.

"Golf-Three-Six," the pilot said over the net. "They've fired on us but missed. We're going to gain some distance and maintain line of sight, over."

About now, the men were sure the Apache pilots wanted to send a Hellfire through the van, but firing missiles and the high-powered thirty-millimeter cannon was strictly prohibited on roads through populated America. Even so, Rob thought he'd give it a shot.

"Alpha-Six-Actual," he said through the speakers. "It's Golf-Three-Five. Archangel-Six has been fired on. Do they have permission to engage, over?"

Rob waited.

"That's a negative!" said the colonel. "You know the ROE (rules of engagement). That would require emergency authority from the top. Since we can't get ahold of POTUS, I contacted the defense secretary personally. He's not willing to make that call. Orders are orders. It's up to you."

The team would have to take out the enemy up close and personal.

"Roger that," Rob replied, kicking the side of the bike. "Damn it!"

But he had an idea. Rob abruptly steered off the road, down a grassy bank, and up a dirt mound. The bikes hopped over the hill as they tore through the countryside.

"Three-Five," Brian said, his back tire hitting the dirt. "I trust you and all, but what the hell are you doing?"

They raced down the dirt road, nothing but a trailing dust cloud left behind.

"I'm gettin' around them," replied Rob. "They're firing the missiles from the back of the van, right? If we can gain some distance in front, we should be able to catch 'em by surprise."

They were getting uncomfortably close to President Tyler's ranch on the outskirts of Denton.

"They ain't going to stop until we stop them!" Rob added, skipping over uneven dirt. "That radical bastard never planned to get out of this alive, anyway!"

The convoy of dirt bikes ran wide open at full speed across the open country. Up on the left, Rob caught the van speeding down the highway in the left lane. He stood up on the bike's pegs and cranked the gas even harder with his hand. They darted up a steep hill, and Rob saw a hunk of metal laid against a jersey barrier next to the highway. He turned the handlebar slightly to the left and aimed for it. The tires hit the solid piece, and Rob's bike launched fifteen feet into the air.

The rest of the team followed behind him. Rob jerked the wheel to the right, hand on the gas, and pushed the bike as hard and fast as it would go. They'd gained close to a mile's distance from the van and braked, sliding onto the shoulder of a highway bridge. Rob quickly retrieved his rifle, as did the others. They saw the vehicle barrel around the curve toward them. With his ACOG fixed to his rifle, Rob aimed for the grill.

"Now!" he said.

All five men pounded the van with a hail of bullets as it

raced toward them. Numerous rounds struck the van's radiator, causing green antifreeze to spill out onto the roadway. White smoke began to rise from the hood as the vehicle rolled toward them. The van cut right, and Rob aimed for the right tire. It blew loudly and deflated, and the driver lost control.

The van coming toward them fast, Rob and the team dove out of the way and onto the hard ground. The van's fender struck the guardrail hard. The van flipped to the side and tumbled twenty feet onto the rocky ground below.

Rob hopped from the pavement and wandered to the metal rail. He peeked over the side at the smoky van resting on its side.

"Don't know if anyone's alive down there," he said, "but we've got to get rid of those missiles."

Rob headed for the pack attached behind his bike seat. He recovered a single block of C-4, wires, and a detonator.

He jumped back onto the bike and made his way around the bridge and to the bottom. As he rolled down the bank, Amir's gunner was barely moving, attempting to crawl through the rear door. Rob brought his HK Rifle up and shot him in the side of the head, blood coating the inside of the door. Rob glanced into the cab of the van. The impact had busted the driver's head wide open. He wasn't moving in the slightest.

Rob moved to the back again, where he found Amir, clutching his broken arm with blood gushing down his head. He lay motionless but was still breathing on the inside of the overturned van. Rob stretched an arm in, gripping Amir's arms and forcing him out past the busted rear doors. He snagged a set of zip cuffs from his side cargo pocket. His rifle slung, Rob wrapped the cuffs around Amir's wrists and the door latch, tightening them hard.

"You want to die for this shit?" Rob asked. "I'll be more than happy to oblige you, asshole."

With the al-Qaeda lieutenant secure, Rob hit his hands and knees and climbed into the back of the van. C-4 in hand, he set it up on top of one of the missile tubes. Rob fastened it to the tube and inserted the blasting cap.

"Enjoy the afterlife, you fucking bastard," Rob said on the way out.

He leaped back onto the bike and dashed back up the hill.

"Well?" Brian asked.

"Well," replied Rob, "this is it."

They suddenly heard Amir scream from down below.

"Allahu Akbar!"

"Yeah," Rob said. "Allahu Akbar, motherfucker."

Rob grinned as he squeezed the remote device. A massive explosion rocked the ground like an earthquake, and the van went up in a fiery mess. Pieces of twisted metal shrapnel shot out from the blast and littered the ground around the hill. The al-Qaeda lieutenant was dead, and the missiles were no more.

"Alpha-Six-Actual," Rob said. "Tangos are down. I repeat, tangos are down, threat is neutralized, over."

Moments later, the colonel responded.

"Roger that, Golf-Three-Five," he replied. "Your country thanks you. I'll have you on the next transport from Sheppard Air Force Base. Come on home, boys. I'd say you've earned a little downtime."

Rob peered down below at the glowing blaze one last time. They heard sirens approaching from down the highway and hightailed it on their motorbikes into the night. But before Rob could rest easy, there was one thing left to do.

FORTY

Riyadh, Saudi Arabia

The temperature that day in the Saudi capital had clocked in at ninety-nine degrees Fahrenheit. Arcadia Square was teaming with a mix of Saudis and expats doing midday shopping and coming and going from the Omar bin Al-Khattab Mosque a few blocks away.

Women wearing hijabs, some holding the hands of their young children, toted shopping bags and ambled along together in groups of two or more. Saudi men with vibrant white and red checkered kufiyah head coverings and wearing white robes conducted business in the several stores around the square.

On the front walk by a sandwich shop, Rob relaxed outside at a round table under an umbrella. Wearing traditional Saudi clothing and black shades, he sipped on a cup of cardamom coffee with his face buried in a local Saudi newspaper. The white robe helped to keep him somewhat cool while he waited under the radiant, cloudless afternoon sky.

Rob was on his own in the country. Though he'd volunteered, he had no backup to speak of. It was a black op. If caught, he'd surely go to prison for espionage or possibly be beheaded. Maintaining diplomatic relations with Saudi Arabia, the US had complete deniability if he was arrested. But Rob was going to end the charade, one way or the other.

He peeked out from behind the unfolded newspaper and spotted a tall man walking among the crowd. It was al-Bashir. He'd just come from the mosque and trudged across the dusty road, his cane in his hand and four of his bodyguards surrounding him.

Rob waited until the terrorist leader's back faced him. As al-Bashir ambled along the curb, Rob tossed the newspaper down and hopped from his chair. He tossed a few bills onto the table and stood, pushing the chair back in. Rob began to follow a hundred meters behind, blending with the large group of Saudis.

The Central Intelligence Agency had finally given the team something they could use. The agency had tracked al-Bashir, who had traveled by airplane under a false name. He and his entourage had landed at Riyadh International Airport early that morning, having fled Lebanon due to Lebanese State Security closing in on them. The country's government was doing a nationwide crackdown in an effort to rid themselves of terrorists within their borders. Al-Bashir had nowhere left to hide.

Rob trampled across the sandy roadway in brown sandals as he trailed al-Bashir and his men to an alley behind a row of tan-colored apartment buildings. As he turned the corner, he spotted the men climbing the stairs to a stone deck and glass back door of an apartment. Rob froze, taking cover behind a fat palm tree. The terrorist leader and three of his guards suddenly faded inside. A fourth, a tall man with a bushy beard and tan prayer cap, remained behind on the deck to guard the door.

Sitting back on a metal patio chair, the man sparked up a cigar and blew a string of smoke. Rob stepped out and strolled through the alleyway, casually passing by the guard overhead. Once the wall blocked his view, Rob took a look around and ducked behind a row of dumpsters. He dropped to one knee. Peeking out from behind the dumpster, he let out a mild whistle.

"Who is there?" the guard asked in Arabic. "Hey, come out now."

Rob waited a few moments. Then he whistled a little louder.

"Hey," the guard added. "That is not funny. If I have to come down there, it will be a bad day for you."

Rob whistled again. This time he heard footsteps coming down the stairs. Rob recovered his neck knife from under his robe and squeezed the grip in his right hand, the blade facing out. The guard rounded the wall separating them, and Rob grabbed him, quickly covering his mouth so he couldn't scream.

He jerked him back and sliced the guard's neck with a swift motion of his arm. Catching the body before it hit the ground, Rob dragged the guard by the arms and dropped him behind the large dumpster. Wiping the blood on the dead man's clothing, Rob popped back out.

He crept his way up the steps and peeked through the glass between the white curtains. With no one in view, Rob softly slid the glass door open. He slipped inside and locked the latch behind him. Rob moved toward the back of the white sofa and hit his knees. Suddenly, another guard appeared out of the hallway and wandered to the kitchen. He opened the refrigerator to grab a drink. The man popped open a soda can and began guzzling it down.

Rob slithered by the white living room furniture and past the stone counter that separated the two rooms. He inched up behind the guard as he took his last sip, but noticing Rob's reflection in the refrigerator, the man drew his gun and quickly spun around. Catching the guard's arm before he could fire, Rob chopped the firearm from his hands. It pinged against the tile floor. Rob kicked the enemy in the gut and, as the man doubled down, he jammed the blade into his body, just under the sternum.

The guard gripped the blade, blood coating his hand. He sneered at Rob with wide eyes and fell to the side. Blood poured over his body, which twitched with his final breath. Rob jerked the knife out and rinsed it in the kitchen sink. He left the body where it fell.

Rob swiped the nine-millimeter Turkish pistol from the floor and continued down the hall from which the guard had come. Pressed against the wall, he moved across the marble floor, past the open bathroom door, and to a staircase that led to the second floor. He could hear men talking in one of the upstairs rooms.

The stench of hookah smoke filled the entire apartment. Rob tiptoed up the marble staircase. He slowly wriggled his way to the top and lurked just under the railing. He peeked around the corner, seeing shadows moving along a wall in the far room to his left. Staying low, Rob headed for a dark room toward the end of the corridor. He could hear al-Bashir speaking with one of his bodyguards on the other side of the wall. Rob peered through the doorway and around the corner.

He spotted the back of the guard getting closer to the door. The man leaned up against the doorframe and spoke to his boss in their native language. Rob made his move, gripping the gun while rushing in, and took the guard by the throat. He pressed the barrel to the side of the man's head.

"You move, asshole," he said, "and you're dead."

Al-Bashir gazed at Rob, rubbing his beard and exhaling hookah smoke. He dropped it onto the coffee table.

"Who are you?" he asked. "How did you get past my men?"

Rob grinned, squeezing the guard's throat tighter. "How do you think?" Rob asked.

Al-Bashir was unaware that most of his guards were now dead.

"What is it you want?" he added.

The guard's face turned bright red. He couldn't breathe with Rob's arm squeezing his throat.

"I want the head of the fucking snake," replied Rob.

Al-Bashir rose from the sofa, shouting in Arabic.

"Haris! Haris!"

"Your men aren't coming," Rob replied. "They're a bit out of commission down there."

Rob took his blade and jabbed it into the guard's chest. He slowly released his grip and retracted the knife as the guard dropped to his knees. The man fell forward, striking his head on the glass table before hitting the floor. A puddle of blood flowed out from under his body and collected on the hard floor.

"I've been waiting a long time for this," said Rob. "For all the people you've killed—women, children, innocent civilians. And for what, some kind of twisted hate for Western society? I don't think there'll be seventy-two virgins waiting for you, you barbaric bastard."

Al-Bashir took a step toward Rob. "The West has sent their soldiers, planes, tanks, and drones to kill innocent Muslims in the name of democracy! I will not be lectured by an infidel who serves an imperialistic master. This will not stop. You can kill me, but the cause will live on. Someone will take my place. And they won't rest until you all are eradicated from our holy lands. Allahu Akbar!"

Rob tipped his head to al-Bashir. "Nice speech," he said.

Al-Bashir went for a gun hidden under a stack of papers on the table. Before he could bring it up, Rob lunged forward and kicked him in the head. The terrorist leader dropped the gun and fell back. Rob dove on top of him, pinning al-Bashir's arms down with his knees.

"You don't deserve a quick death!" he shouted.

Al-Bashir tried to force his way back up, but Rob struck him with a hammer fist to the bridge of the nose, knocking him back down. He pummeled the man, punching him over and over until his face swelled like a balloon. Blood dripped from his nose and poured from his mouth. Rob beat him with both fists until his hands were numb.

Al-Bashir was semiconscious when Rob reached over and snatched the cane leaning against the sofa. He knew the man couldn't move. Rob got up, gripping the cane by the knob, and swung on the terrorist mastermind several times until the solid wood stick snapped over his head.

Al-Bashir was beaten black and blue and nothing more than a bloody mess on the area rug. Though still alive, he could barely move. Rob dropped the other half of the wooden cane to the floor. The terrorist leader attempted to push himself up by his hands, but in his weakened state, he fell to his face.

Rob watched the man try to crawl achingly across the cold floor, a trail of blood running down his arms and onto the surface. With every slight piece of ground he gained, he let out a harrowing whine.

"Look at you," said Rob. "A terrorist master reduced to groveling while you bleed on this dirty-ass floor."

Rob headed to the bathroom to wash the blood off his hands. He dried off with a clean towel on the rack and made his way to the kitchen. He took a seat at the counter and watched al-Bashir slowly crawl toward him. When he made it barely past the bathroom door, Rob hit his feet again. He marched to the other side of the kitchen and disconnected the gas line.

Rob heard a whoosh as the pungent aroma of gas quickly filled the air. Swiping pages from a newspaper on the counter, he wedged them into the toaster and pressed the lever. Rob scowled at al-Bashir one final time.

"Sorry, asshole," he said. "Time for me to go. Give Allah my regards!"

Rob hurried toward the back door. He stepped outside, then clutched the dead guard by the feet and dragged him inside. Rob slipped through the glass door and onto the porch. Making sure no one was around, he marched down the steps, down the alleyway, and toward the street.

He made it a quarter of a kilometer down the road, and an ear-popping concussion shook the ground. Alarms from surrounding homes and cars blared as the blast blew out the windows and engulfed the apartment in flames. Rob faded into the crowd scrambling from the chaos. Emergency sirens sounded not far away as he whistled for a cab. The taxi slowed to a halt by the curb, and Rob climbed into the back.

"Matar!" Rob said in Arabic.

The cab driver wasn't a Saudi but appeared to be Pakistani.

"As you wish," the driver replied in English. "What the hell was that?"

"Not sure," said Rob. "Just get out of here, huh?"

"Yes, sir," replied the cabbie.

The driver hit the gas and the car pulled away, and Saudi police surrounded the scene behind them. Watching in the rearview, the cabbie took a quick right and headed for the Riyadh Airport.

FORTY-ONE

In a corner booth of a small cafe, Rob nursed a strong cup of coffee while watching people through the window pass by on the DC streets. Since he was suffering from a bit of jet lag, the caffeine helped to pep him up a bit.

The Washington neighborhood was full of luxury, with its expensive shops, restaurants, upscale condos, and high-end hotels. It wasn't really Rob's cup of tea. He wasn't there to admire what some would call the finer things in life, though.

It was a cool day in the nation's capital, rain clouds covering the sky outside. Droplets of water began to form on the windows, trickling down the glass and onto the sidewalk. The wind started to pick up a bit, swinging trees that lined the walkway on the opposite side in the gentle gust.

Rob's attention was diverted to a few patrons sitting at the counter across the room. They joked and laughed with a waitress as she wiped the surface down with a damp cloth. A TV on the wall behind her showed the local weather report.

Rob peered again through the wet glass at a law office

building at the end of the street. It was one of the many old, historic structures in that part of town. He checked the time on his watch as another waitress approached his table.

"Can I get you more coffee, sir?" she asked.

Rob smiled up at her. "No thank you, ma'am," he replied. "I'm just fine."

"Okay, hon," she said, wandering to the next table.

Rob was about to leave when he noticed breaking news on the television. The scene unfolding onscreen certainly got his attention. He snapped his fingers and raised a hand.

"Excuse me, miss," he said to the lady behind the counter. "Could you turn that up, please?"

With a click of the remote, the volume increased.

A powerful explosion rocked a wealthy Saudi residential neighborhood block yesterday, crews on the ground are reporting. Saudi investigators and emergency crews are still on the scene, digging through the charred rubble. What they claim was a gas explosion killed five, destroyed a luxury apartment, and damaged two others as the flames spread.

Although the Saudi authorities are tight-lipped about the situation, refusing to comment any further, we are learning from an independent source that Al-Qaeda-in-Lebanon leader, Aasim al-Bashir, was among the dead. The Saudi royal family has long denied his Saudi heritage in an effort to distance the country from its terrorist links.

It is now known that al-Bashir had direct involvement in the attacks on innocent Americans. A few questions still remain. With him gone, what will be the future of the organization he masterminded? Will someone take his place? Or will the terror group simply fade into obscurity?

In addition, the FBI have so far arrested eight people in connection with a slew of shell corporations and a money-laundering scheme that financed the terror group's operations. They're being held in Terre Haute Maximum Security Prison in Indiana. However, the investigation into this is still ongoing.

Rob paid close attention to what was going on behind the news reporter. The wind started to howl, blowing her raincoat to the side as drops flew in from the right side of the screen. She paused a moment, pinching her earpiece and obviously listening to someone.

Ladies and gentlemen, we have just learned of a recent plot to attack the president of the United States. Apparently, it was foiled by a few brave Americans. Oh my, this is unbelievable.

She let go of her earpiece.

Their identity is unknown. But, whoever you are out there, thank you. This is what happens when we come together as a nation. It is truly inspiring, knowing there are those who will fight back regardless of the danger to themselves.

Rob smirked, knowing they would never know who was responsible. He listened while she continued.

Regarding the aftermath of the bombings, victims who've come down with radiation sickness are still being identified and filling up local hospitals. Several federal agencies, making up a joint task force, have been dispatched to deal with the messy result of what they are calling "dirty bombs."

While crews clean and clear debris from streets and neighborhoods, it is unclear just how far the radiation has spread. We anticipate the cleanup will last for quite some time. We are just hoping and praying that not many more folks are effected down the road, though there seems to be a slim chance of that.

We'll update you when more information comes in. This is Nicki Haley reporting live from Chicago.

Rob tossed a ten-dollar bill onto the table and slid out of the booth seat. He fixed his polo shirt, drawing it down over the concealed handgun on the left side of his belt. Rob returned his leather wallet to the back pocket of his dark-tan khaki pants. He snagged his umbrella from the floor and made his way to the cafe exit as he reached up and adjusted his camouflage hat.

As he stepped through the doorway, Rob held it open for an old lady folding an umbrella.

"Thank you, young man," she said as she passed by.

Rob gave her a welcome grin, letting go of the glass door as she passed through. Meandering down the steps, he popped his umbrella open and held it over his head. Rain poured off the canvas entryway cover as he looked down the sidewalk toward the three-way intersection. The rain softened a bit, becoming a misty drizzle while Rob made his way down the street. Light thunder echoed across the sky.

The light at the end went from green to red, and Rob mashed a button on the pole. The pedestrian light turned white after a few seconds, and Rob jogged slowly through the crosswalk to the other side. He wandered down a ways past a black light post, then ascended a set of concrete steps. A large gold sign hung above the green office door:

Law office of Rachel Wilson and Associates.

Rob collapsed his umbrella. He squeezed the door latch, pulled it open, and entered. Stopping to look around, he hung the umbrella on a nearby coat rack. He continued, passing by a waiting room to his left. Rob strolled toward the reception area. The paralegal behind the desk had just finished up a phone call and hung the phone back onto the receiver.

"Hello," she said with a bright smile. "May I help you, sir?"

But a beautiful, tall blonde in a black skirt and blouse appeared from around the corner, and Rob temporarily lost his train of thought.

"Hey, Samantha," she said to the paralegal. "Could you…"

She went silent when she glanced up and saw who was there. She stared at Rob for a moment, as if time stood still. Instead of continuing her conversation with Samantha, she rushed through the door and out into the corridor.

"Rob?" Rachel said, slowly approaching him.

He smiled. "Yup, it's me. Nice place you got here. You in the middle of a big case or anything?"

"I thought…" She sighed. "I thought you forgot about me."

Rob moved closer and placed a hand on her hip. "No, no," he said. "How I could I forget about you? I was just a little preoccupied, that's all. Besides, I don't do flings."

Rachel took Rob's hand and led him to a row of chairs against the wall. They sat next to each other.

"Well," she added. "It's been a little slow this week. Seems I have a break coming."

News of the terrorist attacks and recent developments played in the background. Rachel glanced up at the TV.

"So," she continued, "I'm guessing you know about that, right?"

"Yeah," replied Rob. "I know a little."

"Wow," Rachel added. "I can't believe you're here. It's been a while since we spoke on the phone. Did this have anything to do with you being gone?"

Rob set a hand on her leg. "Even if it did," he replied, "I would have to deny any involvement, sorry."

Rob embraced her hand again and helped her up. "I'll tell you what," he said. "Let me take you out on a proper date this time. I'll tell you everything I can about me, if you promise to end the night with a kiss."

"Hold on," she replied. "Be right back."

Rachel stepped around the corner to retrieve her purse. As she returned, strap over her shoulder, she grabbed Rob's hand, and they headed for the door.

"Sam!" Rachel shouted to her paralegal. "I'll be out for the rest of the afternoon. Take messages for me!"

Samantha grinned while Rob and Rachel headed for the doorway. Rob snatched the umbrella from the rack and gripped the knob. He passed through the doorway and propped it open with his foot. As they made their way down the steps, he held the umbrella over her. It had been a long time since Rob had any time for dating, or much of a social life at all. But he was looking forward to finishing his interrupted vacation.

As he and Rachel strolled down the damp walkway toward Rob's Mustang, he couldn't help but feel a sense of relief. Al-Bashir was dead, his terror network crippled. Several of his associates were headed to death row in a federal prison.

Rob and his team could rest a little easier. However, his job was unpredictable. He could be summoned at any time to go anywhere. He was certain it wouldn't be the last time they heard from al-Qaeda. Someone else would surely rise to fill the void. Until then, he would enjoy life to the fullest, and the great company of a beautiful woman.

THE END

WHAT DID YOU THINK OF AN IMMINENT THREAT?

What did you think of AN IMMINENT THREAT?

Thank you for reading the fourth book in Rob's story. John is currently writing book 5 in the Rob Walker series, SLEEPERS. Find out what happens when Rob and his Delta team are deployed to rescue hostages taken by Hamas in Israel—and discover an Iranian plot to send America back to the stone age.

Did you enjoy **AN IMMINENT THREAT**? Leave a review and let others know!

Visit www.johnetterleebooks.com to sign up to the newsletter

ABOUT THE AUTHOR

John Etterlee is a retired US Army combat veteran, horse and animal lover, adventurer, and author. Born in Augusta, Georgia, he joined the Army shortly after the September 11, 2001, terrorist attacks in the US, and served multiple tours overseas from 2003 to 2013. John was medically retired from the Army for an injury after being medevaced and sent to Landstuhl Army Medical Center in Germany in 2010.

Although John has always enjoyed writing, it wasn't until recovering from surgery that he began to take it more seriously. Writing has since become a passion for him, and he loves to share his stories with the world of book lovers.

John now lives in North Carolina with his wife Elizabeth, whom he met while stationed at Joint Base Lewis-McChord in Washington State in 2011. He is also a lover of cats. John and his wife share their home with a few beautiful Sphynx cats.

In addition, he enjoys traveling and meeting new people. John loves hearing from his readers. You can visit John's website to learn more.

MORE BOOKS BY JOHN ETTERLEE

Rob Walker Books:

THE MESSENGER
RETRIBUTION
BLOOD RED

Roger O'Neil Books:

THE COLD STORM
STRIKE POINT

ROB WALKER BOX SET (BOOKS 1-3)

FOLLOW JOHN

https://www.facebook.com/jbetterlee

https://twitter.com/JEtterleeWrites

https://www.instagram.com/jetterleewrites/

Sign up to John's mailing list and follow him @

www.johnetterleebooks.com

Made in the USA
Middletown, DE
02 March 2024

50682977R00208